BETTY N

THE ULTIMATE (

Betty Neels's novels are loved
by millions of readers around the world,
and this very special *12-volume collection*
offers a unique chance to recapture the pleasure
of some of her most popular stories.

Each month we're bringing you a new volume
containing two timeless classics—irresistible love
stories that belong together, whether they share the
same colourful setting, romantic theme, or follow the
same characters in their continuing lives...

As a special treat, each volume also includes an
introductory letter by a different author. Some of the
most popular names in romance fiction are delighted
to pay tribute to Betty Neels; we hope you enjoy
reading their personal thoughts and memories.

We're proud and privileged to bring you
this very special collection, and hope you enjoy
reading—and keeping—these twelve wonderful
volumes over the coming months.

Volume Nine

—with an introduction from sparkling talent

Paula Marshall

**Two of Betty Neels's
quintessentially English romances:**

*DEAREST MARY JANE
ROMANTIC ENCOUNTER*

We'd like to take this opportunity to pay tribute to **Betty Neels**, *who sadly passed away last year. Betty was one of our best-loved authors. As well as being a wonderfully warm and thoroughly charming individual, Betty led a fascinating life even before becoming a writer, and her publishing record was impressive.*

Betty spent her childhood and youth in Devonshire before training as a nurse and midwife. She was an army nursing sister during the war, married a Dutchman and subsequently lived in Holland for fourteen years. On retirement from nursing Betty started to write, inspired by a lady in a library bemoaning the lack of romantic novels.

Over her thirty-year writing career Betty wrote more than 134 novels and was published in more than one hundred international markets. She continued to write into her ninetieth year, remaining as passionate about her characters and stories then as she was with her very first book.

Betty will be greatly missed, both by her friends at Harlequin Mills & Boon® *and by her legions of loyal readers around the world. Betty was a prolific writer and has left a lasting legacy through her heartwarming novels. She will always be remembered as a truly delightful person who brought great happiness to many.*

THE ULTIMATE COLLECTION

Volume Nine

DEAREST MARY JANE

and

ROMANTIC ENCOUNTER

Two full-length novels

Harlequin Mills & Boon Limited,
Eton House, 18-24 Paradise Road, Richmond, Surrey TW9 1SR

This compilation: THE ULTIMATE COLLECTION
© Harlequin Enterprises II B.V., 2003

First published in Great Britain as:

DEAREST MARY JANE © Betty Neels 1994

ROMANTIC ENCOUNTER © Betty Neels 1992

ISBN 0 263 83651 7

Set in Times Roman 11½ on 12½ pt.
141-0403-104967

Printed and bound in Spain
by Litografia Rosés, S.A., Barcelona

Dear Reader

My mother introduced me to the romances of Betty Neels many years ago. On reading them I could see at once why they were—and still are—so popular. She always tells a good love story in the traditional manner, relying on her character and settings, as well as a strong plot, to hold her readers' interest and keep them turning the page.

Her heroes are powerful and influential men who are successful in their chosen profession, which is often that of a senior doctor. The background details of their work and the descriptions of their homes are very well presented, with the result that the readers feel her characters are living in the real world. Her heroines are invariably attractive with minds of their own, so that the heroes don't take them for granted. Many of her novels are set in Holland, which adds yet another interest to the story.

It is not, then, surprising that her upbeat version of life and love should remain successful in attracting large numbers of readers of all ages over so many years. Now read on—

Paula Marshall

DEAREST MARY JANE

by

Betty Neels

CHAPTER ONE

IT WAS five o'clock and the warm hazy sunshine of a September afternoon was dwindling into the evening's coolness. The Misses Potter, sitting at a table in the window of the tea-shop, put down their teacups reluctantly and prepared to leave. Miss Emily, the elder of the two ladies, rammed her sensible hat more firmly on her head and addressed the girl sitting behind the tiny counter at the back of the room.

'If we might have our bill, Mary Jane?'

The girl came to the table and the two ladies looked at her, wondering, as they frequently did, how whoever had chosen the girl's name could have guessed how aptly it fitted. She looked like a Mary Jane, not tall, a little too thin, with an unremarkable face and light brown hair, straight and long and pinned in an untidy swirl on top of her head. Only when she looked at you the violet eyes, fringed with long curling lashes, made one forget her prosaic person.

She said now in her quiet voice, 'I hope you enjoyed your tea. In another week or two I'll start making teacakes.'

Her customers nodded in unison. 'We shall look forward to that.' Miss Emily opened her purse. 'We mustn't keep you, it's closing time.' She put money on the table and Mary Jane opened the door and waited until they were across the village street before closing it.

She cleared the table, carried everything into the small kitchen behind the tea-room and went to turn the notice to 'Closed' on the door just as a car drew up outside. The door was thrust open before she had time to turn the key and a man came in. He was massively built and tall, so that the small room became even smaller.

'Good,' he said briskly. 'You're not closed. My companion would like tea...'

'But I am closed,' said Mary Jane in a reasonable voice. 'I'm just locking the door, only you pushed it open. You are not very far from Stow-on-the-Wold—there are several hotels there, you'll get tea quite easily.'

The man spoke evenly, rather as though he were addressing a child or someone hard of hearing. 'My companion doesn't wish to wait any longer. A pot of tea is all I am asking for; surely that isn't too much?'

He sounded like a man who liked his own way and got it, but Mary Jane had a lot to do before she could go to her bed; besides, she disliked being browbeaten. 'I'm sorry...'

She was interrupted by the girl who swept into the tearoom. No, not a girl, decided Mary Jane, a woman in her thirties and beautiful, although her looks were marred by her frown and tight mouth.

'Where's my tea?' she demanded. 'Good lord, Thomas, all I want is a cup of tea. Is that too much to ask for? What is this dump, anyway?' She flung herself gracefully into one of the little cane chairs. 'I suppose it will be undrinkable tea-bags, but if there's nothing else...'

Mary Jane gave the man an icy violet stare. 'I do have drinkable tea-bags,' she told him, 'but perhaps the lady would prefer Earl Grey or Orange Pekoe?'

'Earl Grey,' snapped the woman, 'and I hope I shan't have to wait too long.'

'Just while the kettle boils,' said Mary Jane in a dangerously gentle voice.

She went into the kitchen and laid a tray and made the tea and carried it to the table and was very surprised when the man got up and took the tray from her.

In the kitchen she started clearing up. There would be a batch of scones to make after she had had her supper and the sugar bowls to fill and the jam dishes to see to as well as the pastry to make ready for the sausage rolls she served during the lunch-hour. She was putting the last of the crockery away when the man came to the doorway. 'The bill?' he asked.

She went behind the counter and made it out and handed it silently to him and the woman called across. 'I imagine there is no ladies' room here?'

Mary Jane paused in counting change. 'No.' She added deliberately, 'The public lavatories are on the other side of the village square on the road to Moreton.'

The man bit off a laugh and then said with cool politeness, 'Thank you for giving us tea.' He ushered his companion out of the door, turning as he did so to turn the notice to 'Closed'.

Mary Jane watched him drive away. It was a nice car—a dark blue Rolls-Royce. There was a lonely stretch of road before they reached Stow-on-the-Wold, and she hoped they would run out of petrol. It was unlikely, though, he didn't strike her as that kind of man.

She locked the door, tidied the small room with its four tables and went through to the kitchen where she washed the last of the tea things, put her supper in the oven and went up the narrow staircase tucked away behind a door by the dresser. Upstairs, she went first to her bedroom, a low-ceilinged room with a latticed window overlooking the back garden and furnished rather sparsely. The curtains were pretty, however, as was the bedspread and there were flowers in a bowl on the old-fashioned dressing-table. She tidied herself without wasting too much time about it, and crossed the tiny landing to the living-room at the front of the cottage. Quite a large room since it was over the tea-room, and furnished as sparsely as the bedroom. There were flowers here too, and a small gas fire in the tiled grate which she lighted before switching on a reading lamp by the small armchair, so that the room looked welcoming. That done, she went downstairs again to open the kitchen door to allow Brimble, her cat, to come in—a handsome tabby who, despite his cat-flap, preferred to come in and out like anyone else. He wreathed himself round her legs now, wanting his supper and, when she had fed him, went upstairs to lie before the gas fire.

Mary Jane took the shepherd's pie out of the oven, laid the table under the kitchen window and sat down to eat her supper, listening with half an ear to the last of the six o'clock news while she planned her baking for the next day. The bus went into Stow-on-the-Wold on Fridays, returning around four o'clock, and those passengers who lived on the outskirts of the village frequently came in for a pot of tea before they set off for home.

She finished the pie and ate an apple, cleared the table and got out her pastry board and rolling pin. Scones were easy to make and were always popular. She did two batches and then saw to the sausage rolls before going into the tea-room to count the day's takings. Hardly a fortune; she just about paid her way but there was nothing over for holidays or new clothes, though the cottage was hers...

Uncle Matthew had left it to her when he had died two years previously. He had been her guardian ever since her own parents had been killed in their car. She and Felicity, who was older than she was, had been schoolgirls and their uncle and aunt had given them a home and educated them. Felicity, with more than her fair share of good looks, had taken herself off to London as soon as she had left school and had become a successful model, while Mary Jane had stayed at home to run the house for an ailing aunt and an uncle who, although kind, didn't bother with her overmuch. When her aunt had died she had stayed on, looking after him and the house, trying not to think about the future and the years flying by. She had been almost twenty-three when her uncle died and, to her astonished delight, left her the cottage he had owned in the village and five hundred pounds. She had moved into it from his large house at the other end of the village as soon as she could, for Uncle Matthew's heir had disliked her on sight and so had his wife...

She had spent some of the money on second-hand furniture and then, since she had no skills other than that of a good cook, she had opened the tea-room. She was known and liked in the village, which was a help, and after a few uncertain months she was making just enough to live on and pay the bills. Felicity had been to see her, amused at the whole set-up but offering no help. 'You always were the domestic type,' she had observed laughingly. 'I'd die if I had to spend my days here, you know. I'm going to the Caribbean to do some modelling next week—don't you wish you were me?'

Mary Jane had considered the question. 'No, not really,' she said finally. 'I do hope you have a lovely time.'

'I intend to, though the moment I set eyes on a handsome rich man I shall marry him.' She gave Mary Jane a friendly pat on the shoulder. 'Not much hope of that happening to you, darling.'

Mary Jane had agreed pleasantly, reflecting that just to set eyes on a man who hadn't lived all his life in the village and was either married or about to be married would be nice.

She remembered that now as she took the last lot of sausage rolls out of the oven. She had certainly met a man that very afternoon and, unless he had borrowed that car, he was at least comfortably off and handsome to boot. A pity that they hadn't fallen in love with each other at first sight, the way characters did in books. Rather the reverse: he had shown no desire to meet her again and she hadn't liked him. She cleared up once more and went upstairs to sit with Brimble by the fire and presently she went to bed.

It was exactly a week later when Miss Emily Potter came into the shop at the unusual hour—for her—of eleven o'clock in the morning.

Beyond an elderly couple and a young man on a motorbike in a great hurry, Mary Jane had had no customers, which was a good thing, for Miss Emily was extremely agitated.

'I did not know which way to turn,' she began breathlessly, 'and then I thought of you, Mary Jane. Mrs Stokes is away, you know, and Miss Kemble over at the rectory has the young mothers' and toddlers' coffee-morning. The taxi is due in a short time and dear Mabel is quite overwrought.'

Mary Jane saw that she would have to get to the heart of

the matter quickly before Miss Emily became distraught as well. 'Why?'

Miss Potter gave her a startled look. 'She has to see this specialist—her hip, you know. Dr Fellows made the appointment but now she is most unwilling to go. So unfortunate, for this specialist comes very rarely to Cheltenham and the appointment is for two o'clock and I cannot possibly go with her, Didums is poorly and cannot be left...'

'You would like me to have Didums?' asked Mary Jane and sighed inwardly. Didums was a particularly awkward pug dog with a will of her own; Brimble wouldn't like her at all.

'No, no—dear Didums would never go with anyone but myself or my sister. If you would go with Mabel?' Miss Potter gazed rather wildly around the tea-room. 'There's no one here; you could close for an hour or two.'

Mary Jane forbore from pointing out that although there was no one there at the moment, any minute now the place might be filled with people demanding coffee and biscuits. It wasn't likely but there was always a chance. 'When would we get back?' she asked cautiously.

'Well, if the appointment is for two o'clock I don't suppose she will be very long, do you? I'm sure you should be back by four o'clock...'

Miss Potter wrung her hands. 'Oh, dear, I have no idea what to do.'

The taxi would take something over half an hour to get to the hospital. Mary Jane supposed that they would need to get there with half an hour to spare.

'I believe that there is a very good place in the hospital where you can get coffee—dear Mabel will need refreshment.'

Mary Jane thought that after a ride in the taxi with the overwrought Miss Mabel Potter she might be in need of refreshment herself. She said in her calm way, 'I'll be over in half an hour or so, Miss Potter. There's still plenty of time.'

A tearfully grateful Miss Potter went on her way. Mary

Jane closed the tea-room, changed into a blouse and skirt and a cardigan, drank a cup of coffee and ate a scone, made sure that Brimble was cosily asleep on the end of her bed and walked across the village square and along the narrow country lane which led to the Misses Potter's cottage. It was called a cottage but, in fact, it was a rather nice house built of Cotswold stone and much too large for them. They had been born there and intended to live out their lives there, even though they were forced to do so as economically as possible. Mary Jane went up the garden path, rang the bell and was admitted by Miss Emily and led to the drawing-room where Miss Mabel sat surrounded by furniture which had been there before she was born and which neither she nor her sister would dream of changing.

Mary Jane sat down on a nice little Victorian button-back chair and embarked on a cheerful conversation. It was rather like talking to someone condemned to the guillotine; Miss Mabel bore the appearance of someone whose last moment had come. It was a relief when the taxi arrived and the cheerful conversation was scrapped for urgent persuasions to get in.

They were half an hour too early for their appointment, which was a mistake, for the orthopaedic clinic, although it had started punctually, was already running late. It was going on for three o'clock by the time the severe-looking sister called Miss Potter's name and by then she was in such a nervous state that Mary Jane had a job getting her on to her feet and into the consulting-room.

The consultant sitting behind the desk got up and shook Miss Potter's nerveless hand—the man who had demanded tea for his tiresome companion. Mary Jane, never one to think before she spoke, said chattily, 'Oh, hello—it's you—fancy seeing you here.'

She received a look from icy blue eyes in which there was no hint of recollection, although his 'Good afternoon' was uttered with detached civility and she blushed, something she did far too easily however much she tried not to. The stern-

faced sister took no notice. She said briskly, 'You had better
stay with Miss Potter, she seems nervous.'

Mary Jane sat herself down in a corner of the room where
Miss Potter could see her and watched the man wheedle that
lady's complaints and symptoms out of her. He did it very
kindly and without any sign of impatience, even when Miss
Potter sidetracked to explain about the marmalade which
hadn't jelled because she had felt poorly and hadn't given it
her full attention. A nasty, arrogant man, Mary Jane decided,
but he had his good points. She had thought about him once
or twice of course, and with a touch of wistfulness, for handsome giants who drove Rolls-Royce motor cars weren't exactly thick on the ground in her part of the world, but she
hadn't expected to see him again. She wondered about his
beautiful companion and was roused from her thoughts by
Sister leading Miss Mabel away to a curtained-off corner to
be examined.

The man took no notice of Mary Jane but wrote steadily
and very fast until Sister came to tell him that his patient
was ready.

He disappeared behind the curtain and Mary Jane, bored
with sitting still and sure that he would be at least ten
minutes, got up and went over to the desk and peered down
at the notes he had been writing. She wasn't surprised that
she could hardly make head or tail of it, for he had been
writing fast, but presently she began to make sense of it.
There were some rough diagrams too, with arrows pointing
in all directions and what looked like Latin. It was a pity
that no one had seen to it that he wrote a legible hand when
he was a schoolboy.

His voice, gently enquiring as to whether she was interested in orthopaedics, sent her whirling round to bump into
his waistcoat.

'Yes—no, that is...' She had gone scarlet again. 'Your
writing is quite unreadable,' she finished.

'Yes? But as long as I can read it...you're a nosy young
woman.'

'The patients' charter,' said Mary Jane, never at a loss for a word. He gave rather a nasty laugh.

'And a busybody as well,' he observed.

He sat down at his desk again and started to write once more and she went back to her chair and watched him. About thirty-five, she supposed, with brown hair already grizzled at the sides, and the kind of commanding nose he could look down. A firm mouth and a strong chin. She supposed that he could be quite nice when he smiled. He was dressed with understated elegance, the kind which cost a great deal of money, and she wondered what his name was. Not that it mattered, she reminded herself, as Miss Mabel came from behind the curtain, fully dressed even to her hat and gloves.

He got up as she came towards him and Mary Jane liked him for that, and for the manner in which he broke the news to his patient that an operation on her hip would relieve her of pain and disability.

He turned to Mary Jane. 'You are a relation of Miss Potter?' His tone was politely impersonal.

'Me? No. Just someone in the village. Miss Potter's sister couldn't come because of Didums...' His raised eyebrows forced her to explain. 'Their dog—she's not very well, the vet said...' She stopped. It was obvious that he didn't want to know what the vet had said.

'Perhaps you could ask Miss Potter's sister to ring the hospital and she will be told what arrangements will be made to admit her sister.'

He addressed himself to Miss Mabel once more, got to his feet to bid her goodbye, nodded at Mary Jane and Sister ushered them out into the waiting-room again.

'What is his name?' asked Mary Jane.

Sister had her hand on the next case sheets. She gave Mary Jane a frosty look. 'If you mean the consultant you have just seen, his name is Sir Thomas Latimer. Miss Potter is extremely lucky that he will take her as a patient.' She added impressively, 'He is famous in his field.'

'Oh, good.' Mary Jane gave Sister a sunny smile and

guided Miss Mabel out of the hospital and into the forecourt where the taxi was parked.

The return journey was entirely taken up with Miss Mabel's rather muddled version of her examination, the driver's rather lurid account of his wife's varicose veins and their treatment and Mary Jane doing her best to guide the conversation into neutral topics.

It took some time to explain everything once they had reached the cottage. Mary Jane's sensible account interlarded with Miss Mabel's flights of fancy, but presently she was able to wish them goodbye and go home. Brimble was waiting for her, wanting his tea and company. She fed him, made a pot of tea for herself and, since it was almost five o'clock by now, she made no attempt to open the tea-room. She locked up and went upstairs and sat down by the gas fire with Brimble on her lap, thinking of Sir Thomas Latimer.

Nothing happened for several days; the fine weather held and Mary Jane reaped a better harvest than usual from motorists making the best of the last of summer. She had seen nothing of the Misses Potter but she hadn't expected to; they came once a week, as regular as clockwork, on a Thursday to draw their pensions and indulge themselves with tea and scones, so she looked up in surprise when they came into the tea-room at eleven o'clock in the morning, two days early.

'We have had a letter,' observed Miss Emily, 'which we should like you to read, Mary Jane, since it concerns you. And since we are here, I think that we might indulge ourselves with a cup of your excellent coffee.'

Mary Jane poured the coffee and took the letter she was offered. It was very clearly worded: Miss Mabel was to present herself at the hospital in four days' time so that the operation found necessary by Sir Thomas Latimer might be carried out. Mary Jane skimmed over the bit about bringing a nightgown and toiletries and slowed at the next paragraph. It was considered advisable, in view of Miss Mabel's nervous disposition, that the young lady who had accompanied her on her previous visit should do so again so that Miss Potter might be reassured by her company.

'Well, I never,' said Mary Jane and gave the letter back.

'You will do this?' asked Miss Emily in a voice which expected Mary Jane to say yes. 'Most fortunately, you have few customers at this time of year, and an hour or so away will do you no great harm.'

Mary Jane forbore from pointing out that with the fine weather she could reasonably expect enough coffee and tea drinkers, not to mention scone eaters, to make it well worth her while to stay open from nine o'clock until five o'clock. The good weather wouldn't last and business was slack during the winter months. However, she liked the Misses Potter.

'Three o'clock,' she said. 'That means leaving here some time after two o'clock, doesn't it? Yes, of course I'll go and see Miss Mabel safely settled in.'

The ladies looked so relieved that she refilled their cups and didn't charge them for it. 'I hope,' commented Miss Emily, 'that Didums will be well enough for me to leave her so that I may visit Mabel. I do not know how long she will be in the hospital.'

'I'll try and find out for you.' The tea-room door opened and four people came in and she left them to their coffee while she attended to her new customers: two elderly couples who ate a gratifying number of scones and ordered a pot of coffee. Mary Jane took it as a sign that obliging the Misses Potter when she really hadn't wanted to would be rewarded by more customers than usual and more money in the till.

Indeed, it seemed that that was the case; she was kept nicely busy for the next few days so that she turned the 'Open' notice to 'Closed' with reluctance. It was another lovely day, and more people than usual had come in for coffee and if today was anything like yesterday she could have filled the little tea-room for most of the afternoon...

Miss Mabel wore an air of stunned resignation, getting into the taxi without needing to be coaxed, and Mary Jane's warm heart was wrung by the unhappiness on her companion's face. She strove to find cheerful topics of conversation, chattering away in a manner most unusual for her so that by the time they reached the hospital her tongue was cleaving to the roof of her mouth. At least there was no delay; they were taken at once to the ward and Miss Potter was invited to undress and get into bed while Mary Jane recited necessary information to the ward clerk, a jolly, friendly woman who gave her a leaflet about visiting and telephoning and information as to where the canteen was. 'Sister will be coming along in a minute; you might like a word with her.'

Mary Jane went back to Miss Potter's cubicle and found that lady was lying in bed, looking pale although she mustered a smile.

'Sister's coming to see you in a minute,' said Mary Jane. 'I'll take your clothes back with me, shall I, and bring them again when you're getting up?' She cocked an ear at the sound of feet coming down the ward. 'Here's Sister.'

It was Sir Thomas Latimer as well, in a long white coat, his hands in his trouser pockets. He wished Miss Potter a cheerful good afternoon, gave Mary Jane a cool stare and addressed himself to his patient.

He had a lovely bedside manner, Mary Jane reflected, soothing and friendly and yet conveying the firm impression that whatever he said or did would be right. Mary Jane watched Miss Potter relax, even smile a little, and edged towards the curtains; if he was going to examine his patient he wouldn't want her there.

'Stay,' he told her without turning his head.

She very much wanted to say 'I shan't,' but Miss Potter's precarious calm must not be disturbed. She gave the back of his head a look to pierce his skull and stayed where she was.

She had had a busy day and she was a little tired. She eased herself from one foot to the other and wished she could be like Sister, standing on the other side of the bed. A handsome woman, still young and obviously highly efficient. She and Sir Thomas exchanged brief remarks from time to time, none of which made sense to her, not that they were meant to. She stifled a yawn, smiled at Miss Potter and eased a foot out of a shoe.

Sister might be efficient, she was kind too; Miss Potter was getting more and more cheerful by the minute, and when Sir Thomas finally finished and sat down on her side of the bed she smiled, properly this time, and took the hand he offered her, listening to his reassuring voice. It was when he said, 'Now I think we might let Miss...?' that he turned to look at Mary Jane.

'Seymour,' she told him frostily, cramming her foot back into its shoe.

His eyes went from her face to her feet, his face expressionless.

'Miss Potter may be visited the day after tomorrow. Her sister is free to telephone whenever she wishes to. I shall operate tomorrow morning at eight o'clock. Miss Potter should be back in her bed well before noon.' He added, 'You are on the telephone?'

'Me? No. We use the post office and Miss Kemble at the rectory will take a message. Everyone knows the Misses Potter. I've given the ward clerk several numbers she can ring. But someone will phone at noon tomorrow.'

He nodded, smiled very kindly at his patient and went away with Sister as a young nurse took their place. The promise of a cup of tea made Mary Jane's departure easier. She kissed the elderly cheek. 'We'll all be in to see you,' she promised, and took herself off to find the taxi and its patient driver.

By the time they were back in the village and she had explained everything to Miss Emily it was far too late to open the tea-room. She made herself a pot of tea, fed Brimble, and padded around in her stockinged feet getting everything ready for the batch of scones she still had to make ready for the next day. While she did it she thought about Sir Thomas.

The operation was a success; the entire village knew about it and, since they foregathered in Mary Jane's tea-room to

discuss it, she was kept busy with pots of tea and coffee.
Miss Kemble, being the rector's sister, offered to drive to
the hospital on the following day. 'The car will take four—
you will come of course, Miss Emily, and Mrs Stokes, how
fortunate that she is back—and of course my brother.'

Miss Emily put down her cup. 'It would be nice if Mary
Jane could come too....'

'Another day,' said Miss Kemble bossily. 'Besides, who
is to look after Didums? You know she is good with Mary
Jane.'

So it was agreed and the next day, encouraged by Sister's
report that Miss Mabel had had a good night, they set off.
Mary Jane watched them go holding a peevish Didums under
one arm. She took the dog up to the sitting-room presently
and closed the door, thankful that Brimble was taking a nap
on her bed and hadn't noticed anything. She would have
liked to have visited Miss Mabel and now she would have
to wait until she could find someone who would give her a
lift into Cheltenham.

As it turned out, she didn't have to wait long; Mrs
Fellowes popped in for a cup of tea and wanted to know why
Mary Jane hadn't gone with the others. 'That's too bad,' she
declared, 'but not to worry. I'm driving the doctor to
Cheltenham on Sunday—about three o'clock, we'll give you
a lift in, only we shan't be coming back. Do you suppose
you can get back here? There's a bus leaves Cheltenham for
Stratford-upon-Avon, so you could get to Broadway...' She
frowned. 'It's a long way round, but I'm sure there's an
evening bus to Stow-on-the-Wold from there.'

Mary Jane said recklessly, 'Thank you very much, I'd like
a lift. I'm sure I can get a bus home. I'll have a look at the
timetable in the post office.'

It was going to be an awkward, roundabout journey home
and it would depend on her getting on to the bus in
Cheltenham. She would have to keep a sharp eye on the time;
the bus depot was some way from the hospital. All the same
she would go. She wrote a postcard telling Miss Mabel that

she would see her on Sunday afternoon and put it in the letterbox before she could have second, more prudent thoughts.

Miss Emily, coming to collect Didums, had a great deal to say. Her sister was doing well, Sister had said, and she was to get out of bed on the following day. 'Modern surgery,' observed Miss Potter with a shake of the head. 'In my youth we stayed in bed for weeks. That nice man—he operated; Sir someone—came to see her while I was there and told me that the operation had been most successful and that dear Mabel would greatly benefit from it. Nice manners, too.'

Mary Jane muttered under her breath and offered Miss Potter a cup of tea.

She was quite busy for the rest of that week, so that she felt justified on Sunday in taking enough money from the till to cover her journey back home. If the worst came to the worst she could have a taxi; it would mean going without new winter boots, but she liked Miss Mabel.

She usually stayed open for part of Sunday, for that was when motorists tended to stop for tea, but she locked up after lunch, made sure that Brimble was safely indoors and walked through the village to the doctor's house.

Miss Mabel was delighted to see her; she seemed to have taken on a new lease of life since her operation and she insisted on telling Mary Jane every single detail of the treatment. She had got to the momentous moment when she had been out of bed when there was a slight stir in the ward. Sir Thomas Latimer was coming towards them, indeed, he appeared to be about to pass them when he stopped at Miss Mabel's bed.

On his bi-weekly round he had seen Mary Jane's postcard on Miss Mabel's locker and, without quite knowing why, he had decided to be on the ward on Sunday afternoon. It had been easy enough to give a reason—he had operated the day before on an emergency case and what could be more normal than a visit from him to see how his patient progressed? His casual, 'Good afternoon,' was a masterpiece of surprise.

Mary Jane's polite response was quite drowned by Miss Mabel's voice. 'Is it not delightful?' she enquired of him. 'Mary Jane has come to visit me—Dr Fellowes gave her a lift here. She will have to return by bus, though. I'm not sure how she will manage that, it being a Sunday, but she tells me that she has everything arranged.' She beamed at Mary Jane, who wasn't looking. 'I have been telling her how excellent is the treatment here. I shall recommend it to my friends.'

Just as though it were an hotel, thought Mary Jane, carefully not looking at Sir Thomas.

He stayed only a few minutes, bidding them both goodbye with casual politeness, and Mary Jane settled down to hear the rest of Miss Mabel's experiences, until a glance at the clock told her that she would have to go at once if she were to catch the bus. Not easily done, however, for Miss Mabel suddenly thought of numerous messages for her sister so that Mary Jane fairly galloped out of the hospital to pause at the entrance to get her bearings. She wasn't quite sure where the bus depot was and Mrs Fellowes' kindly directions had been vague.

The Rolls-Royce whispered to a halt beside her and its door opened.

'Get in,' said Sir Thomas. 'I'm going through your village.'

'I'm catching a bus.'

'Very unlikely. The Sunday service leaves half an hour earlier—I have that from the head porter, who is never wrong about anything.' He added gently, 'Get in, Miss Seymour, before we are had up for loitering.'

'But I'm not...' she began, and caught his eye. 'All right.' She sounded ungracious. 'Thank you.'

She fastened the seatbelt and sat back in luxury and he drove off without saying anything. Indeed, he didn't speak at all for some time, and then only to observe that Miss Mabel would be returning home very shortly. Mary Jane replied suitably and lapsed into silence once more for the sim-

ple reason that she had no idea what to talk about, but as
they neared the village she made an effort. 'Do you live near
here?'

'No, in London. I have to live near my work.'

'Then why are you here?'

'I visit various hospitals whenever it is found necessary.'

A most unsatisfactory answer. She didn't say anything
more until he drew up before the tea-room.

He got out before she could open her door and opened it
for her, took the old-fashioned key from her and opened the
cottage door.

It was dusk now and he found the switch and turned on
the lights before standing aside to let her pass him.

'Thank you very much,' said Mary Jane once again, and
bent to pick up Brimble who had rushed to meet her.

Sir Thomas leaned against the half-open door in no hurry
to go. 'Your cat?'

'Yes, Brimble. He's—he's company.'

'You live alone?'

'Yes.' She peered up at him. 'You'd better go, Sir Thomas,
if you're going all the way to London.'

Sir Thomas agreed meekly. He had never, he reflected,
been told to go by a girl. On the contrary, they made a point
of asking him to stay. He wasn't a conceited man but now
he was intrigued. He had wanted to meet her again, going
deliberately to the hospital when he knew that she would be
there, wanting to know more about her. The drive had hardly
been successful. He bade her a pleasantly impersonal goodbye. They were unlikely to meet again. He dismissed her
from his thoughts and drove back to London.

CHAPTER TWO

SEPTEMBER was almost over and the weather was changing. Fewer and fewer tourists stopped for coffee or tea although Mary Jane still did a steady trade with the village dwellers—just enough to keep the bills paid. Miss Mabel made steady progress and Mary Jane, graciously offered a lift in the rectory car, visited her again. Sir Thomas had been again, she was told, and Miss Mabel was to return home in a week's time and see him when he came to the hospital in six weeks' time. 'Such a nice man,' sighed Miss Mabel, 'a true gentleman, if you know what I mean.'

Mary Jane wasn't too sure about that but she murmured obligingly.

Miss Mabel's homecoming was something of an event in a village where one day was very like another. The ambulance brought her, deposited her gently in her home, drained Mary Jane's teapots and ate almost all the scones, and departed to be replaced by Miss Kemble, Mrs Stokes and after an interval Dr Fellowes, who tactfully sent them all away and made sure that the Misses Potter were allowed peace and quiet. Mary Jane, slipping through the village with a plate of tea-cakes as a welcome home gift, was prevailed upon to stay for a few minutes while Miss Mabel reiterated her experiences. 'I am to walk each day,' she said proudly, 'but lead a quiet life.' She laughed and Miss Emily laughed too. 'Not that we do anything else, do we, Mary Jane?'

Mary Jane smilingly agreed; that she had dreams of lovely clothes, candlelit dinners for two, dancing night after night and always with someone who adored her, was something she kept strictly to herself. Even Felicity, on the rare occasions when she saw her, took it for granted that she was content.

The mornings were frosty now and the evenings drawing in. The village, after the excitement of Miss Mabel's operation, did settle down. Mary Jane baked fewer scones and some days customers were so few it was hardly worth keeping the tea-room open.

She was preparing to close after an unprofitable Monday when the door was thrust open and a man came in. Mary Jane, wiping down the already clean tables, looked up hopefully, saw who it was and said in a neutral voice, 'Good evening, Oliver.'

Her cousin, Uncle Matthew's heir.

She had known him since her schooldays and had disliked him from the start, just as he had disliked her. She had been given short shrift when her uncle had died and for her part she hadn't been able to leave fast enough, for not only did Oliver dislike her, his wife, a cold woman, pushing her way up the social ladder, disliked her too. She stood, the cloth in her hand, waiting for him to speak.

'Business pretty bad?' he asked.

'It's a quiet time of the year. I'm making a living, thank you, Oliver.'

She was surprised to see that he was trying to be friendly, but not for long.

'Hope you'll do something for me,' he went on. 'Margaret has to go to London to see some specialist or other about her back. I have to go to America on business and someone will have to drive her up and stay with her.' He didn't quite meet her eyes. 'I wondered if you'd do that?' He laughed. 'Blood's thicker than water and all that...'

'I hadn't noticed,' said Mary Jane coldly. 'Margaret has family of her own, hasn't she? Surely there is someone with nothing better to do who could go with her?'

'We did ask around,' said Oliver airily, 'but you know how it is, they lead busy social lives, they simply can't spare the time.'

'And I can?' asked Mary Jane crisply.

'Well, you can't be making a fortune at this time of year.

It won't cost you a penny. Margaret will have to stay the night in town—tests and so forth. She can't drive herself because of this wretched back, and besides she's very nervous.' He added, 'She is in pain, too.'

Mary Jane had a tender heart. Very much against her inclination she agreed, reluctantly, to go with Margaret. It would mean leaving Brimble alone for two days but Mrs Adams next door would feed him and make sure that he was safe. It would mean shutting the tea-room too and, although Oliver made light of the paucity of customers at that time of year, all the same she would be short of two days' takings, however sparse they might be.

Oliver, having got what he wanted, lost no time in going. 'Next Tuesday,' he told her. 'I'll drive Margaret here in the car and you can take over. I leave in the afternoon.'

If he felt gratitude, he didn't show it. Mary Jane watched him get into his car and pulled a face at his back as he drove away.

Oliver returned on the Tuesday morning and Mary Jane, having packed an overnight bag, got into her elderly tweed suit, consigned Brimble to Mrs Adams's kindly hands, and opened the door to him.

He didn't bother with a good morning, a nod seemed the best he could manage. 'Margaret's in the car. Drive carefully; you'll have to fill up with petrol, there's not enough to bring you back.'

Mary Jane gave him a limpid look. 'Margaret has the money for that? I haven't.'

'Good God, girl, surely a small matter of a few gallons of petrol...'

'Well, just as you like. I'm sure Jim at the garage will have a man who can drive Margaret—you pay by the mile I believe, and petrol extra.'

Oliver went a dangerous plum colour. 'No one would think that we were cousins...'

'Well, no, I don't think that they would, I quite often for-

get that too.' She smiled. 'If you go now you'll catch Jim—
he'll be open by now.'

Oliver gave her a look to kill, with no effect whatsoever,
and took out his wallet.

'I shall require a strict account of what you spend,' he told
her crossly, and handed her some notes. 'Now come along,
Margaret is nervous enough already.'

Margaret was tall and what she described to herself as
elegantly thin. She had good features, marred by a down-
turned mouth and a frown; moreover she had a complaining
voice. She moaned now, 'Oh, dear, whatever has kept you?
Can't you see how ill I am? All this waiting about...'

Mary Jane got into the car. She said, 'Good morning, Margaret.' She turned to look at her. 'Before we go I must make
it quite clear to you that I have no money with me—perhaps
Oliver told you already?'

Margaret looked faintly surprised. 'No, he didn't, he
said...well, I've enough with me for both of us.' She added
sourly, 'It will be a nice treat for you, a couple of days in
town, all expenses paid.'

Mary Jane let this pass and, since Oliver did no more than
raise a careless hand to his wife, drove away. Margaret was
going to sulk, which left Mary Jane free to indulge her
thoughts. She toyed with the idea of sending Oliver a bill
for two days' average takings at the tea-rooms, plus the
hourly wages she would earn as a waitress. He would probably choke himself to death on reading it but it was fun to
think about.

'You're driving too fast,' complained Margaret.

Oliver had booked them in at a quiet hotel, near enough
to Wigmore Street for them to be able to walk there for
Margaret's appointment. He had thought of everything,
thought Mary Jane, unpacking Margaret's bag for her since
that lady declared herself to be exhausted; a hotel so quiet
and respectable that there was nothing to do and no one
under fifty staying there. Her room was on the floor above
Margaret's, overlooking a blank wall, furnished with what

she called Hotel Furniture. She unpacked her own bag and
went back to escort Margaret to lunch.

The dining-room was solid Victorian, dimly lit, the tables
laden with silverware and any number of wine glasses. She
cheered up at the sight; breakfast had been a sketchy affair
and she was hungry and the elaborate table settings augered
well for a good meal.

Unfortunately, this didn't turn out to be the case; lunch
was elaborately presented but not very filling: something
fishy on a lettuce leaf, lamb chops with a small side-dish of
vegetables and one potato, and trifle to follow. They drank
water and Mary Jane defiantly ate two rolls.

'I cannot think,' grumbled Margaret picking at her chop,
'why Oliver booked us in at this place. When we come to
town—the theatre, you know, or shopping—we always go to
one of the best hotels.' She thought for a moment. 'Of
course, I suppose he thought that, as you were coming with
me, this would do.'

Mary Jane's eyes glowed with purple fire. 'Now, that was
thoughtful of him. But you have no need to stay here,
Margaret, you can get a room in any hotel, pay the bill here
and I'll drive myself back this afternoon and get someone
from Jim's garage to collect you tomorrow.'

'You wouldn't—how dare you suggest it? Oliver would
never forgive you.'

'I don't suppose he would. I don't suppose he'd forgive
you either for spending his money. I dare say it won't be so
bad; you'll be home again tomorrow.'

'Oliver won't be back for at least a week.' Margaret
paused. 'Why don't you come and stay with me until he is
back? I shall need looking after— all the worry of this examination is really too much for me. I'm alone.'

'There's a housekeeper, isn't there? And two daily maids
and the gardener?' She glanced at her watch. 'Since we have
to walk to this place we had better go and get ready.'

'I feel quite ill at the very thought of being examined,'
observed Margaret as they set out. She had felt well enough

to make up her face very nicely and put on a fetching hat. She pushed past Mary Jane in a cloud of L'Air du Temps and told her sharply to hurry up.

Wigmore Street was quiet and dignified in the early afternoon sun and the specialist's rooms, according to the brass plate on the door, were in a tall red-brick house in the middle of a terrace of similar houses. Mary Jane rang the bell and they were ushered into a narrow hall.

'First floor,' the porter told them and went back to his cubbyhole, advising them that there was a lift if they preferred.

It was very quiet on the first-floor landing, doors on either side and one at the end. 'Ring the bell,' said Margaret and pointed to the door on the left.

It was as Mary Jane put her finger on it that she realised something. The little plate above it was inscribed Sir Thomas Latimer! She had seen it on the doorplate downstairs as well but it hadn't registered. She felt a little thrill of excitement at seeing him again. Not that she liked him in the least, she told herself, as the door was opened and Margaret swept past her, announcing her arrival in a condescending way which Mary Jane could see didn't go down well with the nurse.

They were a little early. The nurse offered chairs, made polite conversation for a few moments and went across to speak to the receptionist sitting at a desk in the corner of the room.

'I didn't expect to wait,' complained Margaret, 'I've come a long way and I'm in a good deal of pain.'

The nurse came back. 'Sir Thomas has many patients, Mrs Seymour, and some need more time than others.'

Five minutes later the door opened and an elderly lady, walking with sticks, came out accompanied by Sir Thomas, who shook her hand and handed her over to the nurse.

He went back into his consulting-room and closed the door and Mary Jane decided that he hadn't noticed her.

However, he had. He put the folder on his desk and went over to the window and looked out, surprised at the pleasure he had felt at the sight of her. He went back to his desk and opened the folder; this Mrs Seymour he was to see must be a sister-in-law—she and Mary Jane came from the same village.

He went and sat down and asked his nurse over the intercom to send in Mrs Seymour.

He could find nothing wrong with her at all; she described endless symptoms in a rather whining voice, none of which he could substantiate. Nevertheless, he sent her to the X-ray unit on the floor above and listened patiently to her renewed complaints when she returned.

'If you will return in the morning,' he told her, 'when the X-ray results will be ready, I hope that I will be able to reassure you. I can find nothing wrong with you, Mrs Seymour, but we can discuss that tomorrow. Shall we say ten o'clock?'

'He is no good,' declared Margaret as they walked back. 'I shall find another specialist...'

'You could at least wait and see what the X-rays show,' suggested Mary Jane sensibly. 'Why not have a rest in your room and an early night after dinner?'

First, though, they had tea in the hotel lounge and since it was, rather surprisingly, quite a substantial one, Mary Jane made the most of it, a little surprised at Margaret, despite her pain, eating a great many sandwiches and cream cakes. Left on her own, she poured a last cup of tea and thought about Sir Thomas. She hadn't expected him to recognise her and after all he had had but the barest glimpse as he had stood in the doorway. As he had ushered Margaret out of his consulting-room he hadn't looked in her direction. All the same, it was interesting to have seen him again in his own environment, as it were. Very remote and professional, thought Mary Jane, eating a last sandwich, not a bit like the man who had pushed his way into her tea-room, demanding tea for his friend. She sighed for no reason at all, picked up a magazine and sat reading, a girl not worth a second glance, until it was time to go up to Margaret's room and warn her that dinner would be in half an hour.

Getting Margaret there by ten o'clock was rather an effort but she managed it, to be told by the nurse that Sir Thomas had been at one of the hospitals since the early hours of the morning operating on an emergency case. He would be with them as soon as possible and in the meantime perhaps they would like coffee?

'Well, this is really too bad,' grumbled Margaret. 'I am a private patient...'

'This was an emergency, Mrs Seymour,' said the nurse smoothly and went to get the coffee.

Mary Jane sat allowing Margaret's indignant whine to pass over her head. Like him or not, she felt sorry for Sir Thomas, up half the night and then having to cope with someone like Margaret instead of having a nap. She hoped he wouldn't be too tired...

When he came presently he looked exactly like a man who had enjoyed a good night's sleep, with time to dress with his usual elegance and eat a good breakfast. Only, when she peeped at him while he was greeting Margaret, she saw that there were tired lines around his eyes. He caught her staring at him when he turned to bid her good morning and she blushed a little. He watched the pretty colour pinken her cheeks and smiled. It was a kind and friendly smile and she was taken by surprise by it.

'Your patient? Was the operation successful?' She went even pinker; perhaps she shouldn't have asked—it wasn't any of her business.

'Entirely, thank you—a good start to my day.' Thank heaven he hadn't sounded annoyed, thought Mary Jane.

The nurse led Margaret away then, and Mary Jane sat and looked at the glossy magazines scattered around her. The models in them looked as though they should still be at school and were so thin that she longed to feed them up on good wholesome food. Some of the clothes were lovely but since she was never likely to wear any of them she took care not to want them too much.

I'm the wrong shape, she told herself, unaware that despite her thinness she had a pretty, curvy figure and nice legs, concealed by the tweed suit.

The door opened and Sir Thomas showed Margaret back into the waiting-room, and it was quite obvious that Margaret was in a dreadful temper whereas he presented an impeturbable manner. He didn't look at Mary Jane but shook Margaret's reluctant hand, wished her goodbye with cool courtesy and went back into his consulting-room.

Margaret took no notice of the nurse's polite goodbyes but flounced down to the street. 'I told you he was no good,' she hissed. 'The man's a fool, he says there is nothing wrong with me.' She gave a nasty little laugh. 'I'm to take more exercise, if you please—walk for an hour, mind you—each day, make beds, work in the garden, be active. I have suffered for years with my back, I'm quite unable to do anything strenuous; if you knew the hours I spend lying on the *chaise longue*...'

'Perhaps that's why your back hurts,' suggested Mary Jane matter-of-factly.

'Don't be stupid. You can drive me home and I shall tell Dr Fellowes exactly what I think of him and his specialist.'

'He must know what he's talking about,' observed Mary Jane rashly, 'otherwise he wouldn't be a consultant, would he?'

'What do you know about it, anyway?' asked Margaret rudely. They had reached the hotel. 'Get your bag and get someone to bring the car round. We're leaving now.'

It was a pleasant autumn day; the drive would have been agreeable too if only Margaret would have stopped talking. Luckily she didn't need any answers, so Mary Jane was able to think her own thoughts.

She wasn't invited in when they arrived at the house. Mary Jane, to whom it had been home for happy years, hadn't expected that anyway. 'You can drive the car round to the garage before you go,' said Margaret without so much as a thank-you.

'Oliver can do that whenever he comes back; if you mind about it being parked outside you can drive it round yourself, Margaret; I'm going home.' She added rather naughtily, 'Don't forget that hour's walk each day.'

'Come back,' ordered Margaret. 'How can you be so cruel, leaving me like this?'

Mary Jane was already walking down the short drive. She called over her shoulder, 'But you're home, Margaret, and Sir Thomas said that there was nothing wrong with you...'

'I'll never speak to you again.'

'Oh, good.'

Mary Jane nipped smartly out of the open gate and down to the village. It was still mid-afternoon; she would open the tea-room in the hope that some passing motorist would fancy a pot of tea and scones. First she would have a meal; breakfast was hours ago and Margaret had refused to stop on the way. Beans on toast, she decided happily, opening her door.

Brimble was waiting for her, she picked him up and tucked him under an arm while she opened windows, turned the sign round to 'Open' and put the kettle on.

Brimble, content after a meal, sat beside her while she ate her own meal and then went upstairs to take a nap, leaving her to see that everything was ready for any customers who might come.

They came presently, much to her pleased surprise; a hiking couple, a family party in a car which looked as though it might fall apart at any moment and a married couple who quarrelled quietly all the while they ate their tea. Mary Jane locked the door with a feeling of satisfaction, got her supper and started on preparations for the next day. While she made a batch of tea-cakes she thought about Sir Thomas.

It was towards the end of October, on a chilly late afternoon, just as Mary Jane was thinking of closing since there was little likelihood of any customers, that Sir Thomas walked in. She had her back to the door, rearranging a shelf at the back of the tea-room and she had neither heard nor seen the Rolls come to a quiet halt outside.

'Too late for tea?' he asked and she spun round, clutching some plates.

'No—yes, I was just going to close.'

'Oh, good.' He turned the sign round. 'We can have a quiet talk without being disturbed.'

'Talk? Whatever about? Is something wrong with Miss Potter? I do hope not.'

'Miss Potter is making excellent progress...'

'Then it's Margaret—Mrs Seymour.'

'Ah, yes, the lady you escorted. As far as I know she is leading her normal life, and why not? There is nothing wrong with her. I came to talk about you.'

'Me. Why?'

'Put the kettle on and I'll tell you.'

Sir Thomas sat down at one of the little tables and ate one of the scones on a plate there, and, since it seemed that he intended to stay there until he had had his tea, Mary Jane put the plates down and went to put on the kettle.

By the time she came back with the teapot he had finished the scones and she fetched another plate, offering them wordlessly.

'You wanted to tell me something?' she prompted.

He sat back in the little cane chair so that it creaked alarmingly, his teacup in his hand. 'Yes...'

The thump on the door stopped him and when it was repeated he got up and unlocked it. The girl who came in flashed him a dazzling smile.

'Hello, Mary Jane. I'm on my way to Cheltenham and it seemed a good idea to look you up.' She pecked Mary Jane's cheek and looked across at Sir Thomas. 'Am I interrupting something?'

'No,' said Mary Jane rather more loudly than necessary. 'This is Sir Thomas Latimer, an orthopaedic surgeon, he— that is, Margaret went to see him about her back and he has a patient in the village.' She glanced at him, still standing by the door. 'This is my sister, Felicity.'

Felicity was looking quite beautiful, of course; she dressed in the height of fashion and somehow the clothes always looked right on her. She had tinted her hair, too, and her make-up was exquisite, making the most of her dark eyes and the perfect oval of her face. She smiled at Sir Thomas now as he came to shake her hand, smiling down at her, holding her hand just a little longer than he need, making some easy light-hearted remark which made Felicity laugh.

Of course, he's fallen for her, reflected Mary Jane; since Felicity had left home to join the glamorous world of fashion she had had a continuous flow of men at her beck and call and she couldn't blame Sir Thomas; her sister was quite lovely. She said, 'Felicity is a well-known model...'

'I can't imagine her being anything else,' observed Sir Thomas gravely. 'Are you staying here with Mary Jane?'

'Lord, no. There's only one bedroom and I'd be terribly in the way—she gets up at the crack of dawn to cook, don't you, darling?' She glanced around her. 'Still making a living? Good. No, I'm booked in at the Queens at Cheltenham, I'm doing a dress show there tomorrow.' She smiled at Sir Thomas. 'I suppose you wouldn't like to come? We could have dinner...?'

'How delightful that would have been, although the dress show hardly appeals, but dinner with you would be another matter.'

The fool, thought Mary Jane fiercely. She had seen Felicity capture a man's attention a dozen times and not really minded but now she did. Sir Thomas was like the rest of them but for some reason she had thought that he was different.

Felicity gave an exaggerated sigh. 'Surely you could manage dinner? I don't know anyone in Cheltenham.'

'I'm on my way back to London,' he told her. 'Then I'm off to a seminar in Holland.'

Felicity said with a hint of sharpness, 'A busy man—are

you a very successful specialist or something, making your millions?'

'I am a busy man, yes.' He smiled charmingly and she turned away to say goodbye to Mary Jane.

'Perhaps I'll drop in as I go back,' she suggested.

He opened the door for her and then walked with her to her car. Mary Jane could hear her sister's laughter before she drove away. She began to clear away the tea tray, she still had to do some baking ready for the next day and Brimble was prowling round, grumbling for his supper.

'We didn't finish our tea,' observed Sir Thomas mildly. He looked at her with questioning eyebrows.

Well, he is not getting another pot, reflected Mary Jane, and told him so, only politely. 'I've a lot of baking to do and I expect you want to get back to London.'

Sir Thomas's eyes gleamed with amusement. 'Then I won't keep you.' He picked up the coat he had tossed over a chair. 'You have a very beautiful sister, Mary Jane.'

'Yes, we're not a bit alike, are we?'

'No, not in the least.' A remark which did nothing to improve her temper. 'And I haven't had the opportunity to talk to you...'

'I don't suppose it was of the least importance.' She spoke tartly. 'You can tell me if we meet again, which isn't very likely.'

He opened the door. 'You are mistaken about a great many things, Mary Jane,' he told her gravely. 'Goodnight.'

She closed the door and bolted it and went back to the kitchen, not wishing to see him go.

She washed the cups and saucers with a good deal of noise, fed Brimble and got out the pastry board, the rolling pin and the ingredients for the scones. Her mind not being wholly on her work, her dough suffered a good deal of rough treatment; notwithstanding, the scones came from the oven nicely risen and golden brown. She cleared away and went upstairs, having lost all appetite for her supper.

Felicity hadn't said when she would come again but she

seldom did, dropping in from time to time when it suited her. When they had been younger she had always treated Mary Jane with a kind of tolerant affection, at the same time making no effort to take much interest in her. It had been inevitable that Mary Jane should stay at home with her aunt and uncle and, even when they had died and she had inherited the cottage, Felicity had made no effort to help in any way. She was earning big money by then but neither she nor, for that matter, Mary Jane had expected her to do anything to make life easier for her young sister. Mary Jane had accepted the fact that Felicity was a success in life, leading a glamorous existence, travelling, picking and choosing for whom she would work and, while she was glad that she had made such a success of her life, she had no wish to be a part of it and certainly she felt no envy. Common sense told her that a plain face and a tendency to stay in the background would never earn her a place in the world of fashion.

Not that she would have liked that, she was content with her tea-room and Brimble and her friends in the village, although it would have been nice to have had a little more money.

The Misses Potter came in for their usual tea on the following day.

Miss Mabel was walking with a stick now and was a changed woman. They had been to Cheltenham on the previous day, they told Mary Jane, and that nice Sir Thomas had said that she need not go to see him anymore, just go for a check-up to Dr Fellowes every few months.

'He's going away,' she explained to Mary Jane, 'to some conference or other, but we heard that he will be going to the Radcliffe Infirmary at Oxford when he gets back. Much sought-after,' said Miss Mabel with satisfaction.

Of course, the village knew all about him calling at the tea-room and, Mary Jane being Mary Jane, her explanation that he had merely called for a cup of tea on his way back to London was accepted without comment. Felicity's visit had also been noticed with rather more interest. Very few

people took *Vogue* or *Harpers and Queen* but those who
visited their dentist or doctor and read the magazines in the
waiting-room were well aware of her fame.

She came a few days later during the morning, walking
into the tea-room and giving the customers there a pleasant
surprise. She was wearing a suede outfit in red with boots in
black leather and a good deal of gold jewellery. Not at all
the kind of clothes the village was used to; even the doctor's
wife and Margaret, not to mention the lady of the manor,
wouldn't have risked wearing such an outfit. She smiled
around her, confident that she was creating an impression.

'Hello, Mary Jane,' she said smilingly, pleased with the
mild sensation she had caused. 'Can you spare me a cup of
coffee? I'm on my way back to town.'

She sat down at one of the tables and Mary Jane, busy
with serving, said, 'Hello, Felicity. Yes, of course, but will
you help yourself? I'm quite busy.'

The customers went presently, leaving the two sisters
alone. Mary Jane collected up cups and saucers and tidied
the tables and Felicity said rather impatiently, 'Oh, do sit
down for a minute, you can wash up after I've gone.'

Mary Jane fetched a cup of coffee for herself, refilled Felicity's cup and sat. 'Did you have a successful show?' she
asked.

'Marvellous. I'm off to the Bahamas next week—*Vogue*
and *Elle*. When I get back it will be time for the dress show
in Paris. Life's all go...'

'Would you like to change it?'

Felicity gave her a surprised stare. 'Change it? My dear
girl, have you any idea of the money I earn?'

'Well no, I don't think that I have...' Mary Jane spoke
without rancour. 'But it must be a great deal.'

'It is. I like money and I spend it. In a year or two I intend
to find a wealthy husband and settle down. Sooner, if I meet
someone I fancy.' She smiled across the little table. 'Like
that man I met when I was here last week. Driving a Rolls

and doing very nicely and just my type. I can't think how you met him, Mary Jane.'

'He operated on a friend of mine here and I met him at the hospital. He stopped for a cup of tea on his way back to London. I don't know anything about him except that he's a specialist in bones.'

'How revolting.' Felicity wrinkled her beautiful nose. 'But of course, he must have a social life. Is he married?'

'I've no idea. I should think it must be very likely, wouldn't you?'

'London, you say? I must find out. What's his name?'

Mary Jane told her but with reluctance. There was no reason why she should mind Felicity's interest in him, indeed she would make a splendid foil for his magnificent size and good looks and presumably he would be able to give Felicity all the luxury she demanded of life.

'He said he was going abroad—to Holland, I think,' she volunteered.

'Good. That gives me time to track him down. Once I know where he lives or works I can meet him again—accidentally of course.'

Well, thought Mary Jane in her sensible way, he's old enough and wise enough to look after himself and there's that other woman who came here with him...

She didn't mention her to her sister.

Felicity didn't stay long. 'Ticking over nicely?' she asked carelessly. 'You always liked a quiet life, didn't you?'

What would Felicity have said if she had declared that she would very much like to wear lovely clothes, go dancing and be surrounded by young men? Mary Jane, loading a tray carefully, agreed placidly.

Since it seemed likely that the quiet life was to be her lot, there wasn't much point in saying anything else.

CHAPTER THREE

OCTOBER, sliding towards November, had turned wet and chilly and customers were sparse. Mary Jane turned out cupboards, washed and polished and cut down on the baking. There were still customers glad of a cup of tea, home from shopping expeditions—or motorists on their way to Cheltenham or Oxford stopped for coffee. More prosperous tea-rooms closed down during the winter months and their owners went to Barbados or California to spend their summer's profits, but Mary Jane's profits weren't large enough for that. Besides, since she lived over the tea-room she might just as well keep it open and get what custom there was.

On this particular morning, since it was raining hard and moreover was a Monday, she was pleased to hear the doorbell tinkle as she set the percolator on the stove. It wasn't a customer, though. Oliver stood there, just inside the door.

She wasn't particularly pleased to see him but she wished him a cheerful good morning.

'I'm just back from the States,' declared Oliver pompously. 'Margaret tells me that you have behaved most unkindly towards her. I should have thought that you could at least have stayed with her and made sure that she was quite comfortable.'

'But she is not ill—Sir Thomas Latimer said so. He said that she should take more exercise and not lie around.'

Oliver's eyes bulged with annoyance. 'I consider you to be a heartless girl, Mary Jane. I shall think twice before asking you to do any small favour...'

'You'd be wasting time,' said Mary Jane matter-of-factly, 'for you're quite able to find someone else if Margaret insists on feeling poorly all the time. I've my living to earn, you know.'

Oliver's eyes slid away from hers. 'As a matter of fact, I have to go away again very shortly...'

'Then you can arrange for someone to be with Margaret; don't waste your time with me, Oliver.'

'You ungrateful...'

She came and stood before him. 'Tell me, what am I ungrateful for?' she invited.

Oliver still didn't meet her eyes. 'Well,' he began.

'Just so, go away, Oliver, before I bang you over the head with my rolling pin.'

'Don't be ridiculous,' he blustered. All the same he edged towards the door.

Which opened to admit the giant-like person of Sir Thomas, his elegant grey suit spattered with rain. He said nothing, only stood there, his eyebrows slightly raised, smiling a little.

Mary Jane had gone pink at the sight of him; blushing was a silly habit she had never quite conquered. She was pleased to see him. Oliver, after a first startled glance, had ignored him. 'You've not heard the last of this, Mary Jane—your own flesh and blood.'

'Ah,' said Sir Thomas, in the gentlest of voices. 'You are, I believe, Mrs Seymour's husband?'

Oliver goggled. 'Yes—yes, I am.' He puffed out his chest in readiness for a few well-chosen words but he was forestalled.

'Delighted to meet you,' said Sir Thomas with suave untruthfulness. 'It gives me the opportunity to tell you that there is nothing wrong with your wife. A change of lifestyle is all that she needs—rather more activity.'

Oliver looked from him to Mary Jane who in her turn was studying the row of glass jars on the shelf on the further wall. 'Really, surely this is hardly the place,' he began.

'Oh, Miss Seymour was with your wife and of course already knows what I have told Mrs Seymour. I thought it might reassure you to mention it. You will, of course, get a report from your own doctor in due course.'

He opened the door invitingly, letting in a good deal of wind and rain, and Oliver, muttering that he was a busy man, hurried out to his car without a word more than a cursory good morning.

Sir Thomas brushed a few drops of rain off his sleeve and Mary Jane said, 'You're wet.'

He glanced at her. 'I was passing in the car and saw you talking to your—cousin? You looked as though you were going to hit him and it seemed a good idea to—er—join you.'

'I threatened him with a rolling pin,' said Mary Jane in a satisfied voice.

'Admirable. A very handy weapon. Do you often use it?' He added gravely, 'As a weapon?'

'Well, of course not. He was annoying me. Do you want coffee?'

'I was hoping that you would ask me. And are there any scones?'

She set a plate on the table and a dish of butter and he spread a scone and bit into it.

'Are you hungry?' asked Mary Jane pointedly.

'Famished. I've been at the Radcliffe all night...'

She poured coffee for them both and sat down opposite him. 'But you're going the wrong way home.'

'Ah, yes. I thought I'd take a day off. I've a clinic at six o'clock this evening. It crossed my mind that it would be pleasant if we were to spend it together. Lunch perhaps? A drive through the countryside?'

'Oughtn't you to go to bed?'

'If you were to offer me a boiled egg or even a rasher or two of bacon I'll doze for ten minutes or so while you do whatever it is you do before you go out for the day.'

'The tea-room...'

'Just for once?' He contrived to look hungry and lonely, although she suspected that he was neither.

'Bacon and eggs,' she told him before she could change her mind. 'And I'll need half an hour.'

'Excellent. I'll come and watch you cook.'

He sat on the kitchen table, Brimble on his knee, while she got out the frying pan and, while the bacon sizzled, sliced bread and made more coffee.

'Two eggs?' She looked up and found him staring at her. It was a thoughtful look and she wondered about it until he spoke.

'Yes, please. Where is your beautiful sister, Mary Jane?'

She cracked the eggs neatly. For some reason his question had made her unhappy although she had no intention of letting it show. 'Well, she went to Barbados but she should be back by now—I think it's the Paris dress shows next week. She lives in London, though. Would you like to have her address?'

'Yes, please, I feel I owe her a dinner. If you remember?'

'Yes, of course.' She wrote on the back of the pad, tore off the page and gave it to him. 'That's her phone number, too.'

She didn't look at him but dished up his breakfast and fetched the coffee-pot.

'I'll go and change while you eat,' she told him. 'Brimble likes the bacon rinds.'

Upstairs she inspected her wardrobe. It would have to be the jersey dress, kept for unlikely occasions such as this one, and the Marks and Spencer mac. Somewhere or other there was a rainproof hat—if only she had the sort of curly hair which looked enchanting when it got wet...

She went downstairs presently and found Sir Thomas, his chair balanced precariously against the wall, his large feet on the table, asleep. He had tidied his breakfast plate away into the sink and Brimble, licking the last of the bacon rinds from his whiskers, was perched on his knees.

Mary Jane stood irresolute. It would be cruel to wake him up; on the other hand he looked very uncomfortable.

'A splendid breakfast,' said Sir Thomas, his eyes still closed. 'I feel like a new man.'

He opened his eyes then. No one would have known that he had been up all night.

'Have you really been up all night?' asked Mary Jane. She blinked at the sudden cold stare.

'I have many faults, but I don't lie.' His voice was as cold as his eyes and she made haste to make amends.

'I'm sorry, I wasn't doubting you, only you look so—so tidy!' she finished lamely.

'Tidy? I have showered and shaved and put on a clean shirt. Is that being tidy?' He lifted Brimble gently from his knee and stood up, towering over her. His gaze swept over her person. 'Most suitably dressed for the weather,' he observed, and she bore his scrutiny silently, aware that the hat, while practical, did nothing for her at all.

She turned the sign to 'Closed', coaxed Brimble into his basket, shut windows and locked doors and pronounced herself ready. The rain was still sheeting down. 'You'll get wet,' she told him. 'I've an umbrella...'

He smiled and took the key from her and locked the tea-room door and went to unlock the car door, bundled her in, gave himself a shake and got in beside her. 'Oxford?' he asked and, when she nodded happily, smiled.

Mary Jane, suddenly shy, was relieved when he started an undemanding conversation, and he, versed in the art of putting people at their ease, kept up a flow of small talk until they reached Oxford. The rain had eased a little, and, with the car safely parked, they set out on a walk around the colleges.

'Did you come here?' asked Mary Jane, craning her neck to see Tom Tower.

'I was at Trinity.'

'Before you trained as a doctor—no, surgeon.'

'I took my MD, and then went over to surgery—ortho-paedics.'

She lowered her gaze from Tom Tower to her companion. 'I expect you're very clever.'

'Everyone is clever at something,' he told her, and took her arm and walked her to the Radcliffe Camera.

'May we go inside?'

'To the reading rooms if you like. It houses the Bodleian Library.'

He took her to the Eastgate Hotel and gave her coffee in the bar, a cheerful place, crowded with students, and then walked her briskly down to the river before popping her back into the car.

'There's a rather nice place for lunch,' he told her casually, 'a few miles away.'

An understatement, Mary Jane decided when they reached Le Manoir aux Quat' Saisons at Great Milton; it was definitely a grand place and the jersey dress was quite inadequate. However, she was given no time to worry about that. She was whisked inside, led away to tidy herself and then settled in the bar with a glass of sherry while Sir Thomas, very much at his ease, sat opposite her studying the menu. He glanced at her presently.

'Dublin Bay prawns?' he suggested. 'And what about *poulet Normand*?'

Mary Jane agreed, she had never tasted Dublin Bay prawns but she was hungry enough to try anything; as for the chicken, she had read the recipe for that in her cookery book—egg yolks and thick cream and brandy, butter and onions—it sounded delicious.

It was. She washed it down with spa water and, when invited, chose an orange cream soufflé—more cream, and Curaço this time. Over coffee she said, in her sensible way, 'This is a delightful place and that was the most gorgeous meal I've had for a long time. You're very kind.'

She caught his eye and went a little pink. 'Oh, dear, I've made it sound like a half-term treat with an...' She stopped just in time and the pink deepened.

'Uncle? Godfather?' he suggested, and she let out a sigh of relief when he laughed. 'I've enjoyed my day too, Mary Jane, you are a very restful companion; you haven't rearranged your hair once or powdered your nose or put on more lipstick and you really enjoyed Oxford, didn't you?'

'Oh, very much. It's a long time since I was there.' She fell silent, remembering how her father used to take Felicity and her there, walking the streets, pointing out the lovely old buildings, and Sir Thomas watched her with faint amusement and vague pity. So independent, he reflected, making a life for herself, and so different from her rather beautiful sister. He must remember to mention her funny little tea-room to his family and friends; drum up some customers for her so that she would have some money to spend on herself. A new hat for a start. No rain hat was becoming but at least it need not be quite as awful as the one she had been wearing all day.

Her quiet voice interrupted his thoughts. 'If you are to be back in London this evening ought we not to be going? I don't want to go,' she added childishly and smiled at him, her violet eyes glowing because she was happy.

'I don't want to go either, but you are quite right.' He had uttered the words almost without thinking and realised to his surprise that he had meant them; he had really enjoyed her company, undemanding, ready to be pleased with everything they had seen and done.

He drove her back to the tea-room, talking about nothing much, at ease with each other, but when she offered him tea he refused. 'I've played truant for long enough. It has been a delightful day, Mary Jane—thank you for your company.'

She offered a small gloved hand. 'Thank you for asking me. It was a treat and so much nicer because I hadn't expected one. I hope you're not too busy this evening so that you can get a good night's sleep, Sir Thomas.'

He concealed a smile. The evening clinic was always busy and there was a pile of work awaiting him on his desk at home.

'I have no doubt of it,' he told her cheerfully, and got into his car and drove away.

She stood at the door until he was out of sight and then

took off her outdoor things, fed a peevish Brimble and put the kettle on. It had been a lovely day; she thought about it, minute by minute, while she sipped her tea. She had too much common sense to suppose that Sir Thomas had actually wished for her company—he had needed a companion to share his day and she had been handy and it was obvious that he had called that morning so that he might get Felicity's address. His invitation had been on the spur of the moment and she was quite sure that she fell far short of his usual companions. And she had seen the look he had cast at the rain hat. She got up and went to examine her face in the small looking glass on the kitchen wall. It was rosy from her day out of doors but she didn't see how her skin glowed with health and how her eyes shone. All she saw was her hair, damp around the edges where it had escaped from the hat, and the lack of make-up.

'You're a plain girl,' she told her reflection, and Brimble looked up from his grooming to mutter an agreement.

Promptly at six o'clock, Sir Thomas sat himself down behind his desk in the clinic consultation-room and listened patiently as one patient after the other took the seat opposite to him, to be led away in turn to be carefully examined by him, and then told, in the kindest possible way, what was wrong and what would have to be done. It was almost nine o'clock by the time the last patient had been shown out and he and his registrar and houseman prepared to leave too. Outpatients Sister stifled a yawn as she collected notes—she hated the evening clinic but she had worked with Sir Thomas for several years now and if he had decided to have a clinic at three o'clock in the morning, she would have agreed cheerfully. He was her—and almost all of the nursing staff's—ideal man, never hurried, always polite, unfailingly patient, apparently unaware of the devotion accorded him. For such a successful man he was singularly unconceited.

He bade everyone goodnight and drove himself to his home; a house in a row of similar elegant houses in Little Venice, facing the Grand Union Canal. It had stopped raining

at last and the late evening was quiet. He opened his front
door and as he did so an elderly man, rather stout and short,
came into the hall.

'Evening, Tremble,' said Sir Thomas, and tossed his coat
on to an elbow chair beside a Georgian mahogany side-table.

Tremble picked up the coat and folded it carefully over
one arm. 'Good evening, sir. Mrs Tremble has a nice little
dinner all ready for you.'

'Thank you.' Sir Thomas was looking through his post.
'Give me ten minutes, will you?'

He took his post and his bag into the study at the back of
the hall and sat down to read the letters before going up to
his room, to return presently and sit by the fire in the big
drawing-room at the front of the house. He was greeted here
by a Labrador dog, who got to elderly feet and lumbered
happily to meet him.

Sir Thomas sat down, a glass of whisky beside him, the
dog's head on his knee. 'A pity you weren't with us, old
fellow,' he said. 'I rather fancy you would have liked her.'

Tremble's voice reminded him that dinner was served and
he crossed the hall with the dog to the dining-room, a room
beautifully furnished with a Regency mahogany twin ped-
estal table surrounded by Hepplewhite chairs; there was an
inlaid mahogany sideboard of the same period against one
wall and the lighting was pleasantly subdued from the brass
sconces on the walls. There were paintings too—Dutch
flower studies and a number of portraits.

Sir Thomas, being a very large man, ate his dinner with
good appetite, exchanging a casual conversation with
Tremble as he was served and offering his dog the last morsel of his cheese.

'Watson had his supper an hour ago, sir,' said Tremble
severely.

'We are told that cheese is good for the digestion,
Tremble; I suppose that applies to dogs as well as humans.'

'I really couldn't say, sir. Will you have your coffee in
the drawing-room?'

'Please, and do tell Mrs Tremble that everything was delicious.'

He went to his study presently with Watson as company, and worked at his desk. He had quite forgotten Mary Jane.

Even if Mary Jane had wanted to forget him she wasn't given that chance. Naturally, in a village that size, she had been seen getting into Sir Thomas's Rolls-Royce, a news item flashed round the village in no time at all, so that when she got out of it again that late afternoon, several ladies living in the cottages on either side of her saw that too.

Trade was brisk the following morning and it was only after she had answered a few oblique questions that she realised why. Since some of the ladies in the tea-room were prone to embroider any titbit of news to make it more exciting, she told them about her day out in a sensible manner which revealed not a whiff of romance.

She was well-liked; disappointed as they were at her prosaic description of her day with Sir Thomas, they were pleased that she had enjoyed herself. She had little enough fun and no opportunity of getting away from the village and meeting young people of her own age. They lingered over their coffee and, when the Misses Potter joined them, the talk turned, naturally enough, to Sir Thomas.

'Such a nice man,' declared Miss Mabel. 'As mild as milk.'

'Even milk boils over from time to time,' muttered Mary Jane, offering a plate of digestive biscuits, the scones had all been eaten long-since.

Sir Thomas, arriving at his consulting-rooms in Wigmore Street the following morning, wished Miss Pink, his secretary and receptionist, a cheerful good morning and paused at her desk.

'What have I got this weekend?' he wanted to know.

'You're making a speech at that dinner on Saturday evening. Miss Thorley phoned and asked would you like to take her to dinner on Sunday evening; she suggested a day out somewhere first.' Miss Pink's voice was dry.

For a moment Mary Jane's happy face, crowned with the deplorable hat, floated before Sir Thomas's eyes. He said at once, 'I intend to go down to my mother's. Would you phone Miss Thorley and tell her I shall be away?'

Miss Pink gave him a thoughtful look and he returned it blandly. 'I'm far too busy to phone her myself.'

Miss Pink allowed herself a gentle smile as Sir Thomas went into his consulting-room; Miss Thorley, on the rare occasions when she had seen her, had looked at her as though she despised her and Miss Pink, of no discernible age, sharp-nosed and spectacled, objected strongly to that.

There was just time before the first patient was announced for Sir Thomas to phone his mother and invite himself for the weekend.

Her elderly, comfortable voice came clearly over the wires. 'How nice, dear. Are you bringing anyone with you?'

He said that no, he wasn't and the fleeting thought that it would be interesting to see his mother and Mary Jane together whisked through his head, to be instantly dismissed as so much nonsense.

Mary Jane's day out, while not exactly a nine-day wonder, kept the village interested for a few days until the local post-man's daughter's wedding. An event which caused the village to turn out *en masse* to crowd into the church and throw confetti afterwards. It brought some welcome custom to Mary Jane, too, for somewhere was needed afterwards where the details of the wedding, the bride's finery and speculation as to the happy couple's future happiness could be mulled over. She did a roaring trade in coffee and scones and, for latecomers, sausage rolls.

She went to bed that night confident that, with luck, she would be able to get a new winter coat.

It was almost midnight by the time Sir Thomas, resplendent in white tie and tails, returned from the banquet which he had been invited to attend. He had made his speech, brief and to the point, and it had been well received and now it was just a question of changing into comfortable clothes, collecting a sleepy Watson and getting into his car once more. It would be late by the time he reached his mother's house, but he had a key. At that time of night, with the roads quiet and a good deal of them motorway, he should be there in little over an hour.

Which he was; he slowed down as he entered the village, its inhabitants long since in bed, and took the car slowly past the church and then, a few hundred yards further, through the open gates of the house beyond.

The night was chilly with a hint of frost and there was bright moonlight. The low, rambling house was in darkness save for a dim light shining through the transom over the door. Sir Thomas got out quietly, opened the door for Watson and stood for a moment while his companion trotted off into the shrubbery at the side of the house, to reappear shortly and, as silent as his master, enter the house.

The hall was square, low-ceilinged and pleasantly warm. There was a note by the lamp on the side-table. Someone had printed 'Coffee on the Aga' on a card and propped it against the elegant china base of the lamp. Sir Thomas smiled a little and went soft-footed to the baize door beside the staircase and so through to the kitchen door where he poured his coffee, gave Watson a drink and presently took himself up to his bed, leaving Watson already asleep on the rug before the Aga.

Four hours later he was up and dressed, drinking tea in the kitchen and talking to his mother's housekeeper, Mrs Beaver.

'And how's that nasty old London?' she wanted to know.

'Well, I don't see a great deal of it, I spend most of my days either at the hospital or my rooms. I often wonder why I don't resign and come and live in peace and quiet here.'

'Go on with you, Sir Thomas, leaving that clever brain of

yours to moulder away doing nothing but walking the dog and shooting pigeons. That's not you. Now if you was to ask me, I'd say get yourself a wife and a clutch of children—no question of you giving up then with all them mouths to feed.'

He put down his mug and gave her a hug, 'You old match-maker,' he told her, and whistled to Watson. It was a fine, chilly morning; there was time to go for a walk before breakfast.

His mother was at the table when he got back, sitting behind the coffee pot; a small, slim woman with pepper and salt hair done in an old-fashioned bun and wearing a beautifully tailored suit.

'There you are, Thomas. How nice to see you, dear, I suppose you can't stay for a few days?'

He bent to kiss her. 'Afraid not, Mama—I'm rather booked up for the next week or so, I'll have to go back very early on Monday morning.'

He helped himself to bacon and eggs, added mushrooms and a tomato or two and sat down beside her. 'The garden looks pretty good...'

'Old Dodds knows his job, though he's a bit pernickety when I want to cut some flowers.' She handed him his coffee, 'Well, what have you been doing, my dear—other than work?'

'Nothing much. A banquet I couldn't miss yesterday evening and one or two dinner parties...'

'What happened to that gorgeous young woman who had begged a lift from you—oh, some weeks ago now?'

He speared a morsel of bacon and topped it neatly with a mushroom.

'Ingrid Bennett. I have no idea.' He smiled suddenly, remembering. 'She insisted on stopping for tea and we did, at a funny little tea-room in a village near Stow-on-the-Wold, run by a small tartar with a sharp tongue.'

'Pretty?'

'No. A great deal of mousy hair and violet eyes.'

His mother buttered toast. 'How unusual—I mean the

eyes. One never knows the hidden delights of remote villages until one has a reason to go to them.' She peeped at him and found him watching her, smiling.

'She interested you?'

'As a person? Perhaps; she was so unlike the elegant young women I usually meet socially. But more than that, I imagine she scratches a bare living from the place and yet she seemed quite content with her lot.'

'No family?'

'A sister. A beautiful creature—a top model, flitting about the world and making a great deal of money, I should imagine.'

'Then she might give something to the tea-shop owner.'

Sir Thomas reached for the marmalade. 'Somehow, I don't think that has occurred to her. Do we have to go to church?'

'Of course. We will have a lovely afternoon reading the Sunday papers and having tea round the fire.'

Mary Jane, always hopeful of customers even on a Monday morning, was taking the first batch of teacakes from the oven when the doorbell rang. She glanced at the clock on the wall; half-past eight and she hadn't even turned the sign round to 'Open' yet. Perhaps it was the postman with a parcel...

Sir Thomas was standing with his back to the door, his hands in his pockets, but he turned round as she unlocked the door and opened it.

She would have turned the sign round too but he put a large hand over hers to prevent that. 'Good morning, Mary Jane. May I beg a cup of coffee from you? I know it's still early.' He sounded meek, not at all as he usually spoke and she jumped at once to the wrong conclusion as he had anticipated.

'You're on your way back to London? You've been up all night?'

Her lovely eyes were soft with sympathy. She didn't wait for an answer, which saved him from perjury, but went on briskly. 'Well, come on in. Coffee won't take more than a few minutes—I could make you some toast...'

'Something smells very appetising.' He followed her into the kitchen.

'Teacakes. I've just made some.' She looked at him over her shoulder. 'Do you want one?'

'Indeed I do.' He wandered back to the door. 'I have my dog with me. Might he come in? Would Brimble object?'

'A dog?' She looked surprised. 'Of course he can come in. Brimble isn't up yet, but I'll shut the stairs door anyway.'

Watson, his nose twitching at the prospect of something to eat, greeted her with gentle dignity. 'Whenever possible he goes everywhere with me,' said Sir Thomas.

Mary Jane fetched a bowl and filled it with water and offered a digestive biscuit. 'The poor lamb, he'll be glad to get home, I expect.' She added shyly, 'You too, Sir Thomas.'

'I'll drop him off before I go to my rooms.'

She poured his coffee, offered a plate of buttered tea-cakes and poured coffee for herself. 'But you'll have to have some rest—you can't possibly do a day's work if you've been up all night. You might make a wrong diagnosis.'

Sir Thomas swallowed a laugh. He should, he reflected, be feeling guilty at his deception, actually he was enjoying himself immensely.

Over his second cup of coffee he asked, 'How's business? And is that cousin of yours bothering you?'

'I make a living,' she told him seriously. 'Oliver hasn't been again—I think that was the second time I've seen him in years. He isn't likely to come again.'

'No other family?' he asked casually.

'No—there's just Felicity and me. He quite likes her though because she's quite famous.'

'And you, Mary Jane, have you no wish to be famous?'

'Me? Famous? What could I be famous for? And I wouldn't want to be, anyway.' She added with a touch of defiance, 'I am very happy here. I've got Brimble and I know almost everyone in the village.'

'You don't wish to marry?'

She got up to refill his cup. 'I've not met many men—not in a village as small as this one. It would be nice to marry but it would have to be someone I—I loved. Could you eat another teacake?'

'I could, but I won't. I must be on my way.'

She watched him drive away, Watson sitting beside him, and went back to make more teacakes and fresh coffee. She didn't expect to be busy on a Monday morning but it was nice to be prepared.

As it turned out, she had several customers; early though it was and after a brief lull the Misses Potter came—most unusually for them on a Monday, to tell her over coffee that their nephew from Canada would be coming to visit them. They in their turn were followed by Mrs Fellowes, to ask her over still more coffee if she would babysit for them on the following Saturday as Dr Fellowes had got tickets for the theatre in Cheltenham. Mary Jane agreed cheerfully; the doctor's children were small and cuddly and once they were asleep they needed very little attention. Mrs Fellowes had been gone only a few moments before two cars stopped, disgorging children and parents and what looked like Granny and Grandpa. They ate all the teacakes and most of the scones, drank a gratifying amount of coffee and lemonade and went away again with noisy cheerfulness, leaving her to clear away, close the tea-room for the lunch-hour and, after a quick sandwich, start on another batch of scones.

No one came during the early afternoon and in a way she was glad for it gave her time to return everything to its usual pristine order. It was almost four o'clock and she was wondering if she should close for the day when a car drew up and a lady got out, opened the door and asked if she might have tea.

'Have a table by the window,' invited Mary Jane. 'It's a nice afternoon and I like this time of day, don't you? Indian or China, and would you like scones or teacakes?'

'China and scones, please. What a charming village.' The

lady smiled at her and Mary Jane smiled back; her customer wasn't young but she was dressed in the kind of tweeds Mary Jane would have liked to be able to afford and her pepper and salt hair was stylishly dressed. She had a very kind face, full of laughter lines.

Mary Jane brought the tea and a plate of scones, butter and a dish of strawberry jam, and Sir Thomas's mother engaged her in idle talk while she studied her. So this was the girl with the violet eyes; the tartar with a sharp tongue. She approved of what she saw and the eyes were certainly startlingly lovely.

'I don't suppose you get many customers at this time of year?' she asked casually.

'Well, no, although today I've been quite busy...'

'You don't open until mid-morning, I suppose,' asked Mrs Latimer, following a train of thought.

'About nine o'clock—I opened early today, though—someone who had been up all night and needed a hot drink.'

Mary Jane's cheeks went nicely pink at the thought of Sir Thomas. To cover her sudden confusion at the thought of him, she went on lightly, 'He had a dog with him—he was called Watson...'

'What an unusual name,' said Mrs Latimer, and silently congratulated herself on her maternal instincts. 'For a dog, I mean. What delicious scones.' She smiled at Mary Jane. 'I am so glad I came here.'

CHAPTER FOUR

THE evenings were closing in and the mornings were crisp. Mary Jane, locking the door after another day almost devoid of customers, thought of Felicity in London from whom she had had a card that morning. The Paris show had been a resounding success and she was having a few days off before another week or so of modelling, this time in the Seychelles. Mary Jane, reading it without envy, wondered why they had to go so far to take photos of clothes which only a tiny percentage of women wore. She wondered who paid for it all—perhaps that was why the clothes were so wildly expensive.

She fed Brimble, had her supper and spent the evening shortening the hem of the jersey dress. Short skirts were the fashion and she had nice legs even if there was no one to notice that.

The morning brought several customers, the last of whom, an elderly man, looked so ill she gave him a second cup of coffee without charging for it. He had a dreadful cough, too, watering eyes and a face as white as paper.

As he got up to go she said diffidently, 'You have got a frightful cold; should you be out?'

'Got a job to do,' he said hoarsely. 'No good giving in, miss.'

Poor fellow, thought Mary Jane, and then forgot him. Closing up for the day later, she peered out into the cold, wet evening and thought with sympathy of Dr and Mrs Fellowes who had gone to London for a few days. It was no weather for a holiday.

She woke up in the night with a sore throat and when she got up she had a headache. There were no customers all day and for once she was glad because she was beginning to feel peculiar. She closed early, locking the door thankfully against persistent rain and a rising wind and, since she wasn't hungry, she fed Brimble, made herself a hot drink and went to bed after a hot bath, but even its warmth and that of the hot water bottle she clasped to her made no difference to the icy shivers running down her spine. Brimble, that most understanding of cats, got on to the bed presently and stretched out against her and soon she slept, fitfully, relieved when it was morning. A cup of tea teamed with a couple of Panadol would make her feel better. She crept downstairs, gave Brimble his breakfast, drank her tea and went back to bed. The weather had worsened during the night and there was no one about; there would certainly be no customers. She went to sleep again, to wake every few hours with a blinding headache and a chest which hurt when she breathed. It was late afternoon when she crawled out of bed again to feed Brimble, wash her face and put on a clean nightie. A night's sleep would surely get her back on her feet, she thought. She ought to make herself a drink, but the very idea of going downstairs again made her feel ill. She got back into bed...

She woke several times aware that she was thirsty, that she should feed Brimble, put on some clothes and knock on Mrs Adams's door and get her to ask Dr Fellowes' locum to come, but somehow she couldn't be bothered to do anything about things. She was dimly aware that Brimble was mewing but she was by now so muddled that she quite thought she had been downstairs to put out his food. She fell into an uneasy doze, not heeding the rain and the wind rattling at the windows.

Sir Thomas, driving himself back from a consultation in Bristol, turned off the motorway at Swindon. He would have to stop for lunch somewhere and he might as well go a little out of his way and have it at Mary Jane's. He had no appointments for the rest of the day and driving was tiring in the appalling weather. It was more than a little out of his

way; from the village he would have to drive to Oxford but
he had reasoned that he could pick up the M40 there, a mere
fifty miles or so from London.

It was just after one o'clock when he stopped at the tea-
room. There was no one around and no traffic, not that there
was ever very much of that and he wasn't surprised to see
the 'Closed' sign on the door. Mary Jane would be having
her lunch. He got out of the car and went to the door and
rang the bell and, since no one came, peered into the little
room. Brimble was sitting on the little counter at the back,
looking anxious, and when Sir Thomas tapped on the glass
he jumped down and came to the door, standing on his hind
legs, mewing urgently.

Sir Thomas rang again and knocked for good measure,
standing patiently in his Burberry, the rain drenching his
head. He stood back from the door and looked up to the
windows above but there was no sign of anyone and after a
moment he walked to the end of the little terrace and went
down the narrow alley which led to the back gardens. Mary
Jane's cottage was halfway along, he opened the flimsy gate,
crossed the small garden and went to peer through the
kitchen window. The kitchen was untidy, not at all in its
usual state with a pan full of milk on the stove and the kettle
and dishes and cutlery lying around. As he looked, Brimble
jumped on to the draining board by the sink and scratched
at the window, which, since he had his own cat-flap, seemed
unnecessary. The cottages on either side were unlit and silent; Sir Thomas took out his Swiss Army penknife, selected
one of its versatile components and eased it into the window
frame.

The window opened easily for the hasp was loose, and he
swung it wide so that Brimble might go out. He didn't want
to. Instead he jumped down and went to the door leading to
the stairs standing half-open.

Sir Thomas took off his Burberry, threw it into the kitchen
and squeezed through the window, no easy task for a man
of his splendid size. He gained the floor and stood for a

moment, listening. When he called, 'Mary Jane,' in a quiet voice, there was silence and he started up the narrow little stairs.

As he reached the tiny landing Mary Jane came wobbling out of the bedroom. She was barefoot and in her nightie and her hair hung down her back and over her shoulders in an appalling tangle. Her pinched face was a nasty colour and her eyelids puffy. Not a pretty sight.

'Oh, it's you,' she said in a hoarse whisper.

Sir Thomas bit back strong language, scooped her up and laid her back in the tumbled bedclothes. She was in no state to answer questions; he went back downstairs, out of the door this time, fetched his bag from the car, paused long enough to fill Brimble's bowl with what he took to be cold milk-pudding in the top of the fridge and took the stairs two at a time.

Mary Jane hadn't moved but she opened her eyes as he sat down on the side of the bed. She was too weary to speak, which was just as well, for he popped a thermometer under her tongue and took her wrist in his large cool hand. It felt comforting and she curled her hot fingers round it and closed her eyes again.

Her temperature was high and her breaths rapid and so was her pulse. He said with reassuring calm, 'You have a nasty bout of flu, Mary Jane. Who's your doctor?'

She opened an eye. 'He's away.'

'Is there anyone to look after you?'

She frowned, not wanting to bother to answer him. 'No.'

He tucked her in firmly. 'I'll be back,' he told her and went out of the back door again and round to the front, to bang on the doors on either side of the tea-room. No one came to answer his thumps and he went to his car and picked up the phone.

Back in the cottage he set to work with quiet speed, clearing the kitchen, shutting and locking the kitchen door, fastening the window and then going upstairs again to fetch his bag. Mary Jane opened her eyes once more. 'Do go away,' she begged. 'I've such a headache.'

'You'll feel better presently,' he assured her, and then asked, 'Have you a box or basket for Brimble?'

'On top of the wardrobe.' She sat up suddenly. 'Why? He's all right, he's not ill?'

'No, but you are. I'm taking you to someone who will look after you both for a day or two. Now be a good girl and stay quiet until I get organised.'

Brimble wasn't pleased to be stuffed gently into his basket, but the hands which picked him up and stowed him away were gentle and he had been easily mellowed by the milk-pudding. He was borne into the tea-room and the basket put on top of one of the tables, next to the bag Sir Thomas had brought downstairs. He unlocked the shop door next and went back upstairs, rolled Mary Jane in the quilt and carried her downstairs. The stairs, being narrow, made things a bit difficult, but Mary Jane was small and slight even if the quilt was bulky. He opened the tea-room door and with some difficulty the car door and arranged his bundle beside his seat, strapped her in and went back for Brimble and his bag before locking the door of the tea-room. He was very wet by now since he hadn't bothered to put his Burberry on again but thrown it into the back of the car, but before he got into the car he stood a moment looking up and down the street. There was no sign of anyone; presumably everyone was indoors, sitting cosily by the fire, no doubt with the TV on very loud to drown the sound of the wind and the rain. He got in, gave a quick look at Mary Jane's sickly face and drove off.

After a minute or so Mary Jane opened her eyes. She felt very ill but she knew vaguely that there were some things she needed to know.

'Not hospital,' she muttered. 'Brimble...'

'Don't fuss,' advised Sir Thomas. 'You're going somewhere so that you can lie in bed for a day or two and get well, and Brimble will be right by you.'

'Oh, good,' said Mary Jane, and, remembering her manners, 'thank you, so sorry to be such a nuisance.'

She dozed off, lulled by his grunt, a reassuring commonplace sound which soothed her. She stirred only slightly when he stopped before his mother's front door and lifted her out as though she had been a bundle of feathers and carried her in. Mrs Latimer, waiting in the hall, took one look at Mary Jane. 'Oh, the poor child. Upstairs, Thomas, the garden room—there's a balcony for the cat.'

He paused for a second by her. 'Bless you, you've thought of everything.'

He went on up the staircase and she received Brimble in his basket and went up after him at a more leisurely pace.

Sir Thomas laid Mary Jane on the bed and carefully unrolled her out of the quilt and Mrs Beaver tucked the bedclothes around her. 'There, there,' she said comfortably, 'the poor young thing. Just you go away, Sir Thomas, and I'll have her put to rights in no time at all. A nice wash and a clean nightie and some of my lemonade.'

Mrs Latimer, coming into the room, nodded her head, set Brimble's basket down on the covered balcony and put a hand on her son's sleeve. 'Shall I get Dr Finney?'

'I'll have a look at her when you've tidied her up. The sooner I get her on to antibiotics the better. You might get him up tomorrow if you would, Mother.'

'Yes, dear. Now go away and have a drink or something and we'll let you know when we are ready for you.'

When he went upstairs again Mary Jane was awake; save for her eyes there was no colour in her face but her hair had been brushed and hung, neatly plaited, over one shoulder and she was wearing one of Mrs Latimer's nighties.

'That's better.' He came and sat on the edge of the bed and felt her pulse. It was galloping along at a fine rate and he frowned a little. 'I'm going to start you off on an antibiotic,' he told her. He spoke with pleasant remoteness, a doctor visiting his patient. 'An injection. I'll get it ready while Mrs Beaver turns you over.'

She couldn't be bothered to answer him; now that she was clean and in a warm bed all she wanted to do was sleep. 'Where's Brimble?' she asked suddenly, and rolled over obedient to Mrs Beaver's kind hands.

'Having a snack on the balcony,' said Sir Thomas, sliding in the needle as Mrs Beaver drew back the bedclothes and ignoring Mary Jane's startled yelp.

'There, dearie, all over,' said Mrs Beaver. 'You just turn over on to the other side and have a little nap.'

'It's sore.' Mary Jane's hoarse voice sounded aggrieved; tears weren't far off.

'Here's Brimble,' said Sir Thomas. She heard his voice, remote and kind and felt Brimble's small furry body beside her, closed her eyes on threatening tears and went to sleep.

Sir Thomas stood for a moment looking down at her. She looked not a day over fifteen...

Downstairs he found his mother sitting in the drawing-room. 'I think I will ring Finney,' he told her, 'explain the circumstances.'

She agreed, 'Yes, dear. I'll take good care of her—it is flu?'

'Yes, but I suspect that there's a mild pneumonia as well. I have no idea how long she was lying there ill.'

'You would have thought that the neighbours would have noticed that the tea-room was closed.'

'Normally, yes, but with this bad weather it would seem normal enough for her not to open, don't you think?'

When he came back from phoning they went to a belated lunch and as they drank their coffee Mrs Latimer asked, 'Has she no family at all? Did you not mention a sister? She should be told.'

'Felicity—yes, of course, if she is in London. I gather that she seldom is, but I have her address and phone number.' He saw his mother's look of surprise and smiled a little. 'I'll look her up. I'm free for the rest of today.'

'If you do see her, Thomas, and she is anxious about Mary

Jane, do tell her that she is very welcome to come here and make sure that she is all right.'

'Thank you, dear.' They were back in the drawing-room and Mrs Latimer began to talk about other things until presently Sir Thomas said, 'I think I'll just take a quick look at Mary Jane before I go. Is Mrs Beaver in the kitchen or in her own room?'

Mrs Latimer glanced at the clock. 'In the kitchen getting the tea-tray ready.'

He went first to look at Mary Jane, deeply asleep now, one arm flung around Brimble. Her washed out face had a little colour now and her breathing was easier; he took her pulse and put a hand on her forehead and then went downstairs to find Mrs Beaver. 'Wake her and wash her and give her plenty to drink and something to eat if she fancies it—yoghurt or something similar. Dr Finney will come in the morning and give you fresh instructions. Thank you, Mrs Beaver—it will only be for a couple of days; I believe she is through the worst of it.'

He drank his tea, promised his mother that he would phone her that evening and drove back to London, leaving his parent thoughtful.

Mary Jane, unaware of his departure and indeed rather hazy as to whether she had seen him at all, woke to find Mrs Latimer sitting by the bed. She still felt ill and weary but her headache was better and she was warm.

When she tried to sit up Mrs Latimer said, 'No, dear, just lie still. We are going to wash your face and hands and make you comfortable and then you are going to eat a little something. Thomas told me to be sure that you did and presently he will telephone to find out if I have done as he asked.'

She smiled so kindly that Mary Jane, to her shame, felt tears fill her eyes and spill down her cheeks. Mrs Latimer said nothing, merely wiped them away and told her that she was getting better and then Mrs Beaver came in with a basin and towels and Brimble was coaxed away to eat his supper on the balcony while she was washed and her hair combed.

She lay passive while the two ladies tidied her, fighting a fresh desire to burst into tears; she had looked after herself for so long that she had forgotten how marvellous it was to be cosseted with such care and gentleness.

Mrs Latimer saw the tears. 'Cry if you want to, my dear. I'm sure you're not a watering pot normally, it's just the flu. You're going to feel so much better in the morning.'

She was quite right. Mary Jane woke feeling as though she had been put through a mangle, but her head was clear; she even wished to get up, to be sternly discouraged by Mrs Beaver, standing over her while she drank her tea and ate some scrambled egg.

'If you would tell me,' began Mary Jane.

'All in good time, miss, you just lie there and get well— bless you, a day or two in bed'll do you all the good in the world and you could do with a bit of flesh on those bones.'

Sir Thomas telephoned as his mother was sitting down to breakfast; he had phoned on the previous evening to tell her that he had rung Felicity and was taking her out to dinner later; now he wanted to know how Mary Jane was and Mrs Latimer said carefully, 'Well, Thomas, I don't know much about it, but she seems better. Very limp and still rather hot but she's had several cups of tea and a few mouthfuls of scrambled egg. I gave her the pills you left for her to take. What did her sister say?'

He didn't answer at once. Felicity had been charming when he had phoned, expressed concern about Mary Jane and begged him to go and see her at her flat. He hadn't wanted to do that; instead he had arranged to take her out to dinner and over that meal he had told her about Mary Jane. She had listened for a few minutes and then smiled charmingly at him across the table. 'She'll be all right, she's awfully tough—it's very kind of you to bother.' She had put out a hand and touched his on the table. 'Could we go somewhere and dance?'

He had refused with beautiful manners, pleading patients to see and the hospital to visit and had driven her back to her flat, and when she had asked him where he lived he had evaded her question.

'She told me that Mary Jane would be all right, that she was tough—oh, and that it was kind of us to bother.'

'I see,' said Mrs Latimer, who didn't. 'Dr Finney will be here presently, will you be at your rooms? He could phone you there.'

'Yes, ask him to do that, will you? I'll phone you this evening— I don't think I'll have time before then.'

He rang off and Mrs Latimer finished her breakfast and went back to Mary Jane. 'My doctor is coming to see you presently; perhaps we can tidy you up first?'

'I could get up,' began Mary Jane. 'I feel much better. I'm giving you so much trouble and you are so kind...'

'It's delightful to have someone to fuss over, my dear. Thomas, as you can imagine, has long outgrown any attempts of mine to cosset him. How would you like a nice warm bath before Dr Finney comes and then pop back into bed?'

Mary Jane was sitting up very clean and fresh in another of her hostess's nighties, still pale and limp but doing her best to appear her normal self, when Dr Finney came. He was elderly and rather slow and very kind.

He examined Mary Jane very thoroughly, tapping her chest and thumping her gently and bidding her say 'nine nine nine' and put out her tongue. All these things done, he said thoughtfully, 'A narrow squeak, young lady; another day and you would have been in hospital with pneumonia. Most fortunate that Thomas found you and acted quickly. Another two days in bed and then you may return to your home. You don't have a job?'

'I run a tea-room.'

'Do you, indeed? How interesting. By all means return to it but don't attempt to exert yourself for a few more days. Take the pills which Thomas has left you and there's no reason why you shouldn't get out of bed from time to time and walk round.' His eye lighted on Brimble who had just come in and had jumped on to the bed. 'A cat? Bless my soul!'

'He is mine, Sir Thomas brought him here with me.'

'Of course. I shall come and see you again in two days' time, young lady, and I expect to find you very much better.'

When Mrs Latimer came back presently Mary Jane said, 'I can't think why Sir Thomas brought me here. That sounds awfully rude but you do understand what I mean, Mrs Latimer. I could have gone to...' She paused because she couldn't think of anywhere, only Margaret, who wouldn't have had her anyway, and Miss Kemble who would have had her and nursed her, too, but only because of a strong sense of duty. All her other friends lived in small houses with children or elderly grannies or grandpas in the spare bedrooms.

'I think,' said Mrs Latimer carefully, 'that Thomas realised that by the time he had found someone in the village who could spare the time to look after you you would have been fit only for the hospital and that would have been such an upheaval, wouldn't it, dear?'

'If I had some clothes I could go home as soon as Dr Finney says I may. I don't want to put you to any more trouble, I can never thank you enough.'

'We can talk about that in two days' time; now you are going to have a nap and presently Mrs Beaver will bring you a little lunch. Remember, my dear, that we are really enjoying having you here even though you aren't well. Allow two elderly ladies to spoil you.'

Mrs Latimer smiled at her and went away and Mary Jane closed her eyes and slept, with the faithful Brimble curled up against her.

It was amazing what two days of good food and ample rest did for Mary Jane. Her hair, washed by Mrs Beaver, shone with soft brown lights, her face lost its pinched look and its colour returned and her eyes regained their sparkle. Not pretty, but nice to look at, reflected Mrs Latimer.

After Dr Finney had been to see her again Mary Jane

asked diffidently if someone could possibly get her clothes so that she might return home, 'For I have trespassed on your kindness too long,' she pointed out. 'If only I had the key, Mrs Adams could go and get me the clothes and send them at once.'

Mrs Latimer looked vague. 'Well, I suppose that Thomas has the key, my dear, but since he will be coming tomorrow, I'm sure he will know what is best to be done.'

So Mary Jane, wrapped in one of her hostess's quilted dressing-gowns, spent a happy day being shown round the house and sitting in Mrs Latimer's pretty little sitting-room at the back of the hall, listening to that lady talking about Thomas. She longed to ask why, at the age of thirty-four, he wasn't married. Perhaps he was divorced or loved someone already married to another man, perhaps she had died young... Mary Jane, with a lively imagination, allowed it to run riot.

He arrived the next day after lunch and he wasn't alone. Felicity got out of the car and accompanied him into the house, was introduced to his mother and made a pretty little speech to her; she had found that she had a couple of days free and on the spur of the moment she had telephoned to Sir Thomas and asked if she might accompany him if and when he next went to his home. 'I have been anxious about Mary Jane,' she added with one of her charming smiles. Mrs Latimer hid her doubts about that, welcomed her warmly and suggested that she might like to go and see Mary Jane at once.

'Oh, yes, please. She isn't infectious, is she? I have several bookings next week; I have to be careful...'

Mrs Latimer led her upstairs, leaving Sir Thomas to go into the drawing-room with Watson where presently she joined him.

'What a very pretty girl,' she observed, sitting down by the fire. Her voice was dry and he looked at her, smiling a little.

'Beautiful. I'm sorry not to have let you know, but I had

no time, I was on the point of leaving when she phoned. I could do nothing else but suggest that she could come.'

'Of course, dear. She expects to stay the night, I dare say.'

'She has an overnight bag with her—said something about putting up at the local pub.'

'No, no, she must stay here. I dare say Mary Jane is delighted to see her.' She didn't look at her son. 'The dear child is so anxious to go back to her tea-room but of course she has no clothes. What do you suggest?'

'I'll drive over presently, take Mrs Beaver with me and fetch what she needs. The place was in a mess; perhaps we could tidy it up a little before I take her back.'

'Do you suppose her sister will go with her and stay a day or two?'

'Unlikely...' He broke off as Felicity came into the room.

'May I come in? Mary Jane is resting so I didn't stay long. What a lovely house you have, Mrs Latimer. I do love old houses; I'd love to see round it.'

She sat down near Sir Thomas and smiled enchantingly at him, and he wondered how two sisters could be so unlike each other. 'I'll go and take a look at her,' he said blandly, 'see if she's fit to go home.'

'I'll come with you,' said Felicity.

'No, no. If she is resting, the fewer visitors she has, the better.'

He took no notice of her pretty little *moue* of disappointment and went away. First to the kitchen to see Mrs Beaver and then upstairs, where he found Mary Jane not resting at all but sitting in a chair with Brimble on her knee, looking out of the window at the dull weather outside.

'Not resting?' he asked, and pulled up a chair to sit beside her. 'Felicity said that you were. How are you?'

'I'm quite well, thank you, Sir Thomas. It was very kind of you to invite Felicity.'

He didn't answer that but observed, 'I hear that you would like to get back to your cottage. I'm going to take Mrs Beaver over there now. Make a list of what you need and we'll bring your things back and I'll drive you over first thing tomorrow morning.'

'I could go as soon as you come back...'

'And so you could, but you're not going to. Another night here won't do you any harm and my mother is loath to let you go.' He got out his pocket-book and a pen and handed them to her. 'Make your list. Mrs Beaver is waiting.'

He was brisk and businesslike so she did her best to be the same, making a careful list with directions as to where everything was. Handing it to him, she tried once more. 'I could go back this afternoon if you wouldn't mind taking me, really I could.'

'Don't be obstinate,' said Sir Thomas, and went away to come back within a few minutes with Mrs Beaver, hatted and coated in case Mary Jane had forgotten something. 'There's no reason why you shouldn't come downstairs and have tea with my mother and Felicity,' he said kindly, and pulled her gently out of her chair. 'Bring Brimble; it's time he and Watson met.'

So she went downstairs and met Watson waiting patiently at the bottom of the stairs for his master. He sniffed delicately at Brimble and Brimble eyed him from the shelter of Mary Jane's arms and muttered before they went into the drawing-room.

'Mary Jane's coming down for tea—we'll be back in good time for dinner.'

'You're not taking Mary Jane back?' Felicity sounded flurried. 'She hasn't any clothes here?'

'We're going to fetch them now.'

'Oh, then I'll come with you...' Felicity had jumped up.

'Mrs Beaver is coming, she knows what to get, but it's good of you to offer.'

He whistled to Watson and went away, leaving the three of them to chat over their tea. At least Felicity did most of the talking, relating titbits of gossip about the people she had met, the glamorous clothes she modelled and the delightful life she led. 'Of course,' she told Mrs Latimer airily, 'I shall give it all up when I marry but it will be so useful—I mean, knowing about clothes and make-up and being social.'

'You are engaged?' asked Mrs Latimer.

'No, not yet. I've had ever so many chances but I know the kind of man I intend to marry—plenty of money, because I'm used to that, a good social background, good looks.' She gave a little tinkling laugh. 'I'll make a good wife to a man with a successful career.'

All the while she talked Mary Jane sat quietly. Sir Thomas, she reflected, was exactly the kind of husband her sister intended to marry, and she was pretty and amusing enough for him to fall in love with her—and he had invited her to come to his mother's home, hadn't he? He had not answered her but he hadn't denied it either. Mrs Latimer quietly took the conversation into her own hands presently and suggested taking Felicity to her room so that she might tidy herself. 'We dine at eight o'clock,' she told her. 'I do hope you will be comfortable; if there is anything you need, do please ask.'

Mary Jane, left alone with Brimble, began making resolute plans for her return. There would be the baking to see to and the place to clean up, for as far as she could remember it had been in something of a pickle when Sir Thomas had fetched her away. He had been so kind and she had put him to a great deal of trouble, she hoped that Mrs Beaver had been able to find everything easily so that he hadn't had to wait too long. The cottage would be cold; she should have asked him to light the gas fire in the sitting-room and sit there...

He hadn't even been into the sitting-room. He and Mrs Beaver had gone into the cold tea-room and through to the kitchen which was indeed in a pickle.

'You go upstairs and get the clothes,' he told Mrs Beaver. 'I'll tidy up here.'

He had taken off his coat and his jacket and rolled up his shirt-sleeves and boiled several kettles of water, washed everything he could see that needed it, dried them and put them away, found a broom and swept the floor and looked in the cupboard. There was tea there, and sugar and a packet of biscuits, cat food and some porridge oats. The fridge held butter and lard, some rather hard cheese and a few rashers of bacon. He went to the foot of the stairs and called up to Mrs Beaver who was trotting to and fro and she peered down at him from the tiny landing. Before he could speak she observed, 'It's a shocking shame, Sir Thomas, that dear child—two of everything, beautifully washed and ironed and mended to death and a cupboard with almost nothing to wear in it. Good stuff, mind you, but dear knows when she went shopping last.' She drew a breath. 'And that sister of hers in them silks and satins—blood's thicker than water, I say and I don't care who hears me say it.'

'Perhaps something can be done about that. I'm going over to the village shop—it should be open still, there's almost no food in the house. Surely the milkman calls...'

'Look outside the back door, sir...'

The milk was there; he fetched it in and put it in the fridge, got into his coat and walked to the shop where he bought what he hoped were the right groceries and bore them back to stack them in the cupboard.

Mrs Beaver was ready by then; they got back into the car and he half listened to Mrs Beaver's indignant but respectful remarks about young girls being left to fend for themselves. She paused for breath at last and added apologetically, 'I do hope I've not put you out, sir, letting me tongue run away with me like that and you likely as not sweet on the young lady. I must own she's pretty enough to catch any gentleman's eye.'

Sir Thomas agreed placidly.

He found his mother and Mary Jane in the drawing-room, bent over a complicated piece of tapestry. They looked up as he went in and Mary Jane got to her feet. 'I'll go and dress,' she said. 'And thank you very much indeed, Sir Thomas.'

He smiled. 'You look very nice as you are, but I dare say you will feel more yourself in a dress.' He held the door for her as she went into the hall. 'Mrs Beaver's taken your case upstairs. Would you like to leave Brimble here? Watson won't hurt him.'

He took the cat from her and watched her go up the staircase before going back into the room.

'Where is our guest?' he asked.

'She went upstairs to tidy herself. Is the cottage all right for Mary Jane to go back?'

'As clean and tidy as we could make it. I fetched some food from the shop—the lady who owns it said they were beginning to wonder where Mary Jane had gone—no one had been out much because of the bad weather and those that had had supposed that she had closed the tea-room since there was no chance of customers. Her neighbours had been away and the Misses Potter, who call regularly, had been indoors with bad colds. A series of unfortunate events.' He sat down opposite her. 'I'm sure that once she is back the village will rally round—she is very well-liked.'

'I'm not surprised...' Mrs Latimer broke off as the door opened and Felicity came into the room. She had changed into a silk sheath of vivid green, its brevity allowing an excellent view of her shapely legs, its neckline, from Mrs Latimer's point of view, immodest. She walked slowly to join them, giving Sir Thomas time to study her charming if unsuitable appearance. It was a pity that he got to his feet almost without a glance and went to get her a drink.

Ten minutes later Mary Jane joined them, wearing the skirt of her suit and a Marks and Spencer blouse, and this time Sir Thomas allowed his gaze to dwell upon her prosaic person. What he thought was nobody's business; all he said was, 'Ah, Mary Jane, come and sit down and have a glass of sherry.'

CHAPTER FIVE

MRS LATIMER spoke. 'Come and sit by me, Mary Jane. How nice to see you dressed and well again. You have recovered so quickly, too. I'm glad for your sake but we shall miss you. Once you are settled in I shall drive over and have tea with you again.'

Mary Jane's quiet answer was drowned by Felicity's voice. 'How I wish that I could live away from London—I do love the country and the quiet life. Sometimes I wish that I would never need to travel so much again. How I envy you, Mary Jane.'

Not easily aroused to bad temper, Mary Jane found these sentiments too hard to swallow. 'Well, I don't suppose it would matter much if you gave up your modelling—there must be dozens of girls... I could do with some help, especially in the summer.' She spoke in a matter-of-fact voice, smiling a little. No one would have known that she was seething; first her dull, sensible clothes, highlighted pitilessly by Felicity's *couture* and now this nonsense about wanting to live in the country. Why, she had run away from it just as soon as she could... Sir Thomas, watching her quiet face from under his eyelids, had a shrewd idea of her thoughts. The contrast between her and her sister was too striking to overlook, especially the clothes; on the other hand, he conceded, Felicity hadn't beautiful eyes the colour of violets.

He said smoothly, 'You would probably find living in the country very dull, Felicity. Are you working at present?'

'Next week—here in London—perhaps we could meet? And then I'm off to New York for the shows. I was there last year and I had a marvellous time. The parties—you have no idea...'

She embarked on a colourful account of her visit and the

three of them listened, Mary Jane with understandable wistfulness, Mrs Latimer with an apparent interest because she had never been ill-mannered in her life, and Sir Thomas with an inscrutable face which gave away nothing of his true feelings.

During dinner, however, Felicity was forced to curb her chatter; Sir Thomas kept the conversation firmly upon mundane matters, and, after drinking coffee with the ladies, he pleaded telephone calls to make and went away to the library, presumably not noticing Felicity's sulky face.

He returned just as Felicity, bored with her companions, declared herself ready for bed.

'Is eight o'clock too early for you?' asked Sir Thomas of Mary Jane. 'I need to be back in town by lunchtime.'

'That's fine,' said Mary Jane. 'But surely I could catch a bus or something...' She frowned. 'All the trouble...'

Felicity had been listening. 'I'll come with you...'

'It would mean getting up at half-past six,' Sir Thomas pointed out suavely.

She hesitated. 'Oh, well, perhaps not. It isn't as if Mary Jane needs anyone any more. I'll be waiting here for you when you get back.'

She smiled her most bewitching smile, quite lost on Sir Thomas who had turned away to speak to his mother.

It was one of those mornings in autumn when night was reluctant to give way to morning. It was raining, too. They left exactly at eight o'clock and Mrs Latimer had come down to see them off. She had embraced Mary Jane warmly and promised to see her again shortly, and now they were in the car driving back to the tea-room, she beside Sir Thomas, Brimble in his basket, indignantly silent on the back seat. There seemed no need for conversation; Mary Jane sensed that her companion had no wish to listen to chatter, not that she was much good at that and at that time of day small talk seemed out of place. However, although for the most part they were silent, it wasn't uneasy. She sat quietly, planning

her week while Sir Thomas thought his own thoughts.
Presumably they were amusing, for once or twice he smiled.

At the tea-room he took no notice of her protests that she
was quite able to be left at its door. He got out, opened the
door, reached into the car for Brimble's basket, took her key
from her and ushered her into her home.

It was chilly and unwelcoming. 'Wait here,' he told her
and went upstairs to light the gas fire, switch on the kitchen
light and set Brimble's basket down on the table. He fetched
her case then, took it upstairs and found her in the kitchen.
'How very clean and tidy it is,' she told him. 'I'm sure I left
it in a frightful mess. Will you have a cup of coffee before
you go?'

'I wish I could but I must get back.' He took her hand in
his, smiling down at her very kindly. 'Take care of yourself,
Mary Jane.'

She stared at him. 'You've been very kind, I can never
thank you or Mrs Latimer enough, and thank you for bringing me back.' She offered a hand and he took it, bending to
kiss her cheek as he did so. She watched him drive away,
wondering if she would ever see him again. Probably not.
On the other hand, if he should fall in love with Felicity, she
would.

She went into the kitchen and released Brimble, made herself a pot of tea, unpacked her few things and put on her
pinny. Customers were unlikely. On the other hand, she had
to be ready for them if they did come. She went to turn the
sign to 'Open' and only then saw the box on the table by
the door. There was a bunch of flowers on it, too—chrysan-
themums, the small ones which lasted for weeks, just what
was needed to cheer up the tea-room...

She took the lid off the box then, and discovered a cooked
chicken, straw potatoes and salad in a covered container, egg
custard in a pottery dish and a crock of Stilton cheese; there
was even a small bottle of wine.

Much cheered, she arranged the flowers on the tables, got
the coffee going and got out her pastry board. As soon as

she had made some scones she would sit down and write to Mrs Latimer—Mrs Beaver too—and thank them for their kindness.

There was no sign of Felicity by the time Sir Thomas reached his mother's house. He went to bid his mother goodbye and went in search of Mrs Beaver. He found her in the kitchen. 'Ask Rosie or Tracey—' the girls who came from the village each day to help in the house '—to go to Miss Seymour's room and tell her that I am leaving in five minutes. If she is unable to be ready by then, Mrs Latimer will get a taxi for her so that she can get to Banbury and get a train to town.'

Felicity was in the hall with a minute to spare and very put out. 'My make-up,' she moaned prettily, 'I haven't had time, and I've thrown my things into my case...' She pouted prettily at Sir Thomas who remained impervious. 'Perhaps we could stop on the way...'

He had beautiful manners. 'I'm so sorry, but there won't be time—I must be at the hospital. Shall we go?'

She bade Mrs Latimer goodbye with the hope that she would see her again. 'For I haven't had time to see your lovely home, have I?' But Mrs Beaver she ignored, sweeping past her to get into the car.

'You'd never know that they were sisters,' declared Mrs Beaver sourly. A thought echoed by Sir Thomas as he swept the Rolls out of the gate and through the village.

Felicity, accustomed to the admiration of the men she met, worked hard to attract Sir Thomas, but although he was a charming companion he remained aloof, and when he stopped the car outside her flat she had the feeling that she had made no impression on him whatsoever. It was a galling thought and a spur to her determination to get him interested in her. Obviously, he had no interest in her success as a model or the glamorous life she led. She would have to change her tactics. She bade him goodbye in a serious voice, with no suggestion that they might meet again and added a rider to the effect that she hoped Mary Jane would be all right. 'I shall take the first opportunity to go down and see her,' she assured him, and he murmured suitably, thinking that the likelihood of that seemed remote. One could never tell, however; beneath that frivolous manner there might be a heart of gold. He thought it unlikely, but he was a tolerant man, ready to think the best of everything and everyone. He dismissed her from his mind and drove to the hospital.

Mary Jane was taking the first batch of scones out of the oven when her first customers came in. A young couple barely on speaking terms, the girl having misread the map and directed her companion in entirely the wrong direction. They sat eyeing each other stormily over the little vase of flowers. Mary Jane brought the coffee and they wanted to know just where they were. She told them and the man muttered, 'We're miles out of our way thanks to my map-reader here.' He glared at the girl.

'No, you're not,' said Mary Jane. 'Just keep on this road and turn right at the first crossroads—you're only a few miles in the wrong direction.'

She left them to their coffee and presently the door opened and the Misses Potter came in.

'Not our usual time, my dear,' said Miss Emily, 'but we were on our way to the stores and saw that you were back. Have you had a nice little break?'

Mary Jane said that, yes, she had and fetched the coffee pot just as Miss Kemble came in. 'I see you're back,' she said briskly. 'You have enjoyed your holiday, Mary Jane?'

It didn't seem worthwhile explaining. Mary Jane said that yes, she had, and poured more coffee. The young couple went presently, on speaking terms once more, and a tall, thin man with a drooping moustache came in and asked for lunch.

She hadn't had time to make sausage rolls and the demand for lunch during the winter was so small that she could only offer soup and sandwiches. She went to the kitchen to open the soup and slice bread, reflecting as she did so that someone had stocked up the fridge while she had been away. She would have to ask Mrs Latimer...

By one o'clock everyone had gone; she made herself some coffee, ate biscuits and cheese, fed Brimble and went upstairs. Beyond a quick look round she had had no time to put anything away and the bed would have to be made up.

That had been done and very neatly too, and so, when she looked, had her nightie been washed and ironed and folded away tidily. The bathroom was spotless and there wasn't a speck of dust anywhere. It was like having a fairy godmother.

She got into her outdoor things and went to the stores, exchanged the time of day with its owner and asked to use the phone. Mrs Latimer sounded pleased to hear from her and Mary Jane thanked her again for her kindness and then asked, 'Someone cleaned the cottage for me and the fridge is full of food and everything is washed and ironed. Did Sir Thomas...no sorry, I'm being silly, I'm sure he's never ironed anything in his life or bought groceries.'

Mrs Latimer chuckled. 'He certainly brought the food and I'm sure if he had to iron he would, and very well too. No, my dear, he took Mrs Beaver with him, she sorted out your things and together they tidied your cottage. Thomas is a dab hand at washing up.'

'Is he really?' said Mary Jane, much astonished. 'If I write him a note could you please send it on to him? And will you thank Mrs Beaver? As soon as I have time I'll write to you and her as well.'

'We look forward to that, my dear. Have you opened your tea-room yet?'

'Yes, and had customers too. I'm going back now to open until five o'clock although I don't expect anyone will come.'

They wished each other goodbye and she rang off and hurried back to her cottage. No one came that afternoon; she locked the door and went to get her supper, carrying the delicacies upstairs to the sitting-room to eat by the gas fire, with Brimble, on the lookout for morsels of chicken, sitting as close as he could get.

Her supper finished, she sat down to write her letters. Those to Mrs Latimer and Mrs Beaver were quickly done, but the note to Sir Thomas needed both time and thought. He had been kind and very helpful but not exactly friendly; it was hard to strike the right note and it took several wasted sheets of paper before she was satisfied with the result. By then it was time to go to bed.

She saw few customers during the following days. Doing her careful sums each evening, she decided that she was barely paying her way; there was certainly nothing to spare once her modest bills were paid. The winter always was a thin time, of course; it was just a question of hanging on until the spring. Looking out of the window at the dull autumn day, the spring looked a long way off. Luckily, there was Christmas; it might not bring more customers but those who came were usually full of the Christmas spirit and inclined to spend more. She was a neat-fingered girl and not easily depressed; in the tiny loft there was an old-fashioned trunk stuffed with old-fashioned clothes which had belonged to her mother. She got on to a chair and poked her head through the narrow opening. The loft was very small and cold and she wriggled into it and heard the scrabble of mouse feet, but mice or no mice she wasn't going to be put off. She leaned in as far as she was able and dragged the trunk over to the opening. She wouldn't be able to get it down into the cottage but she could open it and see if there was anything she could use.

There was. A gauzy scarf, yards of lace, bundles of ribbons, a watered silk petticoat, balls of wool still usable. She dragged them out, closed the trapdoor and examined her finds at her leisure. The wool was fine and in pale colours, splendid for dolls' clothes, even baby clothes, and the lace and ribbons and silk could be turned into the kinds of things people bought at Christmas: pincushions, lavender bags, beribboned nightdress cases—rather useless trifles but people bought them none the less. She went to bed that night, her head full of plans.

There was a card from Felicity in the morning: she was off to New York in two days' time and she had had a meal with Thomas—they would meet again when she got back. She didn't ask how Mary Jane was but Mary Jane hadn't expected that, anyway. She read the card again; she wasn't really surprised that Sir Thomas had been seeing Felicity, but it made her vaguely unhappy. 'And that's silly,' she told Brimble, his whiskered face buried in his breakfast saucer. 'For she's such a very pretty girl and her clothes are lovely. Perhaps she'll come and see us before Christmas,' and then, because that was what she had really been thinking about, she added, 'I wonder what meal it was and where they went?'

Sir Thomas could have told her if he had been there; he had been waylaid—there was no other word for it—by Felicity, who had taken pains to find out where he lived and had just happened to be walking past his house as he returned from the hospital. That she had done this three evenings running without success was something she didn't disclose but she evinced delighted surprise at seeing him again. 'Perhaps we could have dinner together?' she had suggested. 'You must need cheering up after a hard day's work.'

Sir Thomas had been tired, he had wanted his dinner and a peaceful evening with no one but Watson for company while he caught up with the medical journals, but his manners were too nice to have said so; instead he had suggested that they had a drink in a pleasant little bar not too far away, 'For I have to go back to the hospital shortly and I have any amount of work to do this evening.'

She had pouted prettily and agreed and jumped into the car; she had great faith in her charm and good looks, and had no doubt that once they sat down she could persuade him to take her on to dinner—let the hospital wait, he was an important man and must surely do what he wanted to do; he wasn't some junior doctor at everyone's beck and call.

She was, of course, mistaken, and half an hour later she had found herself being put into a taxi with no more than a brisk handshake and regrets that he must cut short an enjoyable meeting. 'I had hoped you could drive me to my flat,' she had complained prettily, and turned her lovely face up to his. 'I do hate going home alone.'

Sir Thomas had handed the cabby some money. 'You must have many friends, Felicity; I'm sure you won't be alone for long.' He had lifted a hand in casual salute as the taxi drove off.

Tremble had come fussing into the hall as he opened the door of his house and Watson had come to meet him.

'You're late, Sir Thomas—a bad day, perhaps?'

'No, no, Tremble, only the last hour or so. Give me ten minutes, will you, while I go through the post?'

He had gone into his study with the faithful Watson and leafed through his letters without paying much attention to them. He had had to waste part of an evening listening to Felicity's airy chatter, and he had found her tedious. 'A beautiful girl,' he told Watson. 'There's no denying that, and charming too. Perhaps I am getting middle-aged...'

It was much later that evening, standing by the French windows leading to the small garden behind the house, waiting for Watson to come in, that he had decided that he would drive down to see how Mary Jane was getting on. Her stiff little note of thanks had amused him, it had so obviously taken time and thought to compose, but she had given no hint as to how she was. It would, he told himself, be only civil to go and see her and make sure that she was quite well again. He was free on Sunday...

Customers had been thin on the ground that week; the Misses Potter came, as usual, of course, and one or two women from the village on their way home from shopping and the very occasional car. Mary Jane told herself that things would improve and started on her needlework. She had neat, clever fingers and a splendid imagination; in no time at all she had a row of mice, fashioned from the petticoat and wearing lace caps on their tiny heads and frilly beribboned skirts. Quite useless but pretty trifles that she hoped someone would buy. She was rather uncertain what she should ask for them and settled on fifty pence, which Miss Emily Potter told her was far too low a price. All the same she bought one and told Miss Kemble about them. That lady bought one too, declaring it was just the thing for a birthday present for her niece. Mary Jane thought it rather a poor sort of present but perhaps she didn't like the niece very much. Selling two of the mice so quickly gave her the heart to continue with her sewing. She sat them on the counter so that anyone paying for their coffee would see them and, very much encouraged by a passing motorist buying three of them, began on a series of frivolous heart-shaped pincushions.

When Sir Thomas drew up outside the tea-room she was standing on the counter stowing away the potted fern which was usually on it so that there was more room for the mice. She had left the 'Open' sign on the door in the hope that a customer or two might come and she turned round as the door was opened and the bell rang.

Sir Thomas's bulk, elegantly clothed in cashmere, filled the doorway. His, 'Good morning, Mary Jane,' was pleasantly casual, which gave her time to change the expression of delight on her face to one of nothing more than polite surprise. But not before Sir Thomas had seen it.

He wasn't a man to mince his words. 'I thought we might have lunch together; may I bring Watson in?'

'Of course bring him in. It's warm in the kitchen. Brimble's there.'

Sir Thomas fetched the dog, shut the door behind him and took off his coat. 'Where would you like to go?' he asked.

'Well, thank you all the same, but I've made a chicken casserole—Mrs Fellowes keeps poultry and she gave me one—already killed, of course. It's in the oven now and I wouldn't like to waste it. It's a French recipe, thyme and parsley and a bay leaf and a small onion. There should be brandy too, but I haven't any so I used the cooking sherry left over from last Christmas.'

Sir Thomas, who had never before had an invitation refused, listened, fascinated. His magnificent nose quivered at the faint aroma coming from the kitchen. With commendable promptness he said, 'Delicious. May I stay to lunch?'

Mary Jane was still standing on the counter. She looked down at him a little uncertainly. 'Well, if you would like to...'

'Indeed I would.' He crossed the room and stretched up and lifted her down, reflecting that she was a little too thin. He saw the mice then and picked one up. 'And what exactly are these bits of nonsense?'

'Well, I'm not very busy at this time of year, so I thought I'd make something to sell—for Christmas you know.'

He studied it and held it in the palm of his hand. 'My mother would love one, and Mrs Beaver. May I have two—how much are they?'

Mary Jane went very pink. 'I would prefer to give them to you, if you don't mind. If you will choose two I will wrap them up.'

He would have to be more careful, Sir Thomas told himself, watching her wrap the mice in tissue paper. Mary Jane was proud-hearted; she might have few possessions but she had the right kind of pride. He asked casually after the Misses Potter, wanted to know if her cousin had been annoying her lately and had her laughing presently over some of Watson's antics.

'Do you mind sitting in the kitchen?' She led the way to where the two animals were sitting amicably enough side by side before the cooking stove. 'I'll make some coffee and put the fire on upstairs.'

'I'll do that,' he said, and when he was downstairs again, he asked, 'Are there any odd jobs to be done while I'm here?'

'Would you reach up and get two plates from that top shelf? I don't often use them but they belonged to my mother.'

He reached up and put them on the table. 'Coalport—the Japan pattern—eighteenth-century? No, early nineteenth, isn't it? Delightful and very valuable, even just two plates.'

'Yes, we always used them when I was a little girl. I never discovered what happened to them all when we came to live with Uncle Matthew. When I came here Cousin Oliver told me that I could take a few plates and cups and saucers with me so I took these. I found them at the back of the china pantry.'

'The casserole will taste twice as good on them. Do you want me to peel potatoes or clean these sprouts?'

She gave him an astonished look. 'But you can't do that. At least, what I mean is you mustn't, you might cut your hands and then you couldn't operate.'

'Then I'll make the coffee...'

The little kitchen was very crowded, what with Sir Thomas and his massive frame taking up most of it and Watson and Brimble getting under their feet. He made the coffee and carried it up to the sitting-room, closely followed by Watson, Mary Jane and Brimble. He had switched on the little reading lamp and the room looked cosy. Sir Thomas stretched out his long legs and drank his coffee. He thought that Mary Jane was very restful; there was no need to talk just for the sake of talking and she was quite unselfconscious. Presently he suggested, 'Would you like to drive around for a while this afternoon? Even in the winter the Cotswolds are always delightful.'

'That would be nice, but isn't there something else you'd rather do?'

He hid a smile, 'No, Mary Jane, there isn't.'

'Well, then, I'd like that very much.' She put down her mug. 'There's the bell.'

Three elderly ladies nipped with the cold, wanting coffee and biscuits and, when the aroma from the casserole reached

them, wanting lunch as well. Sir Thomas could hear Mary
Jane apologising in her pretty voice and reflected that if he
hadn't been there she would have probably offered to share
her dinner with them. As it was, she gave them very careful
instructions as to how to get to Stow-on-the-Wold where,
she assured them they could get an excellent lunch at the
Union Crest.

When they had gone Sir Thomas went downstairs and
locked the door and turned the notice to 'Closed'. 'For nothing,' he explained, 'must hinder my enjoyment of the casserole.'

It was certainly delicious; Mary Jane had creamed the potatoes and cooked the sprouts to exactly the right moment,
grated nutmeg over them and added a dollop of butter, thus
adding to the perfection of the chicken.

Mary Jane had laid the kitchen table with care and, although they drank water from the tap and everything was
dished up from the stove, the meal was as elegant as any in
a West End restaurant. Mary Jane didn't quite believe him
when he said that, but it was nice of him to say so.

They washed up together while Watson and Brimble ate
their own hearty meal and, since the days were getting short
now and the evenings came all too quickly, Sir Thomas took
Watson for a brisk walk while Mary Jane got into her elderly
winter coat, made sure that Brimble was cosy in his basket
and, being a good housewife, went round turning off everything that needed to be turned off, shut windows and locked
the back door securely.

Sir Thomas ushered her into the car, settled Watson on
the back seat and went to lock the tea-room door.

'Have you any preference as to where we should go?' he
asked her.

Mary Jane, very comfortable in the leather seat and quietly
happy at the prospect of his company for an hour or so, had
no preference at all.

He turned the car and went out of the village on the
Gloucester road to turn off after a mile or so into the country.

The road was narrow and there were few villages and almost
no traffic. The big car went smoothly between the hedges
allowing them views on either side.

'You know this part of the country?' asked Sir Thomas.

'No, not well; I've never been on this road before. It's
delightful.'

'It will take us to Broadway. There's another very quiet
road from there to Pershore...'

At Pershore he turned south to Tewkesbury where he
stopped at the Bell and gave her a splendid tea with Watson
under the table, gobbling up the morsels of crumpets and
cake which came his way. 'Your scones are much better,'
declared Sir Thomas.

She thanked him shyly and took another crumpet.

It was already dusk and, in the car once more, he turned
for home, still keeping to the side-roads so that it was almost
dark by the time they got back to the tea-room.

When she would have thanked him and got out of the car
he put a hand over hers on the door-handle. 'No, wait.' And
he took the key and went in to switch on the lights and go
upstairs to turn on the fire. Only then did he come back to
the car.

They went in together and Mary Jane said, 'I don't suppose you would like a cup of coffee?' And when he shook
his head, 'I expect you've got something to do this evening.'
She spoke cheerfully, thinking that he must have found her
dull company. Perhaps he would have a delightful evening
with some beautiful witty girl who would have him laugh.
He hadn't laughed much all day, only smiled from time to
time...

He stood watching her. Her unexpected outing had given
her a pretty colour and her eyes shone. She offered her hand
now. 'It was a lovely day—thank you very much. Please
remember me to your mother and Mrs Beaver when you see
them.' She smiled up at him. 'Did you have a pleasant evening with Felicity? She sent me a card. She's great fun.'

Sir Thomas, versed in the art of concealing his true feelings under a bland face, agreed pleasantly while reflecting that no two sisters could be more unlike each other and why had Felicity made a point of telling Mary Jane that she had spent the evening with him? A gross exaggeration to begin with, and what was the point? To make Mary Jane jealous? That seemed to him to be most unlikely; his friendship with her was of the most prosaic kind, brought about by circumstances.

He got into his car and drove back to London to his quiet house and a long evening in his study, making notes for a lecture he was to give during the coming week. But presently he put his pen down and sat back in his chair. 'You enjoyed your day?' he enquired of Watson, lying half-sleep before the fire. 'Delightful, wasn't it? I think that we must do it again.' He opened his diary. 'Let me see, when do I next go to Cheltenham?'

Watson opened an eye and thumped his tail. 'You agree? Good. Now let me see, whom do we know living not too far from the village?'

Mary Jane watched the tail-lights of the Rolls disappear down the village street and then locked the door and went to feed Brimble. She wasn't very hungry but supper would be something to do. She poached an egg and made some toast and a pot of tea and took the tray upstairs and sat by the gas fire while she ate her small meal. It had been a lovely day but she mustn't allow herself to get too interested in Sir Thomas. The thought occurred to her that perhaps since Felicity wasn't there to be taken out, he had taken the opportunity to see more of her. If he was falling in love with her sister then he would want to be on good terms with herself wouldn't he? She should have talked more about Felicity so that if he had wanted to, he could have talked about her too. For some reason she began to feel unhappy, which was silly since Sir Thomas and Felicity would make a splendid couple. Perhaps she was being a bit premature in supposing that he had fallen in love, but he was bound to if he saw more of her sister; all the men she met fell in love with her sooner or later. Mary Jane was sure of that, for Felicity had told her so.

Autumn had given way to winter without putting up much of a fight and everyone was thinking about Christmas. The village stores stocked up on paper chains for the children to make and a shelf full of sweet biscuits and boxes of sweets. Mary Jane made a cake and iced it and stuck Father Christmas at its centre and put it in her window with two red candles and a 'Merry Christmas' stuck on to the window. Christmas was still a few weeks off, but with the red lampshades she had made the tea-room look welcoming. Surprisingly, for the next day or two she had more customers than she had had for weeks. She sold the mice too, stitching away each evening, replenishing her stock.

She had another card from Felicity. She was back in London to do some modelling for a glossy magazine but she intended to spend Christmas at her flat. There was no point in asking Mary Jane to join her there, she had written, for she knew how much she hated leaving the cottage. She wouldn't have gone, she told herself, even if she had been invited, for she knew none of Felicity's friends and hadn't the right clothes. All the same, it would have been nice to have been asked.

The next day Mrs Latimer came, bringing with her a little dumpling of a woman with a happy face. The Misses Potter were sitting at their usual place but there was no one else there. Mrs Latimer went over to the counter to where Mary Jane was getting out cups and saucers. 'How nice to see you again, my dear, and looking a lot better, too. I've come for tea—some of your nice scones? And come and meet someone who knows about you and your family...

'Mrs Bennett, this is Mary Jane Seymour—Mary Jane, Mrs Bennett was a friend of your mother's.'

The little lady beamed. 'You were a very little girl—you won't remember me, your mother and I lost touch. I heard that you and your sister had gone to live with your uncle and of course Felicity is quite famous, isn't she? However, I had no idea that you were here. I wrote once or twice to your uncle but he never answered. It's lovely to see you again, and with a career too!'

'Well, it's only a tea-room,' said Mary Jane, liking her new customer. 'Do sit down and I'll bring you your tea.'

The Misses Potter, too ladylike to stare, had been listening avidly. Now they had no excuse to stay any longer for the scones were eaten and the teapot drained. They paid their bill, bowed to the two ladies and went home; news of any sort was welcome, and they looked forward to spreading it as soon as possible.

It was long after closing-time when Mrs Latimer and her friend left and the latter by then had wheedled Mary Jane into accepting her invitation to the buffet supper she was giving in ten days' time. It would mean a new dress, but Mary Jane, feeling reckless, had accepted.

That evening Mrs Latimer phoned her son. 'We had tea with Mary Jane—she's coming to Mrs Bennett's party. Tell me, Thomas, how did you discover that she had known Mary Jane's parents?' She paused. 'Or, for that matter, how did you discover Mrs Bennett? A most amiable woman, apparently not in the least surprised to have a visit from a friend of a friend...'

'Easily enough. Felicity mentioned her and I remembered the name—and phoned a few friends around that part of the country. Thank you for your help, my dear.'

Mrs Latimer was frowning as she put down the phone. Thomas was going to a good deal of trouble to liven up Mary Jane's sober life, she hoped it wasn't because he had fallen in love with Felicity. A man in love would go to great lengths to please a girl, and yet, somehow, he wasn't behaving as though he were. He could of course be sorry for Mary Jane. Mrs Latimer smiled suddenly. That young lady wouldn't thank him for that.

CHAPTER SIX

THE problems of a dress kept Mary Jane wakeful for a few nights. She would have to close the tea-room and go to Cheltenham. She couldn't afford to buy a dress; she would have to find the material and make it herself. There wasn't much time for that, especially as she hadn't a sewing-machine. Mrs Stokes had one and so did Mrs Fellowes and now was no time to be shy about asking to borrow from one of them.

Mrs Fellowes agreed to lend hers at once; moreover, when she heard why Mary Jane wanted it, she offered to give her a lift on the following day to Cheltenham.

She found what she wanted: ribbed silk in a soft dove-grey, just right for the pattern she had chosen, a simple dress with a full skirt, a modest neckline and elbow-length sleeves. She bought matching stockings and, in a fit of recklessness, some matching slippers in grey leather. They could be dyed black, she told herself, so they weren't an extravagance.

Customers were few and far between, which was a good thing, for she was able to cut out the dress and sew it. She had a talent for sewing and the dress, when it was finished, would pass muster just as long as it didn't come under the close scrutiny of someone in the world of fashion. She hung it in her bedroom and spent an evening doing her nails and washing her hair, half wishing that she weren't going to the party. Mrs Bennett seemed friendly and sweet but they didn't really know each other; she had said that there would be a lot of people there and Mary Jane wondered if there would be dancing. She loved to dance, but supposing no one wanted to dance with her?

She would be fetched, Mrs Bennett had told her in a letter; friends who lived in Shipton-under-Wychwood would collect her on their way to Bourton-on-the-Hill, where Mrs Bennett lived.

She was ready long before they arrived, wrapped in her elderly winter coat, cold with sudden panic at the idea of meeting a great many strange people. She need not have worried; the estate car which pulled up at her door was crammed with a cheerful family party, quite ready to absorb her into their number, and if they found the winter coat not quite in keeping with the occasion, no one said so. She was made to feel at home and by the time they arrived she had forgotten her sudden fright and went along to the bedroom set aside for their coats, to be further braced by the two girls and their mother admiring her dress. She needed their reassurance, for she could see that, compared with the dresses the other girls were wearing, hers, while quite suitable, was far too modest. Bare shoulders, tiny shoulder straps and bodices which stayed up by some magic of their own seemed to be the norm. She went down the staircase with the others and into the vast drawing-room in Mrs Bennett's house where her hostess was greeting her guests.

Sir Thomas, talking to his host, watched Mary Jane, a sober moth among the butterflies, pause by Mrs Bennett and exchange brief greetings. Her dress, he considered, suited her very well, although he surprised himself by wondering what she would look like in something pink and cut to show rather more of her person. No jewellery either. A pearl choker, he reflected, would look exactly right around her little neck. He listened attentively to his companion's opinion of modern politics, made suitable replies and presently made his way to where Mary Jane, swept along by her new acquaintances, stood with a group of other young people.

She saw him coming towards her and quite forgot to look cool and casual. Her gentle mouth curved into a wide smile and she flushed a little. He took her hand. 'Hello, Mary Jane, I didn't know that you knew the Bennetts.'

She didn't take her hand away. 'I didn't either. Your mother came the other day and brought Mrs Bennett with her. I think she's a friend of a friend and she remembered me when I was a little girl—she knew my mother.'

'What a delightful surprise for you,' said Sir Thomas gravely, not in the least surprised himself. 'Who brought you?'

'Mr and Mrs Elliott—they live at Shipton-under-Wychwood and called for me. They've been very kind...'

'Ah, yes— I've met them. My mother's here—have you seen her yet?'

'No.' She added rather shyly, 'I don't know anyone here.'

'Soon remedied.' He took her arm and made his way round the room, greeting those he knew and introducing her and finally finding his mother.

'There you are, Thomas—and Mary Jane. How pretty you look, my dear, and what a charming dress—I have never seen so many exposed bosoms in all my life and many of them need covering.' She eyed Mary Jane and added, 'Although I don't think your bosom needs to be concealed; you have a pretty figure, my dear.'

Mary Jane, very pink in the cheeks, thanked her faintly and Sir Thomas, standing between them, stifled a laugh. His mother, a gentle soul by nature, could at times be quite outrageous.

'You agree, Thomas?' She smiled up at her son. 'No, probably you don't. Go away and talk to someone; I want a chat with Mary Jane.'

When they were alone she said, 'My dear, I wanted to ask you—where will you be at Christmas? Not alone, I hope?'

'Me? No, Mrs Latimer, Felicity is in London, you know, and I'm going there. I'm looking forward to it.' She told the lie, valiantly glad that Sir Thomas wasn't there to hear her. She was normally a truthful girl but this, she considered, was an occasion when she must bend the truth a little. After all, there was still time for Felicity to invite her...

'I'm glad to hear that. What do you do with your cat?'

Mary Jane was saved from replying by a dashing young man in a coloured waistcoat. 'I say, if I'm not interrupting, shall we dance? They're just starting up. Sir Thomas introduced us just now—Nick Soames? Remember?'

'Run along, dear,' said Mrs Latimer. 'But don't leave without coming to say goodbye, will you?'

So Mary Jane danced. Nick was a good partner and she had always loved dancing and when the dance finished he handed her over to someone called Bill who didn't dance very well but made her laugh a lot. Now and then she saw Sir Thomas, head and shoulders above everyone else, circling the room with a succession of beautifully dressed girls. From the look of them he certainly hadn't agreed with his mother about the over-exposure of bosoms. They're not decent, decided Mary Jane, swanning round the room in the arms of someone called Matt who talked of nothing but horses.

Mrs Bennett had drawn the line at a disco. It was her party, she had pointed out; the young ones could go somewhere and dance their kind of dancing whenever they liked; in her house they would foxtrot and waltz or not dance at all. The band was just striking up a nice old-fashioned waltz when Sir Thomas whisked Mary Jane away from an elderly gentleman who was on the point of asking her to dance with him.

'I was going to dance with that gentleman,' she pointed out tartly.

'Yes, I know, but he's a shocking dancer; your feet would have been black and blue.' He was going round the edge of the big room. 'Are you enjoying yourself?'

'Yes, very much, thank you. I—I was a bit doubtful at first, I mean, I don't know anyone, but Mrs Bennett has been so kind. She's coming to see me one day after Christmas so that we can talk about my mother and father. Uncle Matthew didn't talk to us much, you know; I dare say he didn't like children, although he was a very kind man.'

The music stopped but he didn't let her go and when it started again he went on dancing with her. She was a little flushed now, but her pale brown hair, pinned in its heavy coil, was as neat as when she had arrived and her small person, so demurely clad, was light in his arms.

He waltzed her expertly through an open door and into a small room where a fire was burning and chairs grouped invitingly.

He sat her down by a small table with an inviting display of tasty bits and pieces in little dishes and a bottle of white wine in a cooler. 'Spare me five minutes of your time and tell me how you are.'

'I'm very well thank you, Sir Thomas.' She popped an olive into her mouth—she had had a sketchy lunch and almost no tea and the buffet supper was still an hour or so away.

'Busy?' He poured wine into two glasses. 'I suppose you will be going to Felicity's for Christmas?' His tone was casual though he watched her carefully from under his lids.

'Christmas,' Mary Jane stalled for a time while she thought up a good fib. 'Oh, yes, of course; I always go each year. It's great fun.'

He didn't believe her but nothing in his calm face showed that.

'How do you go?' he wanted to know, still casual.

'Oh, Felicity fetches me,' said Mary Jane, piling fib upon fib. She hadn't looked at him but had busied herself sampling the potato straws. She flashed him a brief smile. 'I expect you go to Mrs Latimer's?'

'Or she comes to stay with me with various other members of the family.'

He handed her a dish of little biscuits and she selected one carefully.

'I'm glad to see you looking so well.' Sir Thomas handed her her glass. 'Let us drink to your continued good health.'

The wine was delicious and very cold. 'And you,' said Mary Jane. 'I hope you have a very happy Christmas and don't have to work. I don't suppose you do, anyhow.'

'You suppose wrongly. People break arms and legs and fracture their skulls every day of the year, you know.'

'Well, yes, of course they do but surely you're too important...' She stopped because he was smiling.

'Not a bit of it; if I'm needed to operate or be consulted then I'm available.'

'Do you ever go to other countries?'

'Frequently.'

She had polished off the potato straws and most of the olives.

'May I have the supper dance?' asked Sir Thomas.

'Will that be soon? I'm awfully hungry...'

He glanced at his watch. 'Half an hour; that will soon pass if you are dancing.'

They went back to the drawing-room and he handed her over quite cheerfully to the horsey Matt, who danced her briskly round the room and gave her a detailed account of his last point-to-point. It was a relief when the music stopped and she was claimed by a tall young man with a melancholy face who had no idea how to dance but shambled round while he told her, in gruesome detail, about his anatomy classes. He was a medical student in his third year and anxious to impress her. 'I saw you dancing with Sir Thomas—do you know him?'

'We're acquainted.'

'He's great—you've no idea—to see him fit a prosthesis...'

'Yes, he seems well-known,' said Mary Jane quickly, anxious to avoid the details.

'Well-known? He's famous!' He trod on her foot and she hoped that he hadn't laddered her stockings or ruined her shoe. 'There's no one who can hold a candle to him. I watched him do a spinal graft last week...' He embarked on the details—every single drop of blood and splinter of bone. Sir Thomas, guiding his hostess round the floor, saw Mary Jane's face and grinned to himself.

The supper dance came next and he went to find her, still listening politely to her companion's description of the instruments needed for the grisly business. Sir Thomas put a large hand on her arm and nodded affably at the young man. 'Our dance, Mary Jane?' he said and led her away.

'It seems you're quite famous,' she observed, her small nose buried in his white shirt-front. 'You never talk about it.'

He said, seriously, 'I don't think I've ever met anyone who would want to hear.'

'How dreadful for you, having to keep it all to yourself.'

'Indeed it is at times but most of my companions wouldn't wish to hear about anything to do with hospitals or patients.'

'No? Well, I wouldn't mind. I'm sure it couldn't be worse than that boy's description of a meni—mensis...'.

'Meniscectomy—the removal of the cartilage of the knee. An operation performed with considerable success and not in the least dramatic.'

He smiled down at her. 'Next time I feel the urge to unburden myself I shall come and see you, Mary Jane.'

She didn't think that he was serious but she said cheerfully, 'You do—I'm not in the least squeamish.'

They went in to supper then, sharing a table with at least half a dozen other guests, eating lobster patties, tiny sausages, cheesey morsels and little squares of toast spread with pâtés and dainty trifles which left Mary Jane feeling hungry still. She drank two glasses of wine, though, and her eyes became an even deeper violet. She would have accepted a third glass of wine if Sir Thomas hadn't pulled her gently to her feet.

'A little exercise?' he suggested suavely, and danced her round the room in a leisurely manner, and when the music stopped took her to where his mother was sitting talking to Mrs Bennett.

'There you are, my dears.' Mrs Latimer beamed at them both. 'Thomas, go away and dance with some of the lovely girls here, I want to talk to Mary Jane.' She realised what she had said, and added, 'I put that very badly, didn't I? Mary Jane is lovely, too.'

Mary Jane smiled a little and sat down and didn't watch Sir Thomas as he went away. It was kind of Mrs Latimer to call her lovely, although it was quite untrue. It would have been nice if Sir Thomas had told her that but of course he never would; she had no illusions as to her mediocre face.

Presently, she was whisked away to dance once more—
never mind her lack of looks, she danced well and the men
had been quick to see that. She didn't lack partners and she
was still full of energy when someone announced the last
waltz and she found Sir Thomas beside her.

'I'll take you back,' he told her. 'Will you explain to the
people who brought you?'

'Won't they mind?'

'I don't suppose so.' He was holding her very correctly,
looking over her head with the air of a man who wasn't very
interested in what he was doing. Most of the other couples
were dancing very close together in a very romantic fashion
but of course, she told herself, there was nothing about her to
inspire romance. Perhaps he was wishing it was Felicity in
his arms. He'd be holding her a lot tighter...!

She thanked him as the dance ended and after a few
minutes of goodbyes went off to fetch her coat. It stood out
like a sore thumb among the elegant shawls and cloaks in the
hall and she wondered if he was ashamed of her and dismissed
the thought as unworthy of him. His place was so sure in
society that he had no need to worry about such things.

Mrs Latimer kissed her goodbye. 'We must see you again
soon, Mary Jane,' a wish echoed by Mrs Bennett. 'We shall
all be busy with Christmas,' she added, 'but in the New Year
you must come and spend the day.'

Mary Jane thanked them both and got into the car and sat
quietly as Sir Thomas drove away.

Clear of the village, he slowed the car. 'A pleasant evening,' he observed. 'Do you go to many parties at this time
of year?'

She couldn't remember when she had last attended a
party—the church social evening, of course, and the Misses
Potters' evening—parsnip wine and ginger nuts—but they
were hardly parties.

'No.' She sought for some light-hearted remark to make
and couldn't think of any.

He didn't seem to notice her reticence but began to talk

about their evening, a casual rambling talk which needed very little reply.

It was profoundly dark when he drew up before her cottage. He said, 'Stay where you are, and give me the key,' and went and opened the door before coming back for her. At the door he said, 'Hot buttered toast and tea would be nice...'

She turned a startled face to his. 'It's half-past two in the morning.' She smiled suddenly. 'Come in, you can make the toast while I put the kettle on.'

They had it in the kitchen, with Brimble, refreshed by a sleep, sitting between them.

'You don't have to go back to London, do you?' asked Mary Jane.

'No, I'm spending the rest of the night at my mother's. I must be back in town by Monday morning, though. And you?'

'Me? Oh, I'm not doing anything. The tea-room will be open, of course, but there won't be many customers.'

'That will give you time to get ready for your trip to London,' he observed smoothly.

She agreed rather too quickly.

He bade her goodnight presently, bending to kiss her cheek with a casual friendliness. 'I dare say we shall see each other again,' and when she looked puzzled, 'At Felicity's.'

She wished then that she could tell him that she would not be there, that she had allowed him to suppose that she would be with her sister, but somehow she couldn't think of the right words. He had gone before she had conjured up another fib.

She had rather more customers than she had hoped for in the last weeks before Christmas and the mice sold well; she began to cherish the hope that she might go to the January sales and look for a coat. The Misses Potter had invited her for Christmas dinner as they had done for several years now and the church bazaar gave her the opportunity to bake some little cakes for Miss Kemble's stall. And on Christmas Eve the postman handed in a big cardboard box from Harrods. It contained caviar, a variety of pâtés, a tin of ham, a small Christmas pudding and a box of crackers, chocolates and a

half-bottle of claret. The slip of paper with it contained a
message from Felicity; she knew that Mary Jane would have
a lovely Christmas, she herself was up to her ears in parties
and there was a wonderful modelling job waiting for her in
Switzerland in the New Year. There was a PS 'Saw Thomas
yesterday'.

Which was to be expected, reflected Mary Jane, shaking off
a sudden sadness.

She went to church at midnight on Christmas Eve and lingered afterwards exchanging greetings with everyone there
and then went back to the cottage to drink hot cocoa and go
to bed with Brimble heavy on her feet. She wasn't sorry for
herself, she told herself stoutly; several people had given her
small gifts and she was going to spend the day with the Misses
Potter. She wondered what Sir Thomas was doing, probably
with Felicity... She fell into a troubled sleep which would
have been less troubled had she known that he was bent over
the operating table, carefully pinning and plating the legs of
a young man who had, under the influence of the Christmas
spirit, jumped out of a window on to a concrete pavement.

She took the wine, the crackers and the chocolates with her
when she went to the Misses Potter. Brimble she had left snug
in his basket, a saucer of his favourite food beside him. Her
elderly friends liked her to stay for tea and by the time she
had washed the delicate china they used on special occasions,
it would be evening. She had put a little Christmas tree in the
cottage window and switched on the lights before she left; it
would be welcoming when she went home.

Miss Emily had roasted a capon and Miss Mabel had set
the table in the small dining-room with a lace-edged cloth,
the remnants of the family silver and china and wine glasses
and had lighted a branched candlestick. Mary Jane wished
them a happy Christmas, kissed their elderly cheeks and
handed over the wine.

'Crackers,' declared Miss Emily. 'How delightful, my dear,
and chocolates—Bendick's—the very best, too. Let us have a
small glass of sherry before lunch.'

It had been a very pleasant day, thought Mary Jane, letting herself into the cottage. Tomorrow she would go for a good walk in the morning and then have a lazy afternoon reading by the fire.

It was raining in the morning and not a soul stirred in the village street. 'It'll be better out than in,' she told Brimble and got into her wellies, her elderly raincoat and tied a scarf over her hair, crammed her hands into woolly gloves and then set out. She took the country road to Icomb, past the old fort, on to Wick Rissington and then she turned for home, very wet and, despite her brisk walking, rather cold.

It was a relief to reach the path at the side of the church, a short cut which would bring her into the main street, opposite the tea-room. She nipped down it smartly and came to a sudden halt. The Rolls was standing before her door and Sir Thomas, apparently impervious to the wind and rain, was leaning against its bonnet, the faithful Watson beside him.

His, 'Good afternoon Mary Jane,' was austere and she had the suspicion that he was concealing ill-humour behind his bland face. It was just bad luck that he should turn up; she was, after all, supposed to be in London, enjoying the high life with Felicity.

She stood in front of him, feeling at a disadvantage; she was wet and bedraggled and the sodden scarf did nothing for her looks.

'Hello, Sir Thomas—how unexpected...'

He took the key from her and opened the door and stood aside to let her enter before following her in. Watson shook himself thankfully and went straight through to the kitchen and Sir Thomas, without asking, took off his coat.

'I expect you'd like a cup of tea,' said Mary Jane, wringing out her headscarf over the sink and kicking off her wellies.

'I expect I would.' He took her raincoat from her and hung it on the hook behind the back door and she went to put on the kettle. It was a little unnerving, she reflected, being confronted like this; she would have to think something up.

She wasn't given the time. 'Well,' said Sir Thomas, 'perhaps you will explain.'

'Explain what?' She busied herself with cups and saucers, wondering if a few more fibs would help the situation. Apparently not.

'Why you are here alone when you should be with Felicity in London.'

'Well...' She spooned tea into the pot and couldn't think of anything to say.

'You told me that you were staying with your sister, and yet I find you here.'

'Yes, well,' began Mary Jane and was halted by his impatient,

'For heaven's sake stop saying "Yes, well"—forget the nonsense and tell me the truth for once.'

She banged the teapot on to the table. 'I always tell you the truth...' She caught his cold stare. 'Well, almost always...'

She sat down opposite him and poured out their tea, handed him a plate of scones and offered Watson a biscuit as Brimble jumped on to her lap.

She decided to take the war into the enemies' camp. 'Why aren't you in London?'

His stern mouth twitched. 'I spent most of Christmas Day with my mother and I'm on my way back to town.'

'You're going the wrong way.'

'Don't be pert. I am well aware which way I am travelling. And now, Mary Jane, since you are unable to string two sentences together, perhaps you will answer my questions.'

'I don't see why I should...'

He ignored this. 'Did Felicity invite you to go to London for Christmas?'

'It's none of your business.' She gave him a defiant look and saw that he had become Sir Thomas Latimer, calm and impersonal and quite sure that he would be answered when he asked a question. She said in a small voice, 'Well, no.' She added idiotically, 'I expect she forgot—you know, she has so many friends and she leads a busy life.'

'Did you not hear from her at all?'

'Oh, yes. She sent me a hamper from Harrods. I don't expect that I would like to go to London anyway, I haven't the right clothes and her friends are awfully clever and witty and I'm not.'

'So why did you lie to me?'

'Well...'

'If you say well just once more, I shall shake you,' he observed pleasantly. 'Tell me, have you ever been to stay with Felicity?'

'W... Actually, no.'

'So why did you lie to me?'

'They were fibs,' she told him sharply. 'Lies hurt people but fibs are useful when you don't want—to interfere or make people feel that they have to help you if you're getting in the way.' She added anxiously, 'Have I made that clear?'

'Oh, yes, in a muddled way. Tell me, Mary Jane, why should you not wish me to know that you would be staying here on your own for Christmas?'

'I have just told you.'

'You think that I have fallen in love with Felicity?'

She looked at him then. 'Everyone falls in love with her, she's so beautiful and she is fun to be with and so successful. Whenever she sends me a card she mentions you so you must know her quite well by now. So you must...yes, I think you must love her.'

She wasn't sure if she liked his smile. 'Would you like me for a brother-in-law, Mary Jane?'

She wondered about the smile; she wouldn't like him for a brother-in-law; she would like him for a husband, and why should she suddenly discover that now of all times, sitting opposite him, being cross-examined as though she were in a witness-box and fighting a great wish to nip round the table and fling her arms round his neck and tell him that she loved him? She would have to say something, for he was watching her.

'Yes, oh, yes, that would be delightful.' She bent to pat

Watson so that he shouldn't see her face and was surprised and relieved when Sir Thomas got up.

'Well, I must be off.' He added smoothly, 'Shall I give your love to Felicity when I see her?'

'Yes, please.' She went to the door with him and she held out her hand. 'Drive carefully,' she told him. 'Goodbye, Sir Thomas.'

His hand on the door, he paused. 'There is something you should know. Falling in love and loving are two quite different things. Goodbye.'

He drove away, Watson sitting beside him, and she went back to the kitchen and began to tidy up. She told herself that it was extremely silly to cry for no reason at all, but she went on weeping and Brimble, wanting his supper and jumping on to her lap to remind her of that, got a shockingly damp coat.

Presently she dried her eyes. 'Well—no, I mustn't say well; what I mean to say is I shall forget this afternoon and take care not to see Sir Thomas again unless I simply must.'

Brimble, drying his fur, agreed.

It was difficult, though, the tea-shop was open, but for several days no one came to drink the coffee or eat the scones she had ready, she filled her days with odd jobs around the cottage, turning out cupboards and drawers with tremendous zeal, making plans for the year ahead; perhaps she should branch out a bit—do hot lunches? But supposing no one ate them? She couldn't afford to waste uneaten meals and her freezer was too small to house more than bare necessities. Felicity, on one of her flying visits, had suggested, half laughingly, that she should sell the cottage and train for something. Mary Jane had asked what and she had said, carelessly, 'Oh, I don't know—something domestic—children's nurse or something worthy—a dietician at a hospital or a social worker, at least you would meet some people. This village is dead or hadn't you noticed?'

Mary Jane recalled the conversation clearly enough now and gave it her serious consideration, deciding that she didn't want to be any of the people Felicity had suggested and, more-over, that the village wasn't dead. Quiet, yes, but at least everyone knew everyone else...

It was the last day of December when Mrs Bennett came. She trotted in, her good natured face wreathed in smiles. 'I'm so glad I found you at home,' she declared, 'and I do so hope you are not doing anything exciting this evening, for I've come to take you back with me—to see the New Year in, my dear.'

She sat herself down and Mary Jane sat down on the other side of the table. 'How very kind of you, Mrs Bennett, but you see it's a bit difficult—there's Brimble and I'd have to come home again...'

Mrs Bennett brushed this aside. 'Put on the coffee-pot, my dear, and we'll put our heads together.' She unbuttoned her coat and settled back in her chair. 'Someone will come over for you at about half-past seven and we'll dine at half-past eight, and I promise you that directly after midnight someone shall bring you back here. There won't be many people, just a few close friends and the family.' She added firmly, 'You can't possibly stay here by yourself, Mary Jane.' She glanced around. 'Your sister isn't here?'

Mary Jane brought the coffee and passed the sugar and milk. 'No, I'm not sure if she is in England—she travels all over the place, you know.'

'So, that settles it,' said Mrs Bennett comfortably. 'Wear that pretty dress you had on at the party, I dare say we shall all be feeling festive, and please don't disappoint me, my dear.'

'I'd love to come, Mrs Bennett, if it's not being too much of a bother collecting me and bringing me back. You're sure the grey dress will do?'

'Quite positive. Now I must be off home and make sure that everything is ready for this evening.'

Mary Jane wasted no time; the contents of a cupboard she had intended to turn out were ruthlessly returned higgledy-piggledy before she set about making her person fit for the evening's entertainment. Her hair washed and hanging still damp down her back, she studied her face, looking for spots. There were none, she had a lovely skin which needed little make-up which was a good thing for she couldn't have afforded it anyway. Her hands needed attention, too...

She was ready long before she needed to be, her hair shining, her small nose powdered, sitting by the little fire with her skirts carefully spread out and Brimble perched carefully on her silken knee. A cheerful tattoo on the door sent her downstairs to open the door to discover that the same family who had taken her to the dance were calling for her. They greeted her with a good deal of friendly noise, waited while she fetched her coat and bade Brimble goodbye and wedged her on to the back seat between the two girls and drove off all talking at once. Such fun, she was told, just a few of us, nothing like the Christmas party but Mrs Bennett always has a splendid meal and lashings of drinks.

They sat down sixteen to dinner and Mary Jane found herself between two faces she recognised, the horsey Matt who it seemed was a nephew of Mrs Bennett's and the medical student, both of whom were in a festive mood and didn't lack for conversation. Dinner lasted a very long time and by the time they had had coffee it was getting on for eleven o'clock and more people were arriving. Mary Jane, listening to an elderly man with a very red face explaining the benefits of exactly the right mulch for roses, allowed her eyes to rove discreetly. It was silly, but she had hoped that perhaps Sir Thomas would be there...but he wasn't.

She was wrong. Calm and immaculate in his dinner-jacket, he arrived with five minutes to spare, just in nice time to take the glass of champagne he was offered and thread his way through the other guests to stand beside her.

CHAPTER SEVEN

MARY JANE saw him coming, and delight at seeing him again swamped every other feeling. She could feel herself going pale, as indeed she was, and her heart thumped so strongly that she trembled so that the glass she was holding wobbled alarmingly. He reached her side, took the glass from her and wished her good evening, adding, 'Did you think that I would not be here?'

He was smiling down at her and she only stopped herself just in time from telling him how wonderful it was to see him. She said instead, 'Well, it's a long way from London and I dare say you've been busy with your patients and—and had lots of invitations to spend the evening there.'

'Oh, yes, indeed, but I wished to spend the evening with my mother—she came over with me.'

She followed her train of thought. 'Isn't Felicity in London?'

He was still smiling but his eyes were cold. 'Yes, she sent you her love.' He might have added that she had wanted him to take her to a party at one of the big hotels and he had made the excuse that he was going to his mother's home. She had said sharply, 'How dull for you, Thomas. I don't suppose you'll see Mary Jane, but if you do or if you meet anyone who knows her send my love, will you?'

Mary Jane said in a wooden voice, 'It's a pity she isn't here...' She was unable to finish for there was a sudden hush as Big Ben began to strike the hour. At its last stroke there were cries of 'Happy New Year!' as the champagne corks were popped and everyone started kissing everyone else. Mary Jane looked at the bland face beside her and said, meaning every word, 'I hope you have a very happy New Year, Sir Thomas.'

He smiled suddenly. 'I hope that we both shall, Mary Jane.' He bent and kissed her, a swift, hard kiss as unlike a conventional social peck as chalk from cheese. It took her breath but before she could get it back Matt had caught her by the hand and whirled her away to be kissed breathless by all the men there. She disentangled herself, laughing, and found Mrs Latimer standing close by.

'My dear, a happy New Year,' said Sir Thomas's mother, 'and how nice to see you enjoying yourself. You lead far too quiet a life.'

Mary Jane wished her a happy New Year in her turn. 'I've just been talking to Sir Thomas.' She blushed brightly, remembering his kiss, and Mrs Latimer just hid a smile.

'He drove down earlier this evening, and he will go back early tomorrow morning—he had made up his mind to be here.'

'He shouldn't work so hard,' said Mary Jane, and blushed again, much to her annoyance. 'What I mean is, he must get so tired.' She added, 'It's none of my business, please forgive me.'

'You're quite right,' observed Mrs Latimer. 'His work is his whole life although I think, when he marries, his wife and children will always come first.'

The very thought hurt; Mary Jane murmured suitably and said that she would have to find her hostess. 'Mrs Bennett kindly said that someone would drive me back as soon after midnight as possible.' She wished her companion goodbye and found Mrs Bennett at the far end of the room talking to Sir Thomas. As Mary Jane got within hearing, she said, 'There you are, my dear. What a pity that you must go but I quite understand…was it fun?'

'I've had a marvellous evening, Mrs Bennett, and thank you very much. I'll get my coat. Shall I wait in the hall and would it be all right if you said goodbye to everyone for me?'

'Of course, child. Sir Thomas is taking you home.'

'Oh, but Mrs Latimer is here, he'll—that is, you will have

to come back for her.' She looked at him and found him smiling.

'The Elliots are driving her back presently.' He spoke placidly but she couldn't very well argue with him. She fetched her coat and got into the Rolls without speaking, only when they were away from the house and out of the village she said,

'I'm sorry to break up your evening.'

He said coolly, 'Not at all, Mary Jane, I had no intention of staying and it is only a slight detour to drop you off before I go back.'

A damping remark which she found difficult to answer but when the silence got too long she tried again. 'Did you bring Watson with you?'

'No—I'm only away for the night and I'll be back to take him for his run tomorrow before I go to my rooms. Tremble will look after him.'

'Won't you be tired?' She added hastily, 'I don't mean to be nosy.'

'I appreciate your concern. I'm not operating tomorrow and I have only a handful of private patients to see later in the day.'

The conversation, she felt, was hardly scintillating. The silence lasted rather longer this time. Presently she ventured, 'It was a very nice party, wasn't it?'

He said mildly, 'Do stop making light conversation, Mary Jane...'

'With pleasure,' she snapped. 'There is nothing more— more boring than trying to be polite to someone who has no idea of the social niceties.' She paused to draw an indignant breath, rather pleased with the remark, and then doubtful as to whether she had been rather too outspoken. His low laugh gave her no clue. She turned her head away to look out at the dark nothingness outside. Where was her good sense, she thought wildly; how could she have fallen in love with this taciturn man who had no more interest in her than he might have in a row of pins? She would forget him the moment she could get into her cottage and shut the door on him.

He drew up gently before her small front door, took the key from her hand and got out and opened it before coming back to open the door of the car for her.

Switching on the tea-room lights, he remarked, 'A cup of tea would be nice.'

'No, it wouldn't,' said Mary Jane flatly. 'Thank you for bringing me home, although I wish you hadn't.' She put a hand on the door, encouraging him to leave, a useless gesture since the door wasn't over-sturdy and his vast person was as unyielding as a tree trunk.

He laughed suddenly. 'Why do you laugh?' she asked sharply.

'If I told you you wouldn't believe me. Tell me, Mary Jane, why did you wish that I hadn't brought you home?'

She said soberly, 'I can't tell you that.' She held out a hand. 'I'm sorry if I've been rude.'

He took her hand between his. 'Goodnight, Mary Jane.' His smile was so kind that she could have wept.

He went out to his car and got in and drove away and she locked up and turned off the lights, gave Brimble an extra supper and took herself off to bed. It was another year, she thought, lying in bed, warmed by the hot water bottle and Brimble's small body. She wondered what it might bring.

It brought, surprisingly, Felicity, sitting beside a rather plump young man with bags under his eyes in a Mercedes. Felicity flung open the tea-shop door with a flourish. 'I just had to wish you a happy New Year,' she cried, and then paused to look around her. The little place was empty except for Mary Jane, who was on her knees hammering down a strip of torn lino by the counter. She got to her feet and turned round and the young man who had followed Felicity said, 'Good lord, is this your sister, darling?'

Mary Jane eyed him; this was not the beginning of a beautiful friendship, she reflected, but all the same she wished him good morning politely and kissed her sister's cheek. 'I'm spring cleaning,' she explained.

Felicity tossed off the cashmere wrap she had flung over her *haute couture* suit. 'Darling, how awful for you, isn't there a char or someone in this dump to do it for you?'

There didn't seem much point in answering that. 'Would you like a cup of coffee?' She waved at two chairs upended on to one of the tables. 'If you'd like to sit down it won't take long.'

Felicity said carelessly, 'This is Monty.' She went over to the table. 'Well, darling, give me a chair to sit on...'

Mary Jane thought that he didn't look capable of lifting a cup of tea let alone a chair and certainly he did it unwillingly. She went into the kitchen and collected cups and saucers while the coffee brewed and presently she went back to ask. 'Are you going somewhere or just driving round?'

'Riding round. It's very flat in town after New Year and I've no bookings until next week. Then it will be Spain, thank heaven. I need the sun and the warmth.'

Mary Jane let that pass, poured the coffee and took the tray across to the table and poured it for the three of them, rather puzzled as to why Felicity had come. She didn't have to wonder for long. 'Have you seen anything of Thomas?' asked Felicity. 'Well, I don't suppose you have but you may have heard something of him—after all, his mother doesn't live so far away, does she? She made a great fuss of you when you had the flu.'

She didn't wait for an answer, which was a good thing. 'I see quite a lot of him in town; I must say he's marvellous to go around with...'

'I say, steady on,' said Monty. 'I'm here, you know.'

Felicity gurgled with laughter. 'Of course you are, darling, and you're such fun.' She leaned across the table and patted his arm. 'But I do have my future to think of—a nice steady husband who adores me and can keep me in the style I've set my heart on...'

'You said you loved me,' complained Monty, and Mary

Jane wondered if they had forgotten that she was there, sitting between them.

'Of course I do, Monty—marrying some well-heeled eminent surgeon won't make any difference to that.'

Mary Jane went into the kitchen. Felicity must be talking about Sir Thomas. If Felicity had been alone she might have talked to her about him and discovered if she were joking; her sister was selfish and uncaring of anyone but herself but there was affection between them; she could at least have discovered if she loved Sir Thomas. But the presence of Monty precluded that. She went back into the tea-room and found Felicity arranging the cashmere stole. 'Well, we're off, darling—lunch at that nice restaurant in Oxford, and then home to the bright lights.' She kissed Mary Jane. 'I'll send you a card from sunny Spain. I must try to see Thomas, I'm sure he could do with a day or two in the sun.'

Monty shook Mary Jane's hand. 'I would never have guessed that you two were sisters.' He shook his head, 'I mean to say...' He had a limp handshake.

Mary Jane put the 'Closed' sign on the door and went back to knocking in nails. Thoughts, most of them unhappy as well as angry, raced round her head. Surely, she told herself, Sir Thomas wasn't foolish enough to fall in love with Felicity, but of course if he really loved her—hadn't he said that loving and being in love were two different things? She forced herself to stop thinking about him.

After a few days customers began to trickle in; the Misses Potter came as usual for their tea and several ladies from the village popped in on their way to or from the January sales; life returned to its normal routine. Mary Jane sternly suppressed the thought of Sir Thomas, not altogether successfully, when a card from Felicity came. She had written on the back, 'Gorgeous weather, here for another week. Pity he has to return on Saturday. Be good. Felicity'.

Mary Jane ignored the last few words, she had no other choice but to be good, but, reading the rest of the scrawled words, she frowned. Felicity had hinted that she would see

Sir Thomas and persuade him to go to Spain with her. It looked as though she had succeeded.

'I suppose the cleverer you are the sillier you get,' said Mary Jane in such a venomous tone that Brimble laid back his ears.

She was setting out the coffee-cups on Saturday morning when the first of the motorcyclists stopped before her door. He was joined by two others and the three of them came into the tea-room. Young men, encased in black leather and talking noisily. They took off their helmets and flung them down on one of the tables, pulled out chairs and sat down. They weren't local men and they stared at her until she felt uneasy.

'Coffee?' she asked. 'And anything to eat?'

'Coffee'll do, darlin', and a plate of whatever there is.' He laughed. 'And not much of that in this hole.' The other two laughed with him and she went into the kitchen to pour the coffee. Before doing so she picked up Brimble and popped him on the stairs and shut the door on him. She wasn't sure why she had done it; she wasn't a timid girl and the men would drink the coffee and go. She put the coffee on the table, then fetched a plate of scones and went back to the kitchen where she had been making pastry for the sausage rolls. She could see them from where she stood at the kitchen table and they seemed quiet enough, their heads close together, talking softly and sniggering. Presently they called for more coffee and ten minutes later they scraped back their chairs and put on their helmets. She took the bill over with an inward sigh of relief, but instead of taking it, the man she offered it to caught her hand and held it fast. 'Expect us to pay for that slop?' he wanted to know.

'Yes,' said Mary Jane calmly. 'I do, and please leave go of my hand.'

'Got a tongue in 'er 'ead, too. An' what'll you do if we don't pay up, Miss High and Mighty?'

'You will pay up. You asked for coffee and scones and I gave you them, so now you'll pay for what you've had.'

'Cor—got a sharp tongue, too, 'asn't she?' He tightened his grip. ''Ave ter teach 'er a lesson, won't we, boys?'

They swept the cups and saucers, the coffee-pot and the empty plates on to the floor and one of them went around treading on the bits of china, crushing them to fragments. The chairs went next, hurled across the room and then the tables. The little vases of dried flowers they threw at walls and all this was done without a word.

She was frightened but she was furiously angry too, she lifted a foot, laced into a sensible shoe, and kicked the man holding her hand. It couldn't have hurt much through all that leather, but it took him by surprise. He wrenched her round with a bellow of rage.

'Why, you little...'

Sir Thomas, on his way to spend a weekend with his mother and at the same time call upon Mary Jane, slowed the car as the tea-room came into view and then stopped at the sight of the motorbikes. He got out, saw the anxious elderly faces peering from the cottages on either side of Mary Jane's home, crossed the narrow pavement in one stride and threw open her door. A man who kept his feelings well under control, he allowed them free rein at the sight of her white face...

Mary Jane wished very much to faint on to a comfortable sofa, but she sidled to the remains of the counter and hung on to it. This was no time to faint; Sir Thomas had his hands full and apparently he was enjoying it, too. The little room seemed full of waving arms and legs. The man who had been holding her was tripped up neatly by one of Sir Thomas's elegantly shod feet and landed with a crash into the debris of tables and chairs which left Sir Thomas free to deal with the two other men. Subdued and scared by this large, silent man who knocked them around like ninepins, they huddled in a corner by their fallen comrade, only anxious to be left alone.

'Any one of you move and I'll break every bone in his

body,' observed Sir Thomas in the mildest of voices, and turned his attention to Mary Jane.

His arm was large and comforting and as steady as a rock. 'Don't, whatever you do, faint,' he begged her, 'for there's nowhere for you to lie down.' Nothing in his kind, impersonal voice and his equally impersonal arm hinted at his great wish to pick her up and drive off with her and never let her go again. 'The police will be along presently; someone must have seen that something was wrong and warned them.' He looked down at the top of her head. 'I'll get a chair from the kitchen...'

She was dimly aware of someone coming to the door then, old Rob from his cottage by the church where he lived with his two sons. 'The Coats lad came running to tell something was amiss. The police is coming and my two boys'll be along in a couple of shakes.' He cast an eye over the three men huddled together. 'Varmints!' He turned a shrewd eye upon Sir Thomas. 'Knock 'em out, did yer? Nice bit of work, I'd say.'

The police, Rob's two sons and the rector arrived together. Not that Mary Jane cared. Let them all come, she reflected; a cup of tea and her bed was all she wanted. The bed was out of the question, but the rector, a meek and kindly man, made tea which she drank with chattering teeth, spilling a good deal of it, thankful that Sir Thomas was dealing with the police so that she needed to answer only essential questions before they marched the three men away to the waiting van. 'You'll need to come to the station on Tuesday morning, miss,' the senior office said. 'Nine o'clock suit you? Have you got a car?'

'I'll bring Miss Seymour, Officer,' said Sir Thomas and he nodded an affable goodbye and turned to old Rob. 'Will you wait while I see Mary Jane up to her bed?'

'I do not want...' began Mary Jane pettishly, not knowing what she was wanting.

'No, of course you don't.' Sir Thomas's voice was soothing. 'But in half an hour or so when you have got over the nasty shock you had, you will think clearly again. Besides, I want to have a look at that wrist.'

She went upstairs, urged on by a firm hand on her back, and found Brimble waiting anxiously on the tiny landing. The sight of his small furry face was too much; she burst into tears, sobbing and sniffing and grizzling into Sir Thomas's shoulder. He waited patiently until the sobs petered out, offered a handkerchief, observing that there was nothing like a good cry and at the same time tossing back the quilt on her bed.

'Half an hour,' he told her, tucking it around her and lifting Brimble on to the bed. 'I'll be back.'

Downstairs, he found old Rob and his sons waiting. 'Ah, yes, I wonder if I might have your help...?' He talked for a few minutes and when old Rob nodded, money changed hands and they bade him goodbye and went off down the village street. Sir Thomas watched them go and then went to let the patient Watson out of the car and get his bag, let himself into the tea-room again and go soft-footed upstairs with Watson hard on his heels.

Mary Jane had fallen asleep, her hair all over the place, her mouth slightly open. She had a little colour now and her nose was pink from crying. Sir Thomas studied her lovingly and then turned his attention to her hand lying outside the quilt. The wrist was discoloured and a little swollen. The man's grasp must have been brutal. He suppressed the wave of rage which shook him and sat down to wait for her to wake up.

Which she did presently, the long lashes sweeping up to reveal the glorious eyes. Sir Thomas spent a few seconds admiring them. 'Better now? I'd like to take a look at that wrist. Does it hurt?'

'Yes.' she sat up in bed and dragged the quilt away. 'But I'm perfectly all right now. Thank you very much for helping me. I mustn't keep you...'

He was holding her hand, examining her wrist. 'This is quite nasty. I'll put a crêpe bandage on for the time being and we'll see about it later. Can you manage to pack a bag with a few things? I'm taking you to stay with my mother for a few days.'

She sat up very straight. 'I can't possibly, there's such a lot to do here, I must get someone to help me clear up and I must see about tables and chairs and cups and saucers and...' She paused, struck by the thought that she had no money to buy these essentials and yet she would have to have them, they were her very livelihood. She would have to borrow, but from whom? Oliver? Certainly not Oliver. Felicity? She might offer to help if she knew about it.

Sir Thomas, watching her, guessed her thoughts and said bracingly, 'There is really nothing you can do for a day or two.' He added vaguely, 'The police, you know. Far better to spend a little time making up your mind what is to be done first.'

'But your mother...'

'She will be delighted to see you again.' He got up and reached down the case on the top of the wardrobe. 'Is Brimble's basket downstairs? I'll get it while you pack—just enough for a week will do. Do you want to leave any messages with anyone? What about the milk and so on?'

'Mrs Adams next door will tell him not to call, and there's food in the fridge...'

'Leave it to me.'

She changed into her suit, packed the jersey dress, undies and a dressing-gown, her few cosmetics, then she did her hair in a perfunctory fashion and found scarf and gloves, out-of-date black court shoes, well-polished, and she burrowed in the back of a drawer and got the few pounds she kept for an emergency. By then, Sir Thomas was calling up the stairs to see if she was ready. He came to fetch her case while she picked up Brimble, carried him down to his basket and fastened him in. She was swept through the ruins of the tea-room before she had time to look round her, popped into the car with the animals on the back seat while he went back to lock the door. He came over to the car then. 'I think it might be a good idea to leave the key with Mrs Adams,' he suggested and she agreed readily, her thoughts busy with ways and means.

A tap on the window made her turn her head. The rector was there, so was his sister, Miss Kemble and Mrs Stokes and hurrying up the street was the shopkeeper. Mary Jane opened the window and a stream of sympathy poured in. 'If only we had known,' declared Miss Kemble, 'we could have come to your assistance.'

'But you did, at least the rector did. A cup of tea was exactly what I needed most! It was all a bit of a shock.'

The shopkeeper poked her head round Mrs Stokes' shoulder. 'A proper shame it is,' she declared. 'No one is safe these days. A good thing you've got the doctor here to take you to his mum. You 'ave a good rest, love—the place'll be as good as new again, don't you worry.'

They clustered round Sir Thomas as he came back to the car and after a few minutes' talk he got into his seat, lifted a hand in farewell and drove away. 'I like your rector,' he observed, 'but his sister terrifies me.'

Which struck her as so absurd that she laughed, which was what he had meant her to do.

He didn't allow her to talk about the disastrous morning either but carried on a steady flow of remarks to which, out of politeness, she was obliged to reply. When they arrived at his mother's house, she was met by that lady with sincere pleasure and no mention as to why she had come. 'We've put you in the room you had when you were here,' she was told. 'And have you brought your nice cat with you?'

Mrs Latimer broke off to offer a cheek to her son and receive Watson's pleased greeting. 'Would you like to go up to your room straight away? Lunch will be in ten minutes or so. Come down and have a drink first.'

The house was warm and welcoming and Mrs Beaver, coming into the hall, beamed at her with heart-warming pleasure. It was like coming home, thought Mary Jane, skipping upstairs behind that lady, only of course it wasn't, but it was nice to pretend...

No one mentioned the morning's events at lunch. The talk was of the village, a forthcoming trip Sir Thomas was to make to the Middle East and whether Mrs Latimer should go to London to do some shopping. Somehow they contrived to include Mary Jane in their conversation so that presently she was emboldened to ask, 'Are you going away for a long time?'

'If all goes well, I should be away for a week, perhaps less. I've several good reasons for wanting to get back as soon as possible.'

Was one of them Felicity? wondered Mary Jane, and Mrs Latimer put the thought into words by asking, 'Have you seen anything of that glamorous sister of yours lately, Mary Jane?'

'No. I'm not sure where she is—she was in Spain but I don't know how long she will be there.'

Sir Thomas leaned back in his chair, his eyes on her face. 'Felicity is in London,' he observed casually.

It was quite true, thought Mary Jane, love did hurt, a physical pain which cut her like a knife. Somehow she was going to have to live with it. 'Perhaps you would like to go and see her?' Sir Thomas went on.

She spoke too quickly. 'No, no, there's no need, I mean, she's always so—that is, she works so hard she wouldn't be able to spare the time.'

She had gone rather red in the face and he said blandly, 'I don't suppose she could do much to help you,' and when his mother suggested that they have their coffee in the drawing-room she got up thankfully.

They had had their coffee and were sitting comfortably before the fire when Sir Thomas asked abruptly, 'Have you any money, Mary Jane?'

She was taken by surprise; there was no time to think up a fib and anyway, what would be the point of that? 'Well, no, I mean I have a few pounds—I keep them hidden at the cottage but I've brought them with me and there's about forty pounds in the post office.' She achieved a smile. 'I shall be able to borrow for the tea-room.' She added hastily, 'I'm not sure who yet, but I've friends in the village.'

'Good. As I said, there's nothing to be done for a day or two; besides, I think that wrist should be X-rayed. I'll take you up to town when I go on Monday morning—I'm operating all day but I'll bring you back in the evening. Someone can take you to my house and Mrs Tremble will look after you until I'm ready.'

He smiled at her. 'You are about to argue but I beg you not to; I'm not putting myself out in the least.'

'It only aches a little.'

'You may have got a cracked bone.' He glanced at her bandaged wrist. He asked mildly, 'What had you done to annoy the man?'

'I kicked him.'

'Quite right too,' said Mrs Latimer. 'What a sensible girl you are. I would have done the same. Do you suppose it hurt?'

He went away presently to make some phone calls and Mrs Latimer said cosily, 'Now my dear, do tell me exactly what happened if you can bear to talk about it. What a brave girl you are. I should never have dared to ask for my money.'

So Mary Jane told her and discovered that talking about it made it seem less awful than she supposed. True, the problem of borrowing money and starting up again was at the moment impossible to solve but as her companion so bracingly remarked, things had a way of turning out better than one might expect. On this optimistic note she bore Mary Jane away to the conservatory at the back of the house to admire two camellias in full bloom.

The three of them had tea round the fire presently and sat talking until Sir Thomas was called to the phone and Mrs Latimer suggested that Mary Jane might like to unpack and then make sure that Mrs Beaver had prepared the right supper for Brimble, who had spent a day after his heart, curled up before the fire. Mary Jane went to her room, bearing him with her; there was some time before dinner and perhaps mother and son would like to be alone. So she stayed there, spending a lot of time before the looking-glass, trying out various hair-styles and then, disheartened by the fact that they didn't improve her looks in the slightest, pinning it in her usual fashion, applied lipstick and powder and, when the gong sounded, went downstairs, leaving Brimble asleep on the bed.

Sir Thomas and his mother were in the drawing-room and he got up at once and invited her to sit down and offered her a drink.

'But the gong's gone...'

He smiled. 'I don't suppose anything will spoil if we dine five minutes later. Did you fall asleep?'

He was making it easy for her and Mrs Latimer said comfortably, 'All that excitement—you must have an early night, my dear.'

They dined presently and Mary Jane discovered that she was hungry. The mushrooms in garlic sauce, beef Wellington and *crème brulée* were delicious and just right—as was the conversation; about nothing much, touching lightly upon any number of subjects and never once on her trying morning. As they got up from the table, Sir Thomas said casually,

'Shall we go for a walk tomorrow, Mary Jane? I enjoy walking at this time of year but perhaps you don't care for it?'

'Oh, but I do.' The prospect of being with him had sent the colour into her cheeks. 'I'd like that very much.'

'Good—after lunch, then. We go to church in the morning—come with us if you would like to.'

'I'd like that, too.'

'Splendid, I've fixed up an appointment for you on Monday morning—half-past nine—we'll have to leave around seven o'clock. I'm operating at ten o'clock.'

'I get up early. Would someone mind feeding Brimble? He'll be quite good on the balcony.'

'Don't worry about him, my dear.' Mrs Latimer was bend-ing her head over an embroidery frame. 'Mrs Beaver and I will keep an eye on him. Thomas, did you bring any work with you?'

'I'm afraid so—there's a paper I have to read at the next seminar.'

'Then go away and read it or write it, or whatever you need to do. Mary Jane and I are going to have a nice gos-sip—I want to tell her all about Mrs Bennett's daughter—she's just got engaged...'

The rest of the evening passed pleasantly. Sir Thomas reappeared after an hour or so and shortly afterwards, in the kindest possible manner, suggested that she might like to go to bed. 'Rather a dull evening for you,' he apologised.

'Dull? It was heavenly.' Had he any idea what it was like to spend almost every evening on one's own even if one were making pastry or polishing tables and chairs? Well, of course he hadn't, he would spend his evenings with friends, going to the theatre, dining out and probably seeing as much of Felicity as possible. The sadness of her face at the thought caused him to stare at her thoughtfully. He wanted to ask her why she was sad, but, not liking him enough to answer, she would give him a chilly look from those lovely eyes and murmur something. He still wasn't sure if she liked him, and even if she did, she had erected an invisible barrier between them. He was going to need a great deal of patience.

She hadn't been expected to sleep but she did, to be wak-ened in the morning by Mrs Beaver with a tray of tea and the news that it was a fine day but very cold. 'Breakfast in half an hour, miss, and take my advice and wear something warm; the church is like an ice-box.'

She had brought her winter coat with her but it wouldn't go over her suit. It would have to be the jersey dress. She dressed under Brimble's watchful eye and went down to breakfast.

That night, curled up in her comfortable bed, she reviewed her day. It had been even better that she had hoped for. The three of them had gone to church and, despite the chill from the ancient building, she had loved every minute of the service, standing between Sir Thomas and his mother, and after lunch she had put on her sensible shoes, tied a scarf over her head and gone with him on the promised walk. It was a pity, she reflected, that they had talked about rather dull matters: politics, the state of the turnip crop on a neighbouring farm, the weather, Watson. She had wanted to talk about Felicity but she hadn't dared and since he hadn't mentioned the tea-room she hadn't liked to say anything about it. After all, he had done a great deal to help her; she was a grown woman, used to being on her own, capable of dealing with things like loans and painting and papering. Women were supposed to be equal to men now, weren't they? She didn't feel equal to Sir Thomas, but she supposed that she would have to do her best. He had been kind and friendly in a detached way but she suspected that she wasn't the kind of girl he would choose for a companion. She would have to go to London with him in the morning to have her wrist X-rayed, although it didn't seem necessary to her, but once she was back here she would go back to her cottage and then she need never see him again. She went to sleep then, feeling sad, and woke in the small hours, suddenly afraid of the future. It would be hard to begin again and it would be even harder never to see Sir Thomas, or worse—if he married Felicity, she would have to see him from time to time. She wouldn't be able to bear that, but of course she would have to. She didn't go to sleep again but lay making plans as to how to open the tea-room as quickly as possible with the least possible expense. She would need a miracle.

CHAPTER EIGHT

IT WAS still dark when they left the next morning. They had breakfast together, wasting no time and, with Watson drowsing on the back seat, had driven away, with no one but Mrs Beaver to see them off. Until they reached the outskirts of the city there was little traffic and they sat in a companionable silence, making desultory conversation from time to time. Crawling through the London streets, Mary Jane thanked heaven that she lived in the country. How could Felicity bear to live in the midst of all the noise and bustle? She asked abruptly, 'Do you like living in London?'

'My work is here, at least for a good part of the time. I escape whenever I can.'

They were in the heart of the city now and the hospital loomed ahead of them. At its entrance he got out, led her across the entrance hall and down a long tiled passage to the X-ray department, where he handed her over to a nurse.

'I'll see you later at my house,' he told her as he prepared to leave.

'Oh, won't you be here?' She was suddenly uncertain.

'I am going home now, but I shall be back presently. By then you will be taken care of by someone. Then Mrs Tremble is expecting you.'

She wanted to ask more questions, but the nurse was watching them with interest and besides, she could see that he was concealing impatience. She said goodbye and went with the nurse to take off her coat and have the bandage taken off her wrist.

The radiographer was young and friendly and she was surprised to find that he knew how her wrist had been injured. 'Sir Thomas phoned,' he told her airily, 'and of course he had to give me a history of the injury. Said you were a brave young lady. Does it bother you at all?'

'It aches but it doesn't feel broken.'

'There may be a bone cracked, though. Let's get it X-rayed—I'll get the radiologist to take a look at it and let Sir Thomas know as soon as possible.'

That done, he bade her goodbye, handed her over to the nurse to have the bandage put on again and then be taken back to the entrance hall.

There was a short, stout man talking to the porter but as she hesitated he came towards her. 'Miss Seymour, Sir Thomas asked me to drive you to his house. I'm Tremble, his butler.'

She offered a hand. 'Thank you, I'm afraid I'm being a nuisance...'

'Not at all, miss. You just come with me. Mrs Tremble has coffee waiting for you. Sir Thomas asked me to tell you that he may be delayed this evening and he hopes that you will dine with him before he drives you back to Mrs Latimer.'

He had ushered her out to the forecourt and into a Jaguar motor car, and as they drove away she asked, 'Where are we going?'

'To Sir Thomas's home, miss.' He had a nice fatherly manner. 'Me and my wife look after him, as you might say. Little Venice, that's where he lives, nice and quiet and not too far from the hospital.'

It wasn't the country, she reflected, but it was certainly quiet and even on a winter's day it was pleasant, with the water close by and the well-cared-for houses. Tremble ushered her in, took her coat and opened a door. Watson came to greet her as she went into the room.

She had found Mrs Latimer's house charming but this drawing-room was even more so. There were easy-chairs drawn up to a blazing fire, a vast sofa between them, covered as they were in a tawny red velvet. A Pembroke table stood behind it and on cither wall were mahogany bow-fronted cabinets, filled with porcelain and silverware. At the window facing the street there was a Georgian library table, flanked by two side-chairs of the same period, and here and there, just where they would be needed, were tripod tables, bearing low table-lamps.

'Just you sit down,' said Tremble, 'and I'll bring you your coffee, miss.'

He went away, leaving her to inspect the room at her leisure with Watson pressed close to her, until she sat down in one of the chairs as Tremble came back. 'Sir Thomas said for you to make yourself at home, miss. There's the library across the hall if you should like to go there presently. Mrs Tremble will be along in a few minutes to make sure that what she's cooking for lunch suits you.'

'Please don't let her bother—I'm sure whatever it is will be delicious. I'm putting you to a great deal of trouble.'

'Not at all, miss. It's a pleasure to have you here. If Watson gets tiresome just open the French window and let him into the garden.'

Left alone, she drank her coffee, shared the biscuits with Watson and presently went to the French window at the back of the room to look out into the garden beyond. It was quite a good-sized garden with a high brick wall and, even on a grey winter day, was a pleasant oasis in the centre of the city. She went and sat down again and presently Mrs Tremble came into the room.

She was a tall, very thin woman with a sharp nose and a severe hairstyle, but she had a friendly smile and shrewd brown eyes. 'You'll be wanting to know where the cloakroom is, miss; I'm sure Tremble forgot to tell you. Forget his own head one day, he will! Now, as to your lunch; I've a nice little Dover sole and one of my castle puddings if that'll suit? Tremble will bring you a sherry and suggest a wine.'

So, later, Mary Jane sat down to her lunch and afterwards went to the library to choose something to read. The shelves were well-filled, mostly by ponderous volumes pertaining to

Sir Thomas's work but she found a local history of that part of London and took it back to read by the fire. Her knowledge of London was scanty and it would be nice to know more about Sir Thomas's private life, even if it was only through reading about his house in a book.

Tremble brought her tea as dusk fell, and drew the red velvet curtains across the windows. 'I'll give Watson his tea now, miss, and take him for a quick run. When Sir Thomas is late home I do that, then the pair of them go for a walk later in the evening.'

Mary Jane ate her tea and, lulled by the warmth of the fire and the gentle lamp-light, she closed her eyes and went to sleep. Voices and Watson's bark woke her and she sat up as the door opened and Sir Thomas came in.

The thought of him had been at the back of her mind all day, mixed in with worried plans for the future of the tea-room. Now the sight of him, calm and self-assured, sent a wave of happiness through her insides.

She remembered just in time about Felicity and greeted him in a sober manner quite at variance with her sparkling eyes.

He wished her good evening in a friendly voice, enquired after her day and voiced the hope that she hadn't found it too tiresome that he had been delayed in driving her back to his mother's house.

'Tiresome? Heavens, no. I've had a lovely day. You can have no idea how delightful it is to eat a meal you haven't cooked for yourself. Such delicious food too! How lucky you are to have Mrs Tremble to cook for you, Sir Thomas—and I've done nothing all day, just lounged around with Watson.' She beamed at him. 'I expect you've been busy?'

He agreed that he had, in a bland voice which didn't betray a long session in Theatre, a ward round, outpatients clinic and two private patients he had seen when he should have been having lunch.

He had sat down opposite her. He had poured her a drink and was sitting with a glass of whisky on the table beside him. She looked exactly right sitting there in her unfashionable clothes; she would be nice to come home to. He dismissed the thought with a sigh; he wanted her for his wife, but only if she loved him, and he wasn't even sure if she liked him! She was grateful for his help, but gratitude was something he chose to ignore.

It was a pity that Mary Jane couldn't read his thoughts. She sat there, making polite conversation until Tremble came to tell them that dinner was served and at the table, sitting opposite him, she continued to make small talk while she ate her salmon mousse, beef *en croûte* and Mrs Tremble's lavish version of Queen of Puddings.

The excellent claret had loosened her tongue so that by the end of their meal she felt emboldened to ask, 'Will you be seeing Felicity? I expect—'

He said silkily, 'I do not know what you expect, Mary Jane, but rid yourself of the idea that I have any interest in your sister. Any meetings we have had have not been of my seeking.'

'Oh, I thought—that is, Felicity said...that you—that you got on well together.'

'In plain terms, that I had fallen in love with her, is that what you are trying to say?' He was suddenly coldly angry. 'You may believe me, Mary Jane, when I tell you that I have no wish to dangle after your sister. I am no longer a callow youth to be taken in by a pretty face.'

She had gone rather red. 'I'm sorry if I've annoyed you. It's none of my business,' and, at his questioning raised eyebrows, she added, 'your private life.'

He debated whether to tell her how mistaken she was and decided not to, and the conversation lapsed while Tremble brought in the coffee tray. When he had gone again, Mary Jane, for some reason, probably the claret, allowed her tongue to run ahead of her good sense. 'Haven't you ever been in love?' she wanted to know.

'On innumerable occasions from the age of sixteen or so. It is a normal habit, you know.'

'Yes, I know. I fell in love with the gym instructor when I was at school and then with the man who came to tune the piano at home. I actually meant enough to want to marry someone...?'

He said gently, 'Yes, Mary Jane. And you?'

'Well, yes.'

'Still the piano-tuner?' He was laughing at her.

She said quickly, 'No,' and managed to laugh too; of course he had found her silly and rather rude, 'I dare say you're wedded to your work.' She spoke lightly.

'Certainly it keeps me fully occupied.' He glanced at his watch. 'Perhaps we had better go...'

She got up at once. 'Of course, I'm sorry, keeping you talking and you've had a long day already.'

She made short work of bidding the Trembles goodbye, saying just the right things in her quiet voice, shaking their hands and smiling a little when Tremble voiced the hope that he would see her again. 'Most unlikely.'

With Watson, drowsy after a good supper and a quick run, on the back seat, Sir Thomas drove away.

Mary Jane, still chatty from the claret, asked, 'Do you like driving?'

'Yes. It is an opportunity to think, especially at this time of night when the roads are fairly clear.'

She kept quiet after that. If he wanted to think then she wouldn't disturb him and if it came to that she had plenty to think about herself. She tore her eyes away from his hands on the wheel and stared ahead of her into the road, lit by the car's headlights. That way she could pretend that he wasn't there sitting beside her and concentrate on her own problems. When eventually he broke the silence it was to remind her that she had an interview with the police in the morning, something she had quite forgotten. 'I've arranged for an officer to come to Mother's house and interview you there,' he added.

'Thank you—I'd forgotten about it. Perhaps he could drive me back to the cottage? I really must start clearing up and getting it ready to open again.' A fanciful remark if ever there was one; she hadn't any idea at the moment how to find the money to start up once more, but he wasn't to know that.

Sir Thomas, who did know, gave a comforting rumble which might have meant anything and said briskly, 'Mother will be disappointed if you don't stay for a few days, and besides, although your wrist has no broken bones, it would be foolish of you to use it for anything more strenuous than lifting a tea-cup. Please do as I ask, Mary Jane, and wait another few days. If it won't bore you too much, I'll take you back home on Saturday morning.'

'Bored?' She was horrified at the thought. 'How could I possibly be bored in that lovely house, and your mother is so kind—I'd almost forgotten how nice mothers are.' There was a wistful note in her voice, and Sir Thomas sternly suppressed his wish to stop the car and comfort her in a manner calculated to make her forget her lack of a parent. Instead, he said in his quiet way, 'Good, that's settled, then.'

It was after ten o'clock when they reached Mrs Latimer's house and found the welcoming lights streaming from the windows and her waiting for them. So was the faithful Mrs Beaver, bustling in with a tray of coffee and sandwiches. 'And there's your bed waiting for you, Mary Jane, and you'd best be into it seeing that Constable Welch'll be here at nine o'clock sharp.'

Mary Jane drank her coffee obediently, ate a sandwich and, although she very much wanted to stay with Sir Thomas, bade them both goodnight.

'I dare say you'll be gone in the morning,' she observed as they walked together to the door.

'I'll be gone in ten minutes or so,' he told her.

She stopped short. 'You're never going back now? You can't—you mustn't, you've been at the hospital all day and driven here and now you want to drive straight back?'

He said placidly, 'I like driving at night and I promise you I'll go straight to bed when I get home.'

She put a hand on his coat sleeve. 'You'll take care, Thomas, do be careful.'

His eyes glinted under their lids. 'I'll be very careful, Mary Jane.' He bent and kissed her then. It was a quick, hard kiss, not at all like the very occasional peck she received from friends. She didn't know much about kisses, but this was definitely no peck. The look she gave him was amethyst fire.

'Oh, Thomas,' she muttered, and flew across the hall and upstairs, happily unaware that she had called him Thomas twice. She woke in the night, however, and she remembered. 'I am a fool,' she told Brimble, curled up on her feet. 'What a good thing he's not here and I must, simply must go away from here before he comes again.'

She had no chance against Mrs Latimer's gentle insistence that she should stay, or Mrs Beaver's more emphatic opinion that she needed more flesh on her bones and, over and above that, Constable Welch, when he came, assured her that there was no need for her return. 'Those men are to stay in custody for a few more days until we get things sorted out,' he told her. 'And there's nothing you can do for a bit.'

So she stayed in the nice old house, keeping Mrs Latimer company, eating the nourishing food Mrs Beaver insisted upon and discovering something of Sir Thomas. For his mother was quick to show her the family photo albums: Thomas as a baby, Thomas as a boy, Thomas as a student, Thomas receiving a knighthood...

'Why?' asked Mary Jane.

'Well, dear, he has done a great deal of work—around the world, I suppose I could say—teaching and getting clinics opened and lecturing, and, of course, operating. His father was a surgeon, too, you know.'

During the next few days she learnt a good deal about Sir Thomas, information freely given by his mother. By the time Saturday came around, Mary Jane felt that she knew quite a lot about him. At least, she told herself, she would have a lot to think about...

Watson's cheerful bark woke her the next morning and a few minutes later Mrs Beaver came in with her morning tea. 'He doesn't get enough rest,' she said, as she pulled back the curtains, revealing a grey February morning. 'Got here in the early hours, and he's up and outside before I could put the kettle on.' She shook her head. 'There's no holding him.'

When she had gone, Mary Jane got out of bed and went to look out of the window. Sir Thomas was at the end of the garden, throwing a ball for Watson. Whatever Mrs Beaver thought, he appeared to be well-rested and full of energy.

He wished her good morning with detached friendliness when she went down to breakfast, and asked if she would be ready to leave after breakfast and applied himself to his bacon and eggs. They had reached the toast and marmalade when he asked, casually, 'Have you any plans, Mary Jane?'

'I'll get cleared up,' she told him, summoning a cheerful voice. 'I can distemper the walls if they're marked, then I'll go to Cheltenham and borrow some money.' She didn't enlarge upon this and he didn't ask her to, which was just as well, because she had no idea how to set about it. She had spent several anxious hours during the nights going over her problems without much success and had come to the conclusion that if the solicitor who had attended to her uncle's affairs was unable to advise her there was nothing for it but to ask Felicity for some money.

They had almost finished when Mrs Latimer joined them. 'I shall miss you, dear,' she told Mary Jane. 'You must come and stay again soon— with Brimble, of course. Do take care of yourself. I shall come and see you and I'll bring Mrs Bennett with me.'

They left shortly after with Watson and Brimble sharing the back seat and Mary Jane very quiet beside Sir Thomas. There seemed nothing to say and since it was still only half light there was no point in admiring the scenery. It wasn't an awkward silence, though, she had the feeling that speech wasn't necessary, that he was content to drive silently, that to make conversation for its own sake was unnecessary. They were almost there when he observed casually, 'I shall be away all next week—Austria. I'll see you when I get back.'

He looked at her and smiled. It was a tender smile and a little amused and she looked away quickly. Then, for something to say, she asked, 'Have you been to Austria before?'

'Several times. Vienna this time—a seminar there.'

He had slowed the car down the village street and he stopped before her cottage, got out and opened the door and let Watson out as he reached in for Brimble's basket. Mary Jane stared.

'Someone's painted the outside—look...'

'So they have,' observed Sir Thomas, showing only a faint interest as he took the key from a pocket and opened the door.

She went in quickly and then stood quite still. 'Inside too,' she said. 'Look at the walls, and there's a new counter and tables and chairs.' She turned to look at him. 'Did you know? But how could...there's no money to pay for it.' She stared into his quiet face. 'It's you, isn't it? You arranged it all.'

'Mr Rob and his sons have done all the work, your friends in the village collected tables and chairs and I imagine that every house in the village contributed the china.'

'You arranged it, though, and you paid for it, too, didn't you?' She smiled widely at him. 'Oh, Sir Thomas, how can I ever thank you? And everyone else of course, and as soon as I've got started again I'll pay you back, every penny.'

'You called me Thomas.' He had come to stand very close to her.

'I expect I forgot,' she told him seriously. 'I hope you didn't mind.'

'On the contrary, I took it as a sign that we were becoming friends.'

She put a hand on his arm. 'How can I ever be anything else after all you've done for me?' She reached up and kissed his cheek. 'I'll never forget you.'

'I rather hope you won't!'

He stared down at her with such intensity that she said hurriedly, 'Will you have a cup of coffee? It won't take a minute.'

He went to fetch her case from the car and she let an impatient Brimble out of his basket and put on the kettle and saw that there were cups and saucers arranged on the kitchen table and an unopened tin of biscuits, sugar in a bowl and milk in the fridge. She knew the reason a moment later for when Sir Thomas came in he was followed by the rector, his sister, old Rob and his sons, the shopkeeper and the Misses Potter.

There was a chorus of, 'Welcome back, Mary Jane,' and a good deal of talk and laughter as she made the coffee and handed round the cups. No one intended to hurry away; they all sat around, admiring their efforts, telling Mary Jane that she had never looked so plump and well. 'And we would never have done any of this if it hadn't been for Sir Thomas,' declared Miss Emily in her penetrating voice. 'He had us all organised in no time.'

It was a pity that presently he declared that he had to go and in the general bustle of handshaking and goodbyes Mary Jane had no chance to speak to him. She did go out to the car with him and stood there on the pavement, impervious to the cold, her hands held in his.

'We can't talk now, Mary Jane, and perhaps it is just as well, but I'm coming to see you. You want to see me, too, don't you?'

'Yes, oh, yes, please, Thomas!'

His kiss was even better than the last one. She stood there watching the Rolls disappear out of sight and would have probably gone on standing, freezing slowly, if Miss Kemble hadn't opened the door and told her to come inside at once. Mary Jane, who never took any notice of Miss Kemble's bossy ways, meekly did as she was told.

She was borne away presently to eat her lunch at the rectory and to be given a great deal of unheeded advice by Miss Kemble. That lady said to her brother later in the day, 'I have never known Mary Jane to be so attentive and willing to take my advice.'

Mary Jane had heard perhaps one word in ten of Miss Kemble's lectures; her head was full of Sir Thomas, going over every word he had said, the way he had looked, his kiss.

Back in her cottage once more, she assured Brimble that she would be sensible, at least until she saw him again. He had said that he wanted to see her again...she forgot about being sensible and fell to daydreaming again.

She was up early the next morning, polishing and dusting, setting out cups and saucers and making a batch of scones. Sunday was a bad day usually, and she seldom opened, only in the height of the tourist season, but she had a feverish wish to get back to her old life as quickly as possible. Her efforts were rewarded, for several cars stopped and when she opened again after lunch there were more customers. It augured well for the future, she told herself, counting the takings at the end of the afternoon.

Her luck held for the first few days, and a steady trickle of customers came; if it continued so, she could make a start on paying back Sir Thomas. She had no idea how much it would be and probably she would be in his debt for years.

Thursday brought Oliver. He marched into the tea-room and stood looking around him. 'Who paid for all this?' he wanted to know.

Mary Jane, her hands floury from her pastry making, stood in the kitchen doorway, looking at him. 'So you did hear about the—incident? The rector told me that he had let you know...'

Oliver blew out his cheeks. 'Naturally, it was his duty to inform me.'

Mary Jane put her neat head on one side. 'And what did you do about it?'

'There was no necessity for me to do anything. The place was being put to rights.' He looked around him. 'It must have cost you a pretty penny. You borrowed, of course?'

'That's my business. Have you just come to see if I'm still
here or do you want something?'

'Since your regrettable treatment of Margaret I would hes-
itate to ask any favours of you.'

'Quite right too, Oliver. So it's just curiosity.'

He said pompously, 'I felt it my duty to come and see how
things were.'

'Oh, stuff,' said Mary Jane rudely. 'Do go away, Oliver,
you're wasting my time.'

'You've wasted enough time with that surgeon,' he
sneered. 'We hear the village gossip as well as everyone else.
Hoping to catch him, are you? Well, I'll tell you something—even if you were pretty, and knew how to dress you
wouldn't stand a chance. That sister of yours has him
hooked. We've been to town and met her—just back from
Vienna. She means to marry him, and I must say this for the
girl, she always gets what she wants.'

She put her hands behind her back because they were
shaking and, although she had gone pale, she said steadily
enough, 'Felicity is beautiful and famous and she works hard
at her job. She deserves to have whatever she wants.'

'Well, from all accounts he's a great catch— loaded, well-
known and handsome. What more could a girl want?' He
laughed nastily. 'So you can stop your silly dreaming and
look around for someone who's not too fussy about looks.'

'Oh, do go. I'm busy.' She added, 'You're getting fat,
Oliver—you ought to go on a diet.'

If he didn't go quickly, she reflected, she would scream
the place down. He was sly and mean and she had no doubt
at all that he had come intending to tell her about Felicity
and Sir Thomas; he had obviously known all about the tea-
room being vandalised and what Sir Thomas had done to
help her. Thankfully, he went with a last, sniggering, 'I don't
expect Felicity will ask you to be a bridesmaid, but you
wouldn't like that, would you? Seeing the man of your
dreams marrying your sister.'

It was too much; she had been cutting up lard to make the

puff pastry for the sausage rolls, and she scooped up a handful and threw it at him as he opened the door. It caught him on the side of his head and slid down his cheek, oozed over his collar and down on to his overcoat.

Rage and surprise rendered him speechless. 'Bye bye, Oliver,' said Mary Jane cheerfully.

She locked the door when he had gone, turned the sign to 'Closed' and went upstairs where she sat down and had a good cry. It had been foolish of her, she told Brimble, to imagine, even for a moment, that Sir Thomas had any deeper feelings for her than those of friendliness and—regrettably— pity, but he could have told her…and he was coming to see her; he wanted to talk. Well, of course he did, he wanted to tell her about Felicity and himself, didn't he? But why couldn't he have told her sooner and only kissed her in a casual manner, so that she couldn't get silly ideas into her head? She blew her red nose, bathed her eyes and went back to her pastry making. Perhaps Oliver had been lying; he was quite capable of that. The thought cheered her so that by the time she had taken the sausage rolls from the oven she felt quite cheerful again.

She had some more customers calling in for coffee and sausage rolls. Several of them remarked upon her heavy cold and she agreed quickly, conscious that her eyes were still puffy and her nose still pink.

Sir Thomas had thoughtfully caused a telephone to be installed when the tea-room had been done up, arguing that as she lived alone it was a sensible thing to have. She had thanked him nicely, wondering how she was going to pay for its rental, let alone any calls she might make.

When it rang just before closing time she lifted the receiver—only he and possibly Mrs Latimer would know the number and, even if her friends in the village knew it, too, they would hardly waste money ringing her up when they only needed to nip down the road. 'Thomas,' she said happily to Brimble, disturbed from a refreshing nap.

It was Felicity.

'Felicity,' said Mary Jane. 'How did you know I had a phone?'

'Thomas told me. Back with your nose to the pastry-board again? What a thrill for you, darling. I'm just back from Vienna and in an absolute daze of happiness, darling. I told you I'd marry when I found the right man—good looks, darling, lots of lovely money and dotes on me.'

Mary Jane found her voice. 'What wonderful news and how exciting. When will you get married?'

'I've one or two modelling dates I can't break but very soon—a few weeks. I wanted to move in with him, but he wouldn't hear of it.' She giggled. 'He's very old-fashioned.'

Mary Jane wasn't sure about Sir Thomas being old-fashioned but she was quite sure that allowing Felicity to move in with him would be something he would never agree to.

'Will you have a big wedding?'

'As big as I am able to arrange in a few weeks. There's a nice little church close by—we've dozens of friends between us and I shall wear white, of course. Bridesmaids, too. A pity you're so far away, darling.'

Which remark Mary Jane took, quite rightly, to be a kinder way of saying that she wasn't expected to be a bridesmaid or even a guest.

'What would you like for a wedding present?'

Felicity laughed. 'Oh, darling, don't bother, I'm sending a list to Harrods. Besides, you haven't any money.'

Mary Jane was pleased to hear how bright and cheerful her voice sounded. 'Let me know the date of the wedding, anyway,' she begged. 'And I'm so glad you're happy, dear.' She was going to burst into tears any minute now. 'I must go, I've scones in the oven.'

'You and your scones,' laughed Felicity, and rang off. Just in time. She locked the door and turned the notice round and switched off the lights, not forgetting to put the milk bottles outside the back door and check the fridge before polishing the tables ready for the morning. All the while she was weeping quietly. Oliver, with his nasty, snide remarks, had been bad enough and she had almost persuaded herself that he had just been malicious, but now Felicity had told her the same story.

Moping would do no good, she told herself presently, and started to clean the stove—a job she hated, but anything was better than having time to think.

She pushed her supper round and round her plate and went to bed. It was a well-known adage that things were always better in the morning.

They were exactly the same, except that now she never wanted to see Thomas again. He had been amusing himself while Felicity was away, playing at being the Good Samaritan. She ground her little white teeth at the thought. If it took her the rest of her life she would pay him back every penny. How dared he kiss her like that, as though he actually wanted to...?

He had said that he would be away for the whole of the week and it was still only Friday; she would have the weekend to decide how she would behave and even if he had to go to the hospital or see his patients he might not come for some days. He might not come at all.

'Which, of course, would be far the best thing,' she told Brimble.

He came the next day just as she was handing a bill to the last of the few people who had been in for tea. She stared at him across the room, her heart somersaulting against her ribs. He looked as he always did, calm and detached, but he was smiling a little. Well he might, reflected Mary Jane, ushering her customers out of the door which Sir Thomas promptly closed, turning the sign round.

'It is not yet five o'clock,' said Mary Jane frostily. Talking to him wasn't going to be difficult at all because she was so angry.

'I got back a day early,' said Sir Thomas, still standing by the door. 'It has been a long week simply because I want to talk to you.'

'Well, you need not have hurried. Felicity phoned me. She's—she's very happy, I hope you will be too.' Despite her efforts her voice began to spiral. 'You could have told me... You've been very kind, more than kind, but I can understand that you wanted to please her.'

'What exactly are you talking about?' he wanted to know, his voice very quiet.

'Oh, do stop pretending you don't know,' she snapped. 'I knew that you would fall in love with her but you didn't tell me, you let me think...did you have a nice time together in Vienna?'

His voice was still quiet but now it was cold as well. 'You believe that I went straight from you to be with Felicity? That I am going to marry her? That I was amusing myself with you?'

'Of course I do. Oliver told me and I didn't quite believe him and then she phoned.'

'Is that what you think of me, Mary Jane?' And when she nodded dumbly he gave her a look of such icy rage that she stepped back. If only he would go, she thought miserably, and had her wish.

CHAPTER NINE

MARY JANE stood in the middle of the sitting-room, listening to the faint whisper of the Rolls-Royce's departure, regretting every word she had uttered. She hadn't given Sir Thomas a chance to speak, and her ingratitude must have shocked him. She should have behaved like a future sister-in-law, congratulated him and expressed her delight. All she had done was to let him see that she had taken him seriously when all the time he was merely being kind. Well, it was too late now. She had cooked her goose, burnt her boats, made her bed and must lie on it. She uttered these wise sayings out loud, but they brought her no comfort.

She felt an icy despair too deep for tears. The thought of a lifetime of serving tea and coffee and baking cakes almost choked her. She could, of course, sell the cottage and go right away, but that would be running away, wouldn't it? Besides, she must owe him a great deal of money...

Leaving church the next morning, Miss Kemble took her aside. 'You must have your lunch with us,' she insisted, overriding Mary Jane's reasons for not doing so. 'Of course you must come, you are still too pale. Do you not sleep? Perhaps you are nervous of being alone?'

Mary Jane said very quickly that she wasn't in the least nervous—only at the thought of Miss Kemble moving in to keep her company. 'Besides,' she pointed out, 'I have a telephone now.'

'Ah, yes, that charming Sir Thomas Latimer, what a good friend he has been to you. I hear from all sides how thoughtful he is of others—always helping lame dogs over stiles.' An unfortunate remark unintentionally made.

They were kind at the rectory. She was given a glass of Miss Kemble's beetroot wine and the rector piled her plate with underdone roast beef which she swallowed down, wishing that Brimble were there to finish it for her. I don't mean to be ungrateful, she reflected, but why does Miss Kemble always make me feel as if I were an object for charity?

She left shortly after their meal with the excuse that she intended to go for a brisk walk. 'For I don't get out a great deal,' she explained, and then wished that she hadn't said that, for Miss Kemble might decide to go with her.

However, there was a visiting parson coming to tea and staying the night, so Miss Kemble was fully occupied. Mary Jane thanked the pair of them sincerely; they had been kind and going to the rectory had filled in some of the long day. Sunday was always a bad day with time lying heavy on her hands, and today was worse than usual. She tired herself out with a long walk; as the days went by it would get easier to forget Sir Thomas and the chances of seeing much of him were slight; Felicity didn't like a country life. She let herself into her cottage, shed her coat and scarf, fed Brimble and spent a long time cooking a supper she hardly touched.

There was a spate of customers on Monday morning to keep her busy and she had promised to make a cake for the Women's Institute meeting during the week, so the baking of it took most of the afternoon.

'Another day gone,' said Mary Jane to Brimble.

Mrs Latimer and Mrs Bennett came the next day. 'We thought we would have a little drive round, dear,' explained Mrs Latimer, 'and we'd love a cup of coffee.'

They sat down, her only customers—and begged her to join them.

'I must say I'm disappointed,' observed Mrs Latimer. 'You don't look at all well, dear. You were quite bonny when I last saw you. Are you working too hard? A few days' rest perhaps? Thomas is back from wherever it was he went to...'

'Vienna.'

'That's right. Has he been to see you?'

Mrs Latimer's blue eyes were guileless.

'Yes.'

For the life of her, Mary Jane couldn't think of anything to add to that. And if Mrs Latimer expected it she gave no sign but made some observation about the life her son led. 'It is really time he settled down,' she declared, which gave Mrs Bennett the chance to talk about her recently engaged daughter, so that any chance Mary Jane had of finding out more about Thomas and Felicity was squashed.

'You must come and see us,' said Mrs Bennett. 'On a Sunday, when you're free. How nice that you're on the telephone—very thoughtful of Thomas to have it put in. I must say it has all been beautifully redecorated.'

'He's been very kind,' said Mary Jane woodenly. 'And the village gave me the china and the tables and chairs. I don't think I could have managed to start again without help. I'm very grateful.'

'My dear child,' said Mrs Latimer, 'I don't know of many girls who would have carved themselves a living out of an old cottage and the pittance your uncle left you, and as for that wretched cousin of yours...'

'I don't see Oliver very often,' said Mary Jane, adding silently, Only when he wants something or has news which he knows might upset me.

The two ladies left presently and, save for a man on a scooter who had taken a wrong turning, she had no more customers that day.

Sir Thomas immersed himself in his work, as calm and courteous and unflappable as he always was, only Tremble was disturbed. 'There's something up,' he confided to Mrs Tremble. 'Don't ask me what, for I don't know, but there's something wrong somewhere.'

'That nice young lady...' began his wife.

'Now don't go getting sentimental ideas in your head,' begged Tremble.

'Mark my words,' said Mrs Tremble, who always managed to have the last word.

That same evening Felicity arrived on Thomas's doorstep.

Tremble, opening the door to her, tried not to look disapproving; he didn't like flighty young ladies with forward manners but he begged her to go into the small sitting-room behind the little dining-room while he enquired if Sir Thomas was free.

Thomas was at his desk writing, with Watson at his feet. He looked up with a frown as Tremble went in. 'Something important, Tremble?'

'A young lady to see you, sir, a Miss Seymour.'

The look on his master's face forced him to remember his wife's words. If this was the young lady who was giving all the trouble then he for one was disappointed. There was no accounting for taste, of course, but somehow she didn't seem right for Sir Thomas.

He followed his master into the hall and opened the sitting-room door and let out a sigh of relief when Sir Thomas exclaimed, 'Felicity—I thought it was Mary Jane.'

'Mary Jane? Whatever would she be doing in London? You might at least look pleased to see me, Thomas. I've news for you—it will be in the papers tomorrow but I thought you might like to know before then. I'm engaged, isn't it fun? A marvellous man—a film director, no less. I've had him dangling for weeks—a girl has to think very carefully about her future, after all. He went to Vienna with me and I decided he'd do. He is in the States now, coming back tomorrow. You'll come to the wedding, of course. I phoned Mary Jane—she won't be coming, she'd be like a fish out of water and she hasn't the right clothes.'

Sir Thomas was still standing, looking down at her, sitting gracefully in a high-backed chair. He said evenly, 'I think it is unlikely that I shall be free to come to your wedding, Felicity. I hope that you will both be very happy. I expect Mary Jane was surprised.'

Felicity shrugged. 'Probably. You were in Vienna, too, were you not? We might have met but I suppose you were lecturing or something dull.'

'Yes. May I offer you a drink?'

'No, thanks, I'm on my way to dine with friends.' She smiled charmingly. 'Do you know, Thomas, I considered you for a husband for a while but it would never have done; all you ever think of is your work.'

He smiled. He didn't choose to tell her how mistaken she was.

On Thursday afternoon the Misses Potter came for tea, as usual. There had been a handful of customers but now the tea-room was empty and Miss Emily said in a satisfied voice, 'I am glad to find that you have no one else here, Mary Jane, for we have brought the newspaper for you to read. There is something of great interest in it. Of course, the *Telegraph* only mentions it, but I persuaded Mrs Stokes to let me have her *Daily Mirror* which has more details.'

The ladies sat themselves down at their usual table and Mary Jane fetched tea and scones and waited patiently while the ladies poured their tea and buttered their scones. This done, Miss Emily took the newspapers from her shopping basket and handed them to her. The *Telegraph* first, the page folded back on 'Forthcoming Marriages'.

Mary Jane's eyes lighted on the announcement at once. 'Mr Theobald Coryman, of New York, to Miss Felicity Seymour of London.' She read it twice just to make sure, and then said, 'I don't understand—is it a mistake?'

'In the *Telegraph*?' Miss Emily was shocked. 'A most reputable newspaper.' She handed over the *Daily Mirror*, which confirmed the *Telegraph*'s genteel announcement in a more flamboyant manner. 'Famous Model to Wed Film Director' said the front-page and under that a large photo of Felicity and a man in horn-rimmed glasses and a wide-brimmed hat. They were arm in arm and Felicity was displaying the ring on her finger.

'It must be a mistake,' said Mary Jane. 'Felicity said...!'

She remembered with clarity what her sister had said— word for word, and Thomas's name had not been mentioned. It was she herself who had made the mistake, jumped to the

wrong conclusion and accused Sir Thomas of behaviour in
a manner which had been nothing short of that of a virago.
She had indeed cooked her goose; worse, she had wronged
him in a manner he wasn't likely to forgive or forget. She
hadn't given him a chance to say anything, either.

The Misses Potter were looking at her in some astonishment. 'You are pleased? Felicity seems to have done very
well for herself.'

'Yes, I'm delighted,' said Mary Jane wildly. 'It's marvellous news. I'm sure she'll—they—will be very happy. He
looks...!' She paused, at a loss to describe her sister's future
husband; there wasn't much of him to see other than the hat
and the glasses. 'Very nice,' she finished lamely.

'They seem very suitable,' remarked Miss Emily drily. 'He
is, so they say, extremely rich.'

'Yes, well, Felicity likes nice things.'

The elderly sisters gave her a thoughtful glance. 'I think
we all do, dear,' said Miss Mabel. 'You look a bit peaked—
have a cup of tea with us.'

Which Mary Jane did; a cup of tea was the panacea for
all ills, at least in the United Kingdom, and it gave her time
to pull herself together.

The Misses Potter went presently, and she was left with
her unhappy thoughts. Would it be a good idea, she wondered, to write to Sir Thomas and apologise; on the other
hand, would it be better to do nothing about it? Had she the
courage, she wondered, to write and tell him that she loved
him and would he forgive her? She went upstairs and found
paper and pen and sat down to compose a letter. An hour
later, with the wastepaper basket overflowing, she gave up
the attempt. Somehow her feelings couldn't be expressed
with pen and ink. 'In any case,' she told Brimble, 'I don't
suppose he has given me a thought.'

In this she was mistaken; Sir Thomas had thought about
her a great deal. Although he shut her away to the back of
his mind while he went about his work, sitting in Sister's
office after a ward round, apparently giving all his attention

to her tart remarks about lack of staff, the modern nurse, the difficulties she experienced in getting enough linen from the laundry—all of which he had heard a hundred times before, he was thinking that he would like to wring Mary Jane's small neck and then, illogically, toss her into his car and drive away to some quiet spot and marry her out of hand. How dared she imagine for one moment that he was amusing himself with her when he loved her to distraction? That he had never allowed his feelings to show was something he hadn't considered.

He promised Sister that he would speak to the hospital committee next time it met, and wandered off to be joined presently by his registrar wanting his opinion about a patient. Stanley Wetherspoon was a good surgeon and his right hand, but a bit prosy. Halfway through his carefully expressed opinion, Sir Thomas said suddenly, 'Why didn't I think of it before? Of course, we were in Vienna at the same time. Naturally...'

Stanley paused in mid-flow and Sir Thomas said hastily, 'So sorry, I've lost the thread—this prosthesis—what do you suggest that we do?'

Presently, Stanley went on his way, reassured, wondering all the same if his boss was overworking and needed a holiday.

Sir Thomas, outwardly his normal pleasantly assured self, went to his rooms, saw several patients and then requested Miss Pink to come into his consulting-room.

'How soon can I get away for a day?'

'Well, it's your weekend on call, Sir Thomas—I could ask your patients booked for Monday to come on Saturday morning—since you'll be here anyway—if you saw them then you could have Monday off.'

'And Tuesday? I know I've got a couple of cases in the afternoon, but is the morning free?'

'It will be if I get Mrs Collyer and Colonel Gregg to come in the afternoon—after three o'clock? That'll give you time to get back to your rooms from hospital and have a meal.'

'Miss Pink, you are a gem of real value to me. Do all that, will you? Then let me know when you've fixed things.'

At the door she asked, 'You'll leave an address, Sir Thomas?'

'Yes. I'll go very early in the morning; if you need anything, get hold of Tremble.'

'Well, well,' said Miss Pink, peering out of the window to watch him getting into his car, and she went in search of his nurse, tidying up in the examination-room. A lady of uncertain age, just as she was, and devoted, just as she was, to Sir Thomas's welfare.

'He looked so happy,' said Miss Pink, and, after a cosy chat of a romantic nature, she went away to reorganise his days for him. A task which necessitated a good deal of wheedling and coaxing, both of which she did most willingly; Sir Thomas had the gift of inspiring loyalty and, in Miss Pink's case, an abiding devotion.

Mary Jane spent the next three days composing letters in her head to Sir Thomas, but somehow when she wrote them down they didn't seem the same. By Sunday evening she had a headache, made worse by a visit from Oliver.

'Well, what do you think of Felicity?' he wanted to know when she opened the door to him.

'I'm very pleased for her, Oliver. You had it all wrong, didn't you?'

He gave her a nasty look. 'I may have been mistaken with the name of her future husband, but there's no denying that she has done very well for herself.'

'Why have you come?' asked Mary Jane, not beating about the bush and anxious for him to go again.

'Margaret and I have had a chat—now that this place is tarted up and equipped again, we think that it might be a good idea if we were to buy you out. You can stay here, of course—the cottage is yours anyway, more's the pity—you can run the place and we will pay you a salary. A little judicial advertising and it should make it worth our while.'

He added smugly, 'We can use the connection with
Felicity—marvellous publicity.'

'Over my dead body,' said Mary Jane fiercely. 'Whatever
will you dream up next? And, if that is why you came, I'll
not keep you.'

She opened the door and ushered him out while he was
still arguing.

When he had gone, however, she wondered if that
wouldn't have solved her problem. Not that she would have
stayed in the cottage. There was no doubt that he would buy
the place from her even if it meant getting someone in to
run it. She would have money and be free to go where she
wanted. She couldn't think of anywhere at the moment, but
no doubt she would if she gave her mind to it. The trouble
was, she thought only of Sir Thomas.

The sun was shining when she got up on Monday morning;
February had allowed a spring day with its blue sky and
feathery clouds to sneak in. Mary Jane turned the door sign
to 'Open', arranged cups and saucers on the four tables and
made a batch of scones. The fine weather might tempt some
out-of-season tourist to explore and come her way. Her op-
timism was rewarded: first one table, then a second and finally a third were occupied. Eight persons drinking coffee at
fifty-five pence a cup and eating their way through the
scones. She did some mental arithmetic, not quite accurate,
but heartening none the less, and made plans to bake another
batch of scones during the lunch hour. It was still only mid-
morning and there might be other customers.

The family of four at one of the tables called for more
coffee and she was pouring it when the door opened and Sir
Thomas came in, Watson at his heels. It was difficult not to
spill the coffee, but she managed it somehow, put the percolator down on the table and, heedless of the customers'
stares, stood gaping at him. He sat down at the remaining
empty table, looking quite at his ease, and requested coffee.
Watson, eager to greet Mary Jane, had, at a quiet word from
his master, subsided under the table. Sir Thomas nodded

vaguely at the other customers and looked at Mary Jane as though he had never seen her before, lifting his eyebrows a little because of her tardy response to his request.

The wave of delight and happiness at the sight of him which had engulfed her was swamped by sudden rage. How could he walk in as though he were a complete stranger and look through her in that casual manner? Coffee, indeed. She would like to throw the coffee-pot at him...

She poured his coffee with a shaky hand, not looking at him but stooping to pat the expectant Watson's head, and then, just to show him that he was only a customer like anyone else, she made out the bill, laid it on the table and held out her hand for the money.

He picked the hand up gently. It was a little red and rough from her chores, but it was a pretty shape and small. He kissed it on its palm and folded her fingers over it and gave the hand back to her.

What would have happened next was anybody's guess, but the two women who had arrived in a small car, having taken a wrong turning, asked loudly for their bill. When they had gone, Mary Jane made herself as small as possible behind the counter, taking care not to look at Sir Thomas, very aware that he was looking at her. The young couple on a walking holiday went next, looking at her curiously as they went out, frankly staring at Sir Thomas, and that left the family of four, a hearty, youngish man, his cheerful loud-voiced wife and two small children. They had watched Sir Thomas with avid interest, in no hurry to be gone, hoping perhaps for further developments. Sir Thomas sat, quite at his ease, silent, his face a blank mask, his eyes on Mary Jane. Unable to spin out their meal any longer, they paid their bill and prepared to go. His wife, looking up from fastening the children's coats, beamed at Mary Jane. 'You'll be glad to see the back of us, love—I dare say he's dying to pop the question—can't take his eyes off you, can he?'

They all went to the door and she turned round as they went out. 'Good luck to you both, bye bye.'

They got into their car and Sir Thomas got up, turned the sign to 'Closed', locked the door and stood leaning against it, his hands in his pockets.

Mary Jane, standing in the middle of the room, waited for him to speak; after a while, when the silence became unbearable, she said the first thing to come into her head.

'Shouldn't you be at the hospital?'

'Indeed I should, but, owing to Miss Pink's zealous juggling of my appointments book, I have given myself the day off.' He smiled suddenly and her heart turned over. 'To see you, my dearest Mary Jane.'

'Me?'

'You believed that I had gone to Vienna to be with Felicity?' He asked the question gravely.

'Well, you see, Oliver told me and then Felicity phoned and she didn't say who it was and I thought it would be you—she said you were famous and rich and good-looking and you are, aren't you? It sounded like you.'

'And then?' he prompted gently.

'Miss Emily showed me two newspapers and one of them had a photo of Felicity and—I've forgotten his name, but he wears a funny hat, and I tried to write you a letter but it was too difficult...'

'You supposed that I had helped you to set this place to rights because you are Felicity's sister?'

She nodded. 'I was a bit upset.'

'And why were you upset, Mary Jane?'

She met his eyes with an effort. 'I'd much rather not say, if you don't mind.'

'I mind very much. I mind about everything you say and do and think. I am deeply in love with you, my dearest girl, you have become part—no, my whole life. I want you with me, to come home to, to talk to, to love.'

Mary Jane was filled with a delicious excitement, and a thankful surprise that sometimes dreams really did come true. She said in a small voice, 'Are you quite sure, Thomas? I love you very much, but Oliver...'

Sir Thomas left the door and caught her close. 'Oliver can go to the devil. Say that again, my darling.'

She began obediently, 'Are you quite sure...?' She peeped at him and saw the look on his face. 'I love you very much.'

'That's what I thought you said, but I had to make sure.'

'But I must tell you...'

'Not another word,' said Sir Thomas, and kissed her. Presently, Mary Jane, a little out of breath, lifted her face to his. 'That was awfully nice,' she told him.

'In which case...'

'Thomas, there's a batch of scones in the oven.' She added hastily, 'It isn't that I don't want you to kiss me, I do, very much, but they'll burn.'

Sir Thomas, quite rightly, took no notice of this remark but presently he said, 'Pack a bag, my love, and urge Brimble into his basket. You may have ten minutes. I will see to things here. No, don't argue, there isn't time—you may argue as much as you wish once we're married.'

She reached up and kissed his chin. 'I'll remember that,' she said and slipped away up the stairs to do as she was told.

He watched her go before going into the kitchen and rescuing the scones, the faithful Watson beside him. Brimble was on the kitchen table, waiting.

'What must I take with me, Thomas?' Mary Jane's voice floated down the little stairs. 'You didn't say where we are going?'

He stood looking up at her anxious face. 'Why, home, of course, my love.' And saw her lovely smile.

ROMANTIC ENCOUNTER

by

Betty Neels

CHAPTER ONE

FLORENCE, cleaning the upstairs windows of the vicarage, heard the car coming up the lane and, when it slowed, poked her head over the top sash to see whom it might be. The elegant dark grey Rolls-Royce, sliding to a halt before her father's front door, was unexpected enough to cause her to lean her splendid person even further out of the window so that she might see who was in it. The passenger got out and she recognised him at once. Mr Wilkins, the consultant surgeon she had worked for before she had left the hospital in order to look after her mother and run the house until she was well again—a lengthy business of almost a year. Perhaps he had come to see if she was ready to return to her ward; unlikely, though, for it had been made clear to her that her post would be filled and she would have to take her chance at getting whatever was offered if she wanted to go to work at Colbert's again; besides, a senior consultant wouldn't come traipsing after a ward sister...

The driver of the car was getting out, a very tall, large man with pepper and salt hair. He stood for a moment, looking around him, waiting for Mr Wilkins to join him, and then looked up at her. His air of amused surprise sent her back inside again, banging her head as she went, but she was forced to lean out again when Mr Wilkins caught sight of her and called up to her to come down and let them in.

There was no time to do more than wrench the clean duster off her fiery hair. She went down to the hall and opened the door.

Mr Wilkins greeted her jovially. 'How are you after all these months?' he enquired; he eyed the apron bunched over an elderly skirt and jumper. 'I do hope we haven't called at an inconvenient time?'

Florence's smile was frosty. 'Not at all, sir, we are spring-cleaning.'

Mr Wilkins, who lived in a house with so many gadgets that it never needed spring-cleaning, looked interested. 'Are you really? But you'll spare us a moment to talk, I hope? May I introduce Mr Fitzgibbon?' He turned to his companion. 'This is Florence Napier.'

She offered a rather soapy hand and had it engulfed in his large one. His, 'How do you do?' was spoken gravely, but she felt that he was amused again, and no wonder—she must look a fright.

Which, of course, she did, but a beautiful fright; nothing could dim the glory of her copper hair, tied back carelessly with a boot-lace, and nothing could detract from her lovely face and big blue eyes with their golden lashes. She gave him a cool look and saw that his eyes were grey and intent, so she looked away quickly and addressed herself to Mr Wilkins.

'Do come into the drawing-room. Mother's in the garden with the boys, and Father's writing his sermon. Would you like to have some coffee?'

She ushered them into the big, rather shabby room, its windows open on to the mild April morning. 'Do sit down,' she begged them. 'I'll let Mother know that you're here and fetch in the coffee.'

'It is you we have come to see, Florence,' said Mr Wilkins.

'Me? Oh, well—all the same, I'm sure Mother will want to meet you.'

She opened the old-fashioned window wide and jumped neatly over the sill with the unselfconsciousness of a child, and Mr Fitzgibbon's firm mouth twitched at the corners. 'She's very professional on the ward,' observed Mr Wilkins, 'and very neat. Of course, if she's cleaning the house I suppose she gets a little untidy.'

Mr Fitzgibbon agreed blandly and then stood up as Florence returned, this time with her mother and using the door. Mrs Napier was small and slim and pretty, and still a little frail after her long illness. Florence made the introductions, settled her mother in a chair and went away to make the coffee.

'Oo's that, then?' asked Mrs Buckett, who came up twice a week from the village to do the rough, and after years of faithful service considered herself one of the family.

'The surgeon I worked for at Colbert's—and he's brought a friend with him.'

'What for?'

'I've no idea. Be a dear and put the kettle on while I lay a tray. I'll let you know as soon as I can find out.'

While the kettle boiled she took off her apron, tugged the jumper into shape and poked at her hair. 'Not that it matters,' she told Mrs Buckett. 'I looked an absolute frump when they arrived.'

'Go on with yer, love—you couldn't look a frump if you tried. Only yer could wash yer 'ands.'

Florence had almost decided that she didn't like Mr Fitzgibbon, but she had to admit that his manners were nice. He got up and took the tray from her and didn't sit down again until she was sitting herself. His bedside manner would be impeccable...

They drank their coffee and made small talk, but not for long. Her mother put her cup down and got to her feet. 'Mr Wilkins tells me that he wants to talk to you, Florence, and I would like to go back to the garden and see what the boys are doing with the cold frame.'

She shook hands and went out of the room, and they all sat down again.

'Your mother is well enough for you to return to work, Florence?'

'Yes. Dr Collins saw her a few days ago. I must find someone to come in for an hour or two each day, but I must find a job first.' She saw that Mr Wilkins couldn't see the sense of that, but Mr Fitzgibbon had understood at once, although he didn't speak.

'Yes, yes, of course,' said Mr Wilkins briskly. 'Well, I've nothing for you, I'm afraid, but Mr Fitzgibbon has.'

'I shall need a nurse at my consulting-rooms in two weeks' time. I mentioned it to Mr Wilkins, and he remembered you and assures me that you would suit me very well.'

What about you suiting me? reflected Florence, and went a little pink because he was staring at her in that amused fashion again, reading her thoughts. 'I don't know anything about that sort of nursing,' she said, 'I've always worked in hospital; I'm not sure—'

'Do not imagine that the job is a sinecure. I have a large practice and I operate in a number of hospitals, specialising in chest surgery. My present nurse accompanies me and scrubs for the cases, but perhaps you don't feel up to that?'

'I've done a good deal of Theatre work, Mr Fitzgibbon,' said Florence, nettled.

'In that case, I think that you might find the job interesting. You would be free at the weekends, although I should warn you that I am occasionally called away at such times and you would need to hold yourself in readiness to accompany me. My rooms are in Wimpole Street, and Sister Brice has lodgings close by. I suppose you might take them over if they suited you. As to salary...'

He mentioned a sum which caused her pretty mouth to drop open.

'That's a great deal more—'

'Of course it is; you would be doing a great deal more work and your hours will have to fit in with mine.'

'This nurse who is leaving,' began Florence.

'To get married.' His voice was silky. 'She has been with me for five years.' He gave her a considered look. 'Think it over and let me know. I'll give you a ring tomorrow—shall we say around three o'clock?'

She had the strong feeling that if she demurred at that he would still telephone then, and expect her to answer, too. 'Very well, Mr Fitzgibbon,' she said in a non-committal voice, at the same time doing rapid and rather inaccurate sums in her head; the money would be a godsend—there would be enough to pay for extra help at the vicarage, they needed a new set of saucepans, and the washing-machine had broken down again...

She bade the two gentlemen goodbye, smiling nicely at Mr Wilkins, whom she liked, and giving Mr Fitzgibbon a candid look as she shook hands. He was very good-looking, with a high-bridged nose and a determined chin and an air of self-possession. He didn't smile as he said goodbye.

Not an easy man to get to know, she decided, watching the Rolls sweep through the vicarage gate.

When she went back indoors her mother had come in from the garden.

'He looked rather nice,' she observed, obviously following a train of thought. 'Why did he come, Florence?'

'He wants a nurse for his practice—a private one, I gather. Mr Wilkins recommended me.'

'How kind, darling. Just at the right moment, too. It will save you hunting around the hospitals and places...'

'I haven't said I'd take it, Mother.'

'Why not, love? I'm very well able to take over the household again—is the pay very bad?'

'It's very generous. I'd have to live in London, but I'd be free every weekend unless I was wanted—Mr Fitzgibbon seems to get around everywhere rather a lot; he specialises in chest surgery.'

'Did Mr Wilkins offer you your old job back, darling?'

'No. There's nothing for me at Colbert's...'

'Then, Florence, you must take this job. It will make a nice change and you'll probably meet nice people.' It was one of Mrs Napier's small worries that her beautiful daughter seldom met men—young men, looking for a wife—after all, she was five and twenty and, although the housemen at the hospital took her out, none of them, as far as she could make out, was of the marrying kind—too young and no money. Now, a nice older man, well established and able to give

Florence all the things she had had to do without... Mrs Napier enjoyed a brief daydream.

'Is he married?' she asked.

'I have no idea, Mother. I should think he might be—I mean, he's not a young man, is he?' Florence, collecting coffee-cups, wasn't very interested. 'I'll talk to Father. It might be a good idea if I took the job for a time until there's a vacancy at Colbert's or one of the top teaching hospitals. I don't want to get out of date.'

'Go and talk to your father now, dear.' Mrs Napier glanced at the clock. 'Either by now he's finished his sermon, or he's got stuck. He'll be glad of the interruption.'

Mr Napier, when appealed to, giving the matter grave thought, decided that Florence would be wise to take the job. 'I do not know this Mr Fitzgibbon,' he observed, 'but if he is known to Mr Wilkins he must be a dependable sort of chap! The salary is a generous one too...not that you should take that into consideration, Florence, if you dislike the idea.'

She didn't point out that the salary was indeed a consideration. With the boys at school and then university, the vicar's modest stipend had been whittled down to its minimum so that there would be money enough for their future. The vicar, a kind, good man, ready to give the coat off his back to anyone in need, was nevertheless blind to broken-down washing-machines, worn-out sauce-pans and the fact that his wife hadn't had a new hat for more than a year.

'I like the idea, Father,' said Florence robustly, 'and I can come home at the weekend too. I'll go and see Miss Payne in the village and arrange for her to come in for an hour or so each day to give Mother a hand. Mrs Buckett can't do everything. I'll pay—it is really a very generous salary.'

'Will you be able to keep yourself in comfort, Florence?'

She assured him that she could perfectly well do that. 'And the lodgings his present nurse has will be vacant if I'd like to take them.'

'It sounds most suitable,' said her father, 'but you must, of course, do what you wish, my dear.'

She wasn't at all sure what she did wish but she had plenty of common sense; she needed to get a job and start earning money again, and she had, by some lucky chance, been offered one without any effort on her part.

When Mr Fitzgibbon telephoned the following day, precisely at three o'clock, and asked her in his cool voice if she had considered his offer, she accepted in a voice as cool as his own.

He didn't say that he was pleased. 'Then perhaps you will come up to town very shortly and talk to Sister Brice. Would next Monday be convenient—in the early afternoon?'

'There is a train from Sherborne just after ten o'clock—I could be at your rooms about one o'clock.'

'That will suit Sister Brice very well. You have the address and the telephone number.'

'Yes, thanks.'

His, 'Very well, goodbye, Miss Napier,' was abrupt, even if uttered politely.

The Reverend Napier, his sermon written and nothing but choir practice to occupy him, drove Florence into Sherborne to catch the morning train. Gussage Tollard was a mere four miles to that town as the crow flew, but, taking into account the elderly Austin and the winding lanes, turning and twisting every hundred yards or so, the distance by car was considerably more.

'Be sure and have a good lunch,' advised her father. 'One can always get a good meal at Lyons.'

Florence said that she would; her father went to London so rarely that he lived comfortably in the past as regarded cafés, bus queues and the like, and she had no intention of disillusioning him.

She bade him goodbye at the station, assured him that she would be on the afternoon train from Waterloo, and was borne away to London.

She had a cup of coffee and a sandwich at Waterloo Station and queued for a bus, got off at Oxford Circus, and, since she had a little time to spare, looked at a few shops along Oxford Street before turning off towards Wimpole Street. The houses were dignified Regency, gleaming with pristine paintwork and shining brass plates. Number eighty-seven would be halfway down, she decided, and wondered where the lodgings were that she might take over. It was comparatively quiet here and the sun was shining; after the bustle and the noise of Oxford Street it was peaceful—as peaceful as one could be in London, she amended, thinking of Gussage Tollard, which hadn't caught up with the modern world yet, and a good thing too.

Mr Fitzgibbon, standing at the window of his consulting-room, his hands in his pockets, watched her coming along the pavement below. With a view to the sobriety of the occasion, she had shrouded a good deal of her brilliant hair under a velvet cap which matched the subdued tones of her French navy jacket and skirt. She was wearing her good shoes too; they pinched a little, but that was in a good cause...

She glanced up as she reached the address she had been given, to see Mr Fitzgibbon staring down at her, unsmiling. He looked out of temper, and she stared back before mounting the few steps to the front door and ringing the bell. The salary he had offered was good, she reflected, but she had a nasty feeling that he would be a hard master.

The door was opened by an elderly porter, who told her civilly that Mr Fitzgibbon's consulting-rooms were on the first floor and would she go up? Once on the landing above there was another door with its highly polished bell, this time opened by a cosily plump middle-aged lady who said in a friendly voice, 'Ah, here you are. I'm Mr Fitzgibbon's receptionist—Mrs Keane. You're to go straight in...'

'I was to see Sister Brice,' began Florence.

'Yes, dear, and so you shall. But Mr Fitzgibbon wants to see you now.' She added in an almost reverent voice, 'He should be going to his lunch, but he decided to see you first.'

Florence thought of several answers to this but uttered none of them; she needed the job too badly.

Mr Fitzgibbon had left the window and was sitting behind his desk. He got up as Mrs Keane showed her in and wished her a cool, 'Good afternoon, Miss Napier,' and begged her to take a seat. Once she was sitting he was in no haste to speak.

Finally he said, 'Sister Brice is at lunch; she will show you exactly what your duties will be. I suggest that you come on a month's trial, and after that period I would ask you to give three months' notice should you wish to leave. I dislike changing my staff.'

'You may not wish me to stay after a month,' Florence pointed out in a matter-of-fact voice.

'There is that possibility. That can be discussed at the end of the month. You are agreeable to your working conditions? I must warn you that this is not a nine-to-five job; your personal life is of no interest to me, but on no account must it infringe upon your work here. I depend upon the loyalty of my staff.'

She was tempted to observe that at the salary she was being offered she was unlikely to be disloyal. She said forthrightly, 'I'm free to do what I like and work where I wish; I like to go to my home whenever I can, but otherwise I have no other interests.'

'No prospects of marriage?'

She opened her beautiful eyes wide. 'Since you ask, no.'

'I'm surprised. I should like you to start—let me see; Sister Brice leaves at the end of next week, a Saturday. Perhaps you will get settled in on the Sunday and start work here on the Monday morning.'

'That will suit me very well.' She did hide a smile at his surprised look; he was probably used to having things his own way. 'Will it be possible for me to see the rooms I am to have?'

He said impatiently, 'Yes, yes, why not? Sister Brice can take you there. Are you spending the night in town?'

'No, I intend to go back on the five o'clock train from Waterloo.'

There was a knock on the door and he called 'come in', and Sister Brice put her head round the door and said cheerfully, 'Shall I take over, sir?' She came into the room and shook Florence's hand.

The phone rang and Mr Fitzgibbon lifted the receiver. 'Yes, please. There's no one until three o'clock, is there? I shall want you here then.'

He glanced at Florence. 'Goodbye, Miss Napier; I expect to see you a week on Monday morning.'

Sister Brice closed the door gently behind them. 'He's marvellous to work for; you mustn't take any notice of his abruptness.'

'I shan't,' said Florence. 'Where do we start?'

The consulting-rooms took up the whole of the first floor. Besides Mr Fitzgibbon's room and the waiting-room, there was a very small, well-equipped dressing-room, an examination-room leading from the consulting-room, a cloakroom and a tiny kitchen. 'He likes his coffee around ten o'clock, but if he has a lot of patients he'll not stop. We get ours when we can. I get here about eight o'clock—the first patient doesn't get here before half-past nine, but everything has to be quite ready. Mr Fitzgibbon quite often goes to the hospital first and takes a look at new patients there; he goes back there around noon or one o'clock and we have our lunch and tidy up and so on, he comes back here about four o'clock unless he's operating, and he sees patients until half-past five. You do Theatre, don't you? He always has the same theatre sister at Colbert's, but if he's operating at another hospital, doesn't matter where, he'll take you with him to scrub.'

'Another hospital in London?'

'Could be; more often than not it's Birmingham or Edinburgh or Bristol—I've been to Brussels several times, the Middle East, and a couple of times to Berlin.'

'I can't speak German...'

Sister Brice laughed. 'You don't need to—he does all the talking; you just carry on as though you were at Colbert's. He did mention that occasionally you have to miss a weekend? It's made up to you, though.' She opened a cupboard with a key from her pocket. 'I've been very happy here and I shall miss the work, but it's a full-time job and there's not much time over from it, certainly not if one is married.' She was pulling out drawers. 'There's everything he needs for operating—he likes his own instruments and it's your job to see that they're all there and ready. They get put in this bag.'

She glanced at her watch. 'There's time to go over to my room; you can meet Mrs Twist and see if it'll suit you. She gets your breakfast and cooks high tea about half-past six. There's a washing-machine and a telephone you may use. She doesn't encourage what she calls gentlemen friends...'

'I haven't got any...'

'You're pretty enough to have half a dozen, if you don't mind my saying so.'

'Thank you. I think I must be hard to please.'

Mrs Twist lived in one of the narrow streets behind Wimpole Street, not five minutes' walk away. The house was small, one of a row, but it was very clean and neat, rather like Mrs Twist—small, too, and bony with pepper and salt hair and a printed cotton pinny. She eyed Florence shrewdly with small blue eyes and led her upstairs to a room overlooking the street, nicely furnished. 'Miss Brice 'as her breakfast downstairs, quarter to eight sharp,' she observed, 'the bathroom's across the landing, there's a machine for yer smalls and yer can 'ang them out in the back garden. I'll cook a meal at half-past six of an evening, something 'ot; if I'm out it'll be in the oven. Me and Miss Brice 'as never 'ad a cross word and I 'opes we'll get on as nicely.'

'Well, I hope so too, Mrs Twist. This is a very nice room and I'm sure I shall appreciate a meal each evening. You must let me know if there's anything—'

'Be sure I will, Miss Napier; I'm one for speaking out, but

Mr Fitzgibbon told me you was a sensible, quiet-spoken young lady, and what 'e says I'll believe.'

Sister Brice was waiting downstairs in the prim front room. 'There's time to go back for half an hour,' she pointed out. 'I'm ready for the first patient; Mr Fitzgibbon won't be back until just before three o'clock, and Mrs Keane will already have got the notes out.'

They bade Mrs Twist goodbye and walked back to Wimpole Street, where Mrs Keane was putting on the kettle. Over cups of tea she and Sister Brice covered the bare bones of Mr Fitzgibbon's information with a wealth of their own, so that by the time Florence left she had a sound idea of what she might expect. Nothing like having a ward in the hospital, she reflected on her way to the station. She would have to make her own routine and keep to it as much as possible, allowing for Mr Fitzgibbon's demands upon her time. All the same, she thought that she would like it; she was answerable to no one but herself and him, of course— her bedsitter was a good deal better than she had expected it to be, and there was the added bonus of going home each weekend. She spent the return journey doing sums on the back of an envelope, and alighted at Sherborne knowing that the saucepans and washing-machine need no longer be pipe-dreams. At the end of the month they would be installed in the vicarage kitchen. What was more, she would be able to refurbish her spring wardrobe.

'Mr Fitzgibbon seems to be an employer of the highest order,' observed her father when she recounted the day's doings to him.

She agreed, but what sort of a man was he? she wondered; she still wasn't sure if she liked him or not.

She spent the next two weeks in a burst of activity; the spring-cleaning had to be finished, a lengthy job in the rambling vicarage, and someone had to be found who would come each day for an hour or so. Mrs Buckett was a splendid worker but, although Mrs Napier was very nearly herself once more, there were tiresome tasks—the ironing, the shopping and the cooking—to be dealt with. Miss Payne, in the village, who had recently lost her very old mother, was only too glad to fill the post for a modest sum.

Florence packed the clothes she decided she would need, added one or two of her more precious books and a batch of family photos to grace the little mantelpiece in her bedsitter, and, after a good deal of thought, a long skirt and top suitable for an evening out. It was unlikely that she would need them, but one never knew. When she had been at the hospital she had never lacked invitations from various members of the medical staff—usually a cinema and coffee and sandwiches on the way home, occasionally a dinner in some popular restaurant—but she had been at home now for nearly a year and she had lost touch. She hadn't minded; she was country born and bred and she hadn't lost her heart to anyone. Occasionally she remembered that she was twenty-five and there was no sign of the man Mrs Buckett coyly described as Mr Right. Florence had the strong suspicion that Mrs Buckett's Mr Right and her own idea of him were two quite different people.

She left home on the Sunday evening and, when it came to the actual moment of departure, with reluctance. The boys had gone back to school and she wouldn't see them again until half-term, but there was the Sunday school class she had always taken for her father, choir practice, the various small duties her mother had had to give up while she had been ill, and there was Charlie Brown, the family cat, and Higgins, the elderly Labrador dog; she had become fond of them during her stay at home.

'I'll be home next weekend,' she told her mother bracingly, 'and I'll phone you this evening.' All the same, the sight of her father's elderly greying figure waving from the platform as the train left made her feel childishly forlorn.

Mrs Twist's home dispelled some of her feelings of strangeness. There was a tray of tea waiting for her in her room and the offer of help if she should need it. 'And there is a bite of supper at eight o'clock, it being Sunday,' said

Mrs Twist, 'and just this once you can use the phone down-stairs. There's a phone box just across the road that Miss Brice used.'

Florence unpacked, arranged the photos and her bits and pieces, phoned her mother to assure her in a cheerful voice that she had settled in nicely and everything was fine, and then went down to her supper.

'Miss Brice was away for most weekends,' said the land-lady, 'but sometimes she 'ad ter work, so we had a bite together.'

So Florence ate her supper in the kitchen with Mrs Twist and listened to that lady's comments upon her neighbours, the cost of everything and her bad back. 'Miss Brice told Mr Fitzgibbon about it,' she confided, 'and he was ever so kind—sent me to the 'ospital with a special note to a friend of 'is. 'E's ever so nice; you'll like working for him.'

'Oh, I'm sure I will,' said Florence, secretly not at all sure about it.

She arrived at the consulting-rooms well before time in the morning. A taciturn elderly man opened the door to her, nodded when she told him who she was, and went to unlock Mr Fitzgibbon's own door. The place had been hoovered and dusted and there were fresh flowers in the vase on the coffee-table. Presumably Mr Fitzgibbon had a fairy godmother who waved her wand and summoned cleaning ladies at unearthly hours. She went through to the cloakroom and found her white uniform laid out for her; there was a frilled muslin cap too. He didn't agree with the modern version of a nurse's uniform, and she registered approval as she changed. She clasped her navy belt with its silver buckle round her neat waist and began a cautious survey of the premises, peering in cupboards and drawers, making sure where everything was; Mr Fitzgibbon wasn't a man to suffer fools gladly, she was sure, and she had no intention of being caught out.

Mrs Keane arrived next, begged Florence to put on the kettle and sorted out the notes of the patients who were ex-pected. 'Time for a cup of tea,' she explained. 'We'll be lucky if we get time for coffee this morning—there's old Lady Trump coming, and even if we allow her twice as long as anyone else she always holds everything up. There's the phone, dear; answer it, will you?'

Mr Fitzgibbon's voice, unflurried, sounded in her ear. 'I shall be about fifteen minutes late. Is Sister Napier there yet?'

'Yes,' said Florence, slightly tartly, 'she is; she came at eight o'clock sharp.'

'The time we agreed upon?' he asked silkily. 'I should warn you that I frown upon unpunctuality.'

'In that case, Mr Fitzgibbon,' said Florence sweetly, 'why don't you have one of those clocking-in machines installed?'

'I frown on impertinence too,' said Mr Fitzgibbon, and hung up.

Mrs Keane had been listening; she didn't say anything but went and made the tea and sat down opposite Florence in the tiny kitchen. 'I'll tell you about the patients coming this morning. One new case—a Mr Willoughby. He's a CA, left lobe, sent to us by his doctor. Lives somewhere in the Midlands—retired. The other three are back for check-ups— Lady Trump first; allow half an hour for her, and she needs a lot of help getting undressed and dressed and so on. Then there is little Miss Powell, who had a lobectomy two months ago, and the last one is a child, Susie Castle—seven years old—a fibrocystic. It's not for me to say, but I think it's a losing battle. Such a dear child, too.'

She glanced at the clock. 'He'll be here in about two minutes...'

She was right; Mr Fitzgibbon came in quietly, wished them good morning and went to his consulting-room.

'Take Mr Willoughby in,' hissed Mrs Keane, 'and stand on the right side of the door. Mr Fitzgibbon will nod when he wants you to show the patient into the examination-room. If it's a man you go back into the consulting-room unless he asks you to stay.'

Florence adjusted her cap just so and took herself off to the waiting-room in time to receive Mr Willoughby, a small, meek man, who gave the impression that he had resigned himself to his fate. An opinion not shared by Mr Fitzgibbon, however. Florence, watching from her corner, had to allow that his quiet assured air convinced his patient that it was by no means hopeless.

'This is a fairly common operation,' he said soothingly, 'and there is no reason why you shouldn't live a normal life for some years to come. Now, Sister will show you the examination-room, and I'll take a look. Your own doctor seems to agree with me, and I think that you should give yourself a chance.'

So Florence led away a more hopeful Mr Willoughby, informed Mr Fitzgibbon that his patient was ready for him, and retired discreetly to the consulting-room.

Upon their return Mr Fitzgibbon said, 'Ah, Sister, will you hand Mr Willoughby over to Mrs Keane, please?' He shook hands with his patient and Florence led him away, a much happier man than when he had come in.

Lady Trump was quite a different matter. A lady in her eighties, who, at Mr Fitzgibbon's behest, had undergone successful surgery and had taken on a new lease of life; moreover, she was proud of the fact and took a good deal of pleasure in boring her family and friends with all the details of her recovery…

'You're new,' she observed, eyeing Florence through old-fashioned gold-rimmed pince-nez.

'Sister Brice is getting married.'

'Hmm—I'm surprised you aren't married yourself.'

Ushered into the consulting-room, where she shook hands with Mr Fitzgibbon, she informed him, 'Well, you won't keep this gel long, she's far too pretty.'

His cold eyes gave Florence's person a cursory glance. His, 'Indeed,' was uttered with complete uninterest. 'Well, Lady Trump, how have you been since I saw you last?'

Mrs Keane had been right: the old lady took twice as long as anyone else. Besides, she had got on all the wrong clothes; she must have known that she would be examined, yet she

was wearing a dress with elaborate fastenings, tiny buttons
running from her neck to her waist, and under that a series
of petticoats and camisoles, all of which had to be removed
to an accompaniment of warnings as to how it should be
done. When at last Florence ushered her back to Mrs Keane's
soothing care, she breathed a sigh of relief.

'Would you like your coffee, sir?' she asked, hoping that
he would say yes so that she might swallow a mug herself.
'Miss Powell hasn't arrived yet.'

'Yes,' said Mr Fitzgibbon without lifting his handsome
head from his notes, 'and have one yourself.'

Miss Powell was small and thin and mouse-like, and he
treated her with a gentle kindness Florence was surprised to
see. The little lady went away presently, reassured as to her
future, and Florence, at Mr Fitzgibbon's brisk bidding, ushered in little Susie Castle and her mother.

Susie was small for her age and wore a look of elderly
resignation, which Florence found heart-rending, but even if
she looked resigned she was full of life just as any healthy
child, and it was obvious that she and Mr Fitzgibbon were
on the best of terms. He teased her gently and made no effort
to stop her when she picked up his pen and began to draw
on the big notepad on his desk.

'How about a few days in hospital, Susie?' he wanted to
know. 'Then I'll have time to come and see you every day;
we might even find time for a game of draughts or domi-
noes.'

'Why?'

'Well, it's so much easier for me to look after you there.
We'll go to X-ray...'

'You'll be there with me? It's always a bit dark.'

'I'll be there. Shall we have a date?'

Susie giggled. 'All right.' She put out a small hand, and
Florence, who was nearest, took it in hers. The child studied
her face for a moment.

'You're very pretty. Haven't you met Prince Charming
yet?'

'Not yet, but I expect I shall one day soon.' Florence squeezed the small hand. 'Will you be my bridesmaid?'

'Yes, of course; who do you want to marry? Mr Fitzgibbon?'

Her mother made a small sound—an apology—but Florence laughed. 'My goodness, no... Now, supposing we get you dressed again so that you can go home.'

It was later that day, after the afternoon patients had gone and she was clearing up the examination-room and putting everything ready for the next day, that Mr Fitzgibbon, on his way home, paused beside her.

'You are happy with your work, Miss Napier?'

'Yes, thank you, sir. I like meeting people...'

'Let us hope that you meet your Prince Charming soon,' he observed blandly, and shut the door quietly behind him.

Leaving her wondering if he was already looking forward to the day when she would want to leave.

CHAPTER TWO

THE days passed quickly; Mr Fitzgibbon allowed few idle moments in his day, and Florence quickly discovered that he didn't expect her to have any either. By the end of the week she had fallen into a routine of sorts, but a very flexible one, for on two evenings she had returned to the consulting-rooms to attend those patients who were unable or who didn't wish to come during the day, and on one afternoon she had been whisked at a moment's notice to a large nursing home to scrub for the biopsy he wished to perform on one of his patients there. The theatre there had been adequate, but only just, and she had acquitted herself well enough. On the way back to his rooms she had asked if he performed major surgery there.

'Good lord, no; biopsies, anything minor, but otherwise they come into Colbert's or one of the big private hospitals.'

They had already established a satisfactory working relationship by the end of the week, but she was no nearer to knowing anything about him than on the first occasion of their meeting. He came and went, leaving telephone numbers for her in case he should be needed, but never mentioning where he was going. His home, for all she knew, might be the moon. As for him, he made no attempt to get to know her either. He had enquired if she was comfortable at Mrs Twist's house, and if she found the work within her scope—a question which ruffled her calm considerably—and told her at the end of the week that she was free to go home for the weekend if she wished. But not, she discovered, on the Friday evening. The last patient didn't leave until six o'clock; she had missed her train and the next one too, and the one after that would get her to Sherborne too late, and she had no intention of keeping her father out of his bed in order to meet the train.

She bade Mr Fitzgibbon goodnight, and when he asked, 'You're going home, Miss Napier?' she answered rather tartly that yes, but in the morning by an early train. To which he answered nothing, only gave her a thoughtful look. She had reached the door when he said, 'You will be back on Sunday evening all right? We shall need to be ready on Monday morning soon after nine o'clock.' With which she had to be content.

It was lovely to be home again. In the kitchen, drinking coffee while her mother sat at the kitchen table, scraping carrots, and Mrs Buckett hovered, anxious not to miss a word, Florence gave a faithful account of her week.

'Do you like working for Mr Fitzgibbon?' asked her mother.

'Oh, yes, he has a very large practice and beds at Colbert's, and he seems to be much in demand for consultations...'

'Is he married?' asked Mrs Napier artlessly.

'I haven't the slightest idea, Mother; in fact, I don't know a thing about him, and he's not the kind of person you would ask.'

'Of course, darling—I just wondered if his receptionist or someone who works for him had mentioned something...'

'The people who work for him never mention him unless it's something to do with work. Probably they're not told or are sworn to secrecy...'

'How very interesting,' observed her mother.

The weekend went too swiftly; Florence dug the garden, walked Higgins and sang in the choir on Sunday, made a batch of cakes for the Mothers' Union tea party to be held during the following week, and visited as many of her friends as she had time for. Sunday evening came much too soon, and she got into the train with reluctance. Once she was back in Mrs Twist's house, eating the supper that good lady had ready for her, she found herself looking forward to the week ahead. Her work was by no means dull, and she enjoyed the challenge of not knowing what each day might offer.

Monday offered nothing special. She was disconcerted to find Mr Fitzgibbon at his desk when she arrived in the morning. He wished her good morning civilly enough and picked up his pen again with a dismissive nod.

'You've been up half the night,' said Florence matter-of-factly, taking in his tired unshaven face, elderly trousers and high-necked sweater. 'I'll make you some coffee.'

She swept out of the room, closing the door gently as she went, put on the kettle and ladled instant coffee into a mug, milked and sugared it lavishly and, with a tin of Rich Tea biscuits, which she and Mrs Keane kept for their elevenses, bore the tray back to the consulting-room.

'There,' she said hearteningly, 'drink that up. The first patient isn't due until half-past nine; you go home and get tidied up. It's a check-up, isn't it? I dare say she'll be late— a name like Witherington-Pugh...'

Mr Fitzgibbon gave a crack of laughter. 'I don't quite see the connection, but yes, she is always unpunctual.'

'There you are, then,' said Florence comfortably. 'Now drink up and go home. You might even have time for a quick nap.'

Mr Fitzgibbon drank his coffee meekly, trying to remember when last anyone had ordered him to drink his coffee and get off home. His childhood probably, he thought sleepily with suddenly vivid memories of Nanny standing over him while he swallowed hot milk.

Rather to his own surprise, he did as he was told, and when Florence went back to the consulting-room with the first batch of notes he had gone. He was back at half-past nine, elegant in a dark grey suit and richly sombre tie, betraying no hint of an almost sleepless night. Indeed, he looked ten years younger, and Florence, eyeing him covertly, wondered how old he was.

Mrs Witherington-Pugh, who had had open chest surgery for an irretractable hernia some years previously, had come for her annual check-up and was as tiresome as Florence had felt in her bones she would be. She was slender to the point of scragginess and swathed in vague, floating garments that took a long time to remove and even longer to put back on. She kept up what Florence privately thought of as a 'poor little me' conversation, and fluttered her artificial eyelashes at Mr Fitzgibbon, who remained unmoved. He pronounced her well, advised her to take more exercise, eat plenty and take up some interest.

'But I dare not eat more than a few mouthfuls,' declared the lady. 'I'm not one of your strapping young women who needs three meals a day.' Her eyes strayed to Florence's Junoesque person. 'If one is well built, of course...'

Florence composed her beautiful features into a calm she didn't feel and avoided Mr Fitzgibbon's eye. 'None the less,' he observed blandly, 'you should eat sensibly; the slenderness of youth gives way to the thinness of middle age, you know.'

Mrs Witherington-Pugh simpered. 'Well, I don't need to worry too much about that for some years yet,' she told him.

Mr Fitzgibbon merely smiled pleasantly and shook her hand.

Florence tidied up and he sat and watched her. 'Bring in Sir Percival Watts,' he said finally. He glanced at his watch. 'We're running late. I shan't need you for ten minutes—go and have your coffee. I'll have mine before the next patient—' he glanced at the pile of notes before him '—Mr Simpson. His tests are back; he'll need surgery.' He didn't look up as she went out of the room.

Sir Percival was on the point of going when she returned, and she ushered in Mr Simpson; at a nod from Mr Fitzgibbon she busied herself in the examination-room while he talked to his patient. She could hear the murmur of their voices and then silence, and she turned to find Mr Fitzgibbon leaning against the door-frame, watching her.

'I'll be at Colbert's if I'm wanted; I'll be back here about two o'clock. You should be able to leave on time this evening. I expect you go out in the evenings when you're free?'

'Me? No, I've nowhere to go—not on my own, that is. Most of my friends at Colbert's have left or got married; besides, by the time I've had supper there's not much of the evening left.'

'I told you the hours were erratic. Take the afternoon off tomorrow, will you? I shall be operating at Colbert's, and Sister will scrub for me. I shall want you here at six o'clock in the evening—there's a new patient coming to see me.'

He wandered away, and Florence muttered, 'And not one single "please"...'

Save for necessary talk concerning patients that afternoon, he had nothing to say to her, and his goodnight was curt. He must be tired, Florence reflected, watching from the window as he crossed the pavement to his car. She hoped that his wife would be waiting for him with a well-cooked dinner. She glanced at her watch: it was early for dinner, so perhaps he would have high tea; he was such a very large man that he would need plenty of good, nourishing food. She began to arrange a menu in her mind—soup, a roast with plenty of baked potatoes and fresh vegetables, and a fruit pie for afters. Rhubarb, she mused; they had had rhubarb pie at home at the weekend with plenty of cream. Probably his wife didn't do the cooking—he must have a sizeable income from his practice as well as the work he did at the hospital, so there would be a cook and someone to do the housework. Her nimble fingers arranged everything ready for the morning while she added an au pair or a nanny for his children. Two boys and a girl... Mrs Keane's voice aroused her from her musings.

'Are you ready to leave, Florence? It's been a nice easy day, hasn't it? There's someone booked for tomorrow evening...'

Florence went to change out of her uniform. 'Yes, Mr Fitzgibbon's given me the afternoon off, but I have to come back at six o'clock.'

'Ah, yes—did he tell you who it was? No? Forgot, I expect. A very well-known person in the theatre world. Using her married name, of course.' Mrs Keane was going around, checking shut windows and doors. 'Very highly strung,' she commented, for still, despite her years of working for Mr Fitzgibbon, she adhered to the picturesque and sometimes inaccurate medical terms of her youth.

Florence, racing out of her uniform and into a skirt and sweater, envisaged a beautiful not-so-young actress who smoked too much and had developed a nasty cough...

The next day brought its quota of patients in the morning and, since the last of them went around noon, she cleared up and then was free to go. 'Mind you're here at six o'clock,' were Mr Fitzgibbon's parting words.

She agreed to that happily; she was free for almost six hours and she knew exactly what she was going to go and do. She couldn't expect lunch at Mrs Twist's; she would go and change and have lunch out, take a look at the shops along the Brompton Road and peek into Harrods, take a brisk walk in the park, have tea and get back in good time.

All of which she did, and, much refreshed, presented herself at the consulting-rooms with ten minutes to spare. All the same, he was there before her.

He bade her good evening with his usual cool courtesy and added, 'You will remain with the patient at all times, Miss Napier,' before returning to his writing.

Mrs Keane wasn't there; Florence waited in the reception-room until the bell rang, and opened the door. She wasn't a theatre-goer herself and she had little time for TV; all the same, she recognised the woman who came in. No longer young, but still striking-looking and expertly made-up, exquisitely dressed, delicately perfumed. She pushed past Florence with a nod.

'I hope I'm not to be kept waiting,' she said sharply. 'You'd better let Mr Fitzgibbon know that I'm here.'

Florence looked down her delicate nose. 'I believe that Mr

Fitzgibbon is ready for you. If you will sit down for a moment I will let him know that you're here.'

She tapped on the consulting-room door and went in, closing it behind her. 'Your patient is here, sir.'

'Good, bring her in and stay.'

The next half-hour was a difficult one. No one liked to be told that they probably had cancer of a lung, but, with few exceptions, they accepted the news with at least a show of courage. Mr Fitzgibbon, after a lengthy examination, offered his news in the kindest possible way and was answered by a storm of abuse, floods of tears and melodramatic threats of suicide.

Florence kept busy with cups of tea, tissues and soothing words, and cringed at the whining voice going on and on about the patient's public, her ruined health and career, her spoilt looks.

When she at length paused for breath Mr Fitzgibbon said suavely, 'My dear lady, your public need know nothing unless you choose to tell them, and I imagine that you are sufficiently well known for a couple of months away from the stage to do no harm. There is no need to tamper with your looks; your continuing—er—appearance is entirely up to you. Fretting and worrying will do more harm than a dozen operations.'

He waited while Florence soothed a fresh outburst of tears and near-hysterics. 'I suggest that you choose which hospital you prefer as soon as possible and I will operate—within the next three weeks. No later than that.'

'You're sure you can cure me?'

'If it is within my powers to do so, yes.'

'I won't be maimed?'

He looked coldly astonished. 'I do not maim my patients; this is an operation which is undertaken very frequently and gives excellent results.'

'I shall need the greatest care and nursing—I am a very sensitive person...'

'Any of the private hospitals in London will guarantee

that. Please let me know when you have made your decision and I will make the necessary arrangements.'

Mr Fitzgibbon got to his feet and bade his patient a polite goodbye, and Florence showed her out.

When she got back he was still sitting at his desk. He took a look at her face and observed, 'I did tell you that it was hard work. At Colbert's I see as many as a dozen a week with the same condition and not one of them utters so much as a whimper.'

'Well,' said Florence, trying to be fair, 'she is famous...'

'Mothers of families are famous too in their own homes, and they face a hazardous future, and what about the middle-aged ladies supporting aged parents, or the women bringing up children on their own?'

Florence so far forgot herself as to sit down on the other side of his desk. 'Well, I didn't know that you were like that...'

'Like what?'

'Minding about people. Oh, doctors and surgeons must mind, I know that, but you...' She paused, at a loss for getting the right words, getting slowly red in the face at the amused mockery on his.

'How fortunate it is, Miss Napier,' he observed gently, 'that my life's happiness does not depend on your good opinion of me.'

She got off the chair. 'I'm sorry, I don't know why I had to say that.' She added ingenuously, 'I often say things without thinking first—Father is always telling me...'

He said carelessly, 'Oh, I shouldn't let it worry you, I don't suppose you ever say anything profound enough to shatter your hearer's finer feelings.'

Florence opened her mouth to answer that back, thought better of it at the last minute, and asked in a wooden voice, 'Do you expect any more patients, sir, or may I tidy up?'

She might not have spoken. 'Do you intend to leave at the end of the month?' he asked idly.

'Leave? Here? No...' She took a sharp breath. 'Do you

want me to? I dare say I annoy you. Not everyone can get on with everyone else,' she explained in a reasonable voice, 'you know, a kind of mutual antipathy...'

He remained grave, but his eyes gleamed with amusement. 'I have no wish for you to leave, Miss Napier; you suit me very well: you are quick and sensible and the patients appear to like you, and any grumbling you may do about awkward hours you keep to yourself. We must contrive to rub along together, must we not?' He stood up. 'Now do whatever it is you have to do and we will go somewhere and have a meal.'

Florence eyed him in astonishment. 'You and I? But Mrs Twist will have something keeping warm in the oven for me...'

He reached for the telephone. 'In that case I will ask her to take it out before it becomes inedible.' He waved a large hand at her. 'Fifteen minutes—I've some notes to write up. Come back here when you're ready.'

There seemed no point in arguing with him; Florence sped away to the examination-room and began to put it to rights. Fifteen minutes wasn't long enough, of course; she would have to see to most of the instruments he had used in the morning—she could come early and do that. She worked fast and efficiently so that under her capable hands the room was pristine once more. The waiting-room needed little done in it; true, on her way out the patient had given vent to her feelings by tossing a few cushions around, but Florence shook them up smartly and repaired to the cloakroom, where she did her face and hair with the speed of light, got out of the uniform and into the jersey dress and matching jacket, thrust her feet into low-heeled pumps, caught up her handbag and went back to the consulting-room.

Mr Fitzgibbon was standing at the window, looking out into the street below, his hands in his pockets. He looked over his shoulder as she went in. 'Do you like living in London?' he wanted to know.

'Well, I don't really live here, do I? I work here, but when

I'm free I go home, so I don't really know what living here is like. At Colbert's I went out a good deal when I was off duty, but I never felt as though I belonged.'

'You prefer the country?'

'Oh, yes. Although I should think that if I lived here in surroundings such as these—' she waved an arm towards the street outside '—London might be quite pleasant.'

He opened the door for her and locked it behind him. 'Do you live in London?' she asked.

'Er—for a good deal of the time, yes.' There was a frosty edge to his voice which warned her not to ask questions. She followed him out to the car and was ushered in in silence.

She hadn't travelled in a Rolls-Royce before and she was impressed by its size; it and Mr Fitzgibbon, she reflected, shared the same vast, dignified appearance. She uttered the thought out loud. 'Of course, this is exactly the right car for you, isn't it?'

He was driving smoothly through quiet streets. 'Why?'

'Well, for one thing the size is right, isn't it?' She paused to think. 'And, of course, it has great dignity.'

Mr Fitzgibbon smiled very slightly. 'I am reassured to think that your opinion of me is improving.'

She couldn't think of the right answer to that; instead she asked, 'Where are we going?'

'Wooburn Common, about half an hour from here. You know the Chequers Inn? I've booked a table.'

'Oh—it's in the country?'

'Yes. I felt that it was the least I could do in the face of your preference for rural parts.'

'Well, that's awfully kind of you to take so much trouble. I mean, there are dozens of little cafés around Wimpole Street—well, not actually very near, but down some of the side-streets.'

'I must bear that in mind. Which reminds me, Mrs Twist asks that you should make sure that the cat doesn't get out as you go in.'

'Oh, Buster. She's devoted to him—he's a splendid tabby; not as fine as our Charlie Brown, though. Do you like cats?'

'Yes, we have one; she keeps my own dog company.'

'We have a Labrador—Higgins. He's elderly.' She fell silent, mulling over the way he had said 'we have one', and Mr Fitzgibbon waited patiently for the next question, knowing what it was going to be.

'Are you married?' asked Florence.

'No—why do you ask?'

'Well, if you were I don't think we should be going out like this without your wife... I expect you think I'm silly.'

'No, but do I strike you as the kind of man who would take a girl out while his wife actually sat at home waiting for him?'

Florence looked sideways at his calm profile. 'No.'

'That, from someone who is still not sure if she likes me or not, is praise indeed.'

They drove on in silence for a few minutes until she said in a small resolute voice, 'I'm sorry if I annoyed you, Mr Fitzgibbon.'

'Contrary to your rather severe opinion of me, I don't annoy easily. Ah—here we are. I hope you're hungry?'

The Chequers Inn was charming. Florence, ushered from the car and gently propelled towards it, stopped a minute to take a deep breath of rural air. It wasn't as good as Dorset, but it compared very favourably with Wimpole Street. The restaurant was just as charming, with a table in a window and a friendly waiter who addressed Mr Fitzgibbon by name and suggested in a quiet voice that the duck, served with a port wine and pink peppercorn sauce, was excellent and might please him and the young lady.

Florence, when consulted, agreed that it sounded delicious, and agreed again when Mr Fitzgibbon suggested that a lobster mousse with cucumber might be pleasant to start their meal.

She knew very little about wine, so she took his word for it that the one poured for her was a pleasant drink, as indeed it was, compared with the occasional bottle of table wine which graced the vicarage table. She remarked upon this in the unselfconscious manner that Mr Fitzgibbon was beginning to enjoy, adding, 'But I dare say there are a great many wines—if one had the interest in them—to choose from.'

He agreed gravely, merely remarking that the vintage wine he offered her was thought to be very agreeable.

The mousse and duck having been eaten with relish, Florence settled upon glazed fruit tart and cream, and presently poured coffee for them both, making conversation with the well-tried experience of a vicar's daughter, and Mr Fitzgibbon, unexpectedly enjoying himself hugely, encouraged her. It was Florence, glancing at the clock, who exclaimed, 'My goodness, look at the time!' She added guiltily, 'I hope you didn't have any plans for your evening—it's almost ten o'clock.' She went on apologetically, 'It was nice to have someone to talk to.'

'One should, whenever possible, relax after a day's work,' observed Mr Fitzgibbon smoothly.

The nearby church clocks were striking eleven o'clock when he stopped before Mrs Twist's little house. Florence, unfastening her seatbelt, began her thank-you speech, which he ignored while he helped her out, took the key from her, unlocked the door and then stood looming over her.

'I find it quite unnecessary to address you as Miss Napier,' he remarked in the mildest of voices. 'I should like to call you Florence.'

'Well, of course you can.' She smiled widely at him, so carried away by his friendly voice that she was about to ask him what his name was. She caught his steely eye just in time, coughed instead, thanked him once again and took back her key.

He opened the door for her. 'Mind Buster,' he reminded her, and shut the door smartly behind her. She stood leaning against it, listening to the silky purr of the car as he drove away. Buster, thwarted in his attempt to spend the night out, waited until she had started up the narrow stairs and then sidled up behind her, to curl up presently on her bed. Strictly forbidden, but Florence never gave him away.

If she had expected a change in Mr Fitzgibbon's remote manner towards her, Florence was to be disappointed. Despite the fact that he addressed her as Florence, it might just as well have been Miss Napier. She wasn't sure what she had expected, but she felt a vague disappointment, which she dismissed as nonsense in her normal matter-of-fact manner, and made a point of addressing him as 'sir' at every opportunity. Something which Mr Fitzgibbon noted with hidden amusement.

It was very nearly the weekend again, and there were no unexpected hold-ups to prevent her catching the evening train. It was almost the middle of May, and the vicarage, as her father brought the car to a halt before its half-open door, looked welcoming in the twilight. Florence nipped inside and down the wide hall to the kitchen, where her mother was taking something from the Aga.

'Macaroni cheese,' cried Florence happily, twitching her beautiful nose. 'Hello, Mother.' She embraced her parent and then stood her back to look at her. 'You're not doing too much? Is Miss Payne being a help?'

'Yes, dear, she's splendid, and I've never felt better. But how are you?'

'Nicely settled in—the work's quite interesting too, and Mrs Twist is very kind.'

'And Mr Fitzgibbon?'

'Oh, he's a very busy man, Mother. He has a large practice besides the various hospitals he goes to...'

'Do you like him, dear?' Mrs Napier sounded offhand.

'He's a very considerate employer,' said Florence airily. 'Shall I fetch Father? He went round to the garage.'

'Please, love.' Mrs Napier watched Florence as she went, wondering why she hadn't answered her question.

Sunday evening came round again far too soon, but as Florence got into the train at Sherborne she found, rather to her surprise, that she was quite looking forward to the week ahead. Hanging out of the window, saying a last goodbye to her father, she told him this, adding, 'It's so interesting, Father—I see so many people.'

A remark which in due course he relayed to his wife.

'Now, isn't that nice?' observed Mrs Napier. Perhaps by next weekend Florence might have more to say about Mr Fitzgibbon. Her motherly nose had smelt a rat concerning that gentleman, and Florence had barely mentioned him...

Florence, rather unwillingly, had found herself thinking about him. Probably because she still wasn't sure if she liked him, even though he had given her a splendid dinner. She walked round to the consulting-rooms in the sunshine of a glorious May morning, and even London—that part of London, at least—looked delightful. Mrs Keane hadn't arrived yet; Florence got the examination-room ready, opened the windows, put everything out for coffee, filled the kettle for the cup of tea she and Mrs Keane had when there was time, and went to look at the appointment book.

The first patient was to come at nine o'clock—a new patient, she noted, so the appointment would be a long one. The two following were short: old patients for check-ups; she could read up their notes presently. She frowned over the next entry, written in Mrs Keane's hand, for it was merely an address—that of a famous stately home open to the public—and when that lady arrived she asked about it.

Mrs Keane came to peer over her shoulder. 'Oh, yes, dear. A patient Mr Fitzgibbon visits—not able to come here. He'll go straight to Colbert's from there. Let's see, he'll be there all the afternoon, I should think—often goes back there in the evening on a Monday, to check on the operation cases, you know. So there's only Lady Hempdon in the afternoon, and she's not until half-past four.' She hung up her jacket and smoothed her neat old-fashioned hairstyle. 'We've time for tea.'

The first patient arrived punctually, which was unfortunate because there was no sign of Mr Fitzgibbon. Mrs Keane was exchanging good-mornings and remarks about the weather, when the phone rang. Florence went into the consulting-room to answer it.

'Mrs Peake there?' It was to be one of those days; no time lost on small courtesies.

'Yes, just arrived, sir.'

'I shall be ten minutes. Do the usual, will you? And take your time.' Mr Fitzgibbon hung up while she was uttering the 'Yes, sir'.

Mrs Peake was thin and flustered and, under her nice manner, scared. Florence led her to the examination-room, explaining that before Mr Fitzgibbon saw new patients he liked them to be weighed, have their blood-pressure taken and so on. She went on talking in her pleasant voice, pausing to make remarks about this and that as she noted down particulars. More than ten minutes had gone by by the time she had finished, and she was relieved to see the small red light over the door leading to the consulting-room flicker. 'If you will come this way, Mrs Peake—I think I have all the details Mr Fitzgibbon needs from me.'

Mr Fitzgibbon rose from his chair as they went in, giving a distinct impression that he had been sitting there for half an hour or more. His, 'Good morning, Mrs Peake,' was uttered in just the right kind of voice—cheerfully confident—and he received Florence's notes with a courteous, 'Thank you, Sister; be good enough to wait.'

As Florence led Mrs Peake away later she had to admit that Mr Fitzgibbon had a number of sides to him which she had been absolutely unaware of; he had treated his patient with the same cheerfulness, nicely tempered by sympathetic patience, while he wormed, word by word, her symptoms from her. Finally when he had finished he told her very simply what was to be done.

'It's quite simple,' he had reassured her. 'I have studied the X-rays which your doctor sent to me; I can remove a small piece of your lung and you will be quite yourself in a very short time—indeed, you will feel a new woman.' He had gone on to talk about hospitals and convenient dates and escorted her to the door, smiling very kindly at her as he had shaken hands.

Mrs Peake had left, actually smiling. At the door she had pressed Florence's hand. 'What a dear man, my dear, and I trust him utterly.'

There was time to take in his coffee before the next patient arrived. Florence, feeling very well disposed towards him, saw at once that it would be a waste of time. He didn't look up. 'Thank you. Show Mr Cranwell in when he comes; I shan't need you, Sister.'

She wasn't needed for the third patient either, and since after a cautious peep she found the examination-room empty, she set it silently to rights. If Mr Fitzgibbon was in one of his lofty moods then it was a good thing he was leaving after his patient had gone.

She ushered the elderly man out and skipped back smartly to the consulting-room in answer to Mr Fitzgibbon's raised voice.

'I shall want you with me. Five minutes to tidy yourself. I'll be outside in the car.'

She flew to the cloakroom, wondering what she had done, and, while she did her face, set her cap at a more becoming angle and made sure her uniform was spotless, she worried. Had she annoyed a patient or forgotten something? Perhaps he had been crossed in love, unable to take his girlfriend out that evening. They might have quarrelled... She would have added to these speculations, only Mrs Keane poked her head round the door.

'He's in the car...'

Mr Fitzgibbon leaned across and opened the door as she reached the car, and she got in without speaking, settled herself without looking at him and stared ahead as he drove away.

He negotiated a tangle of traffic in an unflurried manner before he spoke. 'I can hear your thoughts, Florence.'

So she was Florence now, was she? 'In that case,' she said

crisply, 'there is no need for me to ask where we are going, sir.'

Mr Fitzgibbon allowed his lip to twitch very slightly. 'No—of course, you will have read about it for yourself. You know the place?'

'I've been there with my brothers.'

'The curator has apartments there; his wife is a patient of mine, recently out of hospital. She is a lady of seventy-two and was unfortunate enough to swallow a sliver of glass during a meal, which perforated her oesophagus. I found it necessary to perform a thoracotomy, from which she is recovering. This should be my final visit, although she will come to the consulting-room later on for regular check-ups.'

'Thank you,' said Florence in a businesslike manner. 'Is there anything else that I need to know?'

'No, other than that she is a nervous little lady, which is why I have to take you with me.'

Florence bit back a remark that she had hardly supposed that it was for the pleasure of her company, and neither of them spoke again until they reached their destination.

This, thought Florence, following Mr Fitzgibbon through a relatively small side-door and up an elegant staircase to the private apartments, was something to tell the boys when she wrote to them. The elderly stooping man who had admitted them stood aside for them to go in, and she stopped looking around her and concentrated on the patient.

A dear little lady, sitting in a chair with her husband beside her. Florence led her to a small bedroom presently, and Mr Fitzgibbon examined her without haste before pronouncing her fit and well, and when Florence led her patient back to the sitting-room he was standing at one of the big windows with the curator, discussing the view.

'You will take some refreshment?' suggested the curator, and Florence hoped that Mr Fitzgibbon would say yes; the curator looked a nice, dignified old man who would tell her more about the house...

Mr Fitzgibbon declined with grave courtesy. 'I must get

back to Colbert's,' he explained, 'and Sister must return to the consulting-rooms as soon as possible.'

They made their farewells and went back to the car, and as Mr Fitzgibbon opened the door for her he said, 'I'm already late. I'll take you straight back and drop you off at the door. Lady Hempdon has an appointment for half-past four, has she not?'

She got in, and he got in beside her and drove off. 'Perhaps you would like to drop me off so that I can catch a bus?' asked Florence sweetly.

'How thoughtful of you, Florence, but I think not. We should be back without any delay!'

Mr Fitzgibbon, so often right, was for once wrong.

CHAPTER THREE

MR FITZGIBBON ignored the main road back to the heart of the city. Florence, who wasn't familiar with that part of the metropolis, became quite bewildered by the narrow streets lined with warehouses, most of them derelict, shabby, small brick houses and shops, and here and there newly built blocks of high-rise flats. There was, however, little traffic, and his short cuts would bring him very close to Tower Bridge where, presumably, he intended to cross the river.

She stared out at the derelict wharfs and warehouses they were passing with windows boarded up and walls held upright by wooden props; they looked unsafe and it was a good thing that the terrace of houses on the other side of the street was in a like state. There was nothing on the street save a heavily laden truck ahead of them, loaded with what appeared to be scrap iron. Mr Fitzgibbon had slowed, since it wasn't possible to pass, so that he was able to stop instantly when the truck suddenly veered across the street and hit the wall of a half-ruined warehouse, bringing it down in a shower of bricks.

Mr Fitzgibbon reached behind for his bag and opened the door. 'Phone the police—this is Rosemary Lane—lock the car, and join me.' He had gone striding up the road towards the still tumbling bricks and metal. There was no sign of the truck.

Florence dialled 999, gave a succinct description of the accident and its whereabouts, and added that at the moment the only people there were herself and a doctor and would they please hurry since whoever had been in the truck was buried under the debris. It took no time at all to take the keys, lock the car and run up the street to where she could see Mr Fitzgibbon, his jacket hanging on a convenient iron railing, clearing away bricks and sheets of metal, iron pipes and the like.

'They're coming,' said Florence, not wasting words.

Mr Fitzgibbon grunted. 'Stand there—I'll pass back to you and you toss it behind you, never mind where. The cabin will be just about here—if I could just get a sight of it...'

He shifted an iron sheet very gently and sent a shower of bricks sliding away so that he was able to pull out a miscellany of bricks and rubble. He passed these back piece by piece to Florence, stopping every now and then to listen.

There was a great deal of dust and they were soon covered in it. A sudden thought made Florence say urgently, 'Oh, do be careful of your hands...' She wished she hadn't said it the moment she had spoken—it had been a silly thing to say. What were cuts and bruises when a man's life was possibly at stake? Only the hands belonged to a skilled surgeon...

Seconds later Mr Fitzgibbon stopped suddenly, and Florence, clasping a nasty piece of concrete with wires sticking out of it, stood, hardly breathing, her ears stretched. Somewhere inside the heap of debris a voice was calling feebly. 'Oi,' it said.

Mr Fitzgibbon passed a couple of bricks to Florence. 'Hello, there!' He sounded cheerful. 'Hang on, we're almost there.'

It took several more minutes before he pulled another lump of concrete clear, exposing part of a man's face, coated with dust, just as an ambulance came to a halt beside them, and hard on its heels a police car and a fire engine.

Mr Fitzgibbon withdrew his head cautiously. 'There's a sheet of metal holding most of the stuff—we need the bricks and rubble out of the way so that we can get at him.'

The newcomers were experts; they widened the gap, shored up the metal above the man's head and brought up their equipment for Mr Fitzgibbon's use. He was head and shoulders inside now; Florence could hear him talking to the man, but he emerged very shortly. 'I need access to his legs. Can you clear the rubble from that end? As far as I can see, he's lying in a tunnel. It seems safe enough above his head, but I need to look at his legs. I believe he's pinned down.' He looked over his shoulder. 'Florence, my bag—I want a syringe and a morphia ampoule.'

He checked the drug and told her to draw it up, and slid into the gap again. The men were already busy, carefully shifting rubble from one end over the man's foot, and presently a boot came into view, and then the other foot, and Mr Fitzgibbon went to have a look.

'I'll have my bag,' he said to Florence. 'Tell the medics I want the amputation kit, then cram yourself through the gap and be ready to do what I tell you.' He spoke to the two men who had come to help him, and she slid carefully towards the man, already drowsy from the morphia.

'Cor, lumme,' he whispered, 'getting the VIP treatment, ain't I? And what's a pretty girl like you doin' 'ere?'

The space was small around the man, and Florence found Mr Fitzgibbon's face within inches of her own. He was applying a tourniquet above the man's knee. He said easily, 'Oh, Florence is my right hand. Pretty as a picture, isn't she? You ought to see her when her face is clean. Now, old chap, I'm afraid I shall have to take off part of your leg; you won't know anything about it, and I'll promise you'll be as good as new by the time I've finished with you in hospital. Just below the knee, Florence; let go when I say, and keep an eye open for everything else.'

He stretched behind him. 'I'll have that drip—hang on to your end, will you, while I get the needle in?'

He was busy for a few moments, talking quietly to the man as he worked, and when Florence moved a little and something tore he said, 'I hope that's nothing vital, Florence,' and the man chuckled sleepily.

''Old me 'and,' he told Florence, 'and keep an eye on old sawbones...'

Florence gave the grimy fist a squeeze. 'That's a promise.'

Mr Fitzgibbon shifted his bulk very slightly, and another

face appeared. A young cheerful face, which winked at
Florence. 'Going to put you off to sleep, old chap.'

He had the portable anaesthetic with him, and she said in
a comfortable voice, 'And while he's doing it you can tell
me about yourself. Are you married? Yes? And children, I
expect... Three? I always think that three is a nice number...'
She rambled on for a few more moments until the man was
unconscious, then she took her hand from his and leaned
forward as far as she could, ready to do whatever Mr
Fitzgibbon wanted done.

He was working very fast, his gloved hands, despite their
size, performing their task with gentleness, cutting and tying
and snipping until he said, 'Let go slowly, Florence.'

She loosened the tourniquet very slightly, and then grad-
ually slackened it. Everything held. Mr Fitzgibbon put his
hand behind him for the dressings, and his helper had them
ready. 'How's his pulse?'

'Strong, fast, regular. You'll take him out from your end?'

'Yes, support his head as far as you can reach.'

He disappeared from her view, but presently he and one
of the medics crawled in again and began to shift the man
while the third steadied the leg. It took some time; to
Florence, her shoulders and arms aching from keeping the
man's head and shoulders steady, it seemed like hours. At
last he was free, loaded on to a stretcher and taken to the
ambulance. She began to wriggle out backwards, and halfway there was caught round the waist and swung on to her
feet by Mr Fitzgibbon.

'Stay there,' he told her and went back to talk to the am-
bulancemen, and she stayed, having no wish to move another
step. She ached all over, she was filthy dirty, her mouth was
full of dust and she wanted a cup of tea and a hot bath at
that very minute; she also wanted to have a good cry, just
by way of relieving her feelings.

Her wishes, however, were not to be granted, at least for
the moment. Mr Fitzgibbon came back, took her by the arm

and walked her to his car. 'In you get; I want to get to Colbert's at the same time as that ambulance.'

He waved to the police car and the fire engine as he came abreast of them, and the police car went ahead, its lights flashing and its siren wailing, and the fire engine brought up the rear.

They went very fast and the traffic parted for them rather like the waters of the Red Sea; at any other time Florence would have enjoyed it immensely.

'Has he got a chance?' she asked.

'Yes. I don't think there's much else damaged, but we can't be sure until he's X-rayed. I want to get at that leg, though—I'll need Fortesque! Ring Colbert's, will you, and see if you can get him?'

Mr Fortesque, the orthopaedic consultant, was found, and yes, he would make himself available, and yes, he'd get Theatre Sister on to it right away. Florence relayed the information as Mr Fitzgibbon drove, and was about to hang up when he said, 'Tell them I want a taxi at the hospital to take you home to Mrs Twist. You're not hurt or cut?'

'No, I don't think so.'

'Make sure of that. Go to Casualty if you have any doubts.' He gave her a brief grin. 'Good, we're here. I'll see you later.' He got out and opened her door. 'Get hold of Mrs Keane. I'll phone later.'

He had gone, but not before giving her an urgent shove towards the taxi waiting for her.

The driver got out and helped her into the cab. 'Been in an accident, love?' he wanted to know. 'Not hurt, are you?'

'No, I'm fine, just very dirty. We stopped to help a man trapped in his truck.' She gave him a shaky smile. 'If you'd take me to my rooms, then I can go back on duty...'

'Right away, love...where to?'

He got out and helped her from the cab, and she said, 'Can you wait a minute? I've not got any money with me but I can get some from my room...'

'All taken care of, love. Head porter at Colbert's told me

to call back for it. Just you go in and have a nice cuppa and a lay down.'

He went to the door with her and thumped the knocker and, when Mrs Twist came, handed her over in a fatherly manner. ''Ad an accident,' he told her erroneously. 'I'll leave 'er to your loving 'ands.'

Florence thanked him. 'I'm sure Mrs Twist will give you a cup of tea.'

'Ta, love, but I'd best get back. Take care.'

Mrs Twist shut the door. 'Whatever's happened?' she wanted to know. 'Are you hurt? You're covered in dirt...'

Florence said, 'Not an accident. If you would let me have an old sheet or something I could take these things off here; otherwise the house will get dirty.'

'That's a bit of sense.' Mrs Twist bustled away, arranged an old tablecloth on the spotless lino in the hall, and begged Florence to stand on it. She peeled off everything, with Mrs Twist helping. 'And this dress is ruined,' declared that lady. 'There's a great piece torn out of the back; lucky there wasn't anyone to see your knickers.'

Mr Fitzgibbon must have had a splendid view when he had lifted her out of the truck. 'If I could have a bath and wash my hair, Mrs Twist?'

'That you may, love, and a nice hot cup of tea first. And how about a nice nap in bed?'

'I haven't the time. Mr Fitzgibbon has a patient at half-past four; I must get back to get ready for her.'

'You've not had your dinner?'

'No.'

'I'll have a sandwich or two for you when you've had your bath. Now off you go.'

Later, her head swathed in a towel, comfortable in a dressing-gown and slippers, Florence sat in Mrs Twist's kitchen, gobbling sandwiches and drinking endless cups of tea while she told her landlady all about it. Halfway through she remembered that she had to phone Mrs Keane and, since it was an emergency and Mrs Twist found the whole thing exciting, she was allowed to use the phone. Mrs Keane reacted with calm. 'You come over when you're ready,' she told Florence. 'We'll have a cup of tea, and by then I could ring Colbert's and see if Mr Fitzgibbon has any instructions for us. You're sure you're all right?'

'I'm fine.' Florence put down the phone and, urged by Mrs Twist, went on with her account of the morning's events.

There was more tea waiting for her when she got to the consulting-rooms, and Mrs Keane, despite her discreet manner, was avid to hear the details.

'What I don't understand,' said Florence, 'is why Mr Fitzgibbon was going to operate on the patient—he's a chest man...'

'Yes, dear; he specialises in chest surgery, but he can turn his hand to anything, and this Mr Fortesque is an old friend and colleague. Mr Fitzgibbon is a man who, once having started something, likes to see it through to the end.' She passed the biscuit tin. 'And you, dear, were you hurt at all?'

'No, but my uniform is ruined and I caught the back of the skirt on a nail or something and tore a great rent in it. Mrs Twist said she could see my knickers, which means everyone else saw them too.'

'Knickers?' asked Mrs Keane. 'I didn't think girls wore them any more—only those brief things with lace.'

'Well, yes, but I didn't tell Mrs Twist that—she was horrified enough.'

'Probably no one noticed.'

'Mr Fitzgibbon lifted me down from the truck; I was coming out backwards.'

'Mr Fitzgibbon is a gentleman,' declared her companion. 'Have another cup of tea! We have twenty minutes or so still.'

Florence was arranging the surgical impedimenta Mr Fitzgibbon might need when he came into the consulting-room and thrust wide the half-open door connecting the examination-room. If Florence had hoped for a slightly warmer relationship after their morning's experience she saw at once that she was going to be disappointed. He looked exactly as he always did, immaculate, his linen spotless, not a hair out of place, his manner coolly impersonal.

'Ah, Sister, none the worse for your experience, I hope? You feel able to finish the day's work?'

'Yes. What about that poor man? Did he have any other injuries?'

'Fractured ribs, a perforated lung and a fractured humerus. We've patched him up and he should do. He had plenty of pluck.'

'His wife...?'

'She's with him. She'll stay in the hospital for tonight at least.'

'The children?' Florence went on doggedly.

'With Granny.'

'Oh, good. Someone must have organised everything splendidly.'

'Indeed, yes,' agreed Mr Fitzgibbon, who had done the organising, getting this and that done, throwing his weight around rather, and no one daring to gainsay him. Not that he had been other than his usual cool, courteous self.

'Be good enough to give Mrs Keane details of your ruined uniform so that you can be reimbursed, and—er—for any other garment which may have suffered.'

Florence blushed.

No further reference was made to the morning's happenings, and she went off to her room feeling slightly ill done by. Mr Fitzgibbon could have thanked her, or at least expressed concern as to her feelings—did he consider her to be made of stone? Florence, very much a warm-hearted girl, reflected that there must be something wrong with his life, something which made him uncaring of those people around him. But that wasn't true, she had to remind herself; he had been marvellous with the man in the truck—indeed, he had sounded quite different talking to him. Getting ready for bed, she decided that she was sorry for him; he needed someone or something to shake his unshakeable calm. Underneath that he was probably quite nice to know. Her eyes closed on the praiseworthy resolve to treat him with understanding, not to answer back and to show sympathy if he ever showed signs of needing it.

Full of good resolutions, she went to work the next morning, but there was little opportunity of carrying any of them out. Mr Fitzgibbon was decidedly abrupt in his manner towards her, and in the face of that it was hard to remain meek and sympathetic. Nevertheless, she fetched his coffee and bade him drink it in a motherly fashion, pointed out that it was a lovely morning and suggested that a weekend in the country would do him a world of good, adding that he probably didn't take enough exercise.

He raked her with cold eyes. 'Your solicitude for my health flatters me, Florence, but pray confine your concern to the patients.'

So much for her good intentions.

It was towards the end of the week as she was tidying up after a patient that Mrs Keane came in. 'There's Miss Paton here, Mr Fitzgibbon, wants to see you.' She hesitated. 'I did say that you were about to leave for the hospital.'

He looked up from his desk. 'Ask her to come in, will you, Mrs Keane?' He looked across to the half-open door of the examination-room, where Florence was putting away instruments. 'I shan't need you, Florence; if you haven't finished there perhaps you will come back presently?'

He spoke pleasantly but without warmth. She closed the door and crossed the consulting-room, and reached the door just as it was opened from the other side. Out of the corner of her eye she saw Mr Fitzgibbon get to his feet as a girl came in. Not a girl, she corrected herself, taking in the details with a swift feminine eye, but a woman of thirty, good-looking, delicately made-up, dressed with expensive simplicity. She went past Florence with barely a glance.

'Darling, I simply have to see you. Naughty me, coming

to your rooms, but you weren't at the party and I have so much...'

Florence reluctantly closed the door on the rather high-pitched voice, but not before she had heard Mr Fitzgibbon's, 'My dear Eleanor, this is delightful...'

'Who's she?' asked Florence, and Mrs Keane for once looked put out.

'Well, I can't say for certain, dear. She seems to be very friendly with Mr Fitzgibbon—she's always phoning him, you know, and sometimes he rings her. She's a widow; married an old man. He died a year or so ago. Very smart, she is—goes everywhere.'

'And does she...does he...? Are they going to get married?'

'If she gets her way they will, but you can't tell with him, dear. Never shows his feelings. Very popular he is, lots of friends, could go anywhere he chooses, but you never know what he's thinking, if you know what I mean.'

Florence thought she knew. 'But she's all wrong for him,' she said urgently.

Mrs Keane nodded, 'Yes, dear, he needs someone who doesn't butter him up—someone like you.'

'Me?' Florence said and laughed. 'Are you going home? I'll have to stay and finish the examination-room. I hope they won't be too long. I said I'd be at Colbert's at seven o'clock.'

'Of course, you've got friends there, I expect. I'll be off. The first patient is at nine o'clock tomorrow—a new one, too.'

After Mrs Keane had gone Florence went and sat in the kitchen, and it was another ten minutes before Mr Fitzgibbon and his visitor came out. She came out to meet him and asked if she should lock up, and then bade them goodnight. 'Who's that girl?' she heard Eleanor ask as they left the waiting-room. She wondered what he had replied, then shrugged her shoulders, finished her work and went home in her turn.

She had her supper on a tray in her room, changed quickly and went to catch a bus to Colbert's. The man who had been in the truck was out of Intensive Care and, since she had been on the hospital staff, she had no difficulty in obtaining permission to visit him.

She found him propped up in bed, looking very much the worse for wear but cheerfully determined to get better. His wife was with him; a small, thin woman whose nondescript appearance Florence guessed held as determined a nature as his. She didn't stay long; she arranged the flowers she had brought with her in a vase, expressed her delight at seeing him already on the road to recovery, and prepared to leave.

'Owes 'is life to you and that nice doctor,' said his wife as Florence prepared to say goodbye. 'Bless yer both for saving 'im. And that doctor. 'E's a gent if ever there was one. 'Aving me fetched like 'e did, and all fixed up to stay as long as I want, and the kids seen to. Not to mention the money. A loan, of course; as soon as we can we'll pay 'im back, but there's no denying the cash'll come in handy.'

Going back to her bedsit, Florence reflected that Mr Fitzgibbon was a closed book as far as she was concerned. And likely to remain so.

The next day was Friday and she would be going home in the evening. The day was much as any other; Mr Fitzgibbon never lacked for patients—his appointments book was filled weeks ahead and a good deal of each day was spent at the hospital. Florence cleared up after the last patient that afternoon, glad to be going home. Mr Fitzgibbon had been his usual terse self, and she felt the strong need for the carefree atmosphere of the vicarage.

She tidied away the last dressing towels, wiped the glass top of the small table to a brilliant shine and opened the door into the waiting-room. Mr Fitzgibbon was sitting on the corner of Mrs Keane's desk, talking to her, but he turned to look at Florence and got to his feet.

'I have just agreed to see a patient this evening, Florence. He is unable to come at any other time so we must alter our plans. You were going home this evening?'

She wouldn't have minded so much if she had thought he

had sounded even slightly sympathetic. 'Yes, but there are plenty of morning trains—I can go tomorrow. At what time this evening do you want me here, sir?'

'Half-past six. Telephone your home now, if you wish.'

He nodded and smiled at Mrs Keane, and then went away.

'Hard luck, dear,' said Mrs Keane. 'Is there a later train you could catch?'

'It takes two hours to get to Sherborne and it would be too late for anyone to fetch me. No, it's all right, I'll go on the early train in the morning.'

'Is Mrs Twist home? What about your supper?'

'She's going out, but that's all right, I can open a tin of beans or something. I told her I'd be going home, you see.'

'It's spoilt Mr Fitzgibbon's evening too—he was to have taken someone out to dinner. I dare say it's that woman who came here—that Eleanor...'

'Well, it's nice to know that his evening is spoilt too,' said Florence waspishly. She smiled suddenly. 'And hers.'

Mrs Keane laughed. 'I'll be off; you're coming?'

They went out together, and Mrs Keane said cheerfully, 'See you Monday. He's operating at eight o'clock, so we'll have the morning to ourselves.'

Mrs Twist was put out. 'If I'd known I'd have got you a bit of ham for your supper...'

Florence hastened to placate her. 'If I may open a tin of beans? I'll do some toast. I've no idea how long it's going to take; Mr Fitzgibbon didn't say. I'll catch the early train tomorrow morning...'

'Well, if that's all right with you,' said Mrs Twist reluctantly. 'Just this once. Seeing it's for Mr Fitzgibbon.'

Florence let that pass. She doubted if he would need to open a tin of beans for his supper. She had her tea, tidied her already tidy person, took a quick look at Mrs Twist's *Daily Mirror* and went back to the consulting-room.

Mr Fitzgibbon was already there, brooding over some X-rays. 'Ah, there you are,' he observed, for all the world as though she were late instead of being five minutes early. He went back to his contemplation of the films and she took herself off to the waiting-room, ready to admit the patient.

He arrived fifteen minutes late, and Florence opened the door to him, recognising the famous features so often pictured on the front pages of the daily Press and the evening news on TV. She hoped that her face betrayed no surprise as she wished him good evening and begged him to take a seat. 'Mr Fitzgibbon is here,' she said, 'if you'll wait a moment.'

It struck her much later that one didn't ask men like that to wait a moment, but Mr Fitzgibbon had at that moment thrust open his door and come to shake hands with his patient. He nodded to Florence and she followed them into the consulting-room to hear him assure the man that she was utterly reliable and discreet. 'Sister will prepare the examination-room while I check the details your doctor has given me,' suggested Mr Fitzgibbon smoothly, and Florence, taking the hint, slid away and closed the door.

It seemed a long time before the two men came to the examination-room, and an even lengthier time before Mr Fitzgibbon was finished with his examination. The pair of them went back into the consulting-room, leaving Florence to clear up. Mr Fitzgibbon appeared to have used almost everything usable there—an hour's work at least, she thought, and it was already almost eight o'clock.

She was half finished when he came in. His patient had gone and there was only the reading-lamp on his desk to light the consulting-room.

He said pleasantly, 'I'm sorry that your evening has been spoilt.' He picked up a hand towel from the pile she had just arranged. 'Mrs Twist has supper waiting for you?'

'Oh, yes,' said Florence airily, 'something special.' She said, 'She's a good cook, and I expect we shall have it together...'

Mr Fitzgibbon replaced the towel carefully. 'In that case, there's no point in suggesting that we might have had a meal somewhere together.'

'Was your evening spoilt too?' asked Florence, aware that it had been, but hoping for a few details.

'Spoilt? Hardly. Shall I say that it necessitated a change of plans?'

'Me too,' agreed Florence with a cheerful lack of grammar. 'Never mind, you have the whole weekend.'

'Indeed I have. Be outside Mrs Twist's at half-past eight tomorrow morning, Florence: I will drive you home.'

She arranged everything just so, put the hand towels out of his reach and finally said, 'That is most kind of you, sir, but there is a train I can catch... It only takes two hours; I can be home well before lunchtime.'

'Two hours? I can do it in an hour and a half in the car. I need a breath of country air too.'

'Won't it spoil your day?' asked Florence feebly.

'My dear Florence, if it were going to spoil my day I should not have suggested it in the first place.'

She looked extremely pretty standing there, the last of the sun turning her hair to burnished copper, her face a little tired, for it had been a long day. She gave him a clear look, making sure that he had meant what he had said. 'Then I'd like that very much,' she told him quietly.

'Go home now, Florence. I have some writing to do, so I'll lock up.' He turned back to his desk. 'Goodnight.'

She wished him a good night and made her way to Mrs Twist's, where she kicked off her shoes, opened a tin of baked beans, took the pins out of her hair and sat on the kitchen table, eating her supper. Of course, supper with Mr Fitzgibbon would have been quite a different matter—a well-chosen meal at the end of the day would have been very acceptable, but not acting as a substitute for the glamorous Eleanor.

She fed Buster, had a bath and presently went to bed.

It was a glorious morning; it was almost June and a lovely time of the year. She swapped the dress she had been going to wear for a much prettier one, telling herself it was because it was more suited to the bright sunshine outside, and she skipped downstairs to make a cup of tea. Mrs Twist took things easy on Saturdays and there would be no breakfast, although Florence knew she was free to help herself. The note she had left on the kitchen table for her landlady had gone, and in its place Mrs Twist had left one of her own. 'Don't let Buster out. Have a nice trip, you lucky girl.'

Florence drank her tea, gave Buster his breakfast, picked up her weekend bag and let herself out of the house. She was closing the door gently behind her when the Rolls came to quite a quiet halt and Mr Fitzgibbon got out to open her door.

She wished him good morning and thought how nice he looked in casual clothes; he looked younger too, and his 'good morning' was uttered in a friendly voice. Emboldened, she remarked upon the beauty of the morning, but beyond a brief reply he had nothing to say and she supposed that he wasn't in the mood for conversation. She let out a small surprised yelp when a warm tongue gently licked the back of her neck. She turned her head and found herself looking into a pair of gentle brown eyes in a whiskered face, heavily shrouded in eyebrows and a great deal of light brown hair.

'Ah, I should have mentioned,' said Mr Fitzgibbon casually, 'Monty likes the country too. You don't mind?'

'Mind? No, of course not. She has a beautiful face. What is she?'

'We have often wondered... We settled for a mixed parentage.'

'Did you get her from a breeder or a pet shop?'

'Neither—from a doorway in a street full of boarded-up houses. It took some time for her to achieve the physical perfection she now enjoys, but, even now, it is difficult to decide what her parents might be.'

Florence exchanged another look with the brown eyes behind her. 'She's awfully sweet. Higgins will love her. I'm not sure about Charlie Brown, though—he's our cat.'

'Monty likes cats. Our cat had kittens a couple of weeks

ago and she broods over the whole basketful whenever
Melisande goes walking.'

'Melisande—the cat?'

'Yes. Does your mother know that we're coming?'

'Yes. My brothers are home again for half-term.'

They lapsed into silence again, broken only by Monty's
gentle sighs and mutterings. They were on the A303 by now
and the road was fairly clear, for it was still early. Florence,
sitting back in the comfortable seat with the dog's warm
breath on her neck, felt happy and, since there seemed to be
no need to talk, she took time to wonder why. Of course,
being driven in a Rolls-Royce was enough to make anyone
happy, but it was more than that: she was enjoying Mr
Fitzgibbon's company, even though he was doing nothing at
all to entertain her. She felt quite at ease with him, and the
thought surprised her, for until that moment she had got used
to the idea that she didn't much like him, only, she had to
admit, sometimes.

Presently she ventured to remark that he could turn off at
Sparkford, and then added, 'Oh, sorry, you came with Mr
Wilkins.' Then, because he didn't answer, 'Do you like this
part of England?'

'Very much; an easy drive from town and, once one is away
from the main road, charmingly rural.' He turned off the A303
and took a minor road towards Sherborne, and presently left
it for a narrow country road, its hedges burgeoning with the
foliage of oncoming summer.

Gussage Tollard lay in a hollow; they could see the house-
tops as they went down the hill, and Florence gave a contented
sigh. 'Oh, it is nice to be home,' she said.

'You regret taking the job?' Mr Fitzgibbon wanted to know
sharply. 'You do not like working for me?'

'Of course I like working for you, it's a super job. Only I
wish I knew you better...' She stopped, very red in the face.
'I'm sorry, I don't know what made me say that.'

'Well, if you ever find out, let me know.' He didn't look
at her, for which she was thankful. 'The vicarage is past the

church and along the lane, isn't it?' He sounded so casual that she hoped he might not have heard what she had said, but he must have done because he had told her to tell him... It had been a silly remark and easily forgotten.

She said cheerfully, 'Here we are.' She glanced at her watch. 'It took an hour and twenty-five minutes. You were right.'

'Of course I was.' He spoke without conceit as he got out, opened her door and then let Monty out, giving her the chance to run into the house first.

CHAPTER FOUR

FLORENCE hadn't reached the door before her mother came to meet her, and hard on her heels were her two brothers, with Higgins shoving his way past them to jump up at her, barking his pleasure.

Florence said breathlessly, 'Hello, Mother—boys...here's Mr Fitzgibbon.'

He had followed more slowly, and stood quietly with Monty beside him as they all surged towards him.

'You've met each other,' said Florence to her mother, and added, 'these are my brothers—Tom and Nicky. Oh, and this is Higgins...'

Higgins had sat down deliberately in front of Monty, and presently bent his elderly head to breathe gently over the little dog.

'Oh, good, they're going to be friends,' said Mrs Napier. 'Come in—the coffee is ready. Did you have a decent drive from London?'

She led the way indoors, and Mr Fitzgibbon, at his most urbane, gave all the right answers and, when asked, declared that there was nothing he enjoyed more than coffee in the kitchen.

'You see, I'm getting lunch and we can all talk there while I'm cooking.' Mrs Napier gave him a sweet smile. 'Sit here,' she told him, offering a Windsor chair by the big scrubbed table. 'I'm afraid we use the kitchen a great deal, especially in the winter. This is a nice old house but it is all open fireplaces—there's no heating otherwise, and we spend hours lugging in coals just to keep the sitting-room fire glowing. Thank heaven for an Aga.' She beamed at him. 'Have you one in your home?'

Mr Fitzgibbon hesitated for a moment. 'Er—yes, I believe we have.'

'Well, I'm sure you must need it, leading the kind of life you do...at everybody's beck and call, I dare say.'

She was pouring coffee as she spoke, and Florence picked up a jug of hot milk. 'Black or white?' she asked him. She had been listening to her mother rambling on in her gentle way and not minding in the least; if he didn't like it it was just too bad.

Apparently he didn't mind; he accepted milk and sugar and a large slice of the cake on the table, and entered into a spirited conversation with her brothers concerning cars, although he interlarded this with small talk with her mother, and presently, when she remarked that the vicar had gone to Whitehorse Farm a mile the other side of the village, he suggested he might take the car and give him a lift back. An idea which appealed to the boys and which Mrs Napier instantly accepted. 'Do leave your little dog here if you like; she seems happy enough with Higgins...'

They all went out to the car again, and when Mr Fitzgibbon opened the car doors both dogs got in as well. Florence stood with her mother, watching the car turn smoothly out of the gate, and her mother said, 'I do hope he doesn't mind taking the boys and Higgins; he seems such a nice man—charming manners too. Very considerate to work for, I've no doubt, love.'

'I suppose so, Mother. Nothing is allowed to stand in the way of his work, though, and he's very reserved. He doesn't talk much, only to tell me what he wants done...'

'But, darling, you're not working all the time; you had a two hours' drive from London—you must have talked...?'

Florence cast thoughts back to the morning's journey. 'Well, no, only this and that, you know.'

'I'm surprised that he isn't married,' observed Mrs Napier chattily.

They were in the kitchen, clearing up the coffee-cups. 'I

honestly don't think he's had the time to fall in love, although he must know any number of suitable women...'

'Suitable?'

'Well, you know what I mean, Mother. His kind of female, beautifully dressed and made-up and entertaining and witty and not needing to work...'

Mrs Napier gave a mug an extra polish. 'What makes you think that is his kind of female?'

'A girl—no, a woman came to the consulting-rooms, Eleanor something or other, and he seemed awfully pleased to see her. She had one of those voices you actually hear from yards away even though they're not speaking loudly—you know what I mean?'

'I don't know Mr Fitzgibbon well, but he strikes me as a man who is unlikely to succumb to such a woman. Do you suppose he might stay for lunch?'

'I doubt it,' said Florence. 'Here they are now.'

Her father was the only one to come into the kitchen; the others were outside, and Florence could see two youthful heads on either side of a grizzled one, peering into the Rolls's engine.

Her father kissed her and patted her on the shoulder in a paternal fashion.

'My dear, what a very pleasant man your doctor is...'

'He's a surgeon, Father, and he's not mine...'

'No, no, my dear, I speak lightly. So kind of him to drive over to fetch me, and he's so patient with the boys.' He looked at his wife. 'Might he not be invited to lunch?'

'Of course, it's Saturday—he must be free. I'll ask him.'

Presently, back in the kitchen, he refused. 'There is nothing I would have enjoyed more,' he assured Mrs Napier, 'but I have a date this afternoon, added to which I must get back to town.'

'Well, of course you must,' declared Mrs Napier comfortably. 'I don't suppose you have much time in which to enjoy yourself. It was very kind of you to drive Florence here. It's not like her to miss the train.'

'Ah, but that's why I brought her—she didn't miss the train, she had to stay on Friday evening to attend a patient; I sometimes have consultations at awkward hours.'

Mrs Napier, who had been nurturing the beginnings of a possible romance between this nice man and her daughter, was disappointed.

They went to the door to see him off, and Mrs Napier said wistfully, 'A pity you couldn't stay; I would so enjoy hearing about your work—I really am quite vague as to what exactly Florence does...'

He was getting into the car. 'Works very hard, Mrs Napier; she is also clear-headed and brave, and doesn't make a fuss when her clothes get torn and she gets covered in dust.' He turned to grin at Florence's annoyed face. 'Do ask her about it.'

He waved a hand, and drove away with the minimum of fuss.

'What exactly did he mean?' asked Mrs Napier. 'Come indoors, love, and tell us about it. Have you been in an accident?'

'No,' said Florence crossly, 'and I wasn't going to say anything about it. How tiresome he is.'

'Yes, dear. Now sit down and tell us what happened.'

There was nothing for it but to do as her mother asked. 'Really, I didn't do anything; I mean, only what anyone else would have done. It was Mr Fitzgibbon who rescued the man and amputated his leg. He did it on his hands and knees and it must have been very uncomfortable for him as he's so very large. He went straight to Colbert's and there was further surgery to do. He sent me back to my bedsit in a taxi.'

'How very kind.'

'Yes? He expected me to be on duty at the consulting-rooms later that afternoon.' Florence gave an indignant snort. 'He doesn't spare himself, and he doesn't spare anyone else either.'

'He did bring you home in that Rolls,' Tom pointed out. 'I think he's absolutely super...'

'So do I,' said Nicky. 'He knows a lot about cars too.'

'Pooh,' said Florence, 'who wants to know about cars anyway?' And she flounced out of the room and up to her bedroom, where she hung out of the window and brooded, although she wasn't sure what she was brooding about.

It was impossible to brood for long. The garden below her window was bursting with a mixture of early-summer flowers: roses, entangled with soldiers and sailors, wallflowers, forget-me-nots, pansies, lilies of the valley and buttercups rioted all over the rather neglected flowerbeds of the vicarage garden. Florence took herself off downstairs, firmly resolved to bring a little order to the colourful chaos.

The weekend was over far too quickly; she left the half-weeded garden with reluctance, aware that the hard work she had put into it had done much to assuage the feeling of restlessness. Sitting in the train on the way back to London, she reflected that a week's hard work would get her back to her normal acceptance of life once more.

Her room looked cramped and dreary after the comfortable shabbiness of the vicarage; she arranged the flowers she had brought back with her, unpacked her overnight bag and took a bunch of roses down to the kitchen for Mrs Twist, who was so delighted with them that she opened a tin of soup to add to their supper of corned beef, lettuce and tomatoes.

She walked to work the next morning, the early sunshine already warm. It was going to be a lovely day, and her thoughts turned longingly to the garden at home and all those roses needing her attention. Once at the consulting-rooms and in Mrs Keane's company, she became her usual self. With Mr Fitzgibbon at the hospital, there was the opportunity to give the examination-room a good clean, check the instruments, see that the cupboards and the drawers were stocked, and have a leisurely cup of coffee with Mrs Keane.

'You got home, then?' asked that lady as they drank it.

'Mr Fitzgibbon gave me a lift on Saturday morning.'

'Well, I never did—how very kind of him. Was he spending the weekend in your part of the world, I wonder?'

'Oh, no. He only stayed for a cup of coffee; he said he had a date...'

'That Eleanor woman, I have no doubt. There were two calls from her on the answering machine. Well, he's not likely to take her out this evening—he won't get away from Colbert's much before one o'clock, and there are five appointments starting at two o'clock.'

Mrs Keane took another biscuit. 'He'll be a bit terse, I dare say. Monday morning and all that.' She asked abruptly, 'Are you going to stay? I do hope so.'

'Heavens, the month is almost up, isn't it? Yes, I hope he'll decide to keep me on. The work's interesting, isn't it? And it's nice being able to go home each weekend. And the money, of course...'

'Well, I don't expect you'll get home every weekend. There's an appointment for Wednesday—a query. In the Midlands. You'll probably have to go with him, perhaps stay overnight; it could easily have been the weekend, even though it isn't this time.'

'Well, that's all right.'

'Good. Do you mind if I go out for half an hour? I must get something for supper tonight and we'll probably be too late for the shops this afternoon.'

Left to herself, Florence did some more turning out of cupboards and drawers, and she answered the phone several times and then turned on the answering machine and listened to Eleanor's voice. She sounded snappy; Mr Fitzgibbon hadn't turned up to take her to the theatre, nor had he bothered to let her know why. The second message was even snappier. Florence, while conceding that Mr Fitzgibbon wasn't a man who needed sympathy, being well able to look after himself, felt quite sorry for him.

Mrs Keane was back, and they had eaten their lunch when he came in. His 'good afternoon' was austere, and he looked tired, which wasn't surprising, since he had been operating since eight o'clock, but as Florence ushered in the first of the patients she saw that he had somehow shed his weariness, presenting to his patients a sympathetic calm and a complete concentration.

The last one went just before five o'clock, and she took in a cup of tea Mrs Keane had ready for him.

He glanced up as she went in. 'I'm going back to Colbert's,' he told her. 'My first appointment is for nine o'clock tomorrow morning, isn't it? If I'm late say all the usual, will you? I'll hope to get here, but I can't be certain.'

She murmured and went to the door, to be halted by his, 'By the way, I have to go to Lichfield on Wednesday—a little girl with cystic fibrosis. She's been a patient of mine for some time, but her parents insisted on taking her home... She's a difficult child and I shall want you with me. It is possible that we shall have to spend the night, so bring a bag with you. We shall leave around midday after the morning appointments. I've engaged to meet her local doctor at half-past two.'

'Uniform, sir?'

'Oh, decidedly, and your starchiest manner. The poor child is spoilt by her parents and an old nanny, but she responds quite well to calm authority.'

Florence said, 'Yes, sir,' and took herself out of the room. A couple of days away from the consulting-rooms would be a nice change, but it sounded as though she was going to have her work cut out. She found Mrs Keane in the kitchen, drinking tea, and she poured herself a cup.

'I'm to go to Lichfield,' she explained, 'and probably stay the night there, as you thought.'

'Oh, Phoebe Villiers—Sister Brice dreaded that visit; the child's very difficult and the parents absolutely refuse to let her have further treatment in hospital. They had a house somewhere in Hampstead, and that's how Mr Fitzgibbon took her on as a patient; got her into Colbert's and there really was an improvement, but the parents moved to their other house at Lichfield and discharged her. He could have refused to go on treating her as a patient, but he would never do that, not while there was a chance of keeping the child as fit as possible.'

'So he goes all the way up there to see her?'

'Yes, every three months—she's a private patient, of course, but even if she weren't I believe that he would still go. He doesn't give up easily.'

The next day went smoothly enough; it was just as Mr Fitzgibbon was leaving in the evening after a long afternoon that Florence asked, 'Do I have time to go back to Mrs Twist's tomorrow and fetch my overnight bag?'

'I think not. I want to get away in good time. We shall have to stop for a meal of sorts on the way; you can do whatever you do to your face and hair then.'

Florence muttered a reply. The man needed a wife so that he might have some insight into female ways. She wondered if he treated Eleanor in such an arbitrary fashion, and how she responded if he did. Of course, the occasion would never arise; Eleanor had all the time in the world to make herself ready for any social outing, and this, Florence reminded herself briskly, was by no means to be a social visit—not one of them was likely to notice if her hair was all anyhow and her nose shining.

All the same, she washed her hair that evening, attended to her nicely kept hands and packed an extra uniform. She had dealt with difficult children in hospital and knew how prone they were to throw things...

It wanted ten minutes to noon as Mr Fitzgibbon eased the Rolls away from the kerb. Florence, sitting silently beside him, thought of the small tasks she hadn't had time to do, made a mental inventory of the contents of her overnight bag, and tried not to think about lunch. Her breakfast had been a sketchy one that morning and there had been no time for coffee. She hoped her insides wouldn't rumble. Anyone else, she reflected, and she wouldn't have hesitated to say that she was hungry, but a quick peep at her companion's severe profile made it obvious that he wasn't concerned about food. Getting out of London was uppermost in his mind.

Not knowing that part of the city well, she became quite bewildered with the short cuts and the ins and outs of non-descript streets, and once or twice she wondered if he had got lost, but suddenly they were on the M1, going north, and his well-shod foot went down on the accelerator.

'You're a girl after my own heart,' he said, 'you know when to hold your tongue.' After which astonishing remark he lapsed into silence once more, leaving her to wonder whether he had meant that as a compliment or merely an expression of relief; either way it seemed a good idea to stay silent.

The miles flew by, and they had passed the outskirts of Luton when he slowed the car and turned into Toddington Service Station.

'Twenty minutes and not a minute more. Out you get.'

She got out and followed him into the vast and busy cafeteria. 'Coffee and sandwiches?' he asked as he sat her down at a table. 'Any preference?'

'Cheese, and tea, not coffee.' She added after his retreating back, 'Please.'

The place wasn't too full; he was back quickly with his tray: sandwiches for both of them, coffee for him and a little pot of tea for her—she liked him for that.

They didn't waste time talking, but she liked him even better when he said, 'This is hardly the kind of place to which I would take you, Florence, but we are rather pressed for time. You must allow me to give you dinner one evening as recompense.'

She paused before taking another bite. 'That's all right, sir. These sandwiches are very good, and the tea is heavenly.'

She swallowed a second cup and stood up when he asked her if she was ready.

'I'll meet you at the car—I'll be very quick.' She had whisked herself away, not seeing his quick smile at the unselfconscious remark. The image of Eleanor crossed his mind; in like circumstances she would have talked prettily about powdering her nose and kept him waiting for ten minutes. Of course, she would never allow herself to be in surroundings such as these in the first place.

He was back in the car by now and watched Florence emerge from the Ladies' and make a swift beeline towards him.

He opened the door, shut her in once more and got in beside her. The motorway wasn't busy, since it was the lunch-hour, and the Rolls, kept at a steady pace of seventy miles an hour, made light of the distance. Florence, busy with pleasant plans as to the laying out of her first pay cheque, due the next day, was surprised to see the sign to Lichfield ahead of them. Mr Fitzgibbon turned off the motorway. 'Around twelve miles,' he remarked. He glanced at his watch. 'You will probably have five minutes or so before you meet Phoebe.' He glanced at her. 'You look remarkably neat and tidy.'

'I should hope so,' said Florence tartly. 'You wouldn't employ me for long if I weren't.'

'True. Which reminds me—you intend to stay on?'

'Well, yes, if you're quite satisfied with me, sir.'

'Given time, I see no reason why we shouldn't deal excellently with each other.'

The kind of quelling remark which was enough to tempt a girl to give in her notice then and there.

The Villiers lived a few miles from the town, and Florence glanced around as they drove through the double gates and along a driveway as smooth as silk, running through gardens so well laid out that it might have been painted instead of planted. A far cry from the vicarage garden, always in need of a good weed and the pruning shears, and twice as beautiful. The house matched the garden: with its pristine white walls, sparkling windows and glossy paint, it seemed rather like a stage setting. Mr Fitzgibbon, apparently oblivious to his surroundings, got out, opened her door and walked with her to the wide porch.

Florence, still feeling as though she were on a film set, was ushered into the hall by a maid, very correctly dressed, even to a cap on her head, and stood quietly waiting for whatever would happen next.

'Mr Fitzgibbon and Sister Napier—we are expected,' said Mr Fitzgibbon, and she walked beside him as they were shown into a large room with a lofty ceiling and french windows opening on to the garden, and furnished with modern chairs, deep couches and glass-topped tables. Florence, brought up among well-polished oak and mahogany pieces, winced.

The man and woman who came to meet them matched the room. Well-dressed, the woman beautifully made-up and coiffeured, they were as modern as their surroundings.

Mrs Villiers spoke first. 'Mr Fitzgibbon—so good of you to come. Dr Gibbs will be joining us shortly.' Her eyes swept over Florence. 'A new nurse? What happened to the other one?'

'Sister Brice left me to get married—may I introduce Sister Napier, Mrs Villiers?'

Mrs Villiers nodded in Florence's direction without looking at her. 'Well, do sit down and have a drink... Nurse can go to her room for a moment or two.'

'I should prefer her to meet Phoebe before we examine her.' Mr Fitzgibbon's courteous manner was very cool.

'Oh, if she must. The child's with Nanny. I'll get someone to take her up.'

'I think it might be better if I go too. Perhaps I might be told when Dr Gibbs arrives?'

Mrs Villiers laughed and shrugged her shoulders. 'You must do what you think best, I suppose.' She glanced at her silent husband. 'Archie, ring the bell, will you?'

They were led upstairs by the maid, and then through a closed door and down a passage, which led to the nursery, a room that overlooked the grounds at the back of the house, comfortably furnished with rather a shabby lot of furniture, and much too warm. No wonder, thought Florence; there were no windows open, and there was a quite unnecessary fire in the old-fashioned grate too.

Phoebe was sitting at the table, a painting book and a paintbox before her, and opposite her was an elderly woman with a round, pasty face and beady eyes. She got up as they went in, wished Mr Fitzgibbon a good afternoon and stared at Florence.

He brought his considerable charm to bear upon her, so after a moment she relaxed, nodded a greeting to Florence and told Phoebe to say 'how do you do?' like a little lady.

'Hello,' said Phoebe, and went back to her painting. She would have been a pretty child but her illness had given her the look of an under-nourished waif, with eyes too big for her face and no colour in her cheeks.

Mr Fitzgibbon wasted no time. 'And how is the tipping and tapping going?'

'Well, sir, we don't bother with it—Phoebe doesn't like it, poor little lamb; she's happy to stay in this nice warm room with her old nanny, aren't you, love?'

Phoebe didn't answer her, but after a moment looked sideways at Florence. 'Who's she?'

'I've come to look at you and Sister Napier is here to help me. Dr Gibbs will be here directly.'

'I shan't,' said Phoebe.

Florence pulled out an armchair and sat down beside her. 'Why not?' she asked cheerfully. 'Do tell.'

'Just because...'

'We've come a long way,' said Florence, 'and Mr Fitzgibbon is a very busy man. Still, if you won't there's nothing for us to do but get into the car and drive all the way back to London.' She had picked up a paintbrush and was colouring an elephant bright red.

'Elephants aren't red!' said the child scornfully.

'No. But it's nice to do things wrong sometimes, isn't it?

Roses are red…do you go into the garden each day and smell them?'

'I'm too ill.'

'That's why Mr Fitzgibbon has come to see you; he'll examine you, and perhaps he'll tell you that you're not so ill any more, and then you can go into the garden.'

Florence finished the elephant and started to paint a zebra with purple stripes.

'I'm very highly strung,' said Phoebe, 'did you know?'

'I've often wondered what that meant—do you suppose you swing from the ceiling?'

Phoebe chuckled. 'I like you. I didn't like the other nurse—I bit her.'

'Ah, but you won't need to bite anyone today because you're getting better.'

Mr Fitzgibbon had been talking to Nanny, but he turned to look at Florence now. He asked, 'Aren't you afraid to get bitten, Florence?'

'Me, sir? Not in the least; in any case, I always bite back.'

He laughed, but Nanny frowned, and it was just as well that the door opened then and Dr Gibbs came in. He was elderly with a nice kind face, and he greeted Mr Fitzgibbon warmly.

'This is Sister Napier, who has replaced Sister Brice, and, since we're all here, shall we have an examination and then discuss the situation later? We are to spend the night. Sister Napier will carry out the tipping and tapping in the morning and let me know what progress has been made. I understand that it has been discontinued.'

'Yes, well, I'll tell you about that.' Dr Gibbs shook Florence's hand. 'If Nanny will allow us we can go into Phoebe's room…'

Phoebe was by no means an easy little patient; the examination took twice as long as it needed to, while Florence used all her patience and ingenuity to keep the child reasonably calm and still. The two men went away presently, leaving her to pacify Phoebe as she dressed her again and then handed her back to a suspicious Nanny.

Florence explained that she would have to rouse Phoebe in the morning and bore meekly the other woman's resentment. 'I'm sorry,' said Florence, 'but Mr Fitzgibbon has told me to do this, and he is in charge of the child. I'm sure you want the best possible treatment for her.'

She bade the still complaining child goodbye for the moment and found her way downstairs. Poor little Phoebe was an ill child and she need not have been—given a longer period in hospital and the proper treatment, she would have had a chance to live longer. Florence thought that once they had gone again Nanny would do exactly what she wanted, and any treatment Mr Fitzgibbon had ordered would be ignored.

She wasn't sure where she should go or what she should do—there was no sign of anyone. The two men would be discussing their findings or having tea with the Villierses, which reminded her that a cup of tea would be welcome. As there was no one in sight, she walked through the hall and out of the front door, and strolled along the carefully tended paths; they looked as though no one ever walked along them...

Mr Fitzgibbon, standing at the drawing-room window, listening to Mrs Villiers's peevish voice assuring him that she was far too sensitive to see that the treatment he had ordered was properly carried out and adding a list of her own ailments, allowed his eyes to stray to Florence, strolling along in the afternoon sunshine. Her copper hair glowed under the neat cap, and he thought that even in her severe uniform she looked exactly right in a rose garden.

He heard Mrs Villiers say fretfully, 'Well, I suppose we had better have a cup of tea. Do sit down, Mr Fitzgibbon, and you, Dr Gibbs. I suppose your nurse will want tea?'

'I am sure that Sister Napier would like that. I see that she is walking in the garden.'

'Archie, go and fetch her, will you?'

Conversation over tea was constrained, and Phoebe wasn't mentioned, but when the teacups had been carried away Mr Fitzgibbon observed, at his most bland, 'If I may I shall take Sister Napier into the garden and brief her as to tomorrow morning, and then perhaps we may have a talk about Phoebe.'

They were well away from the house when he asked, 'Well?'

'Well what, sir? If we're talking about Phoebe I think it's a crying shame that her treatment has been so neglected. If it had been carried out properly and she could have gone back into hospital... Can't you make them?' she asked fiercely.

'My dear girl, short of living here and sharing Phoebe's nursery, I see no way of altering things. I have suggested that they employ a nurse to care for the child. Mrs Villiers tells me, however, that Nanny wouldn't agree to that and she categorically refuses to discuss it. Dr Gibbs does what he can but, as you know, one cannot insist on treatment against the patient's wishes or, in the case of Phoebe, her parents'.'

'Nanny is angry that I must disturb Phoebe tomorrow morning.'

'I thought she might be. Would you like me to come along too?'

'At six o'clock in the morning?' She turned to look up at him. 'That wouldn't do at all.'

'I want to be away by nine o'clock. Dr Gibbs will be here at half-past eight—you will be ready?'

'Yes, sir.'

'Do you suppose,' asked Mr Fitzgibbon smoothly, 'that when there is no one around you might stop calling me sir with every other breath?'

Florence considered this. 'No, it wouldn't do at all.'

'It makes me feel elderly.'

'Nonsense, you're not in the least elderly. Do you suppose I'm to dine with you this evening, or have something on a tray?'

He stopped to look down at her with an air of cold surprise which quite shook her. 'Do you imagine that I would allow that? I am surprised at you even suggesting such an idea.'

'Well, I dare say you are, but Mrs Villiers wouldn't be...'

'Let us not waste time talking about her.' They turned to walk back towards the house. 'I'm operating tomorrow afternoon at two o'clock. Theatre Sister is on holiday, so I shall want you to scrub.'

'You tell me now!' exclaimed Florence. 'Really, you are— '

'Yes?' asked Mr Fitzgibbon softly.

'Never mind, sir. What are you going to do?'

'A lobectomy—you can manage that?'

'I shall do my best, sir.' She spoke sweetly, but her blue eyes flashed and the colour came into her cheeks.

'You are quite startlingly beautiful when you're cross,' said Mr Fitzgibbon, and opened the doors into the drawing-room so that she might go ahead of him.

She had been given a room near the nursery. It was pleasant enough, given that it was furnished with the impersonal style of a hotel bedroom. There was a bathroom next door, and she whiled away the hour before dinner lying in a very hot bath, thinking about Mr Fitzgibbon. The thoughts were wispy—odds and ends of conversations, the manner in which he could change from a pleasant companion to a reserved consultant, the expert way in which he handled his car, the way he had tackled what had appeared to be the hopeless task of freeing the man in the truck. 'I shall end up liking him if I go on like this,' said Florence, peering at her lobster-red person in the bathroom mirror.

Later, in bed and half asleep, she went over the evening. Dinner had been very formal, and the sight of Mrs Villiers in black chiffon and sequins had made her very aware of her uniform, even though it was the pristine one she had packed. The conversation had been stilted, with Mrs Villiers talking about her delicate constitution, her husband making very little effort to take part in the conversation, and Mr Fitzgibbon, with his beautiful manners, saying the right things at the right time. As for herself, she had answered when spoken to, listened to Mrs Villiers's grumbles with what she privately called her listening face, and allowed her thoughts to wander. They wandered all over the place and ended up at Mr Fitzgibbon as she fell asleep.

They left at nine o'clock the next morning, and Florence heaved a sigh of relief as Mr Fitzgibbon turned the car on to the road. The morning so far had been horrendous. Phoebe had been a handful, and Nanny had made her worse. Florence had longed to tell her that her cosseting of the child was doing more harm than good, but she guessed that Mr Fitzgibbon had already made that plain. She had eaten a solitary breakfast while he and Dr Gibbs had talked to the Villierses. She stole a look at his stern profile, and decided not to speak until spoken to.

They were more than halfway to the motorway before he said anything.

'We could have done a great deal for that child. Dr Gibbs will continue to urge them to let her go into hospital, but I'm afraid that by the time he does it may be too late to be of much help.'

Florence, despite her kicked shins, agreed with him. 'Poor scrap,' she said.

'You did very well, Florence, and I'm sorry that you weren't treated with better manners.'

'That didn't matter.'

He gave her a quick glance. 'You're a kind girl and you haven't uttered a single grumble. We'll stop at Milton Keynes and have a pot of coffee.'

They joined the M1 presently, travelling for the most part in silence. Florence was quite glad of that: it gave her a chance to check up on her theatre technique.

They stopped at the Post House in Milton Keynes and had their coffee and a plate of buns, not hurrying, and talking in a desultory fashion, and, although they didn't say much for

the rest of the journey, Florence found the silence comfortable. Perhaps their relationship was getting on to a more
friendly footing. She was surprised to realise that she very
much hoped so.

CHAPTER FIVE

MR FITZGIBBON left his consulting-rooms within minutes of arriving, staying only long enough to check Mrs Keane's carefully written messages and go through his post, leaving Florence with the advice that she should be at Colbert's not later than a quarter-past one. 'I have my own instruments there,' he went on, 'but it would be as well for you to check everything before we start.'

Well, of course it would, she agreed silently, and what about her lunch? He had gone without another word.

She said rather worriedly to Mrs Keane, 'Do you suppose I dare pop over to Mrs Twist's and ask her for a sandwich? She doesn't like me going there during the day...'

'I thought of that, dear.' Mrs Keane's cosy voice sounded pleased with itself. 'I bought some sausage rolls for you as I came in this morning. I remembered how poor Sister Brice would come back from somewhere or other, quite famished. I've got the kettle on; we'll have a cup of tea, and I'll eat my sandwiches at the same time and you can tell me all about it.'

Before she went to catch the bus to Colbert's Florence took a look at the appointments book. There were two patients for later that afternoon. She reckoned that Mr Fitzgibbon would have finished before four o'clock, but there were still his instruments to check before they went down to be sterilised and repacked. The first patient was booked for five o'clock; with luck she would be back at the consulting-rooms by then. She joined the queue for the bus and wondered just how quickly she would be able to change back into uniform.

Although she had worked as Staff Nurse in Theatre for some months, she felt uncertain about her reception, but she need not have worried. The staff nurse on duty was newly qualified and nervous.

'I'm glad it's you,' she confided as Florence got into her theatre kit, 'he scares me stiff, and he looks at you...'

'Well, yes,' agreed Florence, and thought that his eyes were rather nice; they could, of course, look like grey steel, but on the other hand they could look warm and amused. 'Now I'd better lay up my trolley.'

The anaesthetist remembered her as she walked in with the trolley, and he nodded to her in a friendly fashion. 'Hello, Florence, how nice to see you back. No chance of you staying with us?'

He checked his patient and settled down on his stool, and when she shook her head observed, 'Working for Fitzgibbon, aren't you? He's a lucky chap!'

Florence's lovely eyes crinkled in a smile behind her mask; a pity Mr Fitzgibbon wasn't there to hear that. He came a moment later, towering over everyone in his green gown. He wished everyone an affable good afternoon, and got down to work. He had his registrar with him and a houseman, rather timidly assisting, very much in awe of his chief. He had no need to be; Mr Fitzgibbon shed the light of his good humour over everyone there, so that the houseman became quite efficient and the little staff nurse, who was good at her job, forgot to be nervous of him. He worked unhurriedly and with the ease of long practice, and Florence, all the well-remembered routine taking over, handed instruments seconds before he held out a hand for them. All the while he carried on a casual conversation with the other men, so that the atmosphere, which had been rather fraught when he had first come in, became decidedly relaxed. In all, reflected Florence, getting out of the gown, a pleasant afternoon. She was carefully checking his instruments, which one of the nurses was washing before sending them to be sterilised, and she was still in her green theatre smock, when he came back into Theatre.

'How long will you be?' he asked.

'Me? Oh, fifteen minutes, sir. I'll be back in time for the first patient.'

'Make sure it is fifteen minutes—I'll be outside in the forecourt.'

'There's no…' She caught his eye, grey steel. 'Very well, sir,' she said, outwardly meek.

'He's never going to take you back with him?' said the little staff nurse.

'Well, I have to be at his consulting-rooms for the first patient, and I might get held up catching a bus,' said Florence practically.

She finished what she was doing calmly, got back into her dress and went down to the forecourt.

He was there, leaning on the car's bonnet, reading the first edition of the evening paper. He folded it away tidily and opened her door. Sitting beside her before starting the engine, he observed, 'You did very well, Florence.'

Her, 'Thank you, sir,' was uttered with just the right amount of meekness.

There was still a little time before the patient would arrive; she was pleased to see that Mrs Keane had the tea-tray ready and surprised when that lady said blithely, 'Tea is made, Mr Fitzgibbon, and I popped out for some of those biscuits you like. How handy the telephone is, to be sure, otherwise I wouldn't have known when you were coming back. I'll bring you a cup…'

'Thank you, Mrs Keane. The second patient has an appointment for half-past five, hasn't he? When you've shown him in, go home. Florence can do whatever else is necessary.'

'Well, if she doesn't mind…'

'Of course I don't mind; there'll be little enough to do anyway.' She eyed the biscuits hungrily. 'I'll get changed before I have my tea…'

Mr Fitzgibbon paused at the door. 'Did you have lunch?' he wanted to know.

'Mrs Keane was kind enough to get some sausage rolls for me this morning.'

'Sausage rolls?' He eyed her shapely person thoughtfully. 'An insufficient diet for one of your build, Florence.'

If he heard her indignant gasp as he turned away he gave no sign.

She had time for three cups of tea and almost all of the biscuits before the patient arrived, a youngish woman with her husband. She was a little frightened, and it was fearfully difficult to get clear answers to Mr Fitzgibbon's gently put questions. Florence, in attendance, reflected that he must be a kind man under his reserved manner. She mulled over the surprising information Mrs Keane had given her over their tea; he didn't only have a large out-patients clinic at Colbert's and operate there twice a week, but he also had another clinic in Bethnal Green, which dealt with the sad regiments of the homeless, sent to him from various charities. So many of them refused to go to a hospital, but the clinic was a different matter. He had willing helpers too—retired nurses, local doctors, social workers. 'Don't you ever mention it,' warned Mrs Keane. 'He never talks about it to anyone. He has to tell me, of course, because I keep his notes and do the bills and the rent and so forth for him. He's helped a good many there, I can tell you; gives them money, finds them jobs, and sometimes helps get them somewhere to live. I don't know how he finds the time, and him with a busy social life too.'

Florence showed the patient and her husband out, saw Mrs Keane on her way and, observant of Mr Fitzgibbon's bell, showed in the last patient.

An elderly, rather shabby man, but very neat; his manners were nice too. He wished her a polite good afternoon, volunteered his name—Mr Clarke—and sat down with the air of one expecting to wait.

'There's Mr Clarke, sir,' said Florence, sliding into the consulting-room.

'Ah, yes. Show him in, Florence, will you? I shan't be needing you for the moment. You could start tidying up.'

She gave him a cross look. Tidying up was none of his business—she was well aware of what had to be done and when. He was writing something, and without looking up he murmured, 'You wished to say something?'

'Yes, but I won't,' said Florence, and swept back into the waiting-room to usher Mr Clarke in.

As she closed the door she heard Mr Fitzgibbon's voice, friendly and calm. 'Mr Clarke, I'm so glad that you could come...'

She went and looked out of the window for a few moments, and then began her clearing up. There wasn't much to do. She put things ready for the morning and went to look at the appointments book. There was a slip of paper tucked into it and she looked at it idly. It was a note in Mr Fitzgibbon's scrawling handwriting, addressed to Mrs Keane, telling her to make an appointment for Mr Clarke, who should by rights have attended his out-patients clinic at Colbert's, but, owing to family circumstances, was unable to do so. 'No fees,' it ended.

Florence put it back where she had found it. It was getting very hard to dislike Mr Fitzgibbon.

She was roused from her thoughts by his voice on Mrs Keane's intercom, bidding her return. Mr Clarke had to be weighed, his blood-pressure taken, his pulse recorded and his respirations noted, and while she did these things she could see that the nice little man was upset and quite determined not to show it. Her small chores done, she went away again and presently showed him out before going into the examination-room to replace towels and the couch cover, clean up generally and stow everything that had been used in the laundry bag. She didn't hurry over this; the evening stretched before her and, although it was a lovely summer one, she was tired, mentally as well as physically. She would eat whatever supper Mrs Twist put before her and go to bed with a book. The appointment book was crammed for the next day and she felt reasonably sure that she wouldn't be able to get the evening train home. That couldn't be helped; she would go on Saturday morning, and in the afternoon she would take her mother into Sherborne and they would buy the washing-machine. Florence fingered the pay envelope in the pocket of her uniform and decided that, uncertain hours or not, it was worth it.

There was no sign of Mr Fitzgibbon and, since she was quite finished, she tapped on his door and went in. 'Is there anything more you would like done, sir?' she asked.

He closed the folder in which he had been writing. 'Nothing—I think we've crammed as much into today as we can, don't you? We've earned ourselves a meal. I've some work to finish here and I must go home. I'll call for you at Mrs Twist's house in an hour's time.'

'Are you inviting me out to dinner, Mr Fitzgibbon?' Her voice was tart.

He looked up briefly. 'Well, of course I am; had I not made myself plain?'

She hesitated: the invitation had sounded more like an order; on the other hand, the dinner he was offering would surely be more appetising than Mrs Twist's reliable but uninspired cooking. 'Thank you, sir, I should like to come.'

'Good, and for God's sake stop calling me sir.'

'Very well, Mr Fitzgibbon,' and then a little shyly, 'Do I need to dress up?'

His fine mouth twitched. 'No, no, there's a nice little place just off Wigmore Street, five minutes' walk from here.' He looked up and smiled at her, a slow, comforting smile. 'You must be tired.'

'I'll be ready in an hour, Mr Fitzgibbon.' She whisked away, very quickly got out of uniform and sped back to Mrs Twist, ready with apologies for not eating the supper which that good lady would have prepared for her, but she had no need of them: Mr Fitzgibbon had telephoned, and her landlady met her with a simpering smile and the opinion that Mr

Fitzgibbon was a gentleman right enough, and was Florence likely to be late back?

'Most unlikely,' said Florence in a matter-of-fact manner. 'We're both tired and tomorrow is booked solid. I may have to stay Friday night and catch an early train home on Saturday morning.'

'Perhaps he'll drive you home again?' suggested Mrs Twist, a woman with a romantic turn of mind.

'Most unlikely, Mrs Twist. Would you mind if I had my bath now instead of this evening?'

'You go ahead, and make the best of yourself,' advised Mrs Twist.

Advice which Florence intended to take. Nicely refreshed from her bath, she examined her wardrobe, searching for something suitable to wear to a nice little place within five minutes' walk. It was a pity, she reflected, that she had no idea what a nice little place consisted of in Mr Fitzgibbon's mind. She decided on a leaf-green crêpe dress with a square neckline and a little matching jacket, piled her copper hair into a chignon, thrust her feet into white sandals, found the little white handbag and put all that she might need into it, and took a last look at herself in the old-fashioned wardrobe mirror. Not being a conceited girl, she decided that she looked all right, thanking heaven that it was a fine evening and that she wouldn't need to take a coat. She hadn't got a suitable one anyway. She would get one on Saturday, she promised herself, and went downstairs, a few minutes early.

Mr Fitzgibbon was in Mrs Twist's front parlour, making himself agreeable to that lady. He had changed into a lighter suit and his tie was slightly less sombre than usual, and gold cuff-links gleamed discreetly from snow-white cuffs. He looked, thought Florence, extremely handsome; no wonder that Eleanor woman was after him. He stood up as she went in.

'Ah, Florence, punctual as always.' He studied her person without appearing to do so, bade Mrs Twist farewell and ushered her outside. 'You don't mind a very short walk? The car is outside the consulting-rooms if you would prefer to drive?'

'I'd like a walk. We don't have much time to take walks, do we?'

'Very little. Do you walk a lot at home?'

'Oh, yes. Miles—I sometimes cycle, though. Father has two villages in the parish as well as Gussage Tollard; when I'm at home I often have to help out with the Mothers' Union and choir practice, and then the bike comes in handy.'

'Do you like country life?'

'I was born and brought up in the vicarage—I went away to boarding-school, but only to Sherborne. I hated London when I came to Colbert's to train.'

'It is hardly a good part in which to live.'

They were walking through the quiet, dignified streets, and she looked round her. 'Well, no, but this is quite different; one could live in any of these streets and be quite content. Though I'd miss the country...'

'A weekend cottage in the country would settle that question, wouldn't it?'

Florence laughed. 'Very nicely. I must look round for a wealthy man with a house round about here and another one in some pretty village.'

He said dreamily, 'There are plenty of wealthy men living in and around this area...'

'I'm sure that there are, only I don't have the chance to meet any of them.'

She looked up at him and laughed. 'Isn't it nice to talk nonsense sometimes?' They were in a narrow side-street, and a moment later he ushered her down some steps into a quite small restaurant, its tables covered in snowy linen and set with gleaming cutlery and lighted by candles. It was fairly full, and Florence was relieved to see that her dress would pass muster. She sat down and glanced around her unself-consciously with frank pleasure. It was an attractive place with white walls, upon which hung some rather nice flower paintings, and the seats were comfortable, the tables not too close together and the waiter, when he came, most attentive.

The menu was impressive and there were no prices upon it, a fact which left her in some doubt as to what to order. Small it might be, but she had a suspicion that it was expensive.

Mr Fitzgibbon, watching her from under drooping lids, smiled to himself.

'I don't know about you,' he observed, 'but I'm hungry. How about crab mousse to start with, noisettes of lamb—they do a splendid sauce with them—and we can choose a sweet later?'

Much relieved, she agreed at once, and agreed again when he suggested a dry sherry while they waited. 'This is a delightful place—why, you wouldn't even know it was here, would you?'

He understood her. 'Nicely hidden away and quiet.'

For something to say she asked, 'I expect you've been here before?'

'Several times.' He smiled at her across the table; she really looked charming sitting there opposite him, the candlelight turning her hair to burnished gold. The dress, he decided, was by no means new or in the forefront of fashion, and she had no jewellery, only a plain gold chain and her watch. He found himself comparing her with Eleanor, who had phoned that evening and demanded that he should take her to some party or other. He had drifted into a casual friendship with her over the years, and although he wasn't in love with her he had found himself wondering if he might marry her. He wanted a wife, a home life and children, but not with Eleanor; the certainty of that had been in his mind for several weeks, although he had ignored it. Now, watching Florence, he acknowledged it.

He began a trivial conversation, touching on a variety of subjects. Over the lamb he asked casually, 'You like reading?'

She popped some delicious garden peas into her mouth. 'Oh, yes. Anything I can lay hands on...'

'Poetry?'

'Well, yes, I like John Donne and the Brownings—oh, and Herrick; I'd rather read a book, though.'

'*Jane Eyre*?' he asked with a twinkle. '*Pride and Prejudice*, *Wuthering Heights*, anything by—what is her name?—M M Kaye?'

Florence speared a baby carrot. 'However did you know? Yes, I read all those. I like gentle books, if you see what I mean.'

'Yes, I see. You're a gentle girl, Florence. Because you're a parson's daughter?'

She took the remark seriously. 'Yes, probably, but I do have a very nasty temper.'

'So do I, Florence, although I flatter myself that I can control it unless I'm severely provoked.'

'Well, I don't suppose that happens very often,' said Florence comfortably. 'People always seem to do what you want straight away, but, of course, you're important, aren't you?'

She looked up, smiling, and met a steely grey stare. 'Are you buttering me up, Florence?'

She refused to be intimidated. 'Good heavens, no. Why should I do that? Anyway, it's true, and I'm sorry if you're mad at me. Father is always telling me to think before I speak.'

'It is I who should apologise, Florence. Feel free to say what you want without thinking first.'

'Excepting when I'm at work, of course.'

'Having settled the matter, let us turn our attention to a sweet. Biscuit glacé, perhaps, with strawberries? Or a crème brûlée?'

'I'd like the biscuit glacé, please; I can make a crème brûlée at home...'

He ordered, and asked for the cheese board for himself. 'You can cook?'

'Well, of course I can, and I had plenty of opportunity to

try out recipes while I was looking after Mother. I suppose all women can cook; it comes naturally, like making beds and ironing shirts.' She was matter-of-fact.

He reflected that he had never had the opportunity of knowing if Eleanor could do any of those things, but it seemed unlikely. He must remember to ask her next time they met. The thought that he was enjoying himself engendered a wish to repeat the occasion.

They had their coffee and walked back presently, and at Mrs Twist's door he took the key from her. 'Do we have to look out for Buster?'

'No, he'll be with Mrs Twist upstairs.' She took back the key. 'Thank you for my dinner, Mr Fitzgibbon; it was a lovely evening.'

'It was a pleasure, Florence.'

He opened the door and she went inside. 'Goodnight, and thank you again.'

His 'Goodnight, Florence,' was quietly said as she closed the door.

She wasn't quite sure what she expected when she got to work the next morning, but it certainly wasn't Mr Fitzgibbon's cold stare and equally cold 'Good morning.' He was seated at his desk, looking so unlike the pleasant companion of the previous evening that the smile faded from her pretty face, and at the first opportunity she sought out Mrs Keane to ask her if she had done or not done something.

'Don't worry, dear,' soothed Mrs Keane, 'I know he's very pleased with your work. Something's on his mind—or someone; that Eleanor, I suppose...'

'Are they engaged or—or anything?'

'No, nor likely to be: he's no more in love with her than I am. He's thirty-six now, and if you ask me he's never been in love—not enough to want to marry. For one thing he's too busy, and for another she'd have to be a girl who could get past that austere manner.'

'He's not always austere,' said Florence, remembering the previous evening.

Mrs Keane gave her a quick look. 'No, dear, but only a few people know that.' She put on the kettle. 'There's time for a cup of tea now if we're quick, before the first patient comes; we can have coffee later. I'll see to the percolator and have the coffee ready, and you can take him a cup then.'

The first patient arrived and Florence turned into an impersonal automaton, doing what was required of her and then melting into the background until she was needed again, carefully not looking higher than Mr Fitzgibbon's firm chin, and when the patient had gone she fetched his coffee and set the cup and saucer down on his desk gently, suppressing a sudden and surprising wish to throw the lot at him. She wasn't at all sure why, but it might have relieved her feelings.

The last patient for the morning had gone when he was called away to the hospital, and half an hour later he rang to say that the afternoon patients would have to be notified that he would be delayed. 'Postpone the first appointment for half an hour,' he told Mrs Keane, 'and the rest for the same time.'

'There goes my chance to get the evening train,' said Florence crossly. 'That's two weekends running. Do you mind if I use the phone to let Mother know?'

'Perhaps that nice Mr Fitzgibbon will drive you down again, love,' said her mother in a pleased voice.

Florence snorted. 'It's the last thing he'll do,' she said snappily, 'and he's not all that nice.'

She was instantly sorry. 'I didn't mean that, Mother. I'm to stay, and I've got my pay packet—we'll go into Sherborne tomorrow afternoon and buy a washing-machine.'

'Oh, darling, how lovely, but I think you should spend your money on some new clothes.'

'Next month, Mother. I must go—see you tomorrow. Let Father know, won't you?'

There were four appointments in the afternoon, and Mr Fitzgibbon took his time over each one of them. Since one patient telephoned to say that she would be unable to come until later in the afternoon, there was a half-hour's wait. Mrs

Keane made tea and Florence got as far as she could with the clearing up, but since there were still two patients to come it seemed a waste of time. She took him a cup of tea, outwardly serene and inwardly seething with impatience.

'You will be unable to go home this evening,' remarked Mr Fitzgibbon. 'A pity, but it cannot be helped. Our friend from the truck had a secondary haemorrhage, and it was necessary to take him back to Theatre.'

'Oh, how awful. Will he be all right? Was it his stump?'

'No, the chest wound. I've had another look and found the trouble. He should do now.' He bent his head over the papers on his desk and she went away, feeling that she would have liked to tell him how mean she felt, moaning because she had had to miss her train while all the while he had been dealing with an emergency. She told Mrs Keane while they drank their tea and was comforted by her sensible observation that, since she hadn't known about it, she had no need to feel guilty.

The delayed patient had come for a check-up and took up a mere twenty minutes of Mr Fitzgibbon's time, but the last patient, a middle-aged and timid lady, accompanied by her husband, took up twice that time, partly because before any examination could be done she needed to be soothed and encouraged. Afterwards, when Florence was helping her to dress again, she felt faint, which delayed her departure for even longer. Florence tucked her up on the examination couch and put a comforting arm around her shoulders while she had a little weep. 'Why does it have to be me?' she demanded tearfully. 'I don't even smoke cigarettes. Do you suppose that Mr Fitzgibbon can really cure me?'

'Certainly he can if he said so,' said Florence stoutly, 'and you don't have to worry about the operation; you really won't know anything about it, and you'll be well again within weeks—you heard him say so. Now I'm going to tell him that you're ready, and you'll go back into the consulting-room and he'll explain everything to you. You can ask him any questions that you want to; he's a kind man and very clever.'

'You are a dear, sweet girl, putting up with an old woman's nonsense.' She patted Florence's arm. 'Shall I see you again?'

'Oh, yes, in a few weeks' time when you come for a check-up after surgery. I shall look forward to seeing you then.'

There was quite a lot to do once the elderly pair had left. Florence took herself off to the examination-room and began to set it to rights, and then put her head round the door to ask if Mr Fitzgibbon would like a cup of coffee.

He refused, still working at his desk, and as she withdrew her head the phone rang. 'Answer that, will you,' he asked her, 'and see who it is?'

Eleanor, thought Florence, and she was right. The piercing voice sounded petulant and demanding, and asked to speak to Mr Fitzgibbon.

'Miss Paton wishes to speak to you, sir.'

He growled something softly and took the phone from her. As Florence went out of the room, closing the door very, very slowly, she heard him say, 'Eleanor, I am extremely busy...' She held the door-handle so that there was still a crack before she closed it, and nodded her head with satisfaction at his, 'No, quite impossible, I shall be working...!'

Mr Fitzgibbon, watching the door-handle soundlessly turning, smiled, paying not the slightest attention to Eleanor's petulant voice.

When Florence went back presently to say that everything was attended to and did he wish her to remain any longer? he lifted his head from his writing to tell her baldly that he needed nothing more and she had no need to stay. He wished her a good night in a voice which suggested that he had no wish to enter into conversation of any kind, and picked up his pen again.

Florence's 'Goodnight,' was crisp. He might at least have expressed regret at her having to miss her evening train. I hope she pesters him to take her out and makes him spend a lot of money at some glitzy restaurant, thought Florence, going back to one of Mrs Twist's wholesome suppers.

Mr Fitzgibbon went home to the charming little Georgian house not ten minutes' drive from his rooms, changed into elderly, beautifully tailored tweeds, told Crib, the elderly man who ran his home with the help of his wife, that he would be back on Sunday night, whistled to Monty, that dog of no known breed, and got back into his car.

Once out of London, he took the A30 and just over two hours later slowed the car as he reached the first grey stone thatched cottages of Mells. It was a small village with a lovely church, a manor-house and a cluster of these same cottages in a charming group dominated by the church and the village inn. Mr Fitzgibbon drove through the centre of the village, and half a mile along a narrow lane turned the car through an open gate and stopped before a low, rambling house built of the same grey and yellow stone as the cottages, but with a red-tiled roof. The front door stood open and he was met on the doorstep by a short, stout woman with a round rosy face and grey hair screwed up into a fierce bun.

'There you are, Mr Alexander, right on time, too. Good thing you phoned when you did—I had time to get Mr Letts to come up with the nicest piece of steak for your supper.' She paused and he bent to hug her.

'Just what I need, Nanny, and how nice to see you.' He let Monty out of the car and they all went indoors, through the stone-flagged hall to a low-ceilinged room with a great inglenook and lattice windows. Doors opened on to the garden behind the house, a lovely place, a riot of roses and summer flowers, with a wide lawn leading down to a narrow stream.

'You're on your own?' asked Nanny unnecessarily.

'Yes, Nanny...'

'Doesn't like the country, does she, that Miss Paton?'

He said evenly, 'No, I'm afraid it isn't quite the life for her.' He had sat down in a great chair and Monty had flopped at his feet. Presently he went on, 'You were quite right, Nanny...'

'Of course I was, Mr Alexander. You just wait until the right girl comes along.'

'She has, but she doesn't know it yet.'

Nanny sat down on a small chair opposite him. She didn't say a word, only waited.

'She's a parson's daughter, a nurse, and she works for me.'

'She likes you?'

'I think so, but not at first, and even now I catch her looking at me as though she wasn't sure of that. On the other hand...'

'Give her time, Mr Alexander.' Nanny got up. 'I'll get your supper; you must be famished, and that nice dog of yours.'

He was up early the next morning and, with Monty beside him, inspected the garden before breakfast. The thought that he was barely an hour's drive away from Florence's home was persistent in his mind but he refused to listen to it. After breakfast he went into the village, where he met the rector and returned with him to have coffee at the rectory. The rector was a keen gardener and the hours passed pleasantly. After lunch he stretched out on the lawn and slept until Nanny called him in to tea. Then he and Monty took themselves off for a long walk before spending a convivial hour in the Talbot Arms. In the evening, after the splendid dinner Nanny put before him, he sat in the lovely drawing-room, thinking about Florence. At length he got up to go to bed, saw Monty into his basket in the kitchen, locked up and turned off the lights before going up the oak staircase to his room. The night was clear and there was a waning moon. He stood by the open window, wondering if Florence was looking at the same moon, and then laughed wryly. 'I'm behaving like a lovesick boy,' he muttered, 'and more than likely she doesn't give a second thought to me...'

Florence wasn't looking at the moon, she was in bed and asleep, but she had from time to time during the day thought about him. She had taken herself to task over this. 'We haven't anything in common except our work,' she told Charlie Brown, snoozing on her bed. 'He lives in London, though I don't know where—in some hideously expensive modern flat, I suppose—and he likes expensive restaurants and big cars, and he hardly ever laughs. And he never looks at me...'

She was wrong, of course, about that.

It was at Sunday lunch that her mother asked, 'I suppose that nice Mr Fitzgibbon has to work at the weekend?'

'I've no idea,' said Florence, 'but I shouldn't think so— he must have a private life.'

'A great many firm friends if he's not married, I expect,' suggested Mrs Napier. 'Handsome single men are always in great demand.'

Florence was filled with a sudden fierce dislike of that. She said, 'I dare say; I really don't know anything about him, Mother.' As she spoke she wished that she did. Where did he go when he left the consulting-rooms, for instance? Did he have parents and live with them, or brothers and sisters? And his friends—surely there must be others than the horrid Eleanor? She could think of no way of finding out, and suddenly she wanted to know quite badly. She reminded herself once again that she was getting too interested in him, and spent the rest of the day gardening with unnecessary energy, and, although she hated leaving home that evening, there was a spark of excitement deep down inside her at the idea of seeing him again.

She went to work a little earlier than usual, a habit she had formed on a Monday morning, to make sure that everything was just so. She was rearranging flowers in a bowl kept filled throughout the year in the waiting-room when Mr Fitzgibbon came in.

A small wave of pleasure at the sight of him left her feeling surprised; there was no particular reason why she should be glad to see him—he hadn't been over-friendly on Friday evening. She bade him good morning and was relieved when he answered her with brisk cheerfulness and a quick smile.

He didn't stop to talk; he went straight to his consulting-room and began on his post, so that when Mrs Keane arrived he called her in at once to take his letters. He saw two patients and then took himself off to Colbert's, leaving Florence and Mrs Keane to get ready for the busy afternoon ahead of them.

Mrs Keane, her hands poised over her typewriter, waited until his footsteps had ceased in the house before observing, 'I wonder what is making him so thoughtful? And absent-minded—he usually rattles off his letters, but this morning he kept going off into a world of his own. There's something on his mind...'

'That Eleanor—she phoned on Friday evening,' said Florence, tucking a clean sheet on the couch and raising her voice through the open door. 'But he said he couldn't take her out. Do you suppose he's met someone he likes better?'

Mrs Keane bent over her notebook. 'I've no doubt of it,' she said with quiet satisfaction.

CHAPTER SIX

THE day's work went smoothly; Mr Fitzgibbon returned directly after lunch and the whole afternoon was taken up with his patients. Usually Mrs Keane booked appointments so that there was a brief lull halfway through the afternoon, enabling them to have a cup of tea, but today there was no let-up, and by five o'clock Florence was tired and a little cross beneath her seemingly composed appearance, and the prospect of the evening spent alone in her room was uninviting. Mrs Twist would be out, spending the evening with friends, and there would only be Buster for company. Showing the last patient out with smiling friendliness, she decided to go out for the evening herself. She had money—not a great deal, but quite enough to take her to some quiet little restaurant where she could get a modest meal. She would have to get a bus to Oxford Street, where there was bound to be somewhere to suit her taste. She bustled around, drank her tea thankfully, took a cup to an unsmiling Mr Fitzgibbon, and, everything being in apple-pie order, asked if there was anything else he wished her to do.

He looked up briefly. 'No, thank you, Florence; enjoy your evening. Are you going out?'

She beamed at him. 'Yes—for a meal. Goodnight, sir.'

He bade her goodnight in a cool voice and sat looking at the closed door after she had gone. It was, he argued to himself, most irritating that the girl treated him in such a manner; he had no idea what she really thought of him. At times he thought that she liked him, and then she withdrew, becoming a cross between tolerant youth making allowances for middle age and a waspish young woman ready to answer back. He sighed, admitting at last to himself that he wanted Florence for his wife but that persuading her to be of like mind would probably be a delicate undertaking. Mr Fitzgibbon sat back and considered how best to set about the matter, unaware that kindly providence was about to lend him a hand.

Florence let herself into Mrs Twist's house, fed Buster, inspected the corned-beef salad in the fridge for her supper, put it back and went to her room to change. It was well past six o'clock but she took the opportunity to have a bath, since Mrs Twist was prone to remind her that hot water cost money so that she felt compelled to have a shower when that lady was home. Now she luxuriated at some length in an extravagant amount of hot water, dressed unhurriedly, coiled her hair in a smooth chignon, made sure that she had her key and enough money, and left the house. Outside on the pavement, she remembered that Mr Fitzgibbon had still been in his rooms when she had left and, for all she knew, he might still be there. She had no wish to encounter him and, remembering Mrs Twist telling her that there was a short cut which would bring her out almost by Cavendish Square, well past the consulting-rooms, she decided to take it.

It was a narrow street with small, neat houses on either side; there were cars parked on one side of it, but otherwise it was empty. It was later than she had intended, for she had dawdled over her dressing and spent ten minutes sitting on the stairs with Buster, who had been feeling lonely, but the June evening was still light and would be for some time to come. She walked on, hardly noticing that the houses were becoming shabby, for she was allowing her imagination full rein; Mr Fitzgibbon would be spending his evening with Eleanor, no doubt; she didn't think that he was very in love with her, though, but Florence guessed that she was too clever to give him a chance to know that. Men, she thought, might be very clever and all that, but they could be singularly blind at times. She looked around her then and saw how the street had changed from neatness to a neglected, rubbish-strewn thoroughfare with paint peeling off the front doors and grubby curtains at the windows. She must have mistaken Mrs Twist's directions, and she was relieved to see a main street ahead of her, busy with cars. She stepped out more briskly and at the same time became aware that she was being followed.

She didn't turn round, nor did she increase her pace, although it was the one thing she would have liked to do. Common sense told her that she was near enough to the end of the street to scream for help if she needed to, and to show unease might spur on whoever it was behind her... Getting closer, too...

She hadn't realised how close: a large, heavy hand caught her by the shoulder and forced her to stop.

Mr Fitzgibbon, on the way home and the last in the queue at the traffic-lights, looked round him idly, marvelling for the hundredth time how it was possible for such neglected, down-at-heel streets to be cheek by jowl with the elegance around them. It was then that providence, metaphorically speaking, tapped him on one massive shoulder so that his glance strayed into the street alongside the car. He saw that copper head of hair immediately; he also saw that its owner was in difficulties. He was out of the car and into the street, oblivious of anything other than the need to get to Florence as fast as possible. For a man of his size, he was a quick mover. He was very nearly there when he saw her kick hard backwards with sufficiently good result to make the man yelp. He was on him then, removing him with a great arm, shaking him like a terrier shook a rat.

'I advise you not to do that again, my man,' said Mr Fitzgibbon without heat, 'or it will be the worse for you.' He let him go and watched him run back down the street before he turned to Florence.

'And what the hell were you doing, strolling down this back street, asking for trouble—a great girl like you...?'

Florence gulped. Being called a great girl in that coldly furious voice was upsetting; worse, it sparked off the temper her parents had been at pains to teach her to control from an early age. She was a bit shaken and a trifle pale, and her voice wobbled just a little, but more with temper than fright. She said with great dignity, 'I am not a great girl...'

'We'll argue about that in the car—I'll be had up for obstruction...'

He took her by the arm and marched her along willy-nilly. 'I don't wish—' she began, but he stowed her into the car without a word, got in himself and drove on.

'A miracle that there is no traffic or police around,' he observed grimly. It wasn't a miracle but providence, of course.

He took the car round Cavendish Square and into Regent Street, turning off into side-streets before he reached Piccadilly and coming out at the lower end of Park Lane and so into Knightsbridge.

Florence, who had sat silently fuming, said, 'This is Knightsbridge; why are you bringing me here?'

He didn't answer but turned into a quiet side-street lined with rather grand houses, and presently turned again under an archway into a narrow tree-lined street. The houses were smaller here but very elegant, painted white, their front doors gleaming with black paint. He stopped before the end house, got out, opened her door and invited her to get out.

'No,' said Florence, and then, catching the look in his eye, she got out, but once on the pavement she didn't budge. 'Why have you brought me here? And where is it anyway? I'm obliged to you for your—your help just now, but...' she paused, pink in the face, her blue eyes flashing '...a great girl like me can look after herself.' She frowned because she suspected that she had got the grammar wrong somewhere.

Mr Fitzgibbon smiled, not very nicely, took her by the arm in a gentle but firm grasp, and marched her to his front door. Crib opened it, and if he was surprised he showed no sign of it, but bade his master a good evening and added a respectful good evening to Florence.

'Ah, Crib, this is Miss Napier, my practice nurse; she has

had an unfortunate encounter in the street. Will you ask Mrs Crib to show her where she can tidy herself?' And, when Crib bustled off down the narrow hall and through a baize door at its end, Mr Fitzgibbon observed in an aloof way, 'You will be better when you have had a drink and a meal.'

'I feel perfectly all right,' snapped Florence, but she couldn't go on because a tall thin woman in a severe grey dress had come through the door and was advancing towards them.

'Good evening, sir,' she smiled at Florence, 'and good evening to you too, miss. If you will come with me?'

She led Florence, speechless and cross, up the graceful little staircase to one side of the hall. 'I hear you've had some kind of accident, miss,' she remarked as they reached the landing. 'There is a cloakroom in the hall, but I dare say you might like a few minutes' peace and quiet if you have been upset.'

She opened a door and ushered Florence into a charming bedroom; its windows overlooked the back of the house and gave a view of a small pretty garden. It was furnished in maple-wood, carpeted in white and curtained in apricot silk. The bedspread on the small bed was of the same material and so were the lampshades, and the walls were a pale tint of the same colour. 'Oh, what a darling room,' said Florence, quite forgetting that she was annoyed.

'One of the guest rooms, miss. The bathroom is through the door there, and if you fancy a nice lie down the *chaise-longue* is very comfortable.'

The housekeeper gave her a kindly smile and went away, and, left to herself, Florence inspected her surroundings more thoroughly. The room was indeed delightful and so was the bathroom, stocked with towels, soap and everything a guest could wish for. Perhaps it had been left ready for a visitor; it seemed a shame to use the soap and one of the fluffy towels so enticingly laid out on one of the glass shelves. However, she had to wash; the man's hand had been dirty, and she could still feel its grimy, sweaty fingers as she had instinctively tried to drag it from her shoulder. She took a look at herself in the wide mirror. There was a dirty mark on her dress and her hair was a mess...!

She went downstairs again some ten minutes later, once more nicely made-up, her fiery head of hair brushed smooth. Her dress had been creased but she couldn't do anything about that, although she had got rid of most of the dirty mark.

There was no one in the hall and she stood, irresolute, at the bottom of the staircase, but only for a moment. Mr Fitzgibbon flung open a door opposite her. 'Come in, come in.' He sounded impatient. 'That's a comfortable chair by the window. What would you like to drink?'

She stood by the door. 'Nothing, thank you, sir. You've been very kind, but I won't trespass upon your time any more.' When he didn't speak she added, 'I'm most grateful...'

He crossed the room, took her by the arm and sat her down in the chair he had indicated. 'A glass of sherry,' he observed, and handed it to her. 'There's nothing like it for restoring ill-humour.'

'I am not ill-humoured,' began Florence, determined to make it clear, which, seeing that she was boiling with rage, hardly made sense.

'You are as cross as two sticks,' said Mr Fitzgibbon genially. 'You are also foolish and most regrettably untruthful.'

Florence had taken a sip of sherry and choked on it, but before she could summon breath to utter he had sat down opposite her, a glass in his hand, the picture of good-natured ease. 'When you have your breath back,' he suggested, 'I should like to know why you were in that disreputable street and why, having told me that you were going out for a meal, you had done no such thing. Did he stand you up?'

'Stand me up? Who?'

'You were intending to dine out alone?'

'Well, what's so funny about that? And I wasn't going to dine. How can you be so silly? On my salary? I was going to Oxford Street to McDonald's or somewhere like that.' She added to make things clearer, 'Mrs Twist's out this evening and it was corned beef and tomatoes.'

Mr Fitzgibbon hid a smile. 'Did you need to fib about it? I am afraid I can't quite see...' He watched the lovely pink creep into her face and saw. 'You were afraid that I might think you were fishing for another meal...'

'What a simply horrid thing to say,' she burst out.

'It's the truth,' he pointed out blandly.

'Well, even if it is, you don't have to say it—I mean, you can think it if you want to but you don't have to put it into words.'

She tossed off the sherry in a defiant way, and he got up and refilled her glass. 'Now I want to know why you were wandering around, asking to be mugged. If you intend to go to Oxford Street you could have kept to Wimpole Street until you came to the bus-stop.'

She managed not to blush this time, but she looked so guilty that Mr Fitzgibbon, watching her from beneath his lids, knew that she was about to tell him some more fibs.

'Well,' began Florence, 'Mrs Twist told me about this short-cut, and it was such a nice evening and the street really looked quite respectable when I started. I thought it would make a nice change.'

It sounded a bit thin, and she could see that Mr Fitzgibbon thought it was too, for his rather stern mouth was turned down at the corners. All the same, what he said was, 'Oh, indeed?' and then, 'I do hope you will give me the pleasure of your company at dinner. I'll drive you back presently.' When she hesitated he added, 'Oxford Street will be packed out with people wanting a meal after the cinema.'

A statement made at random but which reassured her. 'Oh, will it? I hadn't thought of that. We used to go to the local cinema when I was at Colbert's. Are you sure that Mrs Crib won't mind? I mean, will she have cooked enough for two?'

He assured her gravely that Mrs Crib always allowed for the unexpected guest, and began to talk gently about nothing much, putting her at her ease, and when Monty came prancing in from the garden and offered her head for a scratch, looking up at her with melting eyes, she felt all at once quite at home.

'This is a beautiful room,' she told her host. 'You must enjoy coming home to it each evening.'

It was a lovely room, comfortably large, and furnished with a nice mixture of Regency pieces and large chairs and sofas, the kind of sofas where one might put one's feet up or curl into a corner. The curtains at the windows were brocade in what she imagined one would call mulberry-red, and the thin silk carpets scattered on the polished wood floor held the same colour mixed with dull blues and greens. The walls were panelled and for the most part covered by paintings, and there was a bow-fronted cabinet along one wall, filled with fine china and silver. The fireplace was at one end of the room—Adam, she guessed—and in the winter it would hold an open fire. She gave a small sigh, not of envy but of contentment, just because she was enjoying all these things, even if only for an hour or so.

Crib came in to tell them that dinner was served, and they crossed the hall to a smaller room with crimson wallpaper and a rectangular mahogany dining-room table, large enough to seat eight people and set with lace table-mats, sparkling glass and silver. There was a bowl of roses on the table, and Florence asked, 'Are they from your garden?' and, when he nodded, 'The yellow one—isn't that Summer Sunshine? Father plans to get one for next year. I don't suppose you have much time for gardening?'

Crib put a plate of soup before her, and her lovely nose twitched at its delicious aroma. Mr Fitzgibbon studied the nose at some length without appearing to do so. 'No, I should like more time for it. I do potter at intervals, though.'

Florence addressed herself to the soup. Lettuce and cucumber, and not out of a tin either. She had quite forgotten how annoyed she had been at Mr Fitzgibbon's high-handed treatment; indeed, she hadn't felt so happy for a long time, although she didn't trouble to wonder why. The soup plates were removed, and cold chicken, salad and a snowy mound of creamed potatoes were offered. Mr Fitzgibbon poured white wine, passed the pepper and salt and made conversation in an easy manner while he watched Florence enjoying the meal with unselfconscious pleasure, comparing her in his mind with other dinner companions who had shuddered at the idea of a second helping and shunned the potatoes. He frowned a little; he was allowing himself to get too interested in the girl...wanting her for his wife had been a flight of fancy.

Florence saw the frown and some of her happiness ebbed away. After their rather unfortunate encounter that evening—well, fortunate for her, she conceded—even though they hadn't seen eye to eye to begin with, the last half-hour had been delightful, but now he looked forbidding and any moment she would find herself addressing him as 'sir'. She declined more potatoes politely and refused more wine. As soon as she decently could she would think of some excuse to get her out of the house, and the sooner the better.

First there was apple pie and cream to be eaten and polite small talk to be maintained. The small talk became so stilted that he looked at her in surprise. Now what was the matter with the tiresome girl? Still polite and beautifully mannered, but stiff as a poker. She responded willingly to his remarks, but the pleasant feeling that they were old friends, even though they knew very little about each other, had vanished.

They went back to the drawing-room for their coffee, and after half an hour of what Florence privately called polite conversation she said that she should be getting back. 'Mrs Twist might be worried...' she suggested, to which Mr Fitzgibbon made no reply, merely lifted the receiver and phoned that lady, who, it seemed, wasn't in the least worried.

'But, of course,' he said smoothly, 'you would like a good night's sleep—we have a busy day ahead of us tomorrow.'

A gentle reminder that she worked for him and it behoved her to be on duty at the right time. Or so it seemed to her.

She thanked him once again on Mrs Twist's doorstep, and

later, getting ready for bed, reflected on her evening. There had been no need for Mr Fitzgibbon to take her to his home and ask her to dinner, so why had he done it? And why had he become remote, evincing no wish to hinder her from going back to her room at Mrs Twist's? She had thought once or twice just lately that they were on the verge of a cautious friendship. There was no understanding the man, she thought, punching her rather hard pillows into a semblance of softness.

In the morning everything was as usual; he arrived punctually, reminded her that his first patient was deaf, commented upon the delightful morning and made no mention of the previous evening. There was, of course, no reason why he should—all the same, she was unreasonably put out.

The deaf patient took up a good deal of time and made everyone else late, but Mr Fitzgibbon went placidly on as though the morning had ten hours to it instead of five, so that their usual lunch-break was cut short about ten minutes. She and Mrs Keane ate their sandwiches and drank a pot of tea between them, thankful that Mr Fitzgibbon had taken himself off, leaving them free to get the place straight for the afternoon patients.

'Quite a busy day,' said Mrs Keane placidly, arranging the patients' notes in a neat pile on his desk while Florence restored the examination-room to a pristine state. He returned five minutes before his first appointment and spent them on the phone to Colbert's, and after that there was no let-up until after five o'clock. Mr Fitzgibbon was at his desk, writing and being interrupted by the telephone, Mrs Keane had just made a pot of tea, and Florence was carrying a cup to him, when the waiting-room door was thrust open and Eleanor Paton came in on a wave of exquisite scent and looking ravishing in a wild-silk outfit which Florence, in a few seconds' glance, instantly coveted.

Eleanor went past her without speaking, taking the cup and saucer from her as she went, opening the consulting-room door without knocking and going inside.

'Who was that?' asked Mrs Keane, poking her nose round the kitchen door.

'Miss Paton,' said Florence quietly while she damped down rage. 'She just walked in, took his tea and went inside...'

'I'd like to be a fly on the wall,' said Mrs Keane. 'Come and have your tea, dear. Do you suppose we should take in another cup for her?'

'I don't think she would like tea-bags.'

They drank their tea and Florence, who had excellent hearing, listened to Eleanor's high-pitched voice and the occasional rumble of Mr Fitzgibbon's. There was no laughter—it sounded more like an argument, as Eleanor's tones became shrill and his became briefer.

Presently they heard the door open, and the pair of them crossed the waiting-room and out of the door, the signal for Florence to nip to the window. Mr Fitzgibbon's car was outside but he wasn't getting into it, and in a moment she saw Eleanor walking away down the street. And she didn't look round.

Florence withdrew her head cautiously and stepped back; she didn't want Mr Fitzgibbon to see her peering from his window. Her fears were ungrounded, however; he hadn't got into his car—indeed, he was standing so close to her that she felt his waistcoat sticking into the small of her back.

'Snooping?' he asked gently.

She didn't turn round but edged away from him. 'Certainly not,' she said with dignity, fingers crossed because she was telling a fib. 'I thought that you might have gone and forgotten to let us know...'

Being a parson's daughter was a terrible drawback sometimes. She turned to face him. 'No, that was a silly excuse. I looked out of the window to watch you drive Miss Paton away.'

'However, I didn't, and does that please you?'

She met his cold grey eyes steadily. 'It's none of my business, sir. I'm sorry I was—was nosy.'

'You are a very unsettling girl, Florence.' He went into his consulting-room and closed the door quietly, leaving her prey to the thought of getting a month's notice; it seemed like a strong hint that he had changed his mind about taking her on permanently. Perhaps Eleanor had persuaded him that she had been unsuitable, and she had played right into the girl's hands, hadn't she?

She went back into the examination-room, made sure that it was quite ready for the next day and then washed the cups and saucers and tidied everything away while Mrs Keane did the last of her filing. Ten minutes later Mr Fitzgibbon reappeared, bade them both a civil good evening, and went away, so that they were free to leave.

After she had eaten her supper Florence sat in Mrs Twist's small back garden; she had no heart for a walk and, since her landlady was going to spend her evening with a neighbour and had no objection to Florence sitting there if she wished, it offered a few hours of fresh air while she got on with a sweater she was knitting for her father's birthday. Not that the air was all that fresh; Mrs Twist had a neat garden, the tiny grass patch in its centre clipped to within an inch of its life, the flowers planted in rows against the low fence which separated it from the neighbours. Florence, used to a rather untidy garden with not a neighbour in sight, found the next-door children, who hung on the fence on one side, and the garrulous old man on the other side a bit distracting. However, she answered the children's questions readily enough, and when they were sent to bed entered into conversation with the old man, leaning on the top of the fence, smoking a pipe. She wondered what tobacco he used; it smelled like dried tea-leaves and charred paper and caused him to cough alarmingly. However, he was a nice person, prepared to reminisce by the hour about his youth. She gave him her full attention until he went indoors for his supper.

Daylight was fading and she let her knitting fall into her lap, finally allowing her thoughts to turn to what was uppermost in her head: the likelihood of being sacked at the end of the month. It seemed to her that it was what she could expect; looking back over the last few weeks, she reflected that she and Mr Fitzgibbon had an uneasy relationship. It had been her fault; she should never have had dinner with him in the first place—it had allowed her to glimpse him in quite a different light from the impersonal courtesy and rather austere manner he habitually wore. She went to her room and got ready for bed, and then sat up against the pillows with a pen and paper, reckoning what she should do with her salary. Even if he asked her to leave, she would have to wait until he had a replacement and they had agreed on a month's notice on either side, so she could count on six weeks' pay. Thank heaven she had got the washing-machine...

She went to work the next morning resigned to her future. It surprised her a little that she should feel so very sad, and she came to the conclusion that it was because she would be unable to buy all the things she had planned to get. Since she had felt secure in her job, the list was a long one, and now she would only be able to get a very few of the things.

The porter admitted her, wished her a good morning and volunteered the information that Mrs Keane had not yet arrived. Florence let herself into the waiting-room, changed into her uniform, adjusted her cap just so on her bright head, and went to put on the kettle. The first patient wouldn't arrive for another hour, and everything was as ready as it could be. She was in the tiny kitchen when she heard the door open. 'The kettle is on,' she called. 'Were you held up by the buses?'

She turned to see Mr Fitzgibbon, in a thin sweater and flannels, leaning against the door. 'Good morning, Florence; I've been held back by a stove-in chest.' He looked very tired and he needed a shave, and Florence, looking at him, knew why she was feeling sad: it was because if she left she would never see him again, and her heart would break because of that. Why she should have fallen in love with him she had no idea; he had given her no encouragement to do so, and why should he when he had the lovely Eleanor waiting to drop into his arms?

She asked gently, 'If you will go and sit down, will I bring you a cup of tea, sir? I'm sorry you've had a busy night.' He went away and she busied herself with a tray, thinking that she had done this once before, only then she hadn't felt as she did now. She muttered to herself, 'Now, Florence, no nonsense,' and bore the tea and biscuits into the consulting-room and found him writing.

'Must you do that?' she cried. 'Can't it wait until you've had a short sleep and a good hot breakfast?'

He put down his pen. 'You sound like a wife. Unfortunately this can't wait, but when it's done I'll go home and have breakfast and change. Does that satisfy you?'

'Oh, that isn't what I meant, sir. I didn't mean to be bossy, only you do look so tired.' She poured a cup of tea and put it beside him. 'There's Mrs Keane.'

She left him sitting there, staring at the notes he had been writing. She had made him feel every year of his age. He drank his tea, reflecting that she had never looked so young and beautiful. He had no doubt that there were other men who thought the same.

An hour later he was back at his desk, having every appearance of a man who had had a good night's sleep, ample time in which to eat a good breakfast and nothing on his brilliant mind other than his patients. Florence, ushering in the first patient, had time to take a good look at him, back at his desk, immaculately dressed as usual, getting up to shake hands with his patient, a loud-voiced young woman with an aggressive manner which, she suspected, hid nervousness. Mr Fitzgibbon ignored the aggression, examined her with impersonal kindness and finally broke the news to her that she would need to have a bronchoscopy, adding, in his most soothing manner, that if, as he suspected, she might need surgery, he would be prepared to do it. He then waited with patience while Florence dealt with his patient, who had burst into tears, followed by some wild talking. A cup of tea, a handful of tissues and gentle murmurs from Florence worked wonders, so that presently she was able to listen to Mr Fitzgibbon's plans. Showing her out into Mrs Keane's hands, Florence reflected that underneath her aggression she was really quite a nice person.

The next patient was a different kettle of fish: a thin, scholarly man of middle age, who listened quietly to what Mr Fitzgibbon had to tell him, made arrangements to go into hospital without demur and shook hands as he left, expressing his thanks for what could only be described as bad news.

The last two appointments were with children, both with bronchiolitis. Mr Fitzgibbon dealt with them very gently, making them laugh, allowing them to try out his stethoscope, making jokes. Like a nice uncle, thought Florence, stealing a loving glance at his bowed pepper and salt head bending over one small boy.

He had a teaching round that afternoon and there were no patients until four o'clock. She and Mrs Keane ate their lunch together, and then went about their various chores until Mr Fitzgibbon returned just before four o'clock.

'Tea?' he enquired as he went into his room, but before closing the door he turned to say, 'This first appointment—the patient is a frail lady, Florence; be ready with tea and sympathy—they help a lot when it's unpleasant news.'

The little old lady who came ten minutes later looked as though a puff of wind might blow her away, but she had bright blue wide-open eyes and a serene face. Florence settled her in a chair on the other side of the desk and melted into a corner of the room until she would be needed, realising that the two already knew each other, and after a few minutes' chatting Mr Fitzgibbon said, 'Florence, Miss MacFinn was Theatre Sister at Colbert's when I was a very junior houseman—I was terrified of her!'

'Now I should be terrified of you—or at least of what you're going to tell me.' She looked across at Florence and smiled. 'Are you terrified of him, my dear?'

'Me? Heavens, no, Miss MacFinn, and I'm sure you don't need to be, although I know you're not.'

'Well, bad news is never nice, is it? I suppose you want to take a look, Alexander?'

'Indeed I do; will you go with Florence?'

So his name is Alexander, reflected Florence, busy with buttons and hooks and eyes; a very nice name and suitable. Her thoughts seemed to dwell lovingly on Mr Fitzgibbon while she carried on a cheerful conversation calculated to soothe; knowing his name made her feel that she knew something about him at last.

Miss MacFinn was philosophical about having an operation. 'Of course, if you say so, Alexander, but is it sensible at my age?'

'Certainly it is and don't cast doubts on my surgery—I'll wager a hundred pounds that you'll be trotting around on your ninetieth birthday! Will you bet on that?'

Miss MacFinn thought for a moment. 'No, I just might lose my money. You can send me a very large bouquet of flowers instead.' She looked at him straight in the eye. 'Either way!' she added.

'I'll bring them myself.' He got up, smiling, and took her hand. 'You'll go into the private wing as my special patient and no argument. I'll do it myself...'

'Good.' She looked at Florence, standing quietly by. 'It would be nice if this pretty creature would be there too...'

'I'll certainly arrange that.'

The next patient had been waiting for ten minutes or so; Florence showed him in and felt free to clear up the examination-room and get it ready once again, and after him there was only one more appointment and that was for a patient of some months, recovered from surgery and due for a check-up.

It was six o'clock before he had gone, and they began to clear up for the last time. Florence, on her way to the examination-room, was halted by Mr Fitzgibbon.

'I shall be obliged if you will make yourself available

when I operate upon Miss MacFinn. I'll choose a day when Theatre Sister is off duty—you can scrub...'

When she didn't answer he added, 'Miss MacFinn liked you; we think she will need all the help she can get—even a whim satisfied.'

Florence said, 'Very well, sir,' and made for the examination-room once more, only to be stopped again.

'Get Miss Paton on the phone, will you?'

He was writing now and didn't look up.

Eleanor's voice spoke sharply in her ear. 'Yes?'

When Florence said, 'Mr Fitzgibbon wants to speak to you, Miss Paton,' she said even more sharply,

'Well, put him on, then, and don't waste my time.'

Florence handed him the receiver, her eyes sparkling with rage. She said unforgivably, 'And don't ever ask me to do that again, sir.' She swept away, and Mr Fitzgibbon, the receiver in his hand, unheeding of the voice issuing from it, grinned.

He waited until the voice paused for breath and then said quite mildly, 'I'm afraid I'll not be able to take you to the theatre, Eleanor. I'm still at my rooms and shall be for some time, and then I must go back to Colbert's.'

He listened patiently to the peevish voice and then said, 'There are any number of men only too anxious to take my place,' and with that he added, 'and I must hang up, Eleanor, or I shall be here all night.'

He was still at his desk when Florence and Mrs Keane wished him goodnight and left. They parted company on the pavement, and Florence walked slowly back to Mrs Twist's, a prey to worried thoughts. She had allowed her tongue to run away with itself again, and Mr Fitzgibbon would be justified in reprimanding her, and, if it happened that he was feeling bad-tempered, he might even give her the sack. She frowned as she opened Mrs Twist's gate, wondering why she spoke to him like that; she wouldn't have dreamed of addressing any of the patients or the consultants at Colbert's in such a fashion. She went soberly indoors, and presently sat down to sausages and mash and a pot of tea and, since Mrs Twist considered that she looked rather peaky and needed an hour or two in the air, she went obediently into the little garden and sat there, her knitting in her lap and Buster on the knitting. It was pleasant to sit there doing nothing, but a pity that her thoughts were so unsettling. 'I've cooked my goose,' she murmured to Buster, 'not that it matters, for now I have to decide whether I can bear to go on seeing him every day or whether it would be wiser to leave and never see him again. I think I'd better leave—I can say that Mother isn't so well. No, that won't do because he'll probably suggest arranging for her to be re-admitted or some such. I'll just say that she wants me at home...'

Buster rearranged the knitting to his liking and went to sleep, and Florence, closing her eyes, the better to solve her problem, went to sleep too.

CHAPTER SEVEN

FLORENCE went to work in a fine muddle the next morning; uppermost in her head was the thought that she would spend the day, or most of it, in Mr Fitzgibbon's company, but this delightful prospect was overshadowed by the memory of her flash of temper on the previous day. 'One day, my dear girl,' she muttered, 'you'll go too far and get the sack, and have to go home and never see him again.' It was really very upsetting and she dawdled along, making up conversations in her head, all of which had a satisfactory conclusion as such conversations always did.

Mr Fitzgibbon, standing at his window, staring out into the quiet street, rattling the loose change in his pocket, watched her mooning along and wondered what she might be thinking. Nothing cheerful—that was evident. He smiled to himself, studying her neat fiery head and pretty face. She was wearing a cotton dress, one of thousands off the peg, but it was a restful pale green and suited her splendid shape, and she wore it elegantly. He turned away from the window a few moments before Florence instinctively raised her eyes to it as she always did just before she crossed the street. A minute later, when she arrived, he was sitting at his desk, reading his post.

Mrs Keane, coming in on Florence's heels, wished them both good morning and wanted to know with some asperity why Mr Fitzgibbon couldn't have waited for her to deal with his letters. 'For I'm sure I'm able to deal with them far more quickly—and tidily.'

Florence went away to get into her uniform, listening wistfully to the cheerful talk between Mrs Keane and her employer—she could hear him laughing now. He hadn't even smiled at her when she had wished him good morning. Perhaps she was going to get the sack...

However, the busy day came to an end without any mention of it, and at the end of the week she went home again, reluctantly because she wouldn't see Mr Fitzgibbon until Monday morning, but happy to have a day or two in the gentle peacefulness of Gussage Tollard.

The weekend went too fast, and every hour of it had been filled. There were gooseberries and strawberries to pick, currants and some early raspberries all growing higgledy-piggledy in the untidy kitchen garden, and flowers to cut for the church. Mrs Napier, almost her old self once more, was none the less glad to take her ease while Florence took over the cooking, dealt with a load of washing and ironing and went to the village to see how Miss Payne, who had been poorly, was feeling. Well enough to give Mrs Napier a helping hand once more, Florence was assured, to her relief. Now that she had a job she had enough money to pay Miss Payne's modest wage, and the small but necessary chores she did for her mother were worth every penny of it.

In the train, going back to London, Florence mulled over her brief stay. She had enjoyed every minute of it, excepting perhaps the conversation she had had with her mother that afternoon, sitting in the garden after lunch.

'You're not quite happy, are you, darling?' her mother had remarked. 'Is this job too much for you? Is the bedsitter too awful?'

She had denied both vigorously, and Mrs Napier had persisted gently. 'Then it's Mr Fitzgibbon—isn't he kind to you, Florence? Does he work you too hard?'

'No, no,' Florence had said, 'he's very nice to work for, Mother, and it's such an interesting job...' She had been at some pains to give chapter and verse on this, and her mother had uttered a small sigh and said no more, but Florence felt uneasy. If her mother had noticed that something was troubling her, would Mr Fitzgibbon notice it too? It seemed unlikely.

An assumption borne out by his impersonal 'good morning' when he arrived the next day. He left again as soon as
he had seen his post, to go out to his out-patients clinic, for
he had no appointments until the afternoon, but before he
went he put his head round the examination-room door,
where Florence was tidying away the week's linen.

'I shall want you in Theatre tomorrow morning. I'll pick
you up here at eight o'clock sharp. I shall operate upon Miss
MacFinn—if you remember, she wanted to see you again
and, as Theatre Sister is on holiday, it will be most convenient.'

He had gone before she could open her mouth.

'That'll make a nice change for you, dear,' said Mrs
Keane.

They separated and spent a quiet morning, doing small
chores, then sitting over their coffee and finally having their
sandwich lunch, so that they were ready for him when Mr
Fitzgibbon returned. There were several appointments and
two of them stretched into twice their usual length; by five
o'clock Florence was wishing the day were over. Outside the
warm day was dwindling into what was going to be a lovely
evening, but, despite the open windows, the consulting-
rooms were close. She envied Mr Fitzgibbon, sitting back in
his chair, giving his full attention to his patients and looking
cool and at ease. So he should, she reflected grumpily, when
I'm the one who's doing all the running around. When the
last patient finally went she carried in his tea and made for
the door.

'Not so fast, Florence. Before you go I'll sort out the instruments I shall want with me tomorrow morning. Take
them with you and get them sterilised at Colbert's, will you?'
He eyed her quiet face over his teacup. 'A pleasant evening
ahead of you, I trust?'

'Very,' said Florence; there would be shepherd's pie for
supper because it was Monday, and then she would wash her
hair and sit in the tiny garden and knit. Even if anyone, and
by that she meant Mr Fitzgibbon, were to ask her out that

evening, she wouldn't go; she was tired and cross and rather unhappy too. Not that it mattered, of course, for he wouldn't do anything of the sort.

He didn't; he reached for the phone and presently, through the half-open door, she heard him asking Eleanor if they could meet that evening.

She left with Mrs Keane after exchanging polite good evenings. It hadn't been a good day.

It was another lovely morning. She walked round to the consulting-rooms and found the Rolls outside, with Mr Fitzgibbon standing in the doorway, talking to the porter. His 'good morning' was affable, but he wasted no time in small talk. At the hospital he handed her his instruments case and told her to go on up to the theatre block. 'I'll join you in half an hour,' he told her, and walked away towards the consultant's room.

Theatre was ready; the same little staff nurse was on duty and she knew the technician and the two other nurses. She got into her theatre smock and dealt with the instruments, checked that everything was as it should be and went to the anaesthetic-room. Miss MacFinn was there, lying on the trolley, having a drowsy conversation with Dr Sim, the anaesthetist, but when she saw Florence she smiled. 'Alexander promised you'd be here. Such a treat for sore eyes you are, my dear. I've just been talking to him.'

She closed her eyes and Florence gave her hand a squeeze. 'I'll see you later,' she promised, and went to scrub up.

Everything was quite ready as Mr Fitzgibbon came into the theatre. He cast a swift eye around him, waiting while his registrar and a houseman positioned themselves on the other side of the table, asked, 'Ready, Sister?' and bent to his work.

The morning was far advanced by the time he straightened his back for the last time, pronounced himself satisfied and, leaving his registrar to apply the dressing and oversee Miss MacFinn's transfer to the recovery-room, stripped off his gloves, allowed a nurse to help him out of his gown and went away.

Miss MacFinn in safe hands, Florence took off her gown and began to gather up the instruments. She didn't get very far; the theatre maid put a cautious head round the door. 'Sister, you're to go down to the office and have your coffee. Mr Fitzgibbon says so.'

The office was crowded, with the four men perched where they could, waiting for her to pour out. Mr Fitzgibbon gravely offered her Sister's chair, behind the desk, and went to lean his bulk against one wall. She sat down composedly, gave them their mugs in turn, handed round the biscuit tin and sipped her own drink, listening to the men talking about the case. It was rather nice to be back in the hospital, she mused; on the other hand, if she were here permanently, she would see very little of Mr Fitzgibbon. She brooded over this, unaware that they had stopped talking for the moment and were looking at her.

'Hey, Florence, daydreaming? How unkind, when there are four handsome men standing around—wanting more coffee...'

She went a delicate pink. 'Sorry, I was just thinking that it was nice to see you all again.'

She began filling mugs once more, and the registrar observed, 'Which encourages me to invite you out for a meal one evening—I've no money, of course, but we can go to that poky little Chinese place...'

'I remember—they kept looking at us through those bead curtains. I'd like that, Dan.' She smiled at him; they had been out together once or twice in a friendly way; she knew that he was engaged to a girl—a children's nanny, living with a family in Switzerland—and that they planned to get married at the end of the year. Doubtless he wanted to talk about her, and Florence was a very good listener and always had been.

'Oh, good. I'll give you a ring.' He looked across to Mr Fitzgibbon, still lounging against the wall, looking thoughtful and faintly amused. 'Shall I check up on Miss MacFinn, sir?'

'No, I'll go myself, Dan. I'll take Florence back presently and come back here, do the ward-round and cast an eye on Miss MacFinn before I go, right?'

To Florence he said briskly, 'Be ready to leave here in half an hour.'

He went away and the other three men with him, leaving her to sit among the coffee-mugs and biscuit crumbs. She hadn't time to sit about, though; she went back to Theatre, saw to the instruments, checked that the theatre was ready for whatever might be coming to it next, and went away to change. Mr Fitzgibbon has said half an hour, and he wouldn't like to be kept waiting.

She got to the entrance hall a few minutes before he did, which pleased her mightily, for it seemed to her that she was always the one to be last. They got into the car without speaking, and he dropped her off at his rooms, bade her a brief goodbye and drove away. 'Home for lunch,' said Florence, sprinting up the stairs, intent on her sandwiches and tea.

There was one appointment at two o'clock and he was back at his desk five minutes before that. The patient was a middle-aged woman, quiet and composed. She did everything asked of her without demur, answered the questions put to her concisely, listened while Mr Fitzgibbon explained just why it would be necessary to have an operation, agreed to have it when arrangements could be made, thanked him nicely and went away.

Florence, putting a cup of coffee on his desk, remarked, 'What a brave woman; I do hope she has a nice husband or children to comfort her when she gets home.'

'Indeed, yes. I am going back to Colbert's, Florence; I should like you to come with me so that Miss MacFinn can see you. Don't bother to get out of your uniform. If I'm not back by half-past five you and Mrs Keane go home.' He glanced up at her. 'Go and drink your tea—I'm leaving in ten minutes. You can tidy up when you get back.'

'How?' asked Florence. 'How do I get back?'

'I'll bring you.'

She drank her tea in a few gulps, powdered her nose and tucked away a few strands of hair, and then joined him in the waiting-room, just in time to hear him telling Mrs Keane that he wouldn't be back until five or later and would she let anyone who phoned know this?

Eleanor, thought Florence, nipping smartly down the stairs ahead of him.

Miss MacFinn had come round from the anaesthetic and was doing nicely. She was enjoying a refreshing nap when Florence and Mr Fitzgibbon reached her room in the private wing, but within five minutes she had opened her eyes, taken a moment or two to focus them and then murmured in a thread of a voice, 'Admirably suited,' smiled faintly, and closed her eyes once more.

Florence, quite at a loss, glanced at Mr Fitzgibbon and saw that he was smiling, but within a few moments he had become the dignified consultant once again, giving low-voiced instructions to his registrar and then to Sister. That done, he turned to Florence. 'Most satisfactory,' he murmured. 'I'll take you back.'

So he drove her back to Wimpole Street and, beyond observing that Miss MacFinn had every chance of a good recovery, he had nothing else to say during the journey.

Mrs Keane, appraised of the brevity of the visit and Miss MacFinn's remark, looked thoughtful. It was strange, she reflected, that Mr Fitzgibbon treated Florence with nothing more than courteous reserve, but none the less sought her company. As pretty as a picture too, and a fine, big girl, just right for his own massive proportions, not in the least like that awful Miss Paton...

The telephone interrupted her interesting thoughts and, since she was sitting at her desk and Florence was standing by the phone, she said, 'Answer that, dear, will you? It'll be that man you rang about sharpening the surgical scissors; he said he'd ring back...'

It wasn't, it was Eleanor Paton, demanding to speak to Mr Fitzgibbon.

'He won't be back this afternoon,' said Florence politely. 'Would you like to leave a message?'

'Who's that speaking? Are you the woman with the red hair?'

Florence forgot that she was a vicar's daughter and ought to know better. 'Red hair? Brown curls, black eyes, five feet three inches tall, and slim.'

'You're new? She got the sack? Good. No, I won't leave a message...' Miss Paton hung up, and Florence replaced the receiver and looked defiantly at Mrs Keane.

'I didn't tell a fib,' she pointed out. 'If she liked to make what she wanted of it that's her business.'

Mrs Keane began to laugh. 'I'd love to see her face if ever she comes here,' she chortled.

'I wonder why she wants to see him? She sounded very cross; he arranged to see her yesterday evening—I got her on the phone for him. Do you suppose they quarrelled?'

'It must be hard to quarrel with him,' said Mrs Keane, 'it would be like butting one's head against a feather bed wrapped round a block of concrete.'

'Did he get on with Sister Brice?'

'Professionally, yes—but she wasn't his type.'

Florence couldn't stop herself from asking what his type might be.

'I don't think it's Eleanor—we'll have to wait and see.'

Perhaps, thought Florence, he had no idea himself, in which case he might remain single for the rest of his life and she would be able to go on working for him. It would be better than nothing, better than never seeing him again.

At five o'clock Mrs Keane tidied her desk. 'I should think we might go—I've got my in-laws coming to supper; I thought I'd do *coq au vin*...!'

'Then do go, Mrs Keane. I'm not in a hurry; I'll get ready to go and wait until half-past and lock up. It doesn't look as though he's coming back here.'

Mrs Keane went and Florence mooned around for another fifteen minutes. She was on the point of changing out of her uniform when the doorbell was rung. It wouldn't be Mr Fitzgibbon; he had his keys in his pocket—he'd been rattling them when they had been standing by Miss MacFinn's bedside. She opened the door: Eleanor was standing there, beating a tattoo with an impatient foot. She gave a gasp when she saw Florence. 'Why, you're still here—that other girl...' she pushed past Florence '...where is she?'

She turned to glare at Florence, standing by the still open door, saying nothing. 'It was you—there isn't another nurse.'

'I didn't say that there was,' Florence pointed out. 'I'm just locking up, and I'm afraid I must ask you to leave.'

Eleanor sat firmly down on the nearest chair. 'I intend to remain. I insist on remaining.'

They both had their backs to the door and Mr Fitzgibbon's quiet voice made them both start. He said, at his most bland, 'Go home, Florence; I'll lock up.' And when she went without a word to change, closing the door very quietly behind her, he said, 'Come into the consulting-room, Eleanor. I don't know why you've come; I think we have said all there is to say, don't you? And I'm a busy man.'

He opened the door of his consulting-room and he ushered her inside. 'That girl,' spat Eleanor. 'I phoned this afternoon; she said, well, she led me to believe that she had left—she said she was dark-haired, small and slim...'

Florence, going silently to the waiting-room door, paused when she heard his bellow of laughter. They must have made it up, she thought unhappily.

She ate her supper and, feeling restless, got on a bus and got herself taken to Colbert's. The truck driver was still in hospital and she hadn't visited him for a week or more.

He was glad to see her. His wife had just gone home and he was sitting in a chair by his bed, doing the football pools. She pulled up another chair, offered the packet of chocolate biscuits she had brought with her, and sat for half an hour, listening with her full attention to his plans for the future.

No good being a truck driver, was it? he reminded her cheerfully. He'd got a bit of compensation coming to him and he
was going to open a greengrocer's shop. 'And yer know wot,
miss? Mr Fitzgibbon 'ad a nice little place in the Mile End
Road, side-entrance and all to a real classy flat over. Said 'e
was glad ter 'ave it taken off 'is 'ands, too. No rent for a
year, 'e says. 'Ome in a couple of days, though I'll 'ave ter
come for physio and 'ave me leg fitted.' He grinned widely
at her. 'Reckon 'm lucky. The missus isn't 'arf pleased.'

'Oh, I'm so very glad,' said Florence. 'I know you'll make
a success of it. Give me the address, will you? I'll come and
see you.'

She took the scrap of paper he handed her and got up. 'I
must go. Do take care, won't you? And I will come and see
you and your wife.'

He went to the ward door with her, proud of his prowess
with his crutches, and she turned and waved goodbye before
she turned the corner at the end of the corridor.

She was walking along an endless corridor on her way out
when Dan came through a ward door. 'Hey there, I say, I've
had some splendid news—Lucy's coming back. The family
she's with is coming to London; a diplomatic posting—we'll
be able to see quite a lot of each other. I have missed her...'

'What wonderful news, Dan; I'm so glad. Give her my
love and tell her to give me a ring, if you can spare her—
we could have a good gossip.' She smiled widely at Dan and
he beamed back at her, a hand on her arm. It was unfortunate
for Mr Fitzgibbon's peace of mind that he should be coming
towards them; from where he was, they looked absorbed in
each other.

He was very near when they became aware of him, and
Dan said, 'Oh, hello, sir. Have you come in about that
crushed chest, or did you want to see Miss MacFinn?'

'Both,' said Mr Fitzgibbon, 'Miss MacFinn first, I think.'
He slowed his pace, waiting for Dan to join him and, when
he did so, nodded to Florence, smiling blandly, his eyes cold.

'Sorry to interrupt,' he said pleasantly. 'Good evening, Florence.'

The two men went away and Florence loitered along the corridor, wondering what she had done now to make him look like that—coldly angry, and with her. After all, since she'd been a member of the nursing staff at the hospital, no one objected to her coming and going at odd hours, but he had looked at her as though she had no right to be there.

She went off back to Mrs Twist's, highly incensed at his manner.

Two days went by, Mr Fitzgibbon came and went, saw his patients, dictated his letters, and addressed Florence when necessary and not otherwise in an impersonal manner which chilled her to the very marrow.

By the time Friday came she was looking forward to going home; perhaps, away from the scene of her problems, she would be able to solve them. It was halfway through the afternoon when Mrs Keane was struck by a violent migraine. Mr Fitzgibbon was at Colbert's and there were no more patients for that day; they were getting ready to go home. Mrs Keane had been lying down on the examination-room couch, but she had got up to lock her desk before she left, and the phone rang at that moment. Florence, giving the kitchen a final scrutiny, heard Mrs Keane's voice.

'I'll be there at seven o'clock, sir,' she was saying, and, 'I'll bring it with me.'

She put down the receiver and sat down limply. 'Mr Fitzgibbon wants me to go his East End clinic with some vital notes he's left here…'

'Well, you can't,' said Florence very firmly. 'Tell me where to find them and where to go and I'll take them. And I'm getting a taxi for you this very minute. You're not fit to be on your feet.'

'Oh, but I must,' said Mrs Keane feebly.

'Pooh,' said Florence, 'there's no must about it. Where is this folder?'

'You'll miss your train.'

'I'm not going until the morning,' said Florence, thinking it was quite all right and very easy to tell fibs once you got into the bad habit of it.

'You really mean that? The folder is in the left-hand drawer of his desk. It's in a blue cover and it's marked "Confidential". You really don't mind going? I don't know what he'll say...'

Florence wasn't sure either, but all she said was, 'Well, he probably won't notice. Where is it exactly?'

Mrs Keane told her. 'Not a nice district, dear. When I've been I have always had a taxi there and back. On expenses, of course.'

Florence found the folder, locked everything up and put an arm round Mrs Keane, who had her eyes shut and was looking very pale. 'I'd better come with you,' she suggested, but Mrs Keane declared that she would be all right; all the same, when the taxi came Florence begged the driver to keep an eye on his passenger and give her an arm to her front door. The cabbie was elderly and delighted to see such a pretty, charming face at the end of a day of passengers who didn't bother to look at him, only snapped directions as they got in and paid him without a glance.

'Course I will, ducks; got a bad 'ead, 'as she? My old lady gets 'em too.'

Florence said that she was sorry to hear that, and if it hadn't been for a faint moan from Mrs Keane she might have enquired further. She gave him a last smile and waved as the taxi drew away from the kerb.

Mr Fitzgibbon had said seven o'clock, and it would take quite a time to cross London, for the traffic would still be heavy. She explained to Mrs Twist, who gave her a cup of tea and a bun and promised that there would be something in the fridge when she got back, and went to her room to change. Something severe and inconspicuous, she decided, going through her few dresses. The cotton jersey, she supposed, and got into it, subdued her hair into a tidy chignon, thrust her tired feet into sandals, picked up a small handbag she could safeguard if necessary and, with the folder safely in a plastic carrier-bag, went in search of a taxi.

It was a long drive through the City, its blocks of offices silent now, the streets quiet, and then into the lighted streets of the East End, the wholesale dress shops, take-away food shops, amusement arcades, boarded-up houses and here and there high-rise flats alien to their surroundings.

The cabbie turned round once to ask if she was sure she had the right address, 'For this ain't no place for a pretty girl like you, miss.'

She assured him that she had it right. 'It's all right, it's a clinic, and I know the people who work there.'

Anything less like a clinic would be hard to find, she reflected as she got out at last, paid the cabbie, assured him that she was quite safe and crossed the pavement to the half-open door. It was a corner house, its brickwork grimed, two of its three windows boarded up, the third covered with wire netting. She turned to smile reassuringly at the cabbie and pushed open the door. The hall was dark and smelled damp, and from one of several doors there was a subdued volume of sound and a crack of light around its ill-fitting door. Florence opened it and went in.

The room wasn't large, but it was empty of furniture, save for benches against its walls and rows of decrepit chairs taking up every inch of space. It was full of people, though, and those who hadn't got seats were standing against the walls. The babble of talk died down while everyone looked at her; only the noise of the continuous coughing from some of them continued.

'Lost yer way, love?' asked a cheerful stout woman with a small boy on her lap. 'Come ter see Doc?' And, when Florence nodded, 'Well, yer'll 'ave ter take yer turn, ducks, same as the rest of us.'

'I'm not here to see him,' said Florence matter-of-factly, 'I'm a nurse, and I've brought some papers he wants urgently.'

Several voices told her to go through the door at the end

of the room, and a man lounging beside it opened it for her. She thanked him nicely and went through the door on a wave of onions and beer. The atmosphere on the other side of the door was quite a different matter. What fresh air there was in the Mile End Road was pouring in through a window high up in one wall, and the walls were distempered a cheerful pale yellow. The furniture was simple: a desk, a chair behind it and another before it, an examination couch, a cabinet housing the surgery equipment, and a large sink with a pile of towels beside it. Mr Fitzgibbon was bending over a small boy on the couch, Dan was standing opposite, and beside him was the child's mother, a pretty girl with greasy hair, a grubby T-shirt and torn denim trousers. The child was screaming and kicking, and Mr Fitzgibbon had a gentle hand on the small stomach, waiting patiently until he quietened. It was a pity that the girl broke into loud sobs, and when Dan put a soothing hand on her arm flung it off and added her own screams to the child's. Florence put the folder on the desk and joined the group round the couch.

'Now, now,' she said soothingly, and put an arm round the girl's shoulders. 'Come and sit down here so that the doctors can take a look at your little boy. You can tell me all about it...'

She hardly noticed Dan's surprised stare but she couldn't fail to hear Mr Fitzgibbon's terse, 'What the devil—?'

'I'll tell you later,' she announced, and met eyes like cold steel with her own calm blue ones. 'I'll look after Mum,' she added kindly, 'while you get on with what you want to do.'

She led the girl to a chair by a desk in a corner of the room, ignoring his tight-lipped anger. He was probably thinking some very bad language, and most certainly he would have a great deal to say to her later on. But now there was the little matter of getting the girl to stop crying. Florence produced a clean handkerchief, begged her to mop her face, gave her a drink of water from the sink tap and enquired sympathetically as to what was wrong with the child.

The girl was vague; he'd been off colour, wouldn't eat, kept being sick and said his chest hurt him. 'So I brought him here,' she explained, 'seeing as how the doctor here seems to know his stuff.'

She sniffed forlornly, and Florence said, 'Oh, you're right there; he's a very clever man.'

'You his girlfriend?'

'No, no, I'm a nurse—I work for him.'

The girl eyed her with interest, her worries forgotten for the moment. 'Got a bit of a temper, hasn't he? Doesn't show, but you can tell.' She darted a glance at the little group by the couch; the little boy was quiet now, and it was Mr Fitzgibbon talking, making the child chuckle.

He turned his head presently. 'Since you are here, Sister, perhaps you will dress this little chap while I talk to his mother.' His manner was pleasant, but his voice was cold.

It seemed wise not to speak; Florence began to clothe the child in an assortment of garments, listening as best she could to Mr Fitzgibbon at his most soothing, persuading the girl to let him take the child into hospital. He explained cystic fibrosis very simply, enquired as to her circumstances and suggested that she should see the lady at the desk in the room adjoining, who would help her to sort things out. 'I'll get an ambulance,' he told her. 'You can go with Jimmy and then stay the night at the hospital if you wish to; if you want to come back home ask the lady for your fare. Have you any money?'

He sounded so kind that Florence felt the tears crowding her throat, and when Dan came over to see how she was getting on the smile she gave him was so lop-sided that he took a second look at her, but all he said was, 'I'll phone for an ambulance.'

Mother and child were borne away presently, and Dan said, 'I'll get in the next patient, shall I?'

Mr Fitzgibbon was at his desk, finishing a conversation

with Colbert's about the child he had admitted. He put the receiver down and said, 'Not for a moment. Florence, I should like to know why you are here. I spoke to Mrs Keane on the phone...'

She sat down on the chair opposite him. 'Well, it's like this—she had the most awful migraine, so I put her in a taxi and sent her home and came instead of her.' She added in a motherly voice, 'And now I'm here I might as well stay and give a hand. You're bursting with rage, aren't you? But with all these people outside there isn't really time to give vent to it, is there?'

Dan gave a muffled laugh, which he turned into a prolonged cough, but Mr Fitzgibbon didn't smile. He was in a towering rage, all the worse for its being battened down with iron determination. He glanced at his watch. 'You came by taxi?'

She nodded.

'Is it waiting?'

'Heavens, no, that would cost a small fortune, and I was told to put it down to expenses.'

'In that case you had better stay and make yourself useful.' He got up. 'Let's have the next one, Dan.'

He ignored her for the rest of the long evening, but she had little time to worry about that. Wrapped around by a white pinny she found hanging behind the door, she dressed and undressed, applied plasters, redid bandages and cleared up after each patient. The majority of them were old patients who had come for a regular check-up, but nevertheless it was past ten o'clock by the time the last one went away. Florence, helped by the quiet little lady who had been doing the paperwork and attending to the patients' problems, tidied up the place, took off the pinny and followed her to the door, nodding to Dan as she went.

'Not so fast,' said Mr Fitzgibbon, still writing at his desk. 'Dan, go on ahead, will you, and write that child up for something, and make sure his mum's being looked after? I'll be along later.'

Dan hesitated. 'Shall I take Florence with me, sir?'

'I'll take her back to her lodgings.'

Florence advanced a step into the room. 'I shall catch a bus,' she said clearly.

'No, you won't.' He didn't look up. 'Off you go, Dan; I'll see Florence safely back.'

His registrar went with a sidelong smile for Florence and, since Mr Fitzgibbon showed no sign of being ready to leave, she sat down composedly on one of the few chairs in the room.

Presently he closed the folder he was writing in and put away his pen.

'You haven't had your supper?'

'No; Mrs Twist will have left something for me.'

He got up and crossed the room to stand in front of her, making her feel at a disadvantage, since she had to look up a long way to see his face. He put out a hand and hauled her gently to her feet and didn't let her hand go.

'I have been most unkind—will you forgive me?'

He sounded so kind that she had the greatest wish to throw herself on to his chest and have a good cry; instead she looked him in the eye. 'Yes, of course I will. I must have given you a surprise. Do you like to keep all this—' she waved her free hand around '—a secret?'

'As far as I can, yes. Dan knows, of course, and so do several of the local doctors who take it in turns to work here. I've never considered it suitable for women, though.'

'Oh, pooh,' said Florence. 'What about that nice little lady who was here?'

'Ah, yes, well, she's the local school-teacher, and perfectly safe.'

She gave her hand a tug, but he held it fast. 'Well, now I know about it, may I come and work here too? I should very much like to.'

'Why, Florence?'

She had no intention of telling him why; instead she said

matter-of-factly, 'It's worthwhile, isn't it? And I've every evening...'

He lifted his eyebrows. 'Every evening? What about those evenings out with Dan?' He smiled faintly. 'A "poky little Chinese place".'

'That was years ago. I'm glad his fiancée is coming back so soon; she's a dear...'

She glanced at him and was surprised to see what amounted to amused satisfaction on his face. 'If you want to work here I see no reason why you shouldn't, but on the definite condition that I bring you and take you back, and that you stay here in the building. I won't have you roaming the streets...'

She said coldly, 'I'm not in the habit of roaming...' and remembered the unfortunate episode when she had looked for a short-cut to the bus. 'Oh, very well. How often do you come here?'

'Once a week.' He let her hand go, picked up his bag and opened the door. 'It's getting late.'

He stowed her into the car, parked in a scruffy yard behind the house. 'I'm surprised that it's still here,' observed Florence, and then added, 'no, I'm not; they depend on you, don't they?'

'To a certain extent—most of them either need to go into hospital or have just been discharged from it.'

The streets were quiet, and the homeward journey seemed much shorter than her taxi ride.

'Mrs Twist will be in bed?' asked Mr Fitzgibbon.

'Oh, yes, but I have a key.'

'In that case there is no need to disturb her. Mrs Crib will have a meal ready.'

Florence thought longingly of food. 'Well, that's all right for you, isn't it? If you'd just drop me off at the end of this street I can—'

'Don't be silly, Florence, you will eat your supper with me and I'll bring you back afterwards.'

'I don't think—!'

'Good.' He had turned into his street and stopped before his door.

He got out, went round the car and opened her door, and said, 'Out you get,' and, when she didn't budge, scooped her up and set her on her feet on the pavement. He held her for a moment and then bent and kissed her, took her by the arm, opened his street door and urged her inside.

Since she had no means of getting back to Mrs Twist's and there was a delicious aroma coming from the half-open baize door at the back of the hall, Florence, sternly suppressing delighted thoughts about the kiss, decided sensibly to stay for supper.

CHAPTER EIGHT

Mr Fitzgibbon gave Florence a gentle push from behind. 'Straight through to the kitchen. The Cribs will be in bed, but everything will be ready.'

The kitchen was roomy, with an old-fashioned dresser laden with china dishes and plates, a scrubbed wooden table in the centre of the tiled floor, and an Aga stove taking up almost all of one wall. It was flanked by two Windsor armchairs with bright cushions, and between them was Monty, roused from sleep and pleased to see them, weaving round them, uttering whispered barks. Sharing her basket was a cat, stout and matronly, who yawned widely at them and then went to sleep again.

The table had been laid for one person and with the same niceness which would have graced an elegant dining-room. Mr Fitzgibbon opened a drawer and collected spoon and forks and knives, and carried them over to the table and set them tidily beside his own place. He fetched a glass from the dresser, too, and more plates. 'Sit down,' he invited. 'I have my supper here when I go to the clinic, otherwise the Cribs would wait up. You don't mind?'

She shook her head, feeling shy because Mr Fitzgibbon was exhibiting yet another aspect of himself. Quite handy in the kitchen, she reflected, watching him ladle soup into two bowls and set them on the table. Excellent soup too, nothing out of a tin—home-made watercress soup with a blob of cream a-top and fresh brown crusty bread to go with it. After that there were chicken tartlets, kept warm in the oven, with jacket potatoes smothered in butter and a salad from the fridge. Florence forgot to be shy, ate her supper with a splendid appetite and made suitable small talk, all the while conscious of his kiss but trying not to think of it. They had their coffee presently, still sitting at the table, and he asked, 'You're going home for the weekend, Florence?'

'Yes, I promised Mother I would—we're going to make jam.' She glanced at the clock, a large old-fashioned one, hanging above the door. 'If it's convenient I'd like to go back to Mrs Twist's,' and then, by way of making conversation, she added, 'Are you going away for the weekend too?'

'Yes—like you, I'm going into the country.' He got up when she did and said, 'No, leave everything; I'll see to it when I get back.'

He drove her to her room and got out of the car and went with her to Mrs Twist's front door, took her key from her and unlocked it, gave her back her key and asked, 'Do we have to be careful of Buster?'

'No, he'll be upstairs with Mrs Twist. Thank you for a lovely supper, Mr Fitzgibbon, and…and…thank you for letting me come to your clinic each week.' She hesitated. 'But please don't think that I shall expect you to give me supper afterwards.'

'No, no, of course not, but this evening was exceptional, was it not?'

He opened the door and wished her goodnight with a casual friendliness, which for some reason annoyed her. She said 'Goodnight' quickly and went past him, but before he closed the door behind her he said, 'I do believe that we are making progress.' He shut the door before she could ask him what he meant.

Yes, there was a great deal to think about, she reflected as she got ready for bed, taking care to make no sound at all for fear of waking Mrs Twist. She got into bed and started to marshal her thoughts into sense, and went to sleep within minutes. In the morning the last evening's happenings were somehow put into their proper perspective: Mr Fitzgibbon had had every right to be surprised and annoyed at her arrival at the clinic, and common decency and good manners had forced him to take her back to his home for a meal. It was all quite explicable in the light of early morning, all except his kiss, which didn't quite fit in. She decided not to think about it any more.

She caught her train with a minute or so to spare, and sat quietly all the way to Sherborne, daydreaming; if it hadn't been for a child in the carriage excitedly pointing out the castle as they neared the little town she might have been carried on to Yeovil and beyond.

She had phoned her mother from the telephone box opposite Mrs Twist's house, and her father was on the platform waiting for her.

She drove the car back to Gussage Tollard, listening to her father's comments on the week and answering very circumspectly his queries as to her own week, and when they got home her mother, waiting with coffee and seed cake, asked the same questions, but rather more searchingly. Florence answered them all, leaving out as much as possible anything to do with Mr Fitzgibbon, something which her mother was quick to notice.

It was nice to be home; Florence pottered about the house, inspected the garden and then strolled down to the village to purchase one or two groceries her mother had forgotten.

There were several people in the shop, enjoying a gossip while they waited to be served. Florence knew them all and, after enquiring after their respective children, aged parents and whether the jam had set well, answered various enquiries as to her life in London.

'Nasty, smoky place,' observed one lady in house slippers and a printed pinny; she nodded her head wisely so that the row of curlers across her forehead nodded with it. 'No place for kids, I always say. There's Mrs Burge's youngest, went to live with his auntie and now he's in the hospital, having things done to his chest.' She beamed at Florence. 'Same as you worked in, Miss Florence—Colbert's; being looked after by a clever man, too...got a funny name—Fitz something, great big chap, she says, and ever so kind. He's got a house in Mells too; goes there at weekends...'

It was Florence's turn at the counter and she was glad of it; Mr Fitzgibbon's name, uttered so unexpectedly, had sent the colour into her cheeks and she was thankful to bend over the list in her hand.

Mrs Hoskins, serving, put a jar of Bovril on the counter and asked with a kindly curiosity, 'You'll know him, no doubt, Miss Florence? That's the smallest size Bovril I've got, tell your mother.'

'About a pound of Cheddar cheese,' said Florence and, since the village probably knew already that she worked for him but were far too nicely mannered to say so, she said, 'Well, yes, I work for him, you know. He's a very clever surgeon and marvellous with the children.'

There was a satisfied murmur from those around her, and the lady in the printed pinny looked pleased with herself. 'There, didn't I say so?' she wanted to know. 'And him living less than an hour away from here, too.'

Half an hour or so, reflected Florence silently, in that Rolls of his, and she asked for a bottle of cider vinegar, and, since he lived near by, he could quite easily give her a lift if he wanted to. Only he didn't want to.

She frowned so fiercely at the vinegar that Mrs Hoskins said hastily, 'That's the best make, Miss Florence; Mrs Napier won't have any of that nasty cheap stuff, and I won't sell it neither.'

Florence apologised quickly, adding that she had been trying to remember something or other she hadn't put on the list. Which wasn't true, but it made a good excuse. She took her purchases home presently and then went into the garden, where she attacked the weeds with such ferocity that her mother, watching from the open drawing-room window, remarked to the Reverend Mr Napier, sitting beside her, that something had upset Florence. 'I wonder what it can be?' she mused. 'Of course, it's a great help—getting the weeding done.'

Her husband, without lifting his eyes from his newspaper, agreed with her.

One of the Sunday-school teachers was on holiday and Florence had volunteered to take her place with the toddlers' class, but first she intended going off for a walk with Higgins. She was up early on Sunday morning and, with Higgins panting happily at her heels, accompanied her father as far as the church, where he was to take the early service, and then went through the lych-gate, down the narrow lane that led to Mott's Farm, and turned off over the stile into the bridle-path, which would eventually bring her out on the other side of the village. It was a glorious morning and full of the country sounds she missed in London: there were birds singing, sheep bleating, a farm tractor starting up, prepared to make its ponderous way across a field lying fallow, and then the church clock striking the hour of eight. There was plenty of time; her father wouldn't be back until almost nine o'clock, and matins would be at eleven o'clock. She sat down on a fallen log and watched Higgins gallop clumsily from one clump of trees to the other hopeful of finding rabbits, thinking inevitably of Mr Fitzgibbon.

He was at that very moment sitting in her mother's kitchen, drinking tea, looking very much at his ease with Monty at his feet.

Mrs Napier, assembling eggs and bacon and mushrooms for breakfast, had greeted him with no surprise and a great deal of inward satisfaction; it was nice to know that her maternal instincts hadn't been at fault. Here, then, was the reason for her daughter's arduous gardening, her wish to go for long walks with Higgins, her animated conversations about her week at work without any mention of Mr Fitzgibbon. She offered him tea, remarked on the beauty of the morning and volunteered the information that Florence had taken Higgins for a walk. 'Her usual early-morning round when she is at home,' she explained casually, 'down the lane to Mott's Farm, only she goes over the stile and down the bridle-path. It brings her out at the other end of the village in nice time for breakfast.'

She smiled across the kitchen at her visitor. 'Have you come far? Not from London, surely?'

'No, I have a house at Mells—do you know it? It's not so very far from here.'

'A pretty village. Of course, you'll stay and have some breakfast, won't you?'

'That would be delightful. Mr Napier is in church?'

'Yes. He will be back just before nine o'clock. There's matins at eleven, and Florence is taking one of the Sunday-school classes.'

A smile touched the corners of his mouth. He put his mug down. 'Perhaps I could overtake Florence,' he suggested blandly.

'Easily—she doesn't hurry; Higgins likes to hunt for rabbits—he never finds any, but it makes him happy.'

After he had gone Mrs Napier stood for a few minutes, her hands idle over the mushrooms she was peeling, allowing herself a few moments of pleasant daydreaming. A splendid man, she reflected, but possibly proud and reserved and liking his own way, but, on the other hand, utterly dependable and sure of himself and what he wanted. She hoped fervently that he wanted Florence.

Mr Fitzgibbon had no difficulty in finding Florence; she was still sitting on the log, her thoughts miles away, and in any case Monty had seen Higgins and rushed to meet him so noisily that she looked round to see what was happening.

Mr Fitzgibbon, walking slowly towards her, had time to admire the sun glinting on her bronze hair and the faint freckles across the bridge of her nose; he admired the colour creeping up into her cheeks when she saw him too. Her rather faded blue cotton dress and old sandals on her bare feet seemed to him to be exactly right; she was as pretty as a picture; he would have thought the same if she had been wearing a potato sack, although he had at times had the violent urge to hang her around with pearls and jewels and drape her in the very latest of fashions. He controlled his thoughts with an iron will and walked towards her and wished her a casual good morning. 'Such a splendid morning,' he continued blandly, 'and Monty needed a walk.'

Florence eyed him warily. 'All the way from Mells?' and, at his lifted eyebrows, 'Mrs Burge's youngest; they were talking about him in the village shop yesterday and someone said that you lived there.'

He sat down beside her. 'Ah, yes—Billy Burge, a delightful small boy with the heart of a lion—he's a fibrocystic...' He went on smoothly into a detailed account of the child's illness. 'He's almost well enough to go to a convalescent home—it will have to be somewhere round about here so that his family can visit easily.' He glanced at his watch. 'May I join you? Your mother said nine o'clock breakfast—'

'You've been home?'

'I had the urge to explore,' he answered smoothly, 'and I remembered that you lived here.' It seemed that was all the explanation he had to offer.

She got to her feet, and Higgins and Monty bustled up, anxious to be on the move again. 'There's time for us to follow the path round the village; it comes out at the other end of the village by the school. It's not far.'

'I dare say I can manage it,' said Mr Fitzgibbon. He sounded so meek that she gave him a suspicious look, but he was looking away from her, his face devoid of what she had suspected was sarcasm. So they walked on, slipping presently into a comfortable conversation about the country around them, the village and its inhabitants, and the pleasures of the rural life. By the time they reached the vicarage Florence was feeling happier than she had been for some time, although she had no idea why that should be. She only knew, in her mind at least, that she thought of Mr Fitzgibbon as Alexander...

They ate their breakfast in the kitchen, sitting round the solid table with its white starched cloth and blue and white china, and Mr Fitzgibbon made a splendid meal and, very much to Florence's surprise, helped with the washing-up afterwards.

She wasn't sure if she was pleased or not when her father wanted to know if their guest would like to attend morning church.

'Oh, do,' said Mrs Napier, 'and come with us and have lunch here, or if you would rather you can lie about in the garden.'

He agreed very readily to go to church, and accepted his invitation to stay for lunch.

'Oh, good,' said Mrs Napier. 'When do you have to go back to London?'

'This evening—perhaps Florence would like to come back with me?'

He looked across the table at her, faintly smiling. 'It will save you the tiresome trip across town to Mrs Twist's, Florence.'

She said slowly, 'Well, yes, thank you. But don't you want to go to your home—I mean...?' She went a little pink. 'I didn't mean to be rude, but I don't want to spoil your day.'

'Oh, I don't think you'll do that. We can go there on our way back if you don't mind leaving a little earlier than usual.'

Even if she had wanted to refuse it would have been hard with her mother beaming at them both and her father observing that Sunday trains were always late and he had never liked her arriving in London late on Sunday evening.

Mr Fitzgibbon agreed quietly with him, and added blandly, 'That's settled, then. What do we do with the dogs—will they be all right while we are in church?'

'We leave Higgins in the conservatory; he's always quite happy. Monty will probably settle there too.' Mr Napier glanced at his watch. 'Florence, if you're going to take Sunday school you'd better get dressed, my dear.'

Florence went upstairs, feeling rather as though someone had taken the day away from her, rearranged it, and handed it back again. She took off the blue cotton and got into a short-sleeved crêpe dress in pale green, coiled her hair and did her face, found suitable shoes and stockings and went back downstairs, to find Mr Fitzgibbon in a tie and a beautifully tailored blazer. She frowned thoughtfully; she was sure that when he had joined her on the bridle-path he had been wearing an open-necked shirt and no tie. She caught his eye and found him smiling at her. It was a mocking smile, and it made her aware that he knew exactly what she had been thinking.

'I'll be off,' she told the room at large, and whisked herself away with a heightened colour.

Her class was large. Her father's congregation was large too, and there were a great many children in the village. She sat in the small village hall beside the church, telling them Bible stories and drawing on the blackboard to illustrate them, and at the appointed time she marshalled them into a straggling line and marched them into church to take part in the last few minutes of the service.

Mr Fitzgibbon watched her without appearing to do so, gently chivvying her restless brood into suitable quietness with an unselfconscious air which delighted him, and Mrs Napier, beside him, peeping up from under her Sunday hat, heaved a happy, hopeful sigh.

Back at the vicarage, Florence found a dozen reasons why she was unable to spend any time in Mr Fitzgibbon's company. There was the table to lay in the dining-room, the joint of beef, roasting in the oven, to inspect, its accompanying trimmings to deal with and the strawberry tart to arrange on a dish. She did all these things slowly, reluctant to join her parents and Mr Fitzgibbon, sipping sherry in the drawing-room, bewildered by the way in which he had become, as it were, a friend of the family.

'Colossal cheek,' she muttered to Charlie Brown, curled up on a kitchen chair. He flicked a lazy tail by way of answer.

She had to go to the drawing-room eventually, where she

drank her sherry rather faster than she should have done and then urged her father to come and carve the joint, aware that she was not being her usual calm self and unable to do anything about it. Once they were sitting at the table, she regained some of her usual serenity and indeed she began to enjoy herself. There was no doubt about it: Mr Fitzgibbon was a pleasant companion—his manners were beautiful, his conversation interesting, and his ability to listen to other people talking and not to interrupt was unequalled. The meal progressed in a delightful manner, and it wasn't until her mother was serving her mouth-watering fruit tart that Florence looked across the table at Mr Fitzgibbon and knew in a blinding instant that she really was in love with him. The knowledge left her with a slightly open mouth, pale cheeks, a tremendous bubbling excitement and a feeling of relief that now she knew why she had been feeling so cross and vaguely unhappy.

She also realised within seconds of this discovery that on no account must anyone know about it, so that she passed plates, offered cream and remarked on the flavour of the tart in a wooden voice so unlike her usual pretty one that her mother looked sharply at her and Mr Fitzgibbon lowered his lids to hide the gleam in his eyes, watching her face as her thoughts chased themselves across her mind.

Florence removed the plates and fetched the coffee, her feet not quite touching the ground, her head a jumble of thoughts, none of which made sense. An hour on her own would be nice, she thought, but in no way was she to get it; her father declared that he would wash up, and Mr Fitzgibbon offered to help, with the almost careless air of one who always washed up on a Sunday anyway, so she and her mother repaired to the garden to sit in the elderly deckchairs with the dogs lolling beside them.

'Such a handy man,' observed Mrs Napier, 'but I dare say he does quite a lot for himself at home.'

'He has a butler and a cook, Mother—that's in his London

BETTY NEELS 293

house; I don't know about Mells. If it's a small cottage I dare say he has to look after himself.'

'Well, do let me know, my darling—you're going there first on the way back, aren't you?' She closed her eyes. 'We'll have that Victoria sponge for tea—I wonder what time he wants to go?'

'I have no idea,' said Florence snappily. 'I think perhaps I'll change my mind and stay here and go up on the train...'

'Just as you like, love,' said her mother soothingly, 'I'm sure he'll understand.'

Florence sat up. 'Mother, what do you mean?'

'Why, nothing, darling—just an idle remark.'

The two men went for a stroll when they had done their chores, taking the dogs with them, and Florence watched them go with mixed feelings. She felt shy of Mr Fitzgibbon and anxious to present her usual matter-of-fact manner towards him; on the other hand she wanted to spend as much time as possible in his company. Sitting there, with her mother dozing beside her, she tried to decide what she should do. It would be hard to maintain that manner towards him; on the other hand if it was too hard she would have to leave her job and go somewhere where she would never see him again. She was still worrying away at the problem when they came back, and she went indoors to get the tea. Mr Fitzgibbon followed her in presently to carry the tea-tray out into the garden, casually friendly and seemingly unnoticing of her hot cheeks and stilted replies to his undemanding remarks, so that presently she pulled herself together. After all, she reflected, she was the only one who would be affected by her feelings—no one else knew, nor would they ever know. Presently, when they had finished tea, he suggested that they might be going; she agreed with her usual calm manner and went upstairs to get her overnight bag, bade her mother and father goodbye, hugged Charlie Brown and Higgins and got into the car, to hang out of the window at the last minute to call that she would be home again the following weekend. Mindful of her companion, she added, 'I hope.'

Mr Fitzgibbon was at his most urbane as he drove back to Mells; Florence, filled with a mixture of uneasiness and excitement, found herself being soothed into her usual good sense by his reassuring if rambling remarks, none of them touching on anything personal. By the time they reached Mells she had got control of herself and told herself not to behave like a silly girl; it was a situation, she was sure, which occurred over and over again, and she would cope with it.

The first sight of the house took her breath. 'Oh, how can you bear to live in London?' she demanded. 'Just look at those roses...'

Mr Fitzgibbon said mildly, 'Yes, I'm very fond of it, although I like the house in Knightsbridge too. I have the best of both worlds, have I not?'

'Well, you have really worked hard for them,' said Florence, skipping out of the car, closely observed, did she but know it, by Nanny, peering out of the funny little latticed window by the front door.

Nanny went to open the door. This one was the one, then, she reflected with satisfaction, and a nice girl too—beautiful and the proper shape. Nanny had no time for young women like blades of grass. A nice wedding, she thought cosily, and children tumbling about the old house. She opened the door, looking pleased.

Mr Fitzgibbon saw the look and grinned to himself, but he introduced Florence with perfect gravity. 'I've some papers I need to pick up, Nanny—we've had a splendid tea, but perhaps you could find us some supper before we go?'

He watched Florence's face out of the corner of his eye and saw delight, uncertainty and annoyance chase each other across it. 'It's only a couple of hours' drive—less—and I'm sure you would like to see the garden while you're here.'

'You leave it to me, Mr Alexander,' said Nanny briskly. 'A nice little chicken salad and one of my chocolate custards. In half an hour?'

'Splendid, Nanny—we ought to leave by nine o'clock at the latest.'

He turned to Florence, standing between them, feeling rather as though someone had put skates on her feet and given her a push. 'Well...' she began.

'Oh, good. Come along, then; there are some splendid roses at the side of the house, tea-roses, and some spectacular lilies—Casablanca; I put them in last year behind some Peruvian lilies.'

He led the way round the side of the house to where the garden stretched away to a magnificent red-brick wall, almost covered with wistaria, clematis and passion flower, a lawn of green velvet was edged by paths and wide herbaceous borders, bursting with summer flowers, and at the very end there was a circular bed of roses. Monty, trotting to and fro in great contentment, came and nuzzled her hand as she wandered along, very content, to admire the lilies and bend to smell the roses.

'Of course, you have a gardener?' she said presently.

'Oh, yes, but I potter around at the weekends and whenever I have an hour or so to spare.'

'Couldn't you commute?'

'I think it would be possible, but not just yet. Later, when I have a wife and family, perhaps.'

'Eleanor—Miss Paton is very pretty and wears lovely clothes...'

She had hardly been aware that she had spoken her thoughts out loud.

'Oh, quite charming,' agreed Mr Fitzgibbon placidly. 'You like clothes?'

'Well, yes, I do, but I don't have the time,' said Florence crossly and, remembering to whom she was talking, 'and of course, I don't lead that kind of life.'

'You would like to do so?'

His voice was so casual that she answered without thinking. 'Certainly not. I'd be bored stiff.' She paused to examine a rose. 'That's a lovely Super Star. Do you prune in the autumn or in February?'

They strolled round the lovely garden, Monty at their

heels, talking comfortably. I'm not just in love with him, thought Florence, I like him too.

Nanny called them in presently to a supper of cold chicken—a salad, and not just a few lettuce leaves and a tomato, but apples and nuts and grapes, mixed in with chicory and chopped-up mint. There were tiny new potatoes too and a home-made dressing. They drank iced lemonade, since Mr Fitzgibbon would be driving, and finished the meal with the chocolate custards Nanny had promised them.

'I should like to thank your nanny for such a lovely supper,' said Florence, 'but I don't know her name.'

'Nanny.'

'Yes, I know that, but I'm a stranger—it would be very ill-mannered to be so familiar with her.'

'Miss Betts. Run along to the kitchen while I see to Monty. We must go in ten minutes or so.' He opened the door for her. 'It's through that arched doorway by the stairs.'

Florence trod across the hall, wishing very much that she could have seen the rest of the house; the drawing-room was perfect, so was the dining-room, but there were three more doors leading from the hall. She opened the arched door and went down a few steps to another door and, since it was shut, she knocked.

Nanny's comfortable voice bade whoever it was to go in, so she lifted the old-fashioned latch. The kitchen was at the back of the house, a large low-ceilinged room, delightfully old-fashioned but, she suspected, having every labour-saving device that could be wished for. Nanny was standing at the table, picking over a bowl of redcurrants, but she looked up and smiled as Florence went in.

'I wanted to thank you for a lovely supper, Miss Betts,' said Florence. 'And I hope it didn't make a lot of extra work for you.'

'Lor, bless you, Miss Napier, not a bit of it, and it's a treat to see the food eaten. Times I could have cried seeing it being pecked over by Mr Alexander's guests. Here he is

now, come for the currants; Mrs Crib likes to make a nice
fruit tart and there's nothing like your own fruit.'

Florence, aware of Mr Fitzgibbon standing behind her,
agreed with her and turned to go.

'And there's no call to say Miss Betts, Miss Napier—you
call me Nanny, the way Mr Alexander does.' She smiled
widely. 'I dare say we'll meet again.'

To which remark Florence murmured in a non-committal
way, not wishing Mr Fitzgibbon to think that she was expecting to be asked to visit his house again.

They drove away presently with Monty on the back seat,
leaning forward from time to time to breathe gently into the
backs of their necks.

'I expect Monty likes being in the country,' observed Florence, intent on making small talk, and, when her companion
made some brief reply, enlarged upon the subject at some
length, anxious for some reason for there to be no silence.

When she paused for breath, however, Mr Fitzgibbon said
gently, 'Don't try so hard, Florence; your silent company is
contentment enough. And could you call me Alexander when
we aren't working? I begin to dislike my own name, I hear
it so frequently.'

Florence stared ahead of her. Of all the rude men... She
drew a calming breath to damp down her feelings; if he
wanted her silent then that was what he would get. She said
stonily, 'Just as you like.' Nothing was going to make her
say 'Alexander' after his remarks. Let him just wait until
they were back at the consulting-rooms; if he didn't like
being called Mr Fitzgibbon then she would address him as
'sir'.

'Don't sulk,' said Mr Fitzgibbon quietly. 'You have, as
usual, got the wrong end of the stick.' He glanced at her
cross profile. 'I fancy, however, it would be of no use putting
matters right at the moment.'

They travelled some distance in silence until he said, 'I
should like you to come to the hospital to see Miss MacFinn
tomorrow morning. I've a round at nine o'clock; can you be

ready by half-past eight or a little before that at the consulting-rooms? I only intend to look in on her for a few minutes—she has asked to see you again.'

'Very well,' said Florence. 'You have a patient at half-past eleven.'

'Yes, I'll see that you get back as soon as Miss MacFinn has had a word.' He stayed silent for a while and then said, 'I shan't see Mrs Keane before we go to Colbert's; will you ask her to change my appointments on Tuesday morning? I need to be free until one o'clock. Tell her to fit them in in the afternoon and early evening. We shall have to work late.'

'Very well,' said Florence again and looked out of the window. They didn't speak again until they reached Mrs Twist's front door, when she began a thank-you speech, uttered in a high voice quite unlike her usual quiet tones.

He cut her short. 'Oh, don't bother with that,' he begged her, 'you're as cross as two sticks, and I haven't the time to talk to you now.'

He had got out of the car as he spoke and opened her door. Florence got out haughtily, tripped up on the pavement and was set back on her feet with a, 'Tut, tut, pride goes before a fall,' as he took her arm and marched her to the door, unlocked it and, when she would have opened it, put a great hand over hers.

'I should like to think that I know the reason for your peevishness,' he observed blandly, 'but uncertainty forbids me from doing anything about it for the moment; you are like a weathercock being blown to every point of the compass.' He bent suddenly and kissed her quickly. 'Goodnight, Florence.'

He opened the door and shoved her gently into the little hallway beyond, and just as gently shut it behind her.

Florence stood very still and tried to make sense of being called a weathercock, but she had to give up almost at once, for Mrs Twist came out of her front parlour with Buster under one arm.

'I thought I heard a car,' she observed. 'Did you get a lift back? I'm just going to make a cup of tea; have one with me—I could do with a bit of company.'

So Florence stuffed Mr Fitzgibbon and his remarks to the back of her head and sat down on the sofa of Mrs Twist's three-piece, very uncomfortable and covered in cut moquette, and gave her an expunged version of her weekend, excusing herself at length with the plea that she had to be extra early at work in the morning. 'And I dare say you're nicely tired,' said Mrs Twist. 'You'll sleep like a log.'

A remark unfortunately not borne out by Florence, who spent an almost sleepless night, her muddled thoughts going round and round in her head, so that by the time she got up she had a dreadful headache and was no nearer to enlightenment as to Mr Fitzgibbon's remarks on the previous evening and, still more important, why he had kissed her.

CHAPTER NINE

FLORENCE lay awake for a long time and woke from a heavy sleep with no wish to get up and go to work. She had a sketchy breakfast and with an eye on the clock hurried to the consulting-rooms. She reached them at the same time as the Rolls whispered to a stop, and Mr Fitzgibbon thrust open a door, bade her good morning and begged that she should get in, at the same time remarking that she looked washed out. 'You're not sickening for something?' he wanted to know with what she considered to be heartless cheerfulness.

'Certainly not. I never felt better, Mr Fitzgibbon.'

'Alexander.'

'No...'

He was weaving in and out of the morning traffic. 'No? Ah, well, it will take time, I suppose, and you're still as cross as two sticks, aren't you? Is it due to lack of sleep? It's a good thing that we have a busy day ahead of us.'

There really wasn't an answer to this, and she sat silently until they reached Colbert's and there accompanied him to the lifts, very conscious of him standing beside her as they went up to the top floor.

Miss MacFinn was sitting in a well-cushioned chair by her bed, dwarfed by the necessary paraphernalia vital to her recovery. She greeted them with pleasure and bade them sit on the bed. 'Forbidden, I know,' she chuckled, 'but no one will dare say anything to you, Alexander. I hope this is a social visit?' She smiled at Florence. 'So nice to see you again, my dear; you're beautiful, you know, and it acts like a tonic...!'

Florence blushed and looked at her feet, and heard Mr Fitzgibbon's casual, 'Yes, she is, isn't she? And a splendid worker too. So often beauty is accompanied by a bird-brain.'

He got up. 'I must just have a word with Sister; I'll be back presently and run an eye over you before I take Florence back.'

He sauntered away, and Miss MacFinn said, 'Does Alexander work you hard, my dear?'

'No—oh, no, the hours are sometimes irregular, but compared with running a ward it isn't hard at all.'

'He works too hard himself. I'm relieved to know that he intends to marry. It's time he settled down and raised a family.'

Florence, her hands clasped tightly in her lap, agreed quietly, 'I'm sure a wife would be a great asset to him; he's very well-known, isn't he? And I dare say he has any number of friends and a full social life.'

Miss MacFinn coughed. 'Well, dear, I'm not sure about that; he has many friends, but if by social life you mean dinner parties and dances and so on I think you may be mistaken, although I'm sure that, provided he had the right companion, he would enjoy these things.'

'Well, yes, I expect so.'

'Tell me, have you had a pleasant weekend? You live near Sherborne, don't you? A lovely part of the country. I had friends there...'

Mr Fitzgibbon came back presently and, when Florence would have got up, said, 'No, don't go, I shall only be a moment or two.' He sat down on the bed again. 'You're doing well,' he told his patient. 'I'm going to keep you here a little longer than usual, and then you can go to your sister's. I'll listen to your chest if I may...Very satisfactory. We must be off now; I'll be in to see you some time tomorrow.'

'Thank you, Alexander, and thank you, Florence, for coming too. Come and see me again, won't you?'

Florence said that she would. 'In the evening,' she suggested, 'if that's not too late?'

She bent and kissed the elderly cheek, and Miss MacFinn remarked, 'It really is most suitable,' which puzzled Florence and brought a reluctant smile to Mr Fitzgibbon's handsome visage.

The traffic was heavy now. He didn't speak as they drove back, only when they reached the consulting-rooms he reminded her to give Mrs Keane his message about his appointments for the following day.

He had gone to open the door for her and she got out carefully, not wishing to stumble again. She said quietly, 'Very well, sir.'

Then she gasped at his sudden, 'Oh, goodness, now it's sir, is it? Back to square one.'

She paused before she crossed the pavement. 'I don't know what you mean.'

'No? Then think about it, will you? And just as soon as I have the time we'll have a talk. There's a limit to my patience.'

She gave him a startled look—the blandness of his face matched the blandness of his voice, but his eyes were a hard grey from which she flinched. All the same, she might as well give as good as she was getting.

'In that case, Mr Fitzgibbon, let us hope that you will have a few minutes to spare at the earliest opportunity.'

She sailed ahead of him, her coppery head held high, ignoring whatever it was he rumbled in reply. Something rude, she had no doubt.

There were appointments booked until one o'clock and throughout the morning he treated her with a teeth-gritting civility that she did her best to return with a highly professional manner, which, while impressive, she found quite tiring. By the end of the morning she had made up her mind. She was not a particularly impulsive girl, but suddenly the prospect of working for him, seeing him each day and knowing that he didn't care two straws for her, wasn't to be borne. When he got back at two o'clock she gave him five minutes to get settled in his chair, and with an eye on the clock, since his first appointment was barely ten minutes away, she knocked on the door and walked in.

He was writing, but he looked up when she went in. 'Yes?' He glanced at his watch and Florence, who had weakened at the sight of him, bristled.

'I'll not take a moment, Mr Fitzgibbon. I should like to leave. After a month, of course, as we agreed.'

He put down his pen and sat back in his chair. Surprise gave way to a thoughtful look from under his lids, and his smile was full of charm, so that her heart thumped against her ribs and before she could stop herself she had taken a step towards him, brought to a halt, however, by his sudden laugh. 'Splendid; nothing could be better, Florence, and you have no need to stay for a month—I'll let you off that. Go at the end of the week—we will waive our agreement.'

It was the last thing she had expected to hear. 'But you won't have a nurse.'

'I have been interviewing several likely applicants. Mrs Bates, a widow lady, is ready to start work whenever I say so.'

He sat watching her. No doubt expecting me to burst into tears, thought Florence. Well, I won't. She said in a voice that wobbled only very slightly, 'Oh, good. In that case, there's no more to be said, is there?'

'No, not at the moment.' He smiled again. 'Ask Mrs Keane to come in, will you?'

In the waiting-room Mrs Keane looked up from her typewriter. 'Florence, whatever is the matter? You're as white as a ghost. Are you all right?'

'Yes, thank you. Mr Fitzgibbon would like you to go in, Mrs Keane.'

The door was barely closed behind that lady when the first patient arrived, which was a good thing, for Florence was at once caught up in her normal routine. As the afternoon wore on it became apparent that Mrs Keane knew nothing of her departure; Florence had expected Mr Fitzgibbon to tell her, since she was privy to his professional life. She waited until the last patient had been seen and he had left to go to Colbert's, and over a cup of tea broke her news.

'Whatever for?' asked Mrs Keane. 'I thought you were happy here...'

'Well, I like the work very much—that isn't why I'm leaving. In fact, I think Mr Fitzgibbon is glad that I am going; he didn't actually say so, but he knows of a nurse who will start on Monday.'

She looked at Mrs Keane with such sad blue eyes that Mrs Keane, normally the most unsentimental of women, felt a lump in her throat. 'I'm very sorry,' she said slowly, 'and surprised. I thought—well, never mind that now. Have another cup of tea and tell me if you have any plans.'

Florence shook her head. 'Not at the moment, but I'll get another job as soon as I can—not in London, though. I'd quite like to go abroad...'

Mrs Keane, who wasn't so old that she couldn't recognise unrequited love when she saw it, suggested New Zealand in an encouraging voice. 'And the world is so small these days that distance doesn't matter any more.'

She poured more tea. She was going to miss her usual bus home, but she wasn't going to leave Florence, usually such a calm, sensible girl, to mope. 'I heard a bit of gossip this morning. Those two women—Mrs Gregg and Lady Wells, one came early and the other didn't hurry away—they were talking about Eleanor Paton—remember her? She's about to marry the owner of several factories in the Midlands—rich, they said. All I can say is thank heaven she didn't get her claws into Mr Fitzgibbon. She tried hard enough, heaven knows, but of course he was never in love with her. She was fun to take around, I suppose, and he must get lonely.'

'I'm sure that he has no need to be,' said Florence with a snap. 'The world's his oyster, isn't it?'

Florence had got back some of her pretty colour and, judging by her last remark, was feeling belligerent. Mrs Keane, satisfied, got ready to go home. Tomorrow was another day and heaven only knew what it might bring forth.

As for Florence, she went back to Mrs Twist's, ate her supper after a fashion, told that good lady that she was leaving and counteracted a volley of questions by saying simply that she was needed at home. 'Since it's such short notice, Mrs Twist, I'll pay whatever you think is fair, since you'll hardly have time to let my room before I go.'

'As to that,' said Mrs Twist, 'I was thinking of having a bit of a holiday at my sister's. She lives in Margate and I can take Buster with me.' She pressed a second helping on Florence. 'In any case, you have been a good lodger and a nice young lady. I shall miss you.' Which, from Mrs Twist, was high praise indeed.

She had another bad night and went most unwillingly to work in the morning, unnecessarily so, since Mr Fitzgibbon's manner was exactly as it always was: remote courtesy, a few remarks about the weather and a reminder that she was expected at the East End clinic that evening. She muddled through her day, gobbled the tea Mrs Twist had ready for her and took a taxi to the Mile End Road, to find Dan already there, a room packed with patients and a lady in a severe hat taking the place of the gentle soul who usually sat at the desk.

'He's on his way,' Dan told her. 'I say, what's all this about you leaving?'

'Who told you?'

He looked vague. 'Bless me if I can remember—you know how these things get around.' He gave her a friendly smile; it didn't surprise him in the least that Mr Fitzgibbon intended to marry her; he had never said so, of course, but he had taken his devoted registrar aside and warned him that he intended taking a week's holiday and that he, Dan, would have to take over his hospital work while he was away.

Dan knew better than to ask questions, but he had remarked that he and his fiancée had hoped that Mr Fitzgibbon would come to the small party they were planning before they married. 'I shall ask Florence too,' he had added, 'she's an old friend of both of us.'

Mr Fitzgibbon had fixed him with a cold grey stare. 'Florence is leaving at the weekend,' he had said in a voice which had forbidden any further remarks. Dan, however, had eyes in his head and he had seen the way his chief looked at Florence. It was to be hoped that a week's holiday would settle the matter.

Mr Fitzgibbon came in then, greeted everyone much as usual, and they got down to work. It was a long evening and the lady in the hat lacked the smooth handling of the patients so that the clinic lasted longer than usual. When the last patient had gone Mr Fitzgibbon, sitting at his desk, writing, suggested that Dan should take Florence back. 'I shall be some time,' he pointed out, 'and there is no need for her to wait.'

He bade them a pleasant goodnight and returned to his writing.

It was on Friday evening, her packing done, everything left exactly as it should be at the consulting-rooms, that Florence got on a bus and took herself off to Colbert's. She had said that she would visit Miss MacFinn, and this was her last chance.

Miss MacFinn was looking almost as good as new again. She greeted Florence with pleasure and the news that she would be going to her sister's within the next day or so, adding that she would never be sufficiently grateful to Alexander for her recovery. 'The dear man,' she said warmly, 'I'm not surprised that he's so popular with his patients. He's such a good friend too, but I expect you've discovered that for yourself.'

'Yes, oh, yes; I've enjoyed working for him, but I'm leaving tomorrow. I—I'm needed at home.'

Miss MacFinn, who knew all about it anyway, said sympathetically, 'Your mother has been ill, hasn't she? And one's first duty is to one's parents. You will miss your work, though, won't you?'

Florence said steadily, 'Yes, very much. It's most fortunate that Mr Fitzgibbon has found someone to replace me. I—I've enjoyed the work.'

'Well, I'm sure Alexander is going to miss you.' Miss

MacFinn smiled at the determinedly smiling face. 'And I dare say you will miss him, my dear.'

'It was a most interesting job,' said Florence, intent on giving nothing away.

She had already said goodbye to Mrs Keane and, although she had steeled herself to bid Mr Fitzgibbon a formal good-bye, he had forestalled her by leaving unexpectedly early for Colbert's, bidding her a cheerful farewell as he went. 'I'll give you a good reference if you need one,' he had paused at the doorway to tell her. 'I'm sure you'll find an excellent job to suit you.'

He hadn't even shaken hands, she remembered indig-nantly.

Mrs Keane, a silent spectator, had added her own rather more leisurely goodbyes. Being a loyal receptionist and a discreet woman, she had forborn from telling Florence that Mr Fitzgibbon had, with her help, rearranged his appoint-ments so that he would be free for the whole of the next week. He hadn't said why, or where he was going but, as she pointed out to her husband, she hadn't been born yes-terday.

'We shall certainly be asked to the wedding,' she told him happily. 'I shall need a new outfit...'

Florence went home on the early morning train, bidden farewell by a surprisingly tearful Mrs Twist, and if she had hoped against hope to see Mr Fitzgibbon before she went she was doomed to disappointment. She sat and stared out of the window at the countryside, seeing nothing of it, re-viewing her future. She had brought the situation upon her-self, and now she had no job and would never get Alexander Fitzgibbon out of her head or see him again. It didn't bear thinking about. She began resolutely to consider her assets: a month's pay in her pocket, a row of shining new saucepans in the kitchen at home and the washing-machine, and since she was to be home for the time being there would be no need of Miss Payne's services. She thought with longing of the elegant Italian sandals she had intended to buy, and then dismissed them and concentrated on what she should tell her parents. Perhaps she should have telephoned them, but explaining would have taken some time, and anyway what had she to explain? She got out at Sherborne and saw her father waiting for her.

He saw her case at once. 'Holidays, my dear? How delightful.'

'I've left my job, Father.' She had spoken matter-of-factly but when he looked at her face he made no comment other than a remark that her mother would be delighted. 'It's such a splendid time of year to be at home,' he went on gently as he stowed the case into the car and waited patiently while Higgins greeted her.

There was plenty to talk about as they drove home—village gossip, christenings, weddings and urgent repairs to the vicarage roof. She went into the house and found her mother in the kitchen, sitting at the table, shucking peas.

'There you are, darling,' said Mrs Napier. 'You didn't phone, so we knew you'd be home.' She darted a look at her daughter's pale face. 'You look tired, dear; perhaps you should ask for a holiday.'

'I didn't need to do that, Mother—I've left my job,' said Florence bleakly.

Mrs Napier emptied a pod before she spoke. 'If you weren't happy that was the right thing to do, Florence. It will be lovely to have you at home again.'

Florence sat down opposite her mother. 'Just until I find something else. I think I'd rather like to go right away, but I haven't had time to think about it properly.'

'Well, it's nice and quiet here,' observed her mother unworriedly. 'You can take your time deciding, and a few days' doing nothing won't do you any harm.' She smiled suddenly. 'It will be so nice to have you about the place, darling.'

Florence went round the table and kissed her mother's cheek. 'One day I'll tell you about it,' she promised, 'but not just yet.'

Presently she went up to her room and unpacked her case,

arranged the photos and ornaments she had taken with her to London in their original places and got into a cotton dress. An afternoon's gardening would clear her head. To keep busy was vital, because she wouldn't have the chance to think about Alexander, and if she kept busy for long enough perhaps in time she would forget him altogether. She took the pins out of her hair and tied it back carelessly, and went downstairs again to help her mother get the lunch, a meal for which she had no appetite, although she pretended to enjoy it while she talked rather too brightly about the more amusing aspects of her work in Wimpole Street. When the dishes had been washed and she had settled her mother in a garden chair for a snooze, and seen her father off to the church to see one of the church wardens about something or other, she whistled to Higgins; a quick walk before getting down to the gardening seemed a good idea.

When she got back, half an hour later, Mr Fitzgibbon's Rolls-Royce was in the front drive and he was sitting on the grass by her mother's chair. Higgins pranced forward, delighted to see Monty lolling by her master, but Florence stood stock-still as he got slowly to his feet and walked towards her.

'Go away,' said Florence, wishing with all her treacherous heart that he would stay, and then, to make things clearer, she added, 'I don't want to speak to you and, if you want me to go back and work for you, I won't.'

'My dear girl, there is nothing further from my mind.' He looked amused. 'And certainly I am going away, but first I must bid your mother goodbye.'

Which he did, before whistling to Monty, who had gone to have her ears rubbed by Florence, getting into his car and driving away with a casual wave of the hand.

'Well,' said Florence, bursting with rage and love and choked by a great lump of sadness, 'well, why did he come?'

'So kind,' said her mother presently. 'He hadn't forgotten that I had been ill and called to see if I had quite recovered.'

'Very civil of him,' agreed Florence in a colourless voice.

She would telephone all the agencies she knew of on Monday and see if there were any jobs going a long way away. The other side of the world preferably.

With summer holidays in full swing and church-goers sparse, Florence found herself committed to taking the Sunday school the next morning. She was glad to do it—anything to fill the long, empty hours ahead of her. The class was a small one but unruly; she was kept fully occupied keeping law and order, marshalling the children into church for the last hymn and getting them sorted out at the end of the service. Several of them would have to be escorted to their homes in the village, and at the tail-end of the congregation she collected them ready for the short walk across the churchyard and down the village street.

Waiting for the six-year-old Kirk Pike to tie his shoe-lace, she glanced idly around her. The churchyard was peaceful, surrounded by trees and not in the least gloomy. Her father was walking along the path which would lead to the gate to the vicarage, and with him was Mr Fitzgibbon.

There was no mistaking that enormous frame. She watched until the two men disappeared from sight and then led the three small children that were in her care in the opposite direction, answering their questions with only part of her mind while she puzzled as to why he was there, talking to her father. Was he bent on getting her back to work in the consulting-rooms, and hoping to enlist her father's support? 'I'll never go back, never,' said Florence in a sudden loud voice that brought her small companions to a standstill.

She handed them over presently and walked back to the vicarage, going cautiously in case she should encounter Mr Fitzgibbon.

However, he wasn't there; there was no sign of him or his car, and she wondered if she had imagined the whole thing. But her mind was put at rest once they sat down for dinner. 'I had an unexpected visitor after matins,' observed her father, 'Mr Fitzgibbon, on his way to a luncheon party. We had a most interesting talk. He is a man of wide interests and he's interested in medieval architecture. I was telling him about the squint hole and the parvise. He tells me that there is a splendid parvise in Mells church, with a stairs in excellent preservation. He kindly invited me to visit him when he is spending a few days at his home there so that I may see it for myself.'

'How nice,' said Florence rather inadequately.

Her mother sent her to Sherborne in the morning with a list of groceries that the village shop didn't stock, and Florence was glad to go. She would need notepaper and envelopes and any number of stamps if she was going to write to all the agencies listed in the *Nursing Times*. It was a glorious day; she put on the crêpe dress, thrust her feet into sandals and got out the car.

However leisurely she was, the shopping didn't take more than an hour or so. She had coffee in a pleasant café close to the abbey, and went back to the car. Another long walk in the afternoon, she decided, driving home through the narrow winding lanes, and after that she would start her letters. New Zealand would do, she had decided, or, failing that, Canada. They were both a long way from Mr Fitzgibbon.

She took her shopping into the house, to be met by her mother bearing a large cake, covered in foil on a plate.

'Oh, good, darling. Be an angel and run down to the village hall with this, will you? It's for the Mothers' Union tea and I promised a cake. I'd take it myself presently, but old Mrs Symes always likes to cut the cakes before we begin. I don't know why, I'm sure, but one must humour old age, I suppose.'

Florence put the shopping on the kitchen table and took the cake.

'It's a snack lunch,' said Mrs Napier. 'I'll have it ready by the time you get back.'

Carrying the cake in both hands, Florence went down the hall and out of the front door. Mr Fitzgibbon was sitting on the old wooden wheelbarrow no one had bothered to move from the colourful wilderness on the other side of the drive.

He had a dog on either side of him, and all three got up and came towards her as she came to a halt. The dogs barked, but Mr Fitzgibbon didn't say a word.

'Why are you here?' asked Florence fiercely. Her heart was thundering away at a fine pace and her hands were shaking so much that the cake wobbled dangerously.

He took the cake from her. 'I'll tell you as we go,' said Mr Fitzgibbon in a gentle voice calculated to soothe the most agitated of hearts.

'I don't want—!' began Florence weakly.

'Now, now, let us have no more of this. I have a week's holiday, taken at great inconvenience to myself and my patients; I have wasted two days already, and I have no intention of wasting any more.'

They were walking towards the village street; already they had passed the first of the small houses at its end, and the village hall was in sight.

'Give me that cake,' said Florence wildly.

'My dear soul, you're not fit to carry anything—you're shaking like a leaf, and I hope that it's at the sight of me.'

Florence stood still, quite forgetting that she was in full view of anyone who might be in the village shop, let alone those idle enough to be sitting at their windows looking out. She said slowly, 'Of course it's at the sight of you, Alexander; it would be silly to deny it, wouldn't it? Only now I've told you will you please go away?'

'Certainly not. Why do you suppose I've taken this holiday? Somehow the idea of proposing to you in my consulting-room didn't appeal, and on the infrequent occasions when we have been together somehow the right moment didn't occur.' He balanced the cake on one hand and took one of hers in the other. 'Will you marry me, Florence?'

She stared up at him and took a deep, glorious breath, but before she could utter they were hailed from a doorway.

'Miss Florence—is that your mother's cake? Let me have it here. I'm going to the hall now—it will save you a few steps.'

Florence wasn't listening, but Mr Fitzgibbon let her hand go and walked across the street and handed over the cake, and even spent a few moments in polite conversation before he went back to where she was still standing. He took her hand again and drew it under his arm. 'There's a little green bit between the school and the churchyard,' said Florence helpfully, and they walked there unhurriedly, watched by several ladies who had been peeping from the village shop and now crowded to the door to see what would happen next.

It was only a small green patch, but it was quiet. They stopped halfway along it, and Mr Fitzgibbon took her in his arms. 'I asked you to marry me, my darling, but before I ask you again I must tell you that I love you; I've been in love with you for some time now. Indeed, thinking about it—and I have been giving the matter a great deal of thought during the last few weeks—I believe that I loved you the moment I saw you hanging out of the window with a duster on your head.'

'But you never—never even hinted...'

'I have been so afraid that you might not love me; it wasn't until you came storming in declaring that you were going to leave that I thought that you might be a little in love with me. If you won't have me, my dearest heart, I think that I shall go into a monastery or emigrate to some far-flung spot.'

'Don't do that—don't ever go away,' said Florence urgently. 'I couldn't bear it. It took me quite a while to discover that I loved you, but I do and I shan't change.'

Mr Fitzgibbon swept her into his arms. 'I'll see that you don't.' He kissed her then, taking his time about it, and then he kissed her again.

The small green patch was no longer quiet; the village school had let its pupils out for their dinners, and a row of interested faces was watching them over the wall.

''E's kissing and cuddling our Miss Florence,' said a voice. Then there came a shrill, 'Hey, mister, will you get married?'

Mr Fitzgibbon lifted his head. 'That is our intention. Why not go home and tell everybody?'

Florence lifted her head from his shoulder. 'Alexander...'

'Say that again.'

'What? Alexander? Why?'

'It sounds nice...'

She smiled. 'Alexander, darling,' said Florence, and kissed him.

Betty Neels Ultimate Collection
Official Prize Draw Rules

NO PURCHASE NECESSARY

Each book in the Betty Neels Ultimate Collection will contain details for entry into the following prize draw: 4 prizes of a signed Betty Neels book and a weekend break to Amsterdam and 10 prizes of a signed Betty Neels book. No purchase necessary.

To enter the draw, hand print the words "Betty Neels Ultimate Collection Prize Draw", plus your name and address on a postcard. For UK residents please send your postcard entries to: Betty Neels Ultimate Collection Prize Draw, PO Box 236, Croydon, CR9 3RU. For ROI residents please send your postcard to Betty Neels Ultimate Collection Prize Draw, PO Box 4546, Kilcock, County Kildare.

To be eligible all entries must be received by July 31st 2003. No responsibility can be accepted for entries that are lost, delayed or damaged in the post. Proof of postage cannot be accepted as proof of delivery. No correspondence can be entered into and no entry returned. Winners will be determined in a random draw from all eligible entries received. Judges decision is final. One mailed entry per person, per household.

Amsterdam break includes return flights for two, 2 nights accommodation at a 4 star hotel, airport/hotel transfers, insurance and £150 spending money. Holiday must be taken between 1/8/03 and 1/08/04 excluding Bank holidays, Easter and Christmas periods. (Winner has the option of accepting £500 cash in lieu of holiday option.)

All travellers must sign and return a Release of Liability prior to travel and must have a valid 10 year passport. Accommodation and flights are subject to schedule and availability. The Prize Draw is open to residents of the UK and ROI, 18 years of age or older. Employees and immediate family members of Harlequin Mills & Boon Ltd., its affiliates, subsidiaries and all other agencies, entities and persons connected with the use, marketing or conduct of this Prize Draw are not eligible.

Prize winner notification will be made by letter no later than 14 days after the deadline for entry. Limit: one prize per an individual, family or organisation. All applicable laws and regulations apply. If any prize or prize notification is returned as undeliverable, an alternative winner will be drawn from eligible entries. By acceptance of a prize, winner consents to use of his/her name, photograph or other likeness for purpose of advertising, trade and promotion on behalf of Harlequin Mills & Boon Ltd., without further compensation, unless prohibited by law.

For the names of prize winners (available after 31/08/03), send a self-addressed stamped envelope to: For UK residents, Betty Neels Ultimate Collection Prize Draw Winners List, PO Box 236, Croydon, CR9 3RU. For ROI residents, Betty Neels Ultimate Collection Prize Draw Winners List, PO Box 4546, Kilcock, County Kildare.